Naked Ladies

Bilingual Press/Editorial Bilingüe

General Editor
Gary D. Keller

Managing Editor
Karen S. Van Hooft

Associate Editors
Ann Waggoner Aken
Theresa Hannon

Assistant Editor
Linda St. George Thurston

Editorial Consultant
Jennifer Hartfield Lawrence

Editorial Board
Juan Goytisolo
Francisco Jiménez
Eduardo Rivera
Severo Sarduy
Mario Vargas Llosa

Address:
Bilingual Review/Press
Hispanic Research Center
Arizona State University
Box 872702
Tempe, Arizona 85287
(602) 965-3867

Naked Ladies

Alma Luz Villanueva

Bilingual Press/Editorial Bilingüe
TEMPE, ARIZONA

ISBN 0-927534-30-4   cloth
     0-927534-31-2   paper

Library of Congress Cataloging-in-Publication Data

Villanueva, Alma, 1944-
    Naked ladies / by Alma Luz Villanueva.
        p. cm.
    ISBN 0-927534-30-4. — ISBN 0-927534-31-2 (pbk.)
       1. Women—United States—Fiction. 2. United States—Ethnic relations—Fiction. 3. United States—Race relations—Fiction.
    I. Title.
    PS3572.I354N35   1993
    813'.54—dc20   93-30724
                                    CIP

PRINTED IN THE UNITED STATES OF AMERICA

Cover design by Thomas Detrie
Cover art Naked Ladies *by Carmen León*
Back cover photo by W. Q. Castaño

Acknowledgments

Major new marketing initiatives have been made possible by the Lila Wallace-Reader's Digest Literary Publishers Marketing Develop-ment Program, funded through a grant to the Council of Literary Magazines and Presses.

Additional funding provided by a grant from the National Endowment for the Arts in Washington, D.C., a Federal agency.

The quotation on page v is from *Les Guérillères* by Monique Wittig. Copyright © 1969 by Éditions de Minuit. English translation copyright © 1971 by Peter Owen.

The quotation on page 166 is from *For Colored Girls Who Have Considered Suicide When the Rainbow Is Enuf: A Choreo-Poem* by Ntozake Shange (New York: MacMillan, 1977).

Editor's Note

At the request of the author, we have respected certain idiosyncratic and dialectical variants in her writing.

There was a time when you were not a slave,
remember that. You walked alone, full of
laughter, you bathed bare-bellied. You say you
have lost all recollection of it, remember. . . .
You know how to avoid meeting a bear on
the track. You know the winter fear when
you hear the wolves gathering. But you can
remain seated for hours in the tree-tops to
await morning. You say there are no words
to describe this time, you say it does not exist.
But remember. Make an effort to remember.
Or, failing that, invent.

—Monique Wittig, *Les Guérillères*

To Leslie Siegel, always young and beautiful. And to all my women students (and to the men students who listened and were moved) who shared their stories with me (us) and gave me the courage to write this book. They taught me that our small, individual pains and joys have a larger life. Meaning. I see each woman's face, always, naked with her own truth.

Part One

One

Alta noticed the man immediately. He was black, well built, and extraordinarily beautiful in a bright, multicolored jacket. He was walking down the plain cement street like a well-groomed, an escaped, panther.

Alta sighed. She loved dark men. The two kids were quiet for a change. She still turned the morning's argument over in her mind, and she wondered, again, what would happen to her and the kids if she left their father.

"Bastard," Alta murmured, and tears clouded her eyes irritatingly.

Then she saw, at the very corner of her eye, the beautiful panther-man begin to run, holding onto a woman's arm—no, it was her purse wrapped around her arm. In her other arm she held a child who was crying. It seemed, suddenly, as though the universe were absolutely silent, and she, Alta, the only witness. But, no, there were two men across the street, standing and staring as though a television set had just been turned on right before their eyes. And the woman, Alta could hear as she quickly rolled down her window, was saying, "Let go of me, you fucker," in a steady, angry voice.

Within that silent universe there was only one choice: run him over: now. Right now.

The wheel turned without effort, and Alta's aim was perfect. The beautiful panther-man wasn't expecting this, and his face registered shock and pain as the front bumper caught his strong, lovely legs. He'd dragged the woman halfway down the street. Now he let her go and his eyes connected to Alta's.

Alta felt the contact with his body. She heard bone. The choice was hers—live or die—a fence was behind him. She could crush the life from him and she knew it. The color red, behind her eyes, turned to black and white, and she stopped as he limped away in great pain.

"Mom, you hit that man!" Her daughter repeated it like a chant. Her son was silent. Their eyes were enormous and their mouths were slightly open.

"It's okay. I meant to hit him. He was going to hurt that woman."

The woman continued to stand, holding her wrist where the strap had caught. Her child was quiet and clinging to her.

"Are you okay?" Alta shouted, getting out of the car.

"Why in the hell did he do that to *me? Why in the hell me?* I mean, I've worked with underprivileged black kids, signed a zillion petitions against South Africa—the whole damned bit! Damn him!" She began to cry.

Instinctively, Alta put her arms around the woman, and she found herself holding the woman and the child there on the city street as she continued to cry.

"Is everything okay over there?" one of the men across the street yelled.

The woman raised her head and looked at them. "Fuck you! Why didn't you help! Mind your own damned business, you assholes!" she yelled right back.

"Really! They could've been watching TV. I'm Alta, by the way," she said, trying to smile as everything became a little slowed down and real, including the woman.

"Thank you. Thank you, Alta. Jesus, what would've happened if you hadn't been here? My God! I'm Katie."

Katie had thick red hair covering nearly all of her back and her eyes were a dark green like the sea at noon or the forest in summer. There was something lush about her, though anger and fear made her face extremely pale. She was feminine and confident in that—her breasts were swollen to lovely points under her loose-fitting black sweater.

Alta was almost her exact opposite—dark-skinned, nearly black eyes, high cheek bones, with her thick black hair in long twin braids just past her collarbone. Her body was womanly, but she stood almost like a man, with a sense of alert preparation. Alta had grown up in the streets and her instincts for survival were as finely tuned as any wild animal's. Her ancestors had

4

worshipped the jaguar. No wonder the man had caught her eye; only Alta had no idea how much of the jaguar she, herself, embodied.

Katie's coloring and beauty was closer to a bird of paradise. Did jaguars need flowers? Who can say—this was how their friendship began.

It was the summer her grandmother died. Alta followed old Mexican women until they turned around or disappeared behind a door. She never spoke to them; she just wished they'd never turn around or disappear.

It was a beautiful summer, even if it was foggy half the time. The ocean and the secret paths through the Golden Gate park called to her. She rode her bike like a boy and she was still free.

Alta didn't speak to her mother if she didn't have to. If they weren't running away from her crazy stepfather, they were cleaning up the aftereffects of his violence. He beat her mother, broke the furniture or whatever was left of it.

Oh, the summer was beautiful in spite of the fog, death, lack of her own bed, a pillow to fit her head, food. There was still color everywhere, sprayed randomly by the feeble city sun. And she was still free to roam, like a boy, on her bike.

*   *   *

The argument that morning:

"Where do you go, anyway? I mean, how can you spend four hundred dollars in three days? I'm going to have to charge food at Mr. Gong's now till next week. Don't you even think of the kids, Hugh?" There was a terrible despair in Alta's voice. She didn't even expect an answer anymore. All she knew was that her husband took the paycheck and was gone for a few days— sometimes for a week—and when he came back he smelled of alcohol and old vomit and his work clothes were often ripped. He'd stumble to the bedroom and sleep, without a word, filling the room with an odor of decay.

Alta stood in the kitchen holding the forty dollars he'd just given her. It felt strangely like Monopoly money—like she could throw it away and it'd have no value. Why must I clutch the money? she asked herself. And why does he get to throw it away?

"I won't do it again," Hugh muttered as usual. "I don't know why I fucking do it. I just dropped in to have a drink with the boys. Don't make such a big deal. I mean, how often do I do it? A lot of it was overtime, extra money, anyway." His voice was low but menacing, and his body, which was large and muscled from lifting iron and climbing scaffolds, stood facing her, threatening her with its sheer masculine presence.

Hugh stood leaning against the stove, but his hands looked poised to fly and connect to her face, her breasts, her belly. He never said, "Shut up or I'll kick your ass." He didn't have to—his body, his eyes, the tone to his words, his refusal to apologize, told her, "Submit or die." Simple as that. "It's that simple, Alta," the smile at the edge of his lips shouted.

Hugh was still handsome, tall at six foot three, dark from the sun, hazel eyes, French from his father, Russian from his mother. He was twenty-nine; Alta was twenty-seven. They'd met at thirteen and fifteen. April was born when Alta was fifteen, and Alta still loved him like the sun, like the sun. But the sun was killing her. Surely it was killing her to love this man.

Alta fingered the two twenties, noting how oily money feels when it's been passed hand to hand. How the money began to feel like human skin.

"There is no such thing as extra money around here, Hugh. You just blew April's dress I promised her and Ian's birthday next week. What about his bike? Remember?"

"I'll work overtime this week, shit, I'll make it up. Don't sweat it, for Christ's sake. I don't want to hear about it anymore, okay?" His voice was rising.

"Why don't I pick up the check? I hate this waiting every payday to see if you're going to make it home."

"I ain't pussy whipped, Alta. Not by a long shot. That's my money, I'll bring it home."

Alta began to cry. "I have another year and a half to finish my B.A. and then I'm going back to work."

"What're you going to work as, a secretary again and bring home two hundred a week before taxes?" Hugh laughed shortly and then sipped his coffee.

"I'll get something working with kids," Alta said, stopping her tears. "I think I'm doing pretty good considering I'm a high school dropout. Yeah, I think I'm doing pretty good."

"When you make a real wage you're doing pretty good," Hugh said dryly. He lit another cigarette and sat down at the kitchen table with his legs sprawled in front of him.

"Just what is pussy whipped, Hugh?" Alta asked in a soft voice. "I mean, is it your personal definition or one you came up with, collectively, with the boys?"

"Spare me the high and mighty bit, will ya?"

"I mean, if you're in danger of being pussy whipped, I must be prick whipped, right?"

"You don't know what you're even talking about. You're getting carried away again, Alta."

Hugh jumped to his feet and faced the sink with his back to her. He spoke to the stacked breakfast dishes. "Anyway, it's my money."

"It's *our* money. The kids', mine, and yours. You have no right to spend it as you please. You have no right . . ." Alta's voice was high and trembling.

Hugh whirled around and threw his coffee cup, just missing her left shoulder, splattering ceramic all over the kitchen floor.

Ian was standing in the doorway with terror spread on his face. He was ten and big for his age, but now he looked very small.

"Get April, Ian. Get your coats and get to the car." Alta's face was contorted, but her voice was strangely calm.

"I need the car today!" Hugh yelled.

"I'll bring it back by five and then I don't give a shit where you go, you mother fucker!"

They met on the corner at exactly seven. He was sixteen, she was fourteen. It was a foggy, windy night, and they'd probably go have coffee and a piece of pie. There was nowhere else to go. It was too cold to go up on the roof tonight, and they both felt homeless, so they quickly reached to hold hands.

"I think I'm going to have a baby," Alta said in a tight, nervous voice as they began to walk.

Hugh stopped and stared at her. "Why?" he asked softly. "Why do you say that?"

"Because I haven't had my period in almost four months and I feel funny."

"What're we gonna do? I don't think I can marry you. You know, my parents."

They were under a streetlight and it made their faces harsh.

"I'll do something, I guess." Alta felt caught in something as final, and as real, as death; but this reality she carried, alone, in her body.

Hugh just wanted to get away, but instead, he held her hand and refused to believe it was happening.

It was January, when everything seemed to come to a halt. He'd given her a sweater in a large box for Christmas, and she'd opened it, again and again. She would never tell him it was her only present. It was soft against her skin.

It means he loves me, doesn't it? she thought, looking at him.

*   *   *

Alta drove home. The shopping bags were wedged in the very back. She always tried to keep at least a twenty hidden behind her library card. Hugh would have to borrow money from his friends; she wouldn't give him fifty cents. The remaining money would have to last until payday, and Ian's birthday was coming up. He'd have his bike even if it has to be late, she resolved. And my finals are coming up—how can I study?

Did I actually hit that guy? Alta asked herself again. The thrill and the terror returned, sharply. Her breath caught as she parked the car.

"Help me carry, you guys, and then you can watch your programs or whatever."

"Are you going to tell Dad you smacked that guy, Mom?" Ian asked, cautiously.

"Don't say anything, okay? Just don't say anything."

The dining room table was set with long blue candles in the middle and daisies from the backyard. Hugh was cooking in the kitchen. "Dinner's almost ready!" he yelled. "Are you hungry?"

"It smells delicious. What is it?" Alta lifted the lid on the heavy, black skillet. "Is this stuffed lamb chops? Jesus! What're you trying to make up?" She looked at Hugh with happiness, but she didn't smile.

"I suppose I am." Hugh laughed and turned back to the salad.

"Where'd you get the food?"

"Charged it at Gong's. He cut these little pockets for me special. I think that guy's the best butcher in the universe. Anyway, he said, 'No problem, pay me back at end of month.' " Hugh imitated Mr. Gong's Chinese accent.

"Can I help you with anything?" Alta laughed and forgot another squandered paycheck, his three-day absence, his drinking binge. She just couldn't resist him when he was this way. The way he used to be.

"I don't want any interference. This dinner's going to be perfect. How'd you get the groceries, with the forty?"

"My secret stash, sweetie."

"Can I borrow some?" Hugh continued to prepare the salad as Alta put the groceries away.

"Only if you beg."

As they laughed, Ian walked in. "Mom hit a man with the car, Dad. She almost killed the guy, but he was taking someone's purse," Ian said in one breath.

Hugh turned around. "You what?"

Alta told him the story as Hugh repeated "Holy shit," under his breath, whenever she paused.

"Do you think this guy'll figure out where you live? This is serious business, Alta."

"Are you saying I should've let the guy drag her down the street?"

"What I mean is, what if this guy finds you? Holy fucking shit."

"I've thought of that, you know. I guess I'll have to be careful for a while. Tomorrow night Katie invited us all up for dinner. She lives right up the hill from us. You can meet her and her husband—I forget his name."

"Do you get a courage award for this or what?" Hugh's eyes narrowed as he looked at her. "I always knew you could do something like that."

"I didn't. In fact, I still can't really believe it."

"You don't believe you're a real bitch, huh?" Hugh laughed.

"Is that what it means?" Alta blushed involuntarily, but her dark skin hid it.

"Mom almost killed that guy! He had to run for his life!" Ian limped and ran from the room.

"Did April see it?" Hugh laughed briefly.

"Yeah, but I guess she took it in stride or something. She was more worried about Katie and her baby."

"Would you run over me, Alta?" Hugh looked at her playfully, but his tone was serious.

"I guess if I saw you coming out of a bar on payday, I might."

"Thanks a lot." Hugh's face darkened. He rinsed the knife, leaving it to dry on the drain board.

"I mean, aren't you taking money from us?" Alta said softly. She saw his face and added quickly, "Is it ready? I'm really hungry now."

"I bet you are," Hugh said sarcastically. "Ian, April, wash your hands and come to the table!" He turned to Alta. "Did you expect a meal like this? I bet you didn't." He looked triumphant.

"I'll help you serve," Alta said numbly. The delicious food looked like poison to her suddenly, as though something in her brain had uncontrollably switched. Then the kids began to argue in the bathroom, and the last of her energy seeped out. The candles were lit. He would want to make love. She felt a dull pain where her IUD was, in the bloody softness of her womb, and then she went to stop the fighting.

"Come on, let's try it in the bung," Hugh insisted. The word sent a ripple of shock through Alta, and at the same time it made her want to laugh. "The bung?" she echoed.

"You know, the bunghole. Come on, we've been through this before. Let's try it." Hugh let anger creep into his voice. His penis felt limp inside of her, disinterested, after the messy ritual of getting the last of the jelly into the tube. I've been fucking this pussy from the day I was born, Hugh thought sullenly. IUDs *and* diaphragms in her so-called fertile times, Christ . . .

"Come on, Alta, let's try it, okay?" He held her by the waist and back, quickly turning her over. His penis stiffened now with the contact with her buttocks.

"You know, you have an ass like a little boy," Hugh panted in her ear heavily, as he tried to maneuver his penis in to a penetrating position. He suddenly shoved, roughly, but missed.

Alta stifled a scream, slithering out of her stomach position. The pain woke her up, and his words "like a little boy" rang in her ears. She felt slapped and degraded. "Like a little boy."

"I've told you before, Hugh, I'm not going to do that! It hurts! It hurts just to have you try!" She started to cry.

"Oh, come on, it doesn't hurt that much. We could use some Vaseline. Plenty of people do it that way. You act like it's some big deal." Hugh looked at her, through the darkness, with disgust. The bedroom faced another building, so that the effect was claustrophobic at times.

Alta could see his face; all his anger and displeasure were evident, and hadn't she always tried to please him . . . "Like a little boy," the words echoed, over and over. Like Ian, she thought, and the connection made her angry though she couldn't really understand why.

"Hugh, I'm a woman," Alta managed to say through fresh tears that dissipated her anger.

"No shit! Why don't we do something different? I'm sick of this missionary position stuff."

"We do it in lots of different ways and you know it." Then she said, almost in a whisper, "You I know I like it when we sixty-nine."

"It's the only time you come. That gets pretty boring too, you know. And whenever you come you always start crying and talking about how it feels like dying and all that shit. Do you know I dread it?" Hugh sat up, angrily, with his back to her.

Alta felt humiliated beyond words. Now she knew, even her orgasms were despicable, boring, stupid. She began to cry in great, heaving sobs.

"Hey, look, forget it. I'm not in the mood anymore anyway. Too bad we used that goop for nothing." Hugh leapt to his feet; her crying only enraged him.

"Hey, look, forget it. I said forget it, no sweat." He started to walk away.

"Where're you going?" she begged.

"To get a beer," he said irritably and was gone.

The room closed in on her, and she felt like killing herself more than ever. She was good for nothing. A little boy would be better, Alta heard inside her head. I have small, droopy breasts, ugly with stretch marks, and a skinny, little boy's ass. He's right, even my orgasms are ugly. It's true, they do make me feel like I'm dying. That's why I love them—then why don't I just die—why don't I just die?

Then she remembered Rita telling her that her mother drank herself to death in that very bedroom. No one ever said it, but that's what it'd been. Rita lived in the upstairs flat, and Alta paid her the rent though her father owned it. She hadn't thought about Rita's mother in a long time, though it'd frightened her to the point of nausea when she'd heard the story. Rita's mother had died there, in the bedroom, in her sleep.

Now Alta wondered how she could go about killing herself. She wondered who would take care of the children. She thought of her daughter, now almost a woman. She thought of Ian, tall and skinny with his high little boy's voice. This was all that stopped her, the children. Otherwise, who would miss her? I haven't amounted to anything, she answered herself. Going to school, for what? I can't even earn a living. All I make is pocket money. How would I pay the rent, buy food and the rest of it? How can I ever be a counselor—I can't even live for myself.

The words *live for myself* repeated themselves like a cruel joke, a taunting she couldn't control or stop.

A counselor, the unattainable, floated in front of her again. She'd never even said it out loud. Alta knew what Hugh would say: "You can counsel my dick!" His voice was loud and clear inside her head. And, obviously, I can't even do that right, she thought, as the gooey diaphragm jelly seeped out of her vagina with the warmth of her body.

Hugh came back to bed, lying down with a violent thud, nearly taking all the covers from her. Alta lay on her side rigidly, the cold bedroom air surrounding her like a punishment. Hugh burped loudly and for a moment she hated him. No, no, she hated herself. Yes, she would kill herself if it got too bad. Yes, that's what she'd do.

The image of the man's terrified face came back to her, vividly. Only this morning I did that, was the last thing Alta thought, and then the room that killed Rita's mother lost its grip ever so slightly.

April lay on her stomach with her fingers in her mouth. She'd bitten every nail down to the quick. She knew her father would ridicule her tomorrow if they were bleeding, but she couldn't stop. He used to spank her when she was little, but then he gave up. Plus Mom stopped him, April remembered, one time when his big handprints were all over my butt. It would sting so bad, and I just couldn't get away. Mom stopped him even though he left the house and didn't come back all night, and then he was drunk. That's the only time Ian wakes up is when Dad's drunk and yelling or breaking something. He never wakes up when Mom cries, so it's like me and Mom's secret when she cries. We never talk about it or anything, but it's like she knows I know or something.

April listened for her mother, but it was silent now except for the tree outside her window that brushed the side of the house when it was windy. The waning moon shone into the children's room, and April could see Ian asleep on his back with his mouth open and his arms opened wide.

Mom says Ian could sleep through a volcano. I hope I don't sleep that way with my hands sticking out over the sides. Anything could get you that way. Anything.

Mom says I'm going to have my period pretty soon, and I should have my own room. I want a princess bed, April thought, and the image of an enormous white canopy settled itself behind her eyes. But then we'd have to move, she reminded herself. Maybe if we moved he'd just go away. He doesn't even like us, and all he does is make her cry. She forced her raw fingers to her sides and kept them there.

April closed her eyes, sleepily. If I get a princess bed, I'll keep it till I grow up and never get married. And I will never cry. Not like Mom. Never.

Ian began to talk in his sleep, long sentences to the silent darkness. April giggled softly because Ian never believed her the next day.

"Do you want two fried eggs and some bacon, Hugh?" Alta asked in a resigned voice. Her eyes were swollen but not that badly. She'd gotten up early and put ice on them. There were early morning classes today. She wondered if her brain would kick into gear.

"Don't forget, I have to drop you at work today," Alta said, modulating her voice to a careful pitch.

"Give me two, I'm hungry. Shit, I feel like a kid when I can't take my own car to work." Hugh helped himself to four pieces of bacon and drank his coffee, sullenly.

"I'm saving the rest of the bacon for the kids. Do you want some toast?" Alta tried to smile.

"Can't get any. May as well eat."

"The kids are in the next room . . . " Alta's voice trailed off, and a feeling of defeat began nudging itself into her, as though making itself a permanent home in her guts. Hugh ate silently as she fried eggs for April and Ian.

April poured juice for Ian and herself, and then both of them sat at the table, silently waiting for their eggs.

"Looks like a funeral," Hugh said shortly.

"I dreamed a funeral last night. I dreamed we had a dog and it died," Ian said in a careful voice, more to his sister.

"Did your mother run him over?" Hugh laughed loudly.

Ian ignored him. "It was a kind of a sad dream. I had to give a speech and I was trying not to cry or anything." He looked embarrassed. "Dumb dream." Ian's eyes were hazel like his father's and his hair was auburn, but his skin was dark and lovely like his mother's.

Alta served them. "I don't think it's a dumb dream, Ian," She looked at her growing son, and she wanted him always to be so gentle.

"Would you like a dog sometime?" Alta prodded him.

Ian's face lit up. "Yeah, a big one. Could I sleep with it and everything?"

"The last thing we need's a dog," Hugh answered him.

Anger made Alta's heart race. "We've never had a dog. I'd like a dog. How would you like a dog, April? We could all take care of it."

Hugh left the table without another word, leaving relief in his wake. His jaws were clenched. Let them feed the damn dog, he thought, slamming the bathroom door behind him.

April looked at her mother with her large, almost black, eyes, perfect in her dark, high-cheekboned face. Pigtails made her look unmistakably Indian. "Indian from Mexico," April told her friends. "And French, Russian, and Spanish," she'd add, proud of her list.

"I would really like a dog, Mom. I'd love a dog. Do you think we could really get one? I'd feed him and help train him and everything." When April became animated her face became absolutely joyous in contrast to a certain seriousness that usually claimed her features. Like her mother.

April began to laugh and turned toward her brother. "You were saying your speech out loud last night. It was pretty good, for a funeral." She opened her eyes wide to tease him.

"At least I don't snore every night with my mouth open. I bet a mouse crawls in some night," Ian said with a straight face, knowing it drove her crazy.

"I do not, Ian! You lie! Mom, he's lying!"

Ian snickered.

"You little creep!" April made a grab for him.

"I'm getting out to warm the car!" Hugh shouted, opening the front door. "Jesus Christ," he muttered. Then he yelled, "The entire neighborhood's waiting for you two! Get out here! Now!"

Ian ran for the door. April lingered behind.

"Do you think we could really have a dog, Mom?"

"Do you think you two could cool it with the fighting?"

"He really was saying that speech last night. It's kind of scary, like he's talking to someone." April could tell her mother was self-conscious about her eyes being swollen, and she wanted to tell her they weren't that bad.

"You look nice, Mom," April said, turning and running out the door.

Alta could hear the motor running. She grabbed her things and turned off the kitchen light. Her daughter's words made her want to cry. Her eyes filled up and burned. Yeah, I must look like a guppy, Alta thought, and the beginnings of laughter erupted inside her. She looked down the long, dark, drafty hallway that led to her bedroom and closed the door behind her, gently.

They drove the entire way in silence. Hugh always drove. It bothered him to have Alta drive him. As he got out of the car he looked directly into Alta's eyes and said, "You aren't going to start them with this dog thing, are you? Don't you think two kids are enough?"

Before she could answer he added, "See ya tonight at the usual time," and he walked away with a quick stride.

"Bye, Hugh!" Alta called after him.

His crew was in the shack having coffee. Some of the guys put a couple of shots into theirs, offering it around. "It's Frenchy's kid!" one of the older guys yelled loudly. "Wanna shot like yer ol' man, boy? Now, *he* was a man! Drink me under the table, the bastard!"

Everyone laughed except for a couple of younger guys.

"Nah, I'll pass. Had enough the other night. Where's the job, Tony?" Hugh asked his friend. Tony was sitting crouched in a defensive posture with a coffee cup in his hand, waiting for the older men to pick on him.

"These young guys can't take it like the old days. Bunch a pussies in the union now," someone else continued. Grunts of agreement went around.

Tony jumped to his feet, walking over to Hugh. "Downtown, man." He was angry, but it only made him burn with an excess vitality. His icy blue eyes threw off shards of light. "Going straight up, thirty-five floors."

"You know what, Tony? I got skerankas, man. You know, skerankas." Hugh's face was suddenly serious with an intense look of pain.

"What the hell's skerankas, kid?" an older man asked.

"Well, it seems everything I eat turns to shit!" Hugh answered with a booming voice, grabbing the whiskey from the older man's hand and emptying it.

All the men started laughing, beginning to stand up and file out to the trucks.

"Yeah, that's Frenchy's kid!" someone said, and they all echoed it, slapping Hugh on the back as they passed him.

"You didn't have to do that. Fuck the old buzzards." Tony looked at Hugh cooly. He was short, blond, and well built. His arms rippled from working out and working the iron daily. Together, he and Hugh always caused a slight commotion in the street with the office girls. The office girls liked construction guys, especially when they weren't crude or loud. Both of them knew that, and Tony, in particular, collected phone numbers left and right.

Hugh looked back at Tony and laughed, savoring the hard-on he sometimes got when he imagined him and Tony making it. "Come on, man, let's go make a building and check out the pussy!"

"My man! Let's beat those cocksuckers out to the site!" Tony smiled widely.

They jumped into the truck, throwing their tool belts in back and, gunning the motor, sped off.

"My old lady's been raggin' on me, man. You know, that whiskey did taste pretty good."

"Didn't you go right home the other night like you said?"

"Yeah," Hugh lied, "but she was pissed 'cause I spent a fifty. It's my money, ain't it? I should be able to take a fifty once in a while, shit."

"I am never—I mean never—going to get hitched. Bet on it. I mean, your old lady looks good, and I don't know, I kind of think she's a nice lady, but something changes the brand once you own it." Tony looked straight ahead at the traffic.

"Still seeing that cute piece a tail I saw you with last time?" Hugh laughed and licked his lips, flicking his tongue for Tony's benefit.

"Her and two others." Tony laughed with him. "Variety, that's my motto. You know the old saying, why buy the cow when the milk's for free and all that."

Hugh and Tony laughed and whooped. Hugh honked the horn a few times and stuck his head out the window, howling loudly, startling the people in the car next to them.

"Man, did you see their faces? Uptight! You can bet that guy never gets any!" Hugh honked the horn again, making a sharp right taking them directly into downtown San Francisco.

"Did you ever make it with a girl ass backwards? You know, in the old bunghole?" Hugh was almost sorry he'd said it, because Tony looked immediately uncomfortable.

"Well," Tony began slowly, "I hear it's not bad. I mean, lots of people do it, I guess. But, no, I never have. You?"

"Nah, never tried it yet. Alta's not into that kind of stuff. You know, I think my problem with that woman is I'm too fucking faithful. Should make her sweat it a little bit more."

"I guess it's kind of hard, having kids and all. She's a pretty good mother though, isn't she?"

For an instant, Hugh saw Alta's face, sad with swollen eyes. "Yeah, she's a damned good mother. That's for sure. She'll be getting that B.A. bullshit pretty soon too. Sometimes I think she's smarter than me, you know? I mean, I read and all, but just kind of like she *knows* more than me." Hugh gripped the steering wheel.

"Yeah, I know," Tony said, looking at him. "My mother's like that. Can't pull too much on that lady."

Hugh smiled, thinking of last week—the three days away from home. "Yeah, well, fuck it. Dead subject, right?"

After the last class Steve asked Alta to have a cup of coffee, his treat. They walked along talking and laughing. Steve always made her laugh. Black humor always did it to her; it felt like she was going home. All the black and Mexican kids she grew up with—some she liked, some she didn't, but they were always familiar like family.

She wondered why Hugh had married her, or gotten together with her for that matter. He too grew up with the same kids, but a little separate with the watchwords from home hammered into his ears: *spics* and *niggers*. "Spics and niggers ruined this neighborhood. Used to be a good Irish working-class neighborhood before those people started movin' in. Don't be bringin' no spics and niggers 'round this house, Hugh." Then, she'd arrived and they were silent, but not their contempt. "A little dark, ain't she? Do you have to *marry* her? She'll have a dozen kids on ya . . . "

"So, you hit this man on the run, you sayin'?" Steve laughed loudly. "Sounds like the dude had it comin'. Wish I coulda seen that nigger's face."

"You know, Steve, I didn't really want to hit the guy, but I had to." Alta looked around, and she was surrounded by black people. Steve never sat on the white side of the cafeteria, so she always sat here when they got together. Usually she sat somewhere in the middle.

Alta took a sip of her weak cafeteria coffee, and the peach pie she'd bought started to look good. She hadn't eaten breakfast, and now laughing had made her hungry. "You know, even hearing you say 'nigger' bugs me. I mean, if you say it, why can't someone else? Wouldn't that piss you off if someone called you a nigger?"

"I am a nigger, you ol' worryin' little spic." Steve leaned back in his chair and burst out laughing, enjoying himself thoroughly; especially her frown.

Alta started to laugh, nearly spraying coffee out of her mouth. "Oh, fuck it, I can't have a normal conversation with you. What's your secret? I was feeling like shit this morning."

"I could *see* that. When you leavin' that white boy, anyway? *You're* too good for *him*, Alta. Bet he says nigger and means it. Bet he thinks he's too good for you 'cause you're brown."

"One time we were hiking up to Mount Tam with some friends, and we stopped to eat and drink wine and these African guys stopped to ask directions. Hugh ended up talking to them for hours, sharing our wine, really enjoying them. Asking them questions about their country, the whole bit. When those men left they all gave Hugh a hug. A genuine hug. And, you know, I don't think I've ever seen him more surprised or happy in a way. Anyway, I know he felt great."

"Well, the man was friendly enough with me the time I met him," Steve said a little grudgingly. "Just don't like his attitude with you. Anyway, the man's too much of a paradox for me." Steve laughed, cleaning his plate. "Shit, I oughta hike this mother off," he said, indicating his slightly rounded stomach.

"Why don't we take the kids out this weekend? My boy sure likes yours. Bring your book and we'll quiz each other and all that kinda shit."

Alta was thinking about the times Hugh would talk like his father, about not wanting spics and niggers in the Ironworkers. She'd remind him, "I *am* a spic, remember?"

"You aren't in the union, are you?"

"I think we're married, Hugh."

She remembered his face clenched with fury as he stormed out of the house. The word Steve had used. Paradox. Yes, Hugh was a paradox. That was exactly the word she'd needed.

"Ian really likes Richard too. Yeah, why not? I'll bring something to eat. How about Sunday by the playground? I like those drummers on Sunday."

"Good idea. I'll bring a snack and some vino. Lots of vino," Steve laughed. "I dread that quiz." Then, almost as an afterthought, he added, "One thing does puzzle me is why your old man ain't jealous. I can't say as I wouldn't be."

"I don't know, Steve. I guess he just knows I like you as a friend." But Alta had felt his disregard—a cold indifference about other men—before. Then, quickly, she reasoned, it's a hell of a lot better than being chained to the bedpost, and she shrugged it off again.

Alta lay down on April's bed, moving all her dolls aside. She remembered the night April couldn't go to sleep because she couldn't choose the one doll to sleep with. She'd begin to cry when the choice was made. By the fourth doll Alta was exasperated, and then it dawned on her that April didn't have to choose at all.

"April, you can sleep with all your dollies. Here, just put them all around you. See, now they're all happy."

April became instantly calm, lying back down in the middle of about ten dolls.

Alta always felt a calmness when she lay down on April's bed. My little girl, she thought. My sweet, little girl. Alta wanted to get her a princess bed with a canopy and her own room and a puppy and parents who didn't fight and a father who didn't drink and spend the money. And Ian needed that bike and his birthday was next week and she never wanted him to say the words spic or nigger and she never wanted him to be called a spic, wetback, greaser.

Alta cringed. Is that why I married him, to make it easier? She thought about it as far as she could and answered herself the only way she knew how.

Alta imagined Hugh as a teenager, about sixteen. No, nothing could've stopped me. He was tall, handsome, laughing, in her mind's eye. There was something elegant and earthy about him, though she really couldn't put it that way, but she felt it. A peculiar paradox, Alta thought. That word again.

"No, nothing could've stopped me," she murmured to April's dolls.

"This'll help, honey. Try it. It always helps me."

"What is it, Mom?" Alta asked, holding what looked like orange juice. She sniffed it. *"Wow! Smells like a drink."*

"Screwdriver. Just what you need. Do you want to go to the hospital yet?"

Alta and her mother walked the four blocks to the hospital, and then she was left alone so a baby could come out. Unbelievable. (At fifteen it was unbelievable.) Her mother couldn't talk about it or give her advice, but she did make her three stiff screwdrivers, and they laughed on the way to the hospital about how she was really going to have a watermelon. Some watermelon. It was pretty small. (Yes, she was pregnant, but in a dream far away.)

Some instinct drove Alta to buy pink things—a girl. And then a brief dream of a girl—at least that's what Alta had gathered from the quick image of what looked like a baby.

Her mother was doing her best, and at least they weren't fighting as usual, but now she was gone. It was sunset and a muted pink spectrum briefly battled the late April San Francisco fog. Alta got up out of bed after the intense pain where the watermelon was subsided—where the unbelievable that was about to happen to her was stubbornly crouched—to watch the sky; to set her eyes on anything but the blank walls or the awful crucified Christ over her bed—the only color was the dark, red blood on his body—and to escape, if she could, the next horrible pain. (Now, she began to wake up.)

The nun walked in, shocked to see her standing. "Get back into bed, young lady! Do you want to lose that baby?"

She came back in, giving her a shot. When Alta woke up the next morning it was to a pain that gave her no room to breathe. "Give her a saddle block. She's only fifteen," the doctor said impatiently.

The longest needle in her bent-forward spine, the tiny head clamped with forceps, the smallest, slimiest body she'd ever seen. It slid from between her legs.

Wrapped breasts with strips of cloth. Wound round and round, again and again. (Now she was awake.) She wanted to get away from the crushing pain of her breasts, but the nuns only wound them tighter as they caught her first milk.

"If you don't breast-feed this is what happens," a nun said without a trace of sympathy and left.

Someone brings her the watermelon. She opens the soft, worn blanket. It is perfect. Dainty little hands and feet. The miniature face is perfect. The mouth so solemn. Something terrible on the belly button, dark blood on it like a wound. She peeks under the diaper. The watermelon's a girl. "April," Alta whispers as though in captivity.

* * *

23

Katie opened the door and shouted behind her, "It's the woman that saved my life!" She wore a black turtleneck sweater with two buttons pinned on it: "HANDS OFF NICARAGUA" and "ANOTHER MOTHER FOR PEACE." She wore well-fitting, worn jeans and she was barefoot, comfortable, and smiling. Her long, red hair was in a single braid down her back, and Alta noticed again how truly beautiful Katie was. She glanced at Hugh and he was smiling.

"Katie, this is my husband, Hugh. My daughter, April, and my son, Ian, as you didn't get to meet them formally the other day." Alta smiled, meeting Katie's eyes. Then she saw a little boy standing behind her. "Who's this?"

"This is Ethan. Luckily, I left him home that morning. It was bad enough for Erin. Well, come on in. Glad to meet you, Hugh. You must feel safe with this lady around. April, what a pretty name. Were you born in April?"

"Yes," April smiled at Katie. April liked her immediately. Katie had such a generous, open warmth, and April did like all of her mother's friends. She thought they were all pretty and special somehow, and now there was Katie.

"Hi, Ian," Katie smiled at him. "You looked kind of surprised the other day. Not that I blame you."

"I was surprised all right," Ian answered with a deadpan expression. "I guess if he was going to gun us down he'd a done it already."

"Are you prepared?" Katie laughed.

"Not really," Ian said quietly, embarrassed now.

"No one's going to gun us down, Ian. Jesus!" Alta laughed a little nervously.

They entered the front room and a very good-looking man got to his feet. He was quite tall, taller than Hugh, with sandy-gold hair tied back in a ponytail, and he wore a small turquoise earring.

"So, you're the hero," he extended his hand to Alta. He had a slight, but charming, drawl. "I'm the man of the house, Doug, that is." He laughed shortly, with an edge of sarcasm.

"I'm Alta, the hero, though I still find it hard to believe."

"I believe it. You got mean eyes," he laughed more easily now. "Just kiddin' you. You look Indian."

"From Mexico, northern Mexico," Alta answered a little guardedly.

Hugh couldn't keep his eyes off Doug's earring. No, it can't be, he told himself. Gutsy to wear an earring, a big man like that. Hugh extended his slightly trembling hand to Doug, saying, "Glad ta meet ya, Doug," and they began to talk with an unusual ease.

There was bean and guacamole dip on the table, with salsa, and everyone began to eat. There was a feeling of ease and familiarity, in spite of a certain cautiousness, almost as though they were old friends meeting again after a long separation.

"I'm going to law school and working longshore as much as I can. Katie's parents are rich and help us with plastic. Pain in the ass, but it won't be for long."

"I wish Alta's parents were rich. I'd stay home and smoke dope."

"Have some right here." Doug smiled widely and started to roll some. "Where you from, Alta? Mexico?"

"Not quite. I grew up in the Mission District, right here in the city. My family's from northern Mexico."

"You don't look like a city kid somehow. I'm a desert kid, southern California. So's Katie, but a bit more citified. Loves to shop, that woman."

Katie walked in. "Don't talk about me behind my back, that's not fair, Doug." She laughed, but there was an undertone of seriousness to her voice. "Dinner's almost on. About twenty minutes at the most. Do you like that dip, Alta?"

"This is great. Hey, let me help you back there."

"You can come back, but just to talk. Do you want a beer or some wine?"

"Wine sounds good," Alta answered, getting up. She noticed the farmworker's strike poster—HUELGA!—and she smiled with approval.

"I give to that regular, or as regular's I work, that is. Talk ta ya later, Tough City Kid," Doug said, looking at her. He had extremely blue eyes with what looked like a permanent tan, with many wrinkles around his eyes, and creases from squinting in the sun. His tone was friendly with a hint of challenge in it.

"Later, Desert Rat." Alta managed to keep a serious face and left the room, hearing a booming belly laugh behind her.

"She is a trip," Hugh said, almost apologetically. "Uppity women."

"I like 'em uppity. That is, if they aren't mine," Doug said in a confidential tone.

Gross, thought April. Men are gross. She got up and followed Alta to the kitchen. Katie was pouring her mother some wine as she walked in.

Ian followed soon after.

"There's a TV in the kids' room. Do you want some cokes?" Katie asked. "The kids are in there watching something."

Ian took his coke into the bedroom, glad to be able to watch afternoon TV. He rarely got to at home. April stayed in the kitchen and drank hers, listening to the women talk. She knew how to disappear during such conversations and then when to appear again. She knew when her mother paused, knowingly, she would fill in the gory details later.

"Well, I have my B.A. from U.C. Berkeley in history, specializing in the Renaissance. I studied in France for a year. I loved it. But then, like a fool, I got homesick and came back. I wish, now, that I'd stayed. Anyway, I want to go back to school next year and get my master's. I guess I want to teach. What'll you do with your B.A. in psychology? Be a counselor, I bet," Katie said, staring at Alta, waiting for an answer. Her sea green eyes were lively, interested.

April looked at her mother too, expectantly, but carefully; she didn't want her mother to know she was listening to every word.

"I've been thinking about that lately, to tell you the truth, but I think I've got to learn how to counsel me first," Alta finally answered in a quiet voice.

"You know, most analysts get analyzed first before they start in on other people. Have you thought of going into analysis?"

"I've heard of that, of course. I guess I've just never really thought of it for myself, like only rich people do it." Alta hoped she hadn't offended Katie when she realized she'd said "rich people."

"Or crazy people, right?" Katie laughed and emptied her glass. "Shit, I've been to analysis. Granted, my parents are relatively rich, but I don't think I'm nuts." She smiled with amusement. "Well, maybe just a little. Just enough to be healthy, as my father says. Hope he's right."

"Katie, got some more cold beers back there?" Doug's voice boomed over the stereo, which was playing Miles Davis. "Where's the chow, woman?"

Katie rushed to the refrigerator with a slightly embarrassed look, but more, really, of resignation, and got two perfectly cold beers out from the back. She walked quickly down the hall. Then she brought back the empties. "I could be a millionaire from the aluminum," she said bitterly. Then, quickly changing the subject, she said, "Why don't I feed the boys in their room? April can eat with us. You don't want to eat with the boys, right April?"

"I'd rather stick needles in my eyeballs," April answered dryly as her face held the expression of utter truth.

Katie and Alta howled with laughter and poured themselves some more wine. Katie offered April another coke, and to Alta's surprise she declined and decided to wait for dinner.

"My teacher put a nail in a coke overnight. It was really gross. But I figure if I eat with it, it's probably okay."

"How old are you, April?" Katie asked.

"Twelve."

"You look older. You act older too. That's great. Do you ever babysit?"

"Yeah. I like to babysit as long as the kids aren't holy terrors." April smiled shyly.

"She's a good babysitter. She's able to get her brother in a headlock in a minute flat," Alta laughed.

"Well, then maybe she could babysit Doug." The bitter tone returned again for a moment. "Okay, dinner's about done, ladies. April, do you want to set the table? Really, if you can, I'd love you to babysit for me sometime. Hey, maybe we can all go out dancing, Alta. How's that?"

"I love to dance," Alta replied excitedly. "Once in a while my girlfriends and I go out dancing." Alta noticed Katie's face registering surprise. "Just harmless, good fun, of course. Dance 'em and leave 'em. Anyway, most of the guys get it, and, in fact, sometimes we dance with each other or by ourselves. I mean, why not?"

"Well, that sounds like fun. I've never done that actually. I've been meaning to tell you, I love your turquoise necklace. It's beautiful against your skin. I always did want dark skin, but I can't even tan, just blister. Curse of the redhead."

"That's funny because I've been admiring your red hair. So you'll come with us sometime? I know you'll like my friends. Maybe sometime this month. I could use it, especially lately." Alta's face became somber.

"Why is that, if you don't mind my asking."

April's ears pricked up, but she held her head absolutely still and kept looking out the window at a fully blossoming flowery bush covered with millions of tiny, purple buds, clustered together to make a fragrant stalk. A brilliant, green hummingbird appeared and hovered over them. She watched it beating its wings as it dipped its nose into each bud, but she was still listening intently. As it turned its body, here and there, in the last light, it blazed for her like an exquisite, green fire.

"Well," Alta said slowly, as though trying to choose the right words, but in reality she was trying to find them, "things aren't very good between Hugh and me. We've been together for ten years. I had April before we were married. No big deal, of course. We were so young and everything. Anyway, I can't seem to please him no matter what I do and I guess . . . " She paused.

"I guess, I don't want to please him anymore." Her eyes filled with tears, but she stopped them. "I mean, what pleases me? Do you know what I mean, Katie?"

God, Mom's going to cry, April thought. She looked out the window. The hummingbird was gone and the evening wind was kicking up, moving the immense stalks in shudders. Their purple was disappearing with the coming night. "What pleases me" echoed in April's ears and she glanced at her mother. She wasn't crying.

Alta looked at April in a reassuring way, but also with a certain complicity—woman to woman. You *are* sitting there listening, her mother's eyes told her, and then Alta looked away.

"It's like the old Freudian question, 'What do women want' and all that shit. But I think that's too general. I think you're right to ask, 'What do *I* want?' And I know, exactly, what you mean, Alta."

"Hey, Katie, more beer or some chow! The cavemen are gettin' restless!" Doug bellowed from his chair.

"Well, then why don't the cavemen go out and kill a dinosaur, you stupid fuckhead!" Katie said in an angry voice, but not loud enough for Doug to hear.

April laughed, betraying her presence.

"Sorry about the 'fuckhead,' sweetie. Slip of the tongue."

"Well, *why* can't the *fuckhead* get his own beer! I mean, once maybe, but not every time," Alta blurted out.

They all burst out laughing, April included.

"Why don't I serve the little guys, and we could start eating in peace maybe. Maybe we should throw Doug and Hugh in with them."

"Thanks, Alta, good idea. April, do you mind telling Doug and your dad to come on back?" Katie started putting the enchiladas on a large platter.

"Boy, those smell great. I'll go tell the fuckheads dinner's ready," April said, giggling and running down the hall.

"Cool it, April," Alta called after her.

April couldn't stop laughing. She stuck her head in the door and shouted, "It's ready, Cave Persons!"

"This one promises to be worse than her mother," Hugh said in a voice mixed with anger and pride.

Everyone ate with an appetite, but the conversation stayed at a minimum as though a subtle battle line had been drawn and sides had been chosen. Katie kept trying to get a conversation going, but Doug seemed to short-circuit her, and Alta felt shy and awkward under the circumstances. Katie seemed to have training in the social graces; Alta seemed to have none, or rather only what she'd learned on her own.

"Alta's asked me to go dancing with some friends of hers. I kind of like the idea. Then maybe we could all go dancing, Doug." Katie looked at him expectantly.

"You know I don't dance. I'm not a teenager anymore, for Christ's sake, and, besides, after school and work I'm wasted." He turned to Alta. "I didn't know married women went dancing by themselves. I mean, if *you* do, I guess it's okay."

Alta's face burned. "We only go once in a while. I guess Hugh's gotten used to it. Don't you ever go out by yourself with your friends? Hugh sure does, for days. Right, Hugh?" Her anger caught her by surprise.

"Don't start her up, Doug. Jesus," Hugh said. Then fastening his eyes on Alta, he went on. "What I think Doug means is that men can take better care of themselves in strange situations."

"You mean married women aren't as smart as unmarried women?" Alta retorted.

"Well, just like the other day that guy dragging Katie down the street, for Christ's sake," Doug said impatiently.

"You said married women going out, Doug, not just women. Anyway, who ran the guy over?" Alta's voice was trembling.

"Those *men* across the street sure weren't about to do anything," Katie said angrily. "I think if I hadn't been holding Erin I'd have kicked him in the balls."

"Shit, you wouldn't kick anyone in the balls. Not you. That's not proper behavior." Doug's tone of voice was derisive and final, as though his comments were the last word on the subject.

Hugh got up and started for the living room, indicating further that the battle was won. Doug followed after him.

"Bring us a couple of beers, Katie. Good dinner. Yeah, a great dinner." Then he stopped next to Alta. "I guess what I mean is that married women have more to lose."

"Like their virginity?" The words popped out of Alta's mouth.

"Well, you are a trip and I'm too drunk to argue. Maybe next time." Doug started to walk away toward the living room with a slight lurch. "Don't forget the beers!" he yelled.

Alta looked at Katie. April was watching television with the boys, and the kitchen was quiet now as their eyes met.

"It's like talking to a brick wall, Alta. Nothing works." She got up and started for the refrigerator.

"Why are you doing that? Can't he get his own?" Alta couldn't believe she was going to do it.

"His mother always did stuff like that, like a family ritual. If I don't he really goes bananas and it's just not worth it." Katie put the beers on the table. "Do you want some more wine while I'm at it?"

"I do some pretty stupid stuff too, so I'm not putting you down, but don't you think there're limits? I mean, Hugh's mother used to iron his fucking underwear. Do you believe it?"

"Do you?" Katie laughed.

"There's lots of things I won't do," Alta said darkly. "I guess that's why I'm not a good wife, whatever the hell that is."

"Hey, Katie, where's the blessed beer!" Doug's voice split the air with its command.

Something compelled Alta; it was beyond her control. She stood up and said, "Here, give me the blessed beers so I can baptize him."

"So you can what?"

"Alta opened the cans, walked down the hall and entered the living room, putting one beer on the coffee table.

"I'm over here, Alta," Hugh said irritably.

She walked over to Doug. "Here's your blessed beer, Dougie." And she poured it on him.

Doug yelled and jumped to his feet. "What the hell you doin'?" He kept repeating it.

Hugh was speechless as she left the room.

Katie was still standing by the sink. "Did you do it? Did you actually pour it on him?" She started to giggle. "I love it! I love it! Did you actually *baptize* him?"

"Into the order of the most holy of His assholes."

Katie and Alta howled with laughter until tears streamed down their faces.

The kids ran into the room and April asked for all of them, "What's so funny?" Then they heard the shower running as Doug stepped in swearing to himself—"Bitch."

"You're lucky Doug thought it was funny, Alta." Hugh glared at her from across the room. "I mean, I can't get over the fact that you fucking did that. I mean, we just meet the guy and there you are pouring a beer on his head. Jesus!"

"I guess I just couldn't stand it. Like the time I threw the toast on your face after you threw it at me. Remember the jam on your eyebrows?" Alta started to giggle as she took off her shoes. She undressed quickly. The bedroom was always cold at night—even in the day it was cooler than the rest of the house—and, besides, she didn't like Hugh to watch her.

Alta got under the covers and thought of Doug's face. She almost burst out laughing, but she stopped herself. She'd never done anything quite like that. Well, I did hit that guy the other day, she thought, remembering his face. Jesus, she almost said out loud, what's going on with me?

Hugh leapt on the bed, pinning Alta down with his body. "I remember the jam alright." He grabbed her wrists and held them. Her body was wedged tightly underneath him. She could feel his erection through the covers.

"Let go of my wrist, Hugh! It's starting to hurt!"

"No."

"Come on, Hugh! I can hardly breathe!"

He put his mouth on hers, hard. His tongue began to move in and out, slowly, then faster. He relaxed his grip on her wrists slightly, but didn't move his body an inch. He held her firmly, shoving his erection into her belly.

"Roll over!" Alta gasped, turning her face to one side. "I can hardly breathe! I mean it, Hugh, get off!"

"You always say you mean it." Hugh forced her wrists together and held them with one hand. Alta stopped struggling and watched him. A part of her wanted to scream and struggle and fight, and another part of her knew if she'd submit entirely, he'd make it pleasurable. That's usually what happened.

"I want to fuck you. I want to fuck your cunt," Hugh whispered hoarsely. "But first I want to make you come, bitch." His mouth found hers again, and his tongue began darting in and out aggressively. "Do you want me to make you come, Alta? Do you?"

"Yes," she said in a small, submissive voice.

He let go of her wrists, and she lay perfectly still as he turned his body around. "Eat it," he said as he directed his penis into her mouth.

Now she forgot everything except for the golden ring between her legs. Around and around she went, moaning and sweating, moving her hips a little, but not too much, because Hugh didn't like it if she moved too much.

When her fingers slid through the slender circle she wanted to scream, cry and beg for more, but she didn't because Hugh hated her theatrics. Her orgasms.

Then he was on his knees, shoving a pillow under her ass, fucking her with all his might, imagining she was his to kill or let live.

She was in the park, on the playground, in the late afternoon. Her new checkered dress took all of her attention. The skirt was so full it filled with the wind whenever she turned. Eight years old. Tiny pink labia, moist from cotton underpants that clung tightly to her waist, leaving a reddish band she would inspect sometimes alone, feeling its red ridges with her little fingers. She wasn't frightened until he touched her there; until something burned sharply there, between her legs, where she peed and touched herself sometimes, but it never burned when she touched herself there. It just tickled. "If you scream, I'll kill you," he said. The man. The boy. The man. The boy. She never screamed. She never even cried. Later, they caught him. "That's him," she said. But now she knew she would die.

*   *   *

Alta had just gotten back from the park with Steve and the kids. April brought a friend and they'd talked and giggled all day. Ian was filthy from playing with Richard. Hugh was asleep on the couch with two beer cans beside him. One was half full and his dangling fingers threatened to knock it over.

The two girls had been beautiful to watch, lying in the grass, making immense daisy chains, their heads close together as wonderful secrets escaped their lips. Alta had sighed with relief watching her daughter—no one had ever molested her. She was free from that at least.

The two girls had climbed out of sight, and Alta's heart squeezed with pain and fear when she couldn't see them or hear them. As she started to go look for April and Ruby the girls ran back from another direction. Alta filled her eyes with her daughter's innocence. Safe, she thought, safe. Again, you are safe.

"Ya really watch that girl, don't ya? Not that I blame ya, all these jerks slimin' around." Steve offered Alta some more wine.

"Yeah, thanks. I'll be glad when she gets it over with," Alta said, laughing too loud.

"What's that?" Steven asked, looking up with a surprised expression.

"You know, doing it. With the right guy, of course. Someone gentle. Someone she loves." Alta felt herself blush, as though she'd confessed something unspeakable to a man.

Steve looked away toward the boys. They were climbing a tree, throwing rocks at one another.

"Well, my sister was raped when she was barely fourteen. I know it was pretty bad for her. In a weird-ass way, my folks blamed her for it. Well, Mama stuck up for her some, but all in all she was blamed for it like she'd fucked up by having her sorry ass in the wrong place and didn't *she* have more sense than that. Shit." Pain flickered across Steve's face as he remembered his sister's outraged tears finally becoming silent. Then she changed.

"Does she have any kids?" Alta wanted to tell him about an eight-year-old girl, but she just couldn't do it. She watched April walking toward her.

"A couple, married to some fool that can't earn a livin'." Steve's voice trailed off as April approached.

"Mom, can we have some more 7-Up and chips?"

The phone was ringing. Hugh's eyes opened. His hand moved abruptly and he knocked over the beer.

"Shit," he muttered angrily.

"Hello?" Alta said.

"It's me, Jackie. Alta, I just called the cops. Some kids were trying my front and back doors. I mean, big kids, seventeen or so. Can you come over till the cops get here?"

"Are you okay?"

"I'm just scared shitless. Can you come over?" Jackie pleaded. She and Joe had just separated, and she was just getting used to that.

"Sure, I'll be there in about five minutes. Bye."

"What the hell's wrong?" Hugh asked lazily. "I worked on some mobiles—they're down in the basement."

"You should've come to the park with us. It was really nice. There were some good drummers."

"I sat outside a little too. Spilled the fucking beer." Hugh got up and walked toward the kitchen to get the sponge.

"That was Jackie. Something about some guys trying to break in. She called the cops, but she asked me to go over."

"Do you want me to go with you?" He looked at her with a hint of the teenager she remembered. The boy.

"Would you?"

"Sure. Get the kids."

Jackie laughed seeing them all. "That's what I need, muscle! I was about to make dinner. Some tacos. Do you want some?" Then Jackie's face collapsed. "Those guys scared the shit out of me. I guess they didn't think I was home 'cause I parked in the garage. What a neighborhood—you're either mugged or raped." She was shaking.

"Why don't you two take it easy? I'll get the tacos," Hugh said, leaving them alone.

"Is the hamburger fried?" he yelled from the kitchen.

"Not yet, Hugh. Look, you don't have to do that."

"Come on, April and Ian, give me a hand!"

"I'm tired, Mom," Ian complained.

"Ian, get out here! You just have to set the table. Do you wanna eat? Stop that damned whining!"

"Baby," April muttered as she walked back to the kitchen.

"You must love it when he acts like this," Jackie indicated Hugh with her eyes.

Alta smiled and said, "Yeah, it's sure nice to have him take over," but something, deep and mute, felt utterly betrayed. A numbness filled it, so that the anger that circled that desolate place could not enter or leave.

"I was just drinking some tea while waiting for the cops. I'd really like some wine but I've got kind of a hangover from last night. Too much vodka." Jackie poured some tea for Alta. Then she took a fuchsia shawl from the back of the couch, wrapping herself in it.

"Where'd you go last night?" Alta asked, glad for the change of subject.

"To a birthday party for someone at work. Jesus, by the time the cops get here they could kill you and dice you up for a barbecue." Jackie looked attractive in her new short hair. She was dark like Alta, but her face was rounder and she smiled more often. They'd been friends since the seventh grade. "You should wear that color more often. That fuchsia does nice things for your skin." Jackie's darkness glowed against the bright contrast of the shawl. "You look like an orchid." Both of them laughed.

"Well, you know, if this was a rich neighborhood those suckers would've been here before you put the phone down."

"That's the truth. Bastards. And Joe'd love to see me raped and mugged so he could say 'I told you so, you need a man' and all that shit. Anyway, you ought to wear bright colors yourself. Look at yourself. You don't have one bright thing on, but I like your sweater. It looks good on you."

Alta sipped her tea. The word *rape* made her shudder inwardly. Her mind teetered at the edge of its meaning, but then she let it go, wondering what it'd be like to be without Hugh. She picked fuzz balls off her favorite grey sweater. The fog was in completely, swirling around the closed windows.

"Where's little José?" Alta asked, clutching the warmth of the cup with her fingers.

"With his father for the weekend. It's kind of spooky here alone, and now this. Plus, I ain't been laid for a couple of months. I almost did last night, but I chickened out. Got drunk instead." Jackie looked at Alta as a smile formed on her lips. "I miss it. I must admit I do."

Alta drew in a deep breath. They'd talked about almost everything during their long friendship, but not sex itself. Not the actual thing.

"Is Joe good at it? He must be if you miss it." Alta looked out the window, too embarrassed to look directly at Jackie.

"I guess he's pretty good, but I don't come often enough. I didn't even know how to masturbate till a couple of years ago. Pretty retarded, right?" Jackie laughed. "You know, it's like I can finally talk like this 'cause I'm not with anyone. I like it. I hate it. I think I'm going crazy."

Alta looked at Jackie. She looked extraordinarily alive. "I don't think so," she said, smiling at Jackie. "I used to masturbate as a kid. Found the magic button pretty early."

"Do you come enough with Hugh? It's funny we've never really talked about all this stuff. I mean, you don't have to answer if you don't want to. Crazy question, I guess." Jackie laughed, leaning forward with concern on her face because Alta looked like she was about to cry.

"Jackie, it's awful sometimes. I don't even want to come with him anymore. It's like he has to talk me into it." Alta paused. "That is, if you can call it that."

Jackie moved closer, touching Alta's arm. "What do you mean?" The bell rang. "Oh, fuck, there's the cops. Finally." April came in as Jackie rushed out of the room.

"You okay, Mom? Dinner's almost ready, Dad says."

"Yeah, I'm okay. I'm just talking to Jackie. Girl talk and all that."

April didn't believe her, but she didn't know what to say, so she said nothing and went back to the kitchen.

Jackie shut the front door and went back to the front room. She sat down on the couch next to Alta again. "Is something wrong, Alta?"

"I've got to finish school or maybe even get a job part-time until I do. Hugh just blew his last check, and I can't really say anything about it. You know, it's his money."

"Jesus, he did that again?" Jackie sighed, sitting back on the couch. "I guess when Joe hit me again last time, that did it. Do you want to leave him?"

"I don't know. *I* feel crazy. I just don't know. Look, do you remember the woman I was telling you about? Katie?"

Jackie nodded.

"Why don't we all go out soon? Go out dancing. I could sure use it."

"He isn't being rough with you, is he?"

April ran into the room holding some flowers in her hands. "The tacos are ready. I picked some of these flowers from the backyard. I put some on the table too. What do you call these flowers, Jackie?" April asked, handing both women a long, dark, mauve stalk with a delicate pink flower on its tip. The pink was the color of the most tender, innermost flesh: of womb or heart. Or soul. "These are naked ladies. They grow wild back there in the garden." Jackie looked at Alta. "Yeah, these are naked ladies, that's for sure."

The door was locked. Alta's stepfather had locked it. She could hear her mother screaming in a terror she'd never heard anywhere but the movies—but in the movies, it wasn't real. There wasn't the same terrible animal desperation that Alta heard in that moment in her mother's voice. She didn't want to die. Terror. She didn't want to die. Terror. Fear. Terror. Terror. The bedroom door was mainly glass set into panels of wood. Her mother screamed again and again. Terror. Fear. Terror. Fear. He was hitting her mother again, but this time it was worse, much worse. The blows were constant and her mother never stopped screaming. She was afraid for more than herself—yes. Of course. She was pregnant with his child.

Alta put her fist through the thin glass, cutting herself only slightly, and as she pushed the curtain aside she could see her mother, naked, seven months pregnant. Her flesh looked so soft and unnaturally white with red marks on it. Smears. Smears of blood. Little bruises everywhere.

The handle in her hand. She turns it, opening the door. He's drunk but precise in his cruelty. His blows land well and hard. Alta picks up a large marble ashtray. He pays no attention to her. He'll deal with her later, he thinks. Later, after I finish this, he thinks.

There is no sound in the world but the blood in her ears rushing, rushing to her brain, her arms, her fingertips, as she raises the heavy ashtray with its cigarette stubs and used, grey ashes, and brings it down in one swift, lovely movement to his head. His stupid head. His drunken head. She hopes he's dead.

"Get dressed, Mom!"

"You've killed him! Oh, my God, you've killed him!" Alta's mother bends down on her knees, still naked, still bleeding, and touches the blood dripping from his thinning, dark hair. He moans.

"You're a whore!" Alta screams at the top of her lungs. "You're a whore!" Crying, she runs out the front door. Trying to run away from the naked lady.

*   *   *

"Dad has a puppy!" Ian screamed with excitement. "Mom! Dad has a puppy!"

April ran out with him to meet Hugh, who was holding a small, brown, furry creature with tiny quivering ears and a soft wet nose.

Hugh smiled widely, bending down to let the kids get a good look at it. The neighborhood kids surrounded the puppy as well, and Ethan wanted to go out and see it, but Katie told him to wait until Hugh brought the puppy in.

"Can I hold it, Dad? Can I just hold it?" April pleaded.

Hugh regarded his daughter's flushed face, her wide open eyes, the little girl's smile toned down, slightly, by the woman she would become. Soon. Alta in April, Hugh thought and said, "Okay, April, but hang onto him. Don't drop him even if he pees on you. He's peed on me about four times now."

Ian laughed. "Really? Did he really pee on you? Can I hold him too, Dad? I don't care if he pees on me, I really don't." Ian was in absolute ecstasy. The only thing he could see was the puppy's small face, the little fuzzy ears, the tiny, pink tongue, and the soft, so very soft paws dangling over his sister's arms as she cradled him.

"Let me hold him first, Ian. You'll drop him for sure. See, this is how you hold him, real close."

"It's not a baby, April. It's a dog." Ian's voice was filled with envy and longing. "Can't I hold him next, Dad?"

Hugh's smile began to fade with his patience. "Look you two, take the puppy to the backyard and let him check out the bushes, and, April, let Ian hold him too. It's the *family* dog, both of you!"

"Do I have to, Dad?" April whined.

"Maybe I shouldn't have brought a dog home at all. Ian, take this dog food in."

Ian walked past his sister, petting the dog, quickly, on the head. "Take him to the backyard, sister," he said in an infuriating tone.

"Brat," she muttered.

"April, bring the puppy in so we can all see it!" Alta yelled from the top of the stairs.

"Isn't he beautiful, Mom? He's so cute!"

"Yeah, but don't forget, he's Ian's too, kiddo."

The puppy began to pee and April nearly dropped him, screaming all the way to the backyard.

"What made you get the puppy?" Doug asked Hugh after dinner. They sat at the dining room table putting away a bottle of burgundy between them.

"Shit, I don't know. The kids, I guess. Are you really going to finish up this law thing? Going to school must be a fuckin' pain in the ass. I don't think I can even think anymore, to tell you the truth."

"All this shit can take it outta ya, I know. I jes don't take it that seriously anymore or somethin' like that." Doug had more of a drawl at some times than others. Now his drawl was pronounced.

"What do you mean?" Hugh's eyes narrowed.

"Oh, I checked out this little thing in Berkeley, a little blondie, and somehow it put it all in perspective. You know, per-spec-tive," Doug said, lengthening the word, savoring it, and then he licked his lips as though he'd eaten something delicious.

Hugh smiled. "Still like that tight stuff, huh, Doug? Still seein' her?"

"Unfortunately, no. It was brief." Doug's drawl disappeared. "Katie fucking caught on. Some asshole told her."

"Gotta give it some time now, huh?" Hugh split the remaining wine between them.

"Maybe I should get a puppy." Doug laughed, slapping Hugh hard on the back. Their laughter brought two-year-old Erin into the room. The other kids were in the backyard with the puppy.

"Sounds like something good," Alta said, indicating the dining room. "I wonder what they're laughing about, don't you?" She watched the suds disappear from the last of the plates. Only the glasses remained.

"Maybe," Katie said darkly. "Leave the pans for me. I mean it."

"Well, okay. Thanks. So, what do you mean maybe?" Alta looked at Katie closely. Her hair was down tonight like a thick mantle, past her breasts.

"You know, what you don't know can't hurt you. Though I think either way's a bitch."

"Do you know something that's hurt you?" Alta asked gently.

Katie looked up at Alta, and, seeing her sympathy, she answered, "He was seeing this blond broad for a while, while I was home baking cookies. You know, that trip." Tears slid down her cheeks and they felt unusually hot.

"It's gotten to the point that when we're arguing he grabs my face, like the other night," Katie held her own face tightly, to show Alta what she meant. "And he wants me to hold still so he can fucking hit me."

"You're kidding. Why in the hell does he want to hit you? *He's* the one, right?"

"Because I think he's going to see her again and I'm not shutting up about it."

"Has he hit you?"

"He's slapped me. Once. But this fucking holding my face like I'm a retard's degrading."

"What do you do? I mean, how do you handle it?"

Katie's eyes burned into Alta's. "I start crying, just like this." Katie turned her face away. "Fucking incredible, isn't it?"

"Next time grab his hand, Katie. Grab his hand and bite it."

An amazement crept into Katie's eyes as she looked back up at Alta.

"Do you really think I should? I mean, do you really think I should? You seem to be the fucking expert in these matters."

Alta held her breath. Then she said, "Yes, I think you should. Bite him good if he does that again."

"Has Hugh ever hit you?"

Now it was Alta's turn to look away. "He's threatened to hit me a couple of times, but I guess I always shut up at the right time. So, no, he's never hit me." Her voice sounded infinitely sad and infinitely alone. Why is it, she thought, as April burst into the room, that I feel like I'm dead?

After Katie, Doug, and the kids were gone, and April and Ian were asleep, Alta lay awake. First on her stomach, then on her back. Hugh got up to go to the bathroom.

"Piss hard-on," he muttered. He got back into bed, curling around Alta, placing his hand on her breast, twisting her nipple in an irritating way, and pressing his groin into her side. He pulled her face toward him, and his breath was sour with wine.

Alta remembered dismally that the next day was payday. It was an automatic reminder as though a built-in panic button were being pushed. Payday. His payday.

"I'm getting a part-time job until I'm through with my degree. I put an application in at a day-care center close to the college," Alta said evenly, but there was no response from Hugh except for his hand trying to lower her panties.

"Hugh, I'm not in the mood at all. Come on! It's late and you smell like a wino. Cut it out, Hugh!" Alta's voice began to rise.

Hugh jerked into a half-sitting position. "Why the hell get a job? You're only going to make chicken feed. Besides, I make more than enough. I'll let you support me when you make the bucks, how's that?" He lowered himself down next to her.

"If you brush your teeth I might think about it." In the back of her mind was the realization that if they made love the check would probably come home tomorrow. She would take that job if she got it. Teacher's aide, but it was a start.

"Are you serious? You mean, you want me to get up and brush my teeth? Come on, Alta, give me a break, Jesus."

"Give *me* a break—brush your teeth or forget it." Alta's voice was firm, but she waited for his refusal or an outburst of anger. To her surprise he got up. Her advice to Katie burned on her tongue: Bite him. Just bite him. How many times can I back down and just let him fuck me to get it over with, she thought, keeping her breath even and shallow. Or the orgasms he *gives* me. Shit. I used to like it, didn't I? She reached back in her memory. Yes, I did. I did like it. He used to like me to sit up on him. He used to like me to fuck him, he said.

Alta touched her breasts and clitoris lightly, feeling the moisture between her legs. She heard Hugh turn off the water.

"How's this, Queen Alta?" Hugh blew his breath into her face.

"An improvement, thanks. Let me make love to you, Hugh," she said shyly.

"What's the occasion? Does Colgate turn you on? He laughed deep in his throat, remaining in a passive pose on his back. Alta rolled over on him. His body felt huge under hers and he bore her weight without effort. The darkness revealed his features to her. They seemed more familiar to her than her own.

44

"Do you know how much I love you? Do you have any idea? I think I'd die for you," Alta whispered, passion flooding her, and a desire to please him completely, if she could. If only she could.

Hugh remained silent, staring at her through the darkness between them. His hands were at his sides. Alta touched his penis; it was semi-flaccid but hardening.

"Do you love me?" she asked, licking his ear and blowing into it the way he liked it. "Answer me, Hugh. Please. Do you love me?" She kissed his neck, then lowering herself, she licked and sucked his nipples. "Do you? I couldn't stand it if you didn't love me." Tears came to her eyes, and they fell on his belly.

He continued to keep his hands to his sides. He thought of his lover and let her suck him. She was trying so hard. She licked the inside of his shaft with the flat of her tongue.

"Do you love me, Hugh? Answer me," Alta pleaded, openly weeping now.

"Yes, I do, I do, I do," Hugh moaned, thrusting himself deep into her mouth.

This excited her, this absolute position of giving her mouth to him, and his words, "I do, I do, I do," nearly made her come.

She thought of the IUD that made her bleed between periods, but it was worth it now, because she didn't have to stop and fumble with a diaphragm. Alta mounted him, feeling him touch her cervix. This is what it was like, she remembered. Like this. "Come inside me, Hugh. Like this, like this, like this."

"Turn over so I can fuck you from behind. Quick, turn over."

"I like it this way. Please stay this way. Please."

"Come on, put a pillow under you. Come on, what's wrong, you're getting dry, shit."

"Don't hurt me, don't fall out, Hugh, don't hurt me, goddammit."

"Hold still, I'm coming. Hold still!"

Alta held herself still, bracing herself against the deep thrusts of his orgasm.

"Do you want me to finish you with my hand?" Hugh's voice was gentle, but the boredom was unmistakable.

"Why don't you want me to make love to you anymore?"

"You just did, Alta." Hugh's voice trailed off.

Now there was silence except for the occasional car, a cat fight in the distance, the sound of Ian coughing, the puppy whining on the back porch. Dawn was five hours away, and when the sun came up she'd be expected to rise, be a mother, know her name, know her children's names, when, in fact, she'd ceased to exist. What remained could cook, speak when spoken to, pay the bills on time, and endure this terrible humiliation called *love*.

Once she almost left him. She stayed for an office party. She called home. There was no answer. She called Rita. "Where are you, Alta? The kids are here. Hugh went crazy, took the kids for a ride, and just about killed them." Rita's voice was angry as though it were her fault.

Alta began to cry. "I told him I'd be home by eight. Where is he? How're the kids? What do you mean he tried to kill them?" They were six and four. Hugh was on disability so she'd gone to work.

"He wrecked the car, but the kids are alright." Rita's voice softened. "He wrecked the car with a sledgehammer after a wild ride with the kids. It scared them, but they're alright, really they are. They think daddy had an accident and he went to the hospital. We tried to keep him here but he wouldn't stay."

"What did Hugh say? Where did he go? What happened?"

Rita paused. "Well, he said to take the kids because he was afraid he'd hurt them, and then he just split."

Hugh had been dreaming the face of an old woman coming closer and closer to him in the darkness. Alta didn't dream at all. Then he began seeing the old woman wide awake.

"Alta, you've got to let him come home for the night," the family doctor told her. "They can't admit him until tomorrow."

The kids stayed with Rita. Hugh came through the front door, grey and trembling. He lay in her arms like a little boy and he cried. She let him come home. He asked her if she saw the old woman. She was close now, he said.

"No, I don't see anything." Alta's hand shook as she reached for the overhead light.

"Do I have to sign this?" Alta asked.

"Either you or his parents," the director answered her.

Hugh stood staring through the small square of glass as they shut the first door, then the second, metal one that thudded shut. Locked.

"Daddy tried to kill us. He didn't care that we were crying. I asked him to stop, Mommy, but he wouldn't," April said in her solemn six-year-old voice.

* * *

"No school today, huh?" Rita asked, pouring them each a fresh cup of coffee. "I'm going to switch over to a day schedule next semester. Felipe will be in first grade at last." Rita had three children and Felipe was the youngest.

"If I get the job I applied for would you watch the kids after school for a couple of hours, three days a week? That is, if I get it. It's in a child-care center as a teacher's aide."

"Sure, they're no trouble, and April helps me more than anything. You look kind of shot down, mujer. Is anything wrong?" Rita had heard an angry exchange last night, but it'd been brief. Her bedroom was right over Alta's—her mother's, she corrected herself for a split second and then she made her mother's bloated face disappear. It was hard not to hear the anger, the tears, the occasional cries of joy, and she tried very hard to keep theirs—Carl's and hers—below a whisper.

"Oh, it's everything I guess."

"You mean, Hugh, right? That guy puts you through the wringer. He's not seeing things again, is he?" Rita had a way of talking that made the tragic humorous: the tone of her voice, her flippancy in the face of the obvious.

47

Alta laughed, meeting Rita's semi-amused eyes. "You never did visit him there, did you?"

"Not me. They'd keep me, that's for sure," she answered with a laugh. Rita's laugh had an abandon that was hard to resist. Her face was dark with cheekbones as high as Alta's, but even more pronounced. Though she had a very dramatic beauty she chose to play with it rather than take it seriously. Her husband, Carl, was blond and took everything, including himself, much too seriously.

They'd been married for twelve years, and he was always beginning or ending an affair. "It gives me a break," Rita would laugh. Only once did Alta see Rita's anger: "She actually called here and asked for him. Now, that's too much. I can't take *that*."

Her family came from Guatemala where such things were common for the men, and so she continued to shrug it off, the way her mother had learned to shrug it off until she could no longer even see her little daughter crying for help.

Alta laughed with her and even the memory of Hugh's breakdown seemed lighter. "Did I ever tell you about the time I went to visit Hugh, it was a Sunday so lots of visitors were there, and all the visitors were making a concentrated effort to look like everything was perfectly normal, and they weren't scared or anything, right? In other words, it was really uptight," Alta laughed, remembering.

"Anyway, Hugh and I ended up in the TV room—an old W.C. Fields movie was on. No one was even talking. Everyone was just sitting there staring at the movie. I mean, so were we, but here's this hysterical W.C. Fields movie going on before our eyes. It was like everyone was trying to look like *they* weren't crazy, you know? All of a sudden, W.C. jumps into a car, which is inside an immense mansion, and starts driving up the stairs, in and out of all these rooms, like a maniac with this lit cigar protruding from his mouth. I mean, it's stuck in place like with Krazy Glue. I looked at Hugh and we both started howling." Fresh laughter began to rise from the old memory—the insanity of that time.

"That's great. Did you freak everyone out or what?" Rita asked, giggling.

"They started to laugh too. I mean, even the other patients, but, you know, some of those people really were out of it. Some of them laughed like they were crying—like it hurt to laugh. It actually sounded like they were crying, but they kept on laughing, and at the right parts too." Alta paused to catch her breath.

"Do you want some more coffee, loca?"

"Sure. I haven't thought of that in a long time. You know, Hugh's laugh sounded like Santa Claus in there. In a way, he led the laughter, though I helped, I guess." Alta smiled to herself. "That guy wasn't crazy then and he's not crazy now. Shit."

"Well, just watch out that he doesn't make you crazy." Her mother's face came to her again, and she made it go away. "You didn't look so hot when you first got here."

"How do you stand Carl's shit?" A flash of pain and anger went over Rita's face, but Alta continued. "I mean, how can you keep laughing the way you do? I've never talked to anyone else about this."

Rita shrugged her shoulders and tossed her head back as though denial were her one true weapon, her drug. "Well, Jackie knows too. I've told her. Her and you." Her voice was harsh and flat. Then it softened. "Maybe when I laugh, I cry, Alta." For a brief moment Rita's eyes held an unbearable sorrow, and then she looked away.

"Like all the other nuts," she added, laughing loudly at the absurdity of her life, and the pain her father had inflicted on her from the very beginning.

Two

All day Hugh knew he'd do it. There was overtime on his check. What the hell, he thought angrily. "Let's get a couple, okay, Tony?" Hugh carefully placed the large tools and the ropes in the shed. He took his tool belt off, slinging it over his shoulder.

"Gotta hot date." Tony smiled knowingly. "You know, man, gotta shower, shave, and all that shit."

As Hugh crossed the Golden Gate he stuffed forty dollars into his wallet and the rest into the glove compartment under the maps, screwdrivers, and an old drawing Ian had given him when he was eight years old. "DADDY" it said at the bottom. Ian had signed his name in small red letters under the large red letters of DADDY.

The traffic came to a halt. A long stream of cars poured over the bridge, but now they were still, water on every side of them; all of them suspended, end to end, in absolute trust, over their communal death, impatiently.

Hugh drummed the steering wheel with impatience, wondering when the long, unending line of cars would begin to move again over the bridge. Over the bridge his father helped to build. Steel, all of it; man-made steel. Men had died building this bridge, he'd heard his father say, but not to him, never to him.

Hugh remembered his father talking to the men in the kitchen, drinking whiskey with them. He remembered his father's rough pants, his huge hands spread on his knees as he talked, leaning forward. His face squarely built, it'd seemed to him, and perfect like a statue, and his eyebrows, bushy and straight, were glued into place because they hardly moved as he spoke. But his eyes, Hugh remembered, changed often, switching like some kind of inner weather. Hugh noticed that that was when he'd take another drink.

Hugh folded the old, dirty drawing and placed it back in the glove compartment, slamming it with so much force it popped back down. The traffic began to move again slowly, unaware that men had died building the bridge, unaware that Hugh's father had helped build it long ago, unaware of the irrational trust they put in steel, bridges, everyday, common-place death, and Hugh was unaware of how much Ian's drawing looked like his own father. Like a statue. Perfect.

The DADDY in red, the *ian* in red, like blood, like blood-lines unable to touch, some bridge missing between them. One large, one small: DADDY, *ian*. The need between them, equal and immense.

The sky, the air, all around him invited him to breathe as the fog began to swarm all over the cars. Hugh looked up at the giant towers and the fog engulfed them too. It was as though the fog were taking the clear air, confusing him, making him take quick, shallow breaths.

As he approached the last tower, he imagined his father trapped up there in the thickening fog. He's trapped up there forever, Hugh thought. *Let him jump, the bastard.*

The traffic loosened and began to flow, and Hugh turned his back on the bridge, on his father, with a sudden shudder of re-lief. He opened the car window, taking huge gulps of the thick, stinging air. He swerved to miss, running over a dead raccoon; he hated the terrible bump. It made him feel like a coward.

Hugh walked into the bar in Sausalito, a little off-the-road one he liked. It had a pool table in back, and it was al-ways dark the way he liked it. The crowd was mostly young men, the working guys of the area—the waiters, dishwashers, delivery boys, and a few office clerks—and a handful of young women trying to pick them up, imagining what they'd look like in bed. Those broad shoulders, those slim hips, the telling bulge nestled in the crotch. A couple of the truly optimistic women tried picturing some of them as fathers, laughing at themselves. Each one to their own dream; that was the magic of darkened bars.

There were a few older guys dressed in suits, aggressively listing the attributes of the same women as though all they had to do was choose. "Guess this guy didn't have time to wash," one of them laughed as Hugh sat a few stools away.

There was oil on his shirt and pants from the machinery he grabbed and worked with all day without any caution to cleanliness. He enjoyed looking at himself at the end of the day, like a mischievous kid.

"Hope he doesn't stink," one of the other suits said in a perceptible voice. They all chuckled, attempting to keep it between them.

The bartender recognized Hugh and came over eyeing the men. "Insurance agents, I bet. What'll ya have, buddy? Whiskey or the hot brandy?"

"Hey, Jim. Yeah, I'm probably building the fuckin' office they'll be moving into so they can sit on their fat asses in style." Hugh's voice was loud and some of the younger men began to laugh.

Someone yelled, "Right on!" Then more laughter. The men in the suits looked down at their drinks quietly.

"I'll take a glass of Dubonnet, Jim, for starters. Get somethin' for yourself while you're at it."

"Dubonnet?" the smaller man of the group echoed with exaggerated disbelief.

Hugh turned and stared at them, his face deceptively calm while a vein on the side of his forehead throbbed visibly, as it did whenever he was about to lose his temper. "Do you guys have a problem with Dubonnet?"

"Hey, man, I'll take a fucking Dubonnet on the fucking rocks!" A good-looking young man sat down on the empty bar stool next to Hugh.

Hugh turned to face him and laughed as he met his eyes. He was maybe twenty-two, blond, with a boyish, enthusiastic face—the nice shoulders, the slim hips, the telling bulge nestled in the crotch. "A man of taste, I gather."

"Yeah, that's me alright. I thought you might regret smearing those assholes all over the wall tomorrow morning." He had a direct, personal gaze—the gaze of a pleasure seeker, but an honest one. There was a distinct appetite for life in his presence and Hugh liked that. In fact, Hugh hungered for that very thing.

"You just might've spoiled my fun." Hugh smiled at him. "I didn't get your name. Mine's Hugh." Hugh met his gaze.

"It's Chris. Chris Mahoney. Play any pool?"

Their drinks arrived.

"Sure do. What's your next drink, Chris?"

"I'll take a tap beer. Catch you next time."

"Hey, Jim, two tap beers and a double whiskey. Get another one for yourself."

Hugh's voice was sluggish and slurred, filled with an old, aching longing. "Hey, Bill, can I come up? Is anyone there, man? See ya in a while. I'm drunk, ya guessed it. Well, can I come up or what?"

The older man laughed softly, softly.

Hugh's eyes burned, his stomach burned, his mind burned. At the very first hint of sexual interest Chris had fled with disgust written all over his face. No amount of booze was going to break down Chris's inhibitions; he just wasn't interested, period.

Hugh had known Bill since he was seventeen; the same year he'd escaped into the Marines from his parents, Alta and April, and then Bill.

They'd met in a restaurant in San Francisco. Bill liked young men, though he had a lover his own age. He was fatherly, understanding, and gentle.

53

The speedometer hit eighty-five. Tomorrow or the next day he'd have to face Alta, but for now it was just himself, the night, and the side of the mountain that took him, much too slowly, to Bill's where everything was always understood, though it didn't last. It never lasted like everything else in his life. "Why does everything good have to end so fucking fast?" Hugh yelled out loud, taking a curve too close. His heart pounded, and the brush with his death sobered him a notch or two.

It'll be good tonight. Yes, Hugh thought, I'm just where I should be—a willing, slightly awake drunk. His laughter filled the car, but there were also tears in his eyes.

Tonight he'd let Bill penetrate him. Tonight he was in the mood. Then he'd let Bill suck him off, letting the circles and circles of loneliness escape him. He would lose control, lose all control to Bill, and then Bill would take care of him softly, softly, until he became husband, father, again. Until he became Frenchy's kid.

The children were asleep and the dishes were done, drying placidly in a lovely order on the rack. Everything was in order as far as she could see. The door and windows were locked, the floor swept, the table cleared, her bed untouched, still made from the morning.

Alta waited for the soothing sound of the key in the carefully locked door, but she knew she wouldn't hear it tonight. He's done it again, my fucking god, he's done it again, she moaned to herself. Despair spread in helpless ripples throughout her body as she sat rigidly on the couch. She wondered how they'd survive this time. No money! her mind screamed. "Damn him! Damn him!" Alta hissed. Standing up, she walked to the window. A dark, swift figure was running toward the stairs, then up them.

"Alta, it's me, Katie!" Her knock was continuous until Alta opened the door. Katie burst through the door bringing the night with her, a sense of escape. She stood in the middle of the front room, angry and defiant. "Well, I bit him. I actually made the sucker bleed."

"Was he doing that stupid bit again?" Alta began to smile in spite of herself.

"Yeah, and I took an incredible bite out of his hand." Katie's eyes glittered as a laugh bubbled out of her.

"Do you want a glass of wine? I've been sitting here contemplating suicide. Hugh's disappeared again with the fucking paycheck." Alta couldn't hide her misery. There was something defeated about her posture, the tone of her voice, flat and listless, and a darkness hovered in her large, watchful eyes.

Katie put her arm around Alta, pulling her close. "I wonder what the malfunction is, you know? What if we started acting like that? Selfish bastards."

Alta poured the wine to the brim. "I'll drink to that," she said, trying to laugh but she couldn't.

"You aren't serious about this suicide thing, are you?" Katie unbuttoned her coat, revealing a cotton nightgown. She kept her eyes on Alta's.

"Sometimes I feel like it. I guess I really do," Alta said in a whisper. Tears sprang to her eyes, pushing themselves out from her lower lids like angry babies. They stung her, but they demanded birth.

"Don't you dare," Katie said softly. "Do you understand me, Alta? I really mean it. Don't you dare even think it." Katie didn't know what else to say so she reached over, brushing back Alta's thick, black hair that hid her face as it fell forward like a curtain. Katie knew that trick, that feminine comfort, of hiding behind her loose, red hair, so she let go of Alta's black hair, not wanting to intrude that far.

Alta got up, wet a kitchen towel, and wiped her face with cold water. "It's only a feeling, really, Katie. I don't even have any idea how I'd do it. I can't stand the idea of hurting myself—you know, guns and knives. So for me it'd have to be chocolate-covered sleeping pills."

"Why don't you leave him? I mean, if it's that bad, if you even contemplate suicide, even for a moment, leave him, throw him out. Fuck it, Alta."

"I've thought of that too, much in the same way as dying—vaguely. I don't know how I'd do it. Like the chocolate-covered sleeping pills, maybe if someone sent me a million-dollar check." Alta laughed sarcastically, with sorrow running right behind it. "And how do you go about not loving someone anymore? How do you turn that one off?"

"Maybe with a chocolate-covered man. Maybe if you eat this guy—I mean, this guy would be six feet, right?—you wouldn't need any more love or men," Katie said with an ironic smile, and her eyes blazed with a secret humor. "Maybe, as the shrinks say, the man would be inside of us, and we could train this guy to like women, and then maybe we could like ourselves. Jesus, I oughta tape this for future reference. My future reference." Katie laughed, mostly at herself.

"I like that. Somehow it makes a lot of sense. I like the idea of eating a man whole." The image made her laugh out loud. "We'd save the genitals for dessert, or would you eat those first?"

"Would they be chocolate covered?" Katie's laugh was rich and throaty. "No, no, I know; they'd be solid chocolate."

As Alta's laughter subsided, her arms and legs hanging loosely over the couch, she said, "I hate to say this, but I'm getting hungry. I didn't eat dinner. Do you want something?"

"Sure. All this talk about solid-chocolate dicks has definitely made me hungry. Am I glad I came down. I almost didn't. I was afraid you'd think I was nuts or something."

"And then you walk in and hear me going on about suicide. I'm really glad you came. Maybe we could special order a six-foot chocolate man."

"We could try. Start a fad. Men could eat chocolate women for the same therapeutic effect." Katie's laughter came in loud gusts, and Alta's laugh, when she didn't censor it, had a crazy edge that fed on itself endlessly.

It was going on two o'clock as Alta melted the margarine for the first omelette. The phone rang.

"If that's Doug, would you tell him I'll be home before he has to take off. I don't feel like talking to him. I feel too good."

"I understand." Alta picked up the phone, imagining at the same time it was a hospital with the news that Hugh was dead. "Doug? Look, Katie says she'll be home before you have to leave." She tried to keep her voice neutral.

"May I speak to her, Alta?" Doug was definitely angry.

"She says she'd rather not. Look, she'll be there in a couple of hours."

"Goddammit, Alta, I want to talk to her! I'm not kidding! I want to talk to her, now!"

"Look here, Doug, she wouldn't be here if you hadn't tried to hit her, so why don't you have some cool and try growing up or something."

Doug was silent, so Alta hung up.

"Thanks. I'll do the same for you sometime. I mean, I'd better. I already owe you my life." Then with a worried look Katie added, "I hope Doug doesn't try anything else. I mean, what choice do I have with the kids and all?"

"We have a choice; we just don't fucking know it yet," Alta said in a tired voice. The wine and the late hour were starting to lull her. Even Hugh seemed unimportant. Just the omelette in the pan had importance, its buttery scent, its rising center, the melted cheese in the middle.

"That's the morning star, or so my father used to tell me," Katie said, pointing to the small, white blaze. All the other stars looked silly next to it as they began to fade. This was the hour the night was darkest and most profoundly still. The hour the sun would decide to live or die.

The women stepped outside, shivering in the predawn cold. They embraced, both of them silent as Katie walked toward her car. Alta watched until she'd started the motor. The darkness was soothing and quiet. The city was so quiet at that hour.

Like camping out, Alta thought suddenly, and the old urge to be exposed to the night filled her.

"I remember the night," she murmured, making herself look up to the still arrogant star. It only seemed to grow brighter, fierce with light, as the others grew dull and shy.

Alta shut the door and locked it, walking quickly toward the perfectly made bed.

"I'm picking up the check from now on, Hugh. I can't take it anymore." Tomorrow was payday and just thinking about it made her sick to her stomach.

"What's the problem? Didn't I give you everything but forty last week? Anyway, they won't give you the check. It's in my name and only I can pick it up."

"I'm picking up the check, Hugh. Also, I'm going camping with my friends this weekend, so you can do anything you want, which you do anyway."

"What does that mean?"

"Where'd you stay for two nights? I never really know where you are. The way you just walked in Sunday morning without any explanation. Do you think you have it made because I'm so stupid?"

"I stayed at Tony's. I mean, why should I come home to this?"

Usually, this was the point where Alta would relent and then she'd pretend nothing had ever happened.

"All I know is, I'm picking up the check, and I'll see you Sunday, if you're here."

"Shit, you've never camped without me. Do any of you feminists know how to start a fire?" Hugh had an overwhelming urge to punch her right in the face, to knock her down, to make her bleed. *To make her.*

Alta saw his anger and, reading his eyes, she recoiled. He'd always loomed over her, threatening her with his face, body, hands, but he'd never hit her. Alta had always known to become silent—angry, but silent. Either that or the usual tears.

There was something relentless in Alta's eyes. It'd been there when she was twelve, and it peeked through again now. Hugh brushed past her, knocking her slightly off balance, slamming the door so hard she was surprised every window in the house didn't break.

April stood at the bedroom door. "Was that Dad? What's wrong, Mom?"

April was twelve, almost a woman, and her eyes were clear and direct, confident. She's so beautiful, Alta thought. She's still so strong.

"Nothing's really wrong. He's just mad because I'm picking up the check tomorrow. Are you excited about going camping?"

April sat down on the bed. She didn't know anymore whether she should curl up with her mother or sit with her legs crossed at a distance. She was almost as tall as Alta.

"We've never been camping without Dad. Is it safe and all?"

"Katie and Jackie'll be with us. Rita's just going to come out for a barbecue," Alta said, pushing April's thick, black hair back. She loved her daughter's profile. It never failed to move her, inexplicably. "You know Rita, she hates camping. She told me she's even afraid of worms." Alta laughed.

"Mom, do you think my you-know-what's going to happen pretty soon? You were twelve, right?"

"Yes, I was twelve. I bet you do start your menstrual real soon. Any day, in fact. Do you ever have kind of sore breasts?"

April looked away, embarrassed. "Yeah, and they're getting bigger too." She turned, meeting Alta's eyes. "Do you like being a woman and everything, Mom?"

Alta's heart stopped. Her daughter's eyes wanted truth and she'd never lied to her, not about the important things. They were so connected in that realm that April would feel the shift of evasion if Alta didn't speak the truth.

"You know, April, sometimes I have trouble liking myself, just who I am. I think everyone does that stuff to some extent. But I think, if anything, being a woman has made me feel good about myself—like having you and Ian. I guess I don't always

59

like having my menstruals, but I think I'd miss it if I didn't have it anymore. It kind of feels like everything's new after my period. Colors look brighter, food tastes better."

Alta reached back in her memory to an old woman's words and continued. "In a way, being a woman is kind of a miracle." She saw that her daughter's eyes were fastened on her. "*We can make life* in our wombs."

"I remember when you told me that I had a womb when I was little and you showed me in a book where it is and I felt like I had a really great secret. I told some of my friends they had wombs too, but they wouldn't believe me." April yawned, lying across the bed on her stomach. "It'll be fun camping with Katie and Jackie. I just wish they had a kid my age. Are we all going to sleep in one tent?"

"We're bringing two tents. I was pretty young when I had you, kiddo. Anyway, don't forget, if you see blood on your panties it's just your menstrual, and tell me right away. You'll get to wear a Kotex." Alta remembered her first period; she'd been terrified, then angry. Angry that she finally had to be a woman, a woman like her mother. "Mother," she murmured involuntarily, as her daughter closed her eyes.

The old anger and the old longing overtook Alta as she watched April sleep. A fierce protectiveness, mingled with sadness, rose up in her. "You're my daughter and I'll never let anyone, ever, hurt you. Never, as long as I live." Alta's words echoed in the suspended silence, and her daughter's breath was even with trust.

The thought of walking into the office and asking for Hugh's check filled her with dread and humiliation—but she had to do it. She just had to.

"My little woman," Alta murmured softly, watching April sleep. "Niña mujer." Tears came to Alta's eyes as she remembered her grandmother's name for her. The soft profile of her daughter came from her grandmother's people. Then Alta thought, Maybe Hugh resents the kids being dark like me. Then she thought of Ian's eyes, exactly like his father's (and those of his father's father), and she sighed, exhausted, because nothing she ever did seemed to be enough.

"April, get up, honey. Here, I'll help you to get to bed."

"I thought I was just talking to you, Mom."

"You were, niña, but you fell asleep on me. Good dreams, April. Fly far, far away, but always come back to me. Tell me your dreams in the morning." Her grandmother's words were automatic to her, and they comforted as she repeated them, as though someone were saying it again to her.

Alta's dreams were no longer clear and vivid as they'd been as a child. They'd stopped coming, and whenever she did dream, she quickly forgot their bits and pieces. So she encouraged her children to dream, especially April, as though their dreams were the one link that held her to the lost world of her grandmother.

As Alta tucked April in Hugh's key turned in the door. It brought her no relief this time, only dread. The house was so silent when the children were asleep. Everything hinged on the beating of her heart.

"Let's camp here by the creek! It's perfect! God, I'm starved to the death!" Jackie was yelling with excitement.

"This looks fine to me!" Alta yelled back. "I'll light the lantern so we can see what we're doing. It smells so good here—redwoods, redwoods, redwoods! Fuck, how I love the smell of redwoods!"

A light rain had fallen that morning and the scent of the forest was all around them, exquisite in the settling dusk. A muted pink-orange sunset was fading, and a few small stars poked through as the other stars prepared themselves to join the growing expanse of darkness.

"First star!" Ian yelled, pointing to the west.

"There's at least four out now, dummy!" April returned irritably.

"Hey, cool it, April, and don't you call Ian dummy, okay?"

April groaned, "Then why does he act like a dummy?"

61

"You apologize to your brother, now! Do you hear me? Now!"

"Sorry," she said, barely letting the word out of her mouth.

"April, would you give me a hand with Erin? I'm afraid to let him down in the dark. Would you stay in the car with him? Here're some tapes if you want." Katie got out of the car to make room for April.

April smiled, pleased that she wouldn't have to help unload everything. She was tempted to stick her tongue out at Ian on the sly, but thought better of it. She popped in a tape and played with Erin, who giggled and jumped on her over and over with great delight.

The secretary had looked at Alta with a confused, irritated expression at first and then comprehension had taken its place. "What was the name again, dear?"

Alta had cashed the check, leaving forty dollars for Hugh on the kitchen table, under the mat. The rest was in her wallet, safe and sound. She'd make out money orders for bills Monday. Maybe I'll open a checking account in my name only and not tell Hugh. These money orders are expensive, she thought, and next week my job starts. He will not get hold of the money again, Alta told herself.

"If you get here before noon every Friday I'll have the check waiting for you, honey." The older woman had given Alta a knowing look and a reassuring smile. "I know what it's like trying to raise kids, what it takes."

"Thank you very much," Alta replied, struck speechless by the older woman's understanding and kindness.

"No problem. No problem at all, dear."

With some fumbling and tripping over stones and fallen branches, the women set up the two tents, spread out the sleeping bags, and unpacked the food for dinner.

Alta placed the shredded paper, then the kindling, then the larger pieces of wood, with painstaking care. Finally, on the fourth try it caught hold. Not too much big wood until the kindling catches, Alta noted for the next time.

"Let's get these babies on!" Jackie began unpacking the steaks from the cooler.

"The potato salad's in my cooler," Katie said with a broad smile on her face.

"Hey, let's break out the vino, ladies!" Jackie yelled as she reached for the still-cold colombard.

After dinner it was so late even April fell asleep without protest. Alta added some good-sized pieces to the fire for warmth. The children were safe within the nylon tents, and the women's shadows were huge as they moved from place to place, silently, talking in quiet voices. Their laughter, as it rose from time to time, was gentle, floating away toward the distant stars. There was something infinitely gentle and nurturing, something very old—ancient—about mothers and children surrounded by darkness, filled with good food, stories, warmth, safety.

The mothers' immense shadows moved surely, creating the last comforts for those that depended on them, and, for the moment, there was no conflict with the larger shadows of men.

"Why don't we sleep outside? It's a lot nicer out here, and it's not going to rain tonight. I mean, look at those stars." Alta shivered with delight, looking up at the vivid clusters. She slipped into her sleeping bag as Katie and Jackie prepared to do the same. Now sleep began to claim her. She dreaded being the last one awake; only then would she be afraid.

"It sure beats smelling farts all night, that's for sure. If you're not smelling your own farts, you're smelling your kids'. Actually, I like my own." Jackie laughed and took another sip of wine.

"Or your old man's. I think I'm used to my kids' farts but not Doug's. Hey, put the tarp right here. We can hold hands if we get scared. Are you guys scared yet? You know, I've never camped without a man." Katie instantly wished she hadn't admitted it, but she went on anyway. "I've only camped with my father and Doug. Pathetic, isn't it? Do you guys have knives or anything?" Katie laughed nervously.

"I camped out with a woman I lived with for a while when I was kid, but this is the first time as the-one-in-charge. She was a tough lady, that lady, and, come to think of it, she did sleep with a knife," Alta remembered. "Get out the butcher knives, ladies," she giggled, but the darkness had begun to look formidable to her as well.

"Yeah, and we went and picked a real private spot too," Jackie added with a groan.

"You picked it, Jackie," Alta reminded her. "I like it though, can't hear anyone else."

"Which means they can't hear us either. Oh, shit, hand me a goddamned knife. Do you suppose we'll qualify as amazons after this ordeal?" Jackie looked at the knife in her hand, feeling its sharp edge with her fingers.

"First we'll have to slice off a tit. Guess it'll have to be the right one, that's the one that gets in the way being that I'm right-handed. Either that or both, they're both pretty big. Like I have these big tits," Jackie laughed. "It's funny. I used to like them when I was younger. Now I'm getting tired of them. I should lose weight. I'm getting fucking fat. Anyway, off with the tits, amazons." There was an unmistakable sadness in Jackie's voice.

"Why should we maim ourselves? Maim the men, I say." Katie sighed. She knew her voice held no conviction. "I want to be an amazon, but without the tit sacrifice, if you please."

"Is Rita coming tomorrow?" Jackie asked in a muffled voice.

"Yeah, around noon, just for the day. You know, she hates camping. Guess she'll never be an amazon," Alta said, closing her eyes, laughing softly.

"Why do suppose she stays with that bastard, anyway?" Jackie really didn't expect an answer.

"Why do I stay with that bastard?" Alta replied. Her eyes began to burn with sleep.

"We used to call it love, remember?" Katie's voice was small and tired. She fingered the wooden handle of her butcher's knife.

"Fuck love. It's sex I crave." Jackie turned on her side, away from her friends and stared out at the night, at the trees silhouetted in various shapes against the sky. The vivid stars only made her feel small and insignificant. Our father who art in heaven came to mind, but she banished it angrily.

"Hope no stray perverts heard that one," she laughed nervously. "It's either called love or rape, isn't it? Jesus, men are assholes."

Jackie's words triggered a series of images in Alta's mind, ending with Hugh's face staring at her angrily, saying, "You know, your bunghole." Anger filled her. She wondered who she hated more at the moment, Hugh or herself. "Bastard," she murmured.

"Have you told Jackie about the chocolate men, Alta?" Katie's voice trailed off. They were cozy against each other, and Katie was in the middle. The fire in front of them leaped to sharp yellow points, sending out its warmth in every direction.

Alta mentally turned Hugh into a piece, an enormous piece, of chocolate. She started to giggle, and immediately she was seized by a hilarious fit of laughter.

"She's off her rocker," Jackie muttered, laughter hidden behind her voice.

Alta blew her nose, wiping her eyes. She could barely keep them open. "It's like this, Jackie; we have to dip the men in our lives in chocolate and then eat them. Penis and all."

"I'm game. I'll donate Joe. I'll save his pecker as a fucking memento." Jackie was mumbling now. She looked up at the sky and thought, And if there is a male god, I'll eat that bastard too. The infinite chocolate bar, the Milky Way, His Highness with Almonds . . . women don't count except as worshipers, but what's a god without worshipers? You blew it man, she rambled on mentally. A strange loneliness engulfed her; the sense of the infinite waiting to be eaten was horrible.

"Alta? Hey, Katie, you awake?" She could hear them breathing. She wondered if they were pretending to be asleep, but decided against speaking again. Jackie closed her eyes. The sky tilted, scooping her up with its rough tongue like a black, green-eyed cat, and Joe and god were only ghosts trying to haunt her.

She dreams: Jackie

An immense wall is in front of her, and, as she looks up, it reaches up to the sky as far as she can see. She pushes on the wall, and it's solidly fastened to the earth. She touches it and it feels smooth and almost warm. She leans forward and licks the wall. A strange ecstasy fills her: chocolate. "I will never be hungry again." She wants to bite, but she can only lick, lick, lick. Lick.

She dreams: Alta

She holds a large clay pot. She takes a stick and, starting at the top, carves a straight line downward. Then, with great difficulty, as though something wants to stop her, she places the stick to the left and carves, with as much concentration as she possesses, a straight line across. A cross. It fills her with a great joy to see it, as though she's finally created something wonderful with her own two hands.

She dreams: Katie

A beautiful woman dressed in a dark purple cape, with its hood slightly shielding her averted face, holds a pure, white dove in her hands. She lets it go. Katie wants to weep, but the beautiful woman is so calm.

* * *

"I can't believe you crazy women spent the night here by yourselves. My God, how primitive," Rita said, laughing.

"We are now amazons, Rita baby. Better watch your ass," Jackie said, walking over to give her a hand with her packages.

"So, what did you bring for the feast?" Alta asked. "I think I'm hungry already."

"Marinated chicken, or is that amazon food? Also, champagne, French bread, and more."

"You always were my favorite person; you know, Rita?" Jackie peeked into the cooler. "Goddamn, woman, you weren't just a whistlin' dixie! Fuckin' A! How 'bout poppin' this baby before it goes flat!"

"At ten in the morning?" A frown crossed Katie's face.

"What are you, a girl scout? Pop that mama!" Jackie reached for the champagne.

"Hey, I'll take some of that. I mean, how often do we drink champagne in the morning, in the woods, after a treacherous night of fending off perverts and wolves, right?" Alta smiled, looking at Katie.

"If you guys are that hungry, I've got some cheese and crackers here," Rita offered.

"Welcome Rita, welcome Rita, welcome Rita," Jackie chanted.

"Well, I certainly didn't mean to come off like a girl scout," Katie said defensively. "I was just thinking of the kids and all."

"We're not going to get drunk, come on. We're just going to enjoy ourselves, right?" Jackie laughed and handed Katie the first glass. "Come on, woman, loosen up and shake them hips." Jackie started dancing, curling her toes into the warm, soft summer earth as she sipped her champagne.

The early morning sun, as it filtered through the immense mother redwoods, made the four women look young. Extraordinarily young. Like girls.

Katie laughed and took a sip.

"If these women start gettin' too wild on us we'll have to tie 'em to a tree till they come to their godgiven and proper senses." Rita rolled her eyes, looking at Alta.

"Hey, where's my champagne? Greedy little thing, aren't you?" Alta took her champagne and started dancing with

Jackie in the silence. Katie started to sway, humming "Light My Fire" so softly no one else could hear her.

There was only the sound of the creek in the distance and the wind blowing gently at the very tips of the redwoods. All the kids, including April, were down by the creek playing in the water. Ethan played quietly in the shallows with his toys, wishing he were old enough to leap from the rope. He felt like a baby. April and Ian took turns watching Erin and jumping from the huge, knotted rope that dangled over the cool, green depths. It looked like a clear, glittering emerald in the morning sun, and it invited the children to jump, swinging from the cottonwood over the water in wide, lovely swoops. Then, screaming at the top of their lungs they let go of the rope, flying for an instant like birds as they plunged into the chilly morning creek like fish.

"You shoulda seen your face when you let go of the rope, Rita! I thought you were gonna shit a brick! I wish I had a camera." Alta laughed, remembering Rita's face. "I didn't even know you could swim," she gasped, unable to control her fit of hilarity.

"You call that swimming? That, Alta la loca, is the perro paddle. Under normal circumstances I never would've done that. Too much vino malo." Rita put her hands to her head exaggeratedly. Then she laughed loudly without restraint. "I thought I was going to *die* when I let go of that damned rope, and the water's so damned cold."

"I thought Katie was going to die jumping from the second branch like that. No more wine for you in the morning, girl." Jackie shook her head and laughed loudly.

"Tomorrow I'll try for the second branch," Alta said, licking her fingers. The barbecued chicken was incredible.

"Can I try, too, Mom?"

Alta had stopped April from jumping so high that afternoon, and now her daughter had her cornered.

"Okay, April. I suppose if you're not afraid to, you can do it." Alta turned to Rita. "Why don't you stay the night? You brought sleeping bags and we have enough food. The kids could split up into the tents. Come on, stay."

"I understand I have to slice off my tit, as Jackie says, to stay, so I'm afraid I can't."

"Keep your tits, just stay. We'll protect you, Rita," Jackie said, flexing her arm muscles playfully.

"You should see our knives," Katie said as though she were revealing a well-kept secret. "We are dangerous, Rita, no shit."

A brief look of sorrow crossed her face as she remembered something from her childhood, something she'd never told anyone. Her mother was dead and only her father knew. There'd been no one to protect her then from her father. No one. Their playful offer to protect her now touched her in a strange way. Even her mother hadn't been able to.

Rita smiled, erasing her sadness. "If anyone came through here you'd all run in different directions." She tried to laugh, but the looks on her friends' faces stopped her.

"I really don't think anyone's going to bother us, but if anyone tried to I sure wouldn't run," Alta said a little angrily.

"No, no, I really can't stay. Personal preference. You know how I hate this camping out business." Rita looked at Alta, saying, "I suppose after that business with the purse snatcher I should know you wouldn't run, shouldn't I?"

"Oh, come off it, Rita; Carl's not going anywhere. I mean, Alta's here with Hugh the Horrible on the loose." Jackie laughed at her own pun.

Alta saw Rita's instant anger and interjected, "But this time I have the money, so the damage will be minimal."

Rita sprang to her feet. "My not staying has nothing to do with Carl or you, Jackie." Tears came to her eyes but she willed them away. "We all have our cross to bear, don't we?"

"I'm not bearing any crosses, that's for damned sure," Jackie said in a low voice.

Rita ignored her. "Anyway, my kids are almost falling asleep, so I'd better be going."

"Your chicken was delicious, Rita," Katie said. "Stay another hour at least. It's such a great time of day."

Jackie stood up to face Rita. "Rita, what I said wasn't meant to be insulting. I mean, Joe, as you know, is a total bastard-asshole-fuckhead. So I'm not trying to put you on the spot. I mean, we know Carl has affairs, and we know José has affairs. What about you, Katie?"

Rita was clearly uncomfortable, but she stood there frozen to the spot. April sat, amazed at the conversation she was being allowed to witness. It felt like a bomb was about to go off. The sky behind Rita's head was a mixture of reds and purples streaked across the horizon. The sun was setting fast, and it was as though the colors radiated from Rita's dark, still head. She held herself absolutely rigid.

Rita exploded. "I don't want to hear this! Why should I want to know if Katie's husband is having an affair? How in the hell would that help me? That's enough, Jackie!" She began packing her things and throwing everything in the back of the car. Two of her children were already sleeping in the backseat. The third was playing with Ian in the tent, but now she poked her head out to see why her mother's voice was so angry.

Jackie continued in an even voice. "Because maybe then you wouldn't feel so fucking alone, Rita. Because maybe then you'd know it's not your fucking fault. That's why. And because I care about you."

"Jackie's right." Alta couldn't help it; she had to say it out loud. "I haven't caught Hugh with anyone but I know something's going on. Is that my fault? I mean, is it your fault, Rita?"

"I don't have to listen to this. This is my private life, and I will not discuss it like a news item." Rita gathered her daughter, started the car, and drove away. Once her anger died down, passing Sausalito, she wondered if Carl would be home. Or would there be a quickly written excuse—lie—on the bedroom dresser under her favorite perfume bottle? Would there be fresh flowers next to it as well? she wondered.

Now she felt alone with her lie, with the truth. Now she wept silently as her children slept—her daughter, the oldest, curled beside her. Now she wished she were surrounded by dangerous women, the ones with butcher knives. Even Jackie. They were her friends and she knew it.

Katie lowered her bathing suit top to oil the fleshy, white rim of her breasts. "No men as far's I can see. Actually, I feel like taking off the top entirely. My boobs get so sweaty in this thing."

"I've always been jealous that men get to walk around half naked with no hassles," Alta replied as she stretched her top, letting the cooling air touch the hidden skin beneath. "Although, I suppose, if I did bare all no one would jump me, being that I'm nearly built like a boy." Alta glanced down at her breasts and then quickly looked back at the water.

"I think you have a nice body. You don't look like a boy to me, lady, and you'd definitely get arrested for walking down the street with your breasts exposed. And jumped too, probably." Katie laughed. "I think that's really a trip, getting arrested and all for taking off our tops. Shit." The sun felt delicious on her breasts.

Jackie was sunbathing on the opposite bank with her arm flung over her face. She was still wet. She watched the drops of water lengthen on her arm as they began to fall, knowing she'd have to get right back in the moment she dried off. It was hot in the noon sun, and her body fluttered with rainbows pooled here and there as she breathed.

What I wouldn't give for a *cold* margarita, she thought. Right here next to me. She sat up, eyeing the water irritably.

"What is that on your breast, Katie, a spider bite or what?" Alta asked, indicating a large, red swelling.

Katie covered herself quickly. "Oh, it's nothing, I guess. I've had it for about a year." She paused, then continued. "It was very small at first, and, well, now it's this damned size."

"Have you had it checked? That should be checked." Alta suddenly felt chilled although the sun burned her body. Even her sweat seemed suspended.

"I went in and about a dozen doctors saw me. They said it was from my birth control pills, so I stopped taking them." Katie's eyes pleaded with Alta for understanding.

Alta met her eyes. "Have you had a biopsy of that?" Her mouth felt dry and the children's playing seemed very far away. April climbed to the second branch and leaped, straddling the rope fearlessly. She swung twice across the creek, then bracing her feet on the knot, she pushed off and dove with a shriek of delight. Surfacing, she spun in a little circle with her hand scooping the light-filled water ahead of her.

"They said it was nothing," Katie answered in a hypnotized voice.

"But did you get a biopsy of it?" Alta insisted, getting angry.

"Well, no. The doctors said it was really nothing." Katie turned away because she knew she couldn't hide anymore.

"Do you mean to say it's been getting bigger all year and you haven't gone back?" Alta almost hated to keep pushing, but it was as though she couldn't help herself.

Katie shook her head.

"You've got to get a biopsy right away, when you get back. Damn it, you have to demand a damned biopsy. Fuck this looking-at-it-shit!"

"I'll do it. I promise." Katie's voice was weary as though she'd come to the end of an exhausting journey with a secret she'd been forced to keep, and somehow she'd only been waiting for someone to say, "I know your secret."

"I'm not going to stop bugging you until you get a biopsy. I mean it, Katie. I can't believe it's gotten bigger all year. Call the minute you get home. Do you promise me?"

"I want cookies, Mommy," Erin whined, pulling on his mother.

"I promise. I'll call." Katie looked pale. Huge tears blinded her as she groped for the package of cookies.

Erin hummed softly as he ate. One of the cookies dropped into the creek, floating away. He began to cry, pointing at it. Katie rushed forward to replace it and, instantly, he was comforted. She sat next to the creek, putting Erin on her lap, watching Jackie swim toward her.

"I'm not ready to go home!" Jackie yelled. "What about you guys?" She smiled straight up into the sun, repeating her smooth breast stroke evenly. "The only fucking thing that tempts me to go back to fucking civilization is a fucking chilled margarita!"

Jackie turned over on her back and submerged herself entirely.

Alta laughed shortly, glancing at Katie who sat quietly with Erin on her lap and muttered, "My sentiments, exactly," thinking of Hugh. She'd never picked up the check before, and she wondered how she'd gotten the guts to do it. She couldn't imagine doing it again. Then she thought of the money safe in her purse and relief flooded her. She wondered if Hugh would be home, but a strange thought skittered across her mind: It'd be better if he weren't, it'd be quiet, it'd be peaceful. It'd be safe.

Katie's heart couldn't stop racing, as though it wanted to get ahead of her, to kill her and get it over with. Tears ran down her face. It's just a stupid lump that'll go away like all those doctors said. They are the doctors, aren't they? she asked herself. If they don't know, who does? Yet the word *cancer* whispered itself dully each time she looked at the red growth on her breast.

If I died, she thought, Doug would find someone else in six months, I know, that motherfucker. But the kids, my children. She held Erin, feeling his baby fat next to her body. The baby fat she, herself, had pumped into him from her own body. From her own breasts. His baby body, the body she, Katie, had given him. Now an undeniable despair filled her, and it was as though the quick, clear creek were suddenly polluted by invisible, deadly chemicals, poisonous to all life—as though the sky were filled with radiation fallout and no birds would ever sing again forever—as though a terrible, endless, killing winter had settled itself on the Earth. But she forced herself to see the light on the water for Erin and Ethan's sake. Erin's feet dangled in its coolness and Ethan played in it farther up stream.

"Katie, are you okay?" Alta asked, sitting next to her. "Katie?" Alta touched her smooth, sunburned shoulder. In the sunlight, Katie's red hair looked like living fire as it blazed with an arrogance of its own.

"Has anyone ever told you, you look like a bird of paradise?" Alta's voice was soft with a strange tenderness, and she was surprised she'd said it, but at the same time she was filled with a curious joy.

Katie smiled, mostly to herself, and turned to look at Alta. "Has anyone ever told you, you look like a tiger?" Katie paused. "No, that's not it. I mean, a jaguar."

Alta's face narrowed with pleasure for a moment. "Are you okay, Katie?"

The winter returned with a roar. "I don't know, Alta. You know?"

Hugh tried to work on the delicate steel mobile in the basement. It was getting huge and the balance was interesting, but who in the hell would ever see it besides a few friends, he thought to himself with a familiar mixture of boredom and bitterness. He added the intricate steel piece and spun it, and now the left side hung too low. He felt like smashing the whole thing to pieces: six months' work. All the little stupid scraps of steel I've collected, stuffing them into my lunch box like a good, little boy.

"Fucking spic bitch!" Hugh spit the words angrily into the stale air as he thought of Alta picking up his check and cashing it, not putting a penny of it into the checking account. "Just keep the whole damn thing, *my fucking money*, in your twat, bitch!"

He allowed the rage to fill him, and, without knowing it, Alta fused with his mother, Sarah, and, for a moment, he was a boy of five tied up in a chair, screaming his lungs out to a shut kitchen door. Sometimes he fell asleep from his rages and later the thin, red marks of his mother's clothesline would burn.

"Bitch! Fucking bitch!" He wanted to weep. It started sometimes in his stomach and died somewhere as it lurched past his grown man's heart.

He remembered walking down the steel beam the other day—the wind had stopped dead, as he'd leaned into it, keeping his balance, with only enough room to put his feet one after another, and six floors below. He'd caught himself upright, ready to fling himself flat onto the cold, steel beam.

"That's how I earn my money, bitch! With my goddamned life!" If Hugh would've added, "I wear the pants in this family!" his father would've been quoted fully and correctly.

Hugh pushed the mobile so hard it hit the cement basement wall, clattering like a sad, metal bird. "Hugh the artist, what a laugh," he muttered.

Bill was home. He'd go to Bill's sober for a change. It'd been a while. Maybe he'd work in the studio and watch Bill's strong, skilled hands mold the clay flat, round, high, wide. Then later those same hands might take warmed oil and massage him flat, round, high, wide. They might lie in the hot tub and suck each other's tongues, each other's dicks, then do it all over again, muscle to hard muscle. Bill's broad, hairy body, his hard masculine hands squeezing every last drop of pleasure out of him. Hugh smiled lazily, and he was hard as he pulled into traffic.

The front door was open so Hugh knew Bill was in the studio. There were fresh flowers everywhere in large, beautiful jars. An immense plant in the front room window grew in a container that Bill had thrown using the entire length of his arms and chest to center it. Hugh had laughed, watching him twelve years ago. The sight of the raw clay covering Bill's arms and chest had excited him. They'd made love covered in the wet, slippery clay.

Bill looked up and smiled. He wore shorts and a T-shirt splattered with clay. He was a good-looking man with his slightly long, grey hair and faded blue eyes. There was kindness in his eyes, and amusement, and a flickering steel light that rarely failed him when he wished to see the truth.

"I have to get a job done today. So it looks like I'll be working another three hours. Tomorrow I fire. How're you doing?"

Hugh smiled hesitantly and asked, "Can I spend the night? That is, if no one's coming by," implying Bill's older, steady lover.

"I'd like that, Hugh. Why don't you work on the kick wheel, get a drink, take off your shirt so I can look at you. I always like to look at you when you're around, you know."

Hugh couldn't help beaming at the older man's acceptance; tears stung his eyes.

"Do you want me to pound some of this clay? I could get into that," Hugh said, picking up a huge rectangular piece. "Then maybe I'll try throwing a couple of pots."

Bill took off his T-shirt, exposing his tanned, well-muscled chest, slightly rounded at the shoulders from stooping over his work. "I've got a big piece to do later. If you'd punch that clay, that'd certainly help."

Hugh took off his pants, shirt, and undershirt, leaving on the black, low-cut bikini Alta had bought him. It showed his masculinity off well—his smooth, muscled thighs; long, tapered legs; his chest tanner than the rest of his body with its lush patch of dark hair narrowing like an arrow to his groin; his shoulders broad, yet graceful; his neck and the tilt of his head almost like a dancer's from walking the narrow, steel beams in the high wind, balancing.

"God, you're beautiful," Bill murmured.

Hugh blushed, looking up shyly yet exultantly. "Do you really think so?" His voice sounded low and feminine. Young.

"Come here and I'll show you."

Hugh's movements were a little awkward in spite of the wide, wooden floor beneath him as though he were taking his first steps. His body felt thick with its sudden heat and his temples pounded.

Bill turned off the potter's wheel, swivelling around in his seat to face Hugh. He placed his hands on Hugh's waist, leaving his imprints on each side, laughing deep in his throat, almost growling. Then he slid his hands up over Hugh's chest, leaving trails of clay that began drying, almost instantly, with the heat of his skin. Bill picked up a glob of wet clay sitting in its bowl and began painting again, turning Hugh around. Hugh stood passively, yet alert, with his hands to his sides, and Bill, beginning at the small of his back, trailed upward following the long, firm spine. He extended both hands, simultaneously, to the breadth of Hugh's shoulders. Those shoulders that carried steel and iron and other men's lives, Bill imagined. *Other men, like us,* Bill almost said out loud, but he didn't, and the silence in the studio, surrounded by forest on the side of a mountain at the end of a dirt road, was audible.

No voices pierced the air here—certainly no woman's voice, no child's—only the delicate, ragged breath of two men, alike, exactly of one mind for the moment, feeling the pleasurable swelling of their penises, the pleasant ache of their balls for each other. Only their delicate, ragged breath filled the air.

Hugh moaned, throwing his head back in feminine abandon. Now Bill dipped his hands once more into the wet, slippery clay, trailing his hands down Hugh's slim, mannish hips. His breath caught as he inserted his fingers into Hugh's black bikini, exposing his firm, tense ass. White, white like the moon, Bill thought gratefully. He knelt down on both knees, placing his arms around Hugh's legs and began licking the center of that mysterious planet, that loveliness.

Hugh moaned louder in a sustained kind of song, coming so deeply from the center of his being his legs began to tremble violently.

Bill let his saliva run down Hugh's ass, and turning him gently, he lowered his bikini, exposing the taut, sweet penis. He took it entirely into his mouth at once and inserted his finger into the dark side of the moon, imagining the white flesh shining as he explored Hugh with his probing finger.

As Hugh came, spurting in wide, wild circles, splattering the walls, the floor, and Bill with his hot, stinging life, he cried, "Daddy, Daddy! I love you, Daddy!" in a hoarse, horrible, utterly triumphant voice. No woman caught this sperm. No would grow from it. This sperm was free and wild, shooting toward the stars. Star spoor. Man spoor. Spoor of the father.

"I love you, too, Hugh. I love you, too. Now bend over here," Bill said, placing Hugh carefully over his worktable, chest down. "Daddy needs to love you too. Daddy needs to love you . . . " Why is the first thrust the best? Bill wondered with a violent shudder. Like piercing the cosmos, dead center, it is. Yes, it is. Yes. But first Bill placed a rubber on his penis. He only trusted his steady lover. You never know what you might catch from these young guys, he thought as he fumbled with it.

"Forget the rubber, I don't care," Hugh moaned.

"There, got it. Now just hold still, like that . . . "

Now there was nothing in the world but two men, alone, making fire.

Carl was brushing his teeth and the kids were arguing in the front room.

"Get ready for bed!" Rita yelled angrily. Instantly, she regretted it. He'd been home, hadn't he? No note, no excuses, no flowers. He'd been in the backyard sunbathing in the nude, in the corner where no one could see unless they stood on the fence.

Rita herded the kids into bed as Carl took a long, hot shower. The relief she'd felt seeing him lying on the grass flooded her again. Relief and gratitude. Looking at his blond hair from the back porch door she'd imagined, in her burning joy, that she owned that hair. That head.

The children were still talking quietly. She could hear her daughter's voice, her laughter. Almost the age, in another year, when her father . . . No, she wouldn't think of it. She refused to think of it.

Carl turned off the shower. Rita thought of her friends and imagined them in their sleeping bags, or maybe they were sitting by the fire drinking wine. Maybe they were talking about her and what a sap she was to take Carl's crap. But Carl was home tonight, she reminded herself.

Rita pulled down the covers, then the sheets, and she noticed the bed wasn't very well made. And then she noticed, as she readjusted the pillows, the smears of a very bright pink lipstick.

José was asleep by the time Jackie got home, so she carried him in and undressed him. He's getting so big, she thought, and a sharp, mothering tenderness flooded her. He never woke up or made a sound as she put his pajamas on. His little boy's penis flopped over, utterly vulnerable, and it made her want to cry. She covered her son up to his neck, and then, as usual, she put his baby blanket on top of his regular ones. She sighed deeply, remembering the countless times she'd told him the story of coming home from the hospital wrapped in it. "You were the size of a puppy . . . "

The house was silent except for the sound of José's breathing, the little mouth wide open—the mouth that had sucked her breasts, drunk her milk. The night his father had beaten her, it seemed he'd purposely aimed for her breasts as though he were jealous of their wordless serenity, of the simple act of feeding and being fed. Joe felt excluded. Yes, he'd aimed for her breasts.

"Black and blue," Jackie said out loud to the silent house. "Black and blue." She got the bottle of vodka out of the freezer, some crackers and smoked Gouda cheese. Slowly she poured the thick, translucent, almost frozen, liquid into a wine glass, tilting it from side to side as it moved like a tempting, edible mercury. She took a sip, and the mercury exploded in her mouth, telling her what she wanted to know.

Next weekend I'm getting laid whether I know the guy's name or not. José will be with Joe. I'll do as I damn well please. "I'm not carrying any fucking cross," she said out loud as the refrigerator kicked into gear. It sounded like a jet in the silence, especially after the silence of the nights spent outdoors.

Jackie quickly walked over to the window, opening it wide, but the fog was in. The fog depressed her. It reminded her of her childhood, the muted cruelty of her father's blows, her mother never screaming; but she'd heard it all her life through the thin walls. She'd always blamed the fog somehow.

"The fucking fog," Jackie murmured. Tears stung her eyes. "Why don't you just demolish the stars, why don't you? Fuck." When she was ten her father began to hit her hard with his fists, but she had screamed. She screamed loud and long and bloodcurdling, and he hated her for it, and she hated him. He went back to hitting her mother, who remained silent. Who was still silent. Fat, saggy, and silent, Jackie thought angrily.

She wanted to sob, but she couldn't. She wanted to write a poem, but she couldn't. Poems, my ass, she thought, berating herself. General masturbation no one's ever going to fucking read. She slammed the window closed against the thick, menacing fog.

Jackie poured the next glass full to the brim and sipped the mercury slowly, sensually. At that moment she would've settled for Joe gladly.

"Are you seeing that bitch again?" Katie screamed.

"What do you care? I took third place after the kids were born. I don't even make any money—any real money, that is. You'd probably be better off without me. Then your parents could support you while you go back to school in style." Doug glared at her from the other side of the room, but his voice sounded, at bottom, disinterested.

"That's not true, Doug." Katie began to cry. "That's just not true! I can't imagine being without you, but I can't stand you doing this."

"Doing what?" Doug challenged her cruelly.

Katie was hysterical now. "You know what, you bastard, you know what!" She fell on the couch, holding her stomach, doubled over with pain.

Doug jumped to his feet, yelling, "This is the shit I can't stand! This martyr bit. You'd think you were dying. What a crock of shit!"

All hope escaped her. She simply felt no hope. She wanted to scream, scream, and never stop screaming: I am dying! The red spot isn't going away! You've got to love me now because I really am dying . . .

Ethan was standing in the front room door, so small and dark, like a spirit or a lost child's shadow, but the voice was human enough: "Mommy, I'm scared."

"Christ, the kids should be sleeping," Doug said angrily.

Katie looked at Doug. "I hate you." She wiped her face and got up, bending over to pick up her son. Hate and love wrenched her soul equally.

Alta woke up as the front door shut. Hugh had tried to close it quietly, but the wind was blowing hard. When he finally came to bed, slipping in as carefully as he could, she pretended to be asleep, staying on her stomach protectively, breathing evenly in and out. His breath finally settled, and he never once tried to touch her. In fact, he slept turned away from her, and she was glad.

Alta lay there remembering the stars and the fire. The night. It seemed so far away. Their laughter. Their conversations without lies. It seemed so far away.

Three

Katie was late. She should've been back over an hour ago, and Alta was beginning to get a little worried. Ethan was playing in the yard with Ian's toy cars making tracks in the dirt and then parking them in the large, block building he'd built. It was multicolored and imaginative with its series of spires, almost like a church. His expression was solemn as though he were deciding grave things, as he brought out the red car for a run, then the yellow, then the sleek, black, low one with red racing stripes on its sides (Ian's favorite). Ethan held the black racing car up to his eyes and pushed on one of its tiny rubber wheels till it came off. He looked up at the house guiltily and shoved it in his jean pocket, pressing the rubber wheel once between his fingers.

After Erin had fallen asleep, Alta began frying hamburger and chorizo for tacos. There was some chilled Chablis in the refrigerator with sliced oranges floating in it, waiting for Katie. As Alta had carried Erin to Ian's bed from the front room floor, she had imagined Katie, at the same moment, being told the results of her biopsy. She'd tried to imagine Katie's face, the expression: good or bad. But she couldn't, so she looked down at Erin's two-year-old face, perfect with sleep—almost like death, she'd thought, as a shudder ran the length of her body.

Then she bent her face to Erin's open mouth, and his warm, quick breath had comforted her. She'd smiled at the dry, sticky popsicle stains around his mouth, shutting the bedroom door behind her.

The afternoon wind began to kick up as Alta finished frying the corn tortillas, placing them, folded, to drain on a paper towel. Ian and April would be home in an hour. Ethan was in the backyard eating his taco, making the cars greasy and shiny. That pleased him. A large yellow monarch landed on his multicolored block building as though on a flower. It stretched its wings in the sun and flew away before Ethan could see it.

Katie came in without knocking and walked straight toward the kitchen where Alta was. She clenched herself the way she'd been clenching herself from the moment they'd told her, but now that she saw Alta's startled face, she crumbled.

"There's nothing they can do. It's too late." Katie's face and voice had no defense as she looked at Alta. Her courage and anguish were almost too much to bear, but Alta continued to meet her gaze.

"I'm going to die. It's in my glands, everything. I'm going to die." Except for the dark circles under Katie's eyes, she looked beautiful and young. She looked undeniably young.

"How long do they say?" Alta whispered.

"Maybe six months." Katie's shoulders hunched forward as the first moans rose up from her belly. She hid her face in her hands and wept. "Why? Why in the fuck me?" Katie raised her head. "Why?" she asked Alta as though Alta were death and could answer her logically, patiently. Tenderly.

Alta walked over to Katie, as in a dream, taking her into her arms. She felt Katie's round, soft breasts between them, with her own small breasts meeting hers. She began to cry, "Oh, Katie, I'm so sorry, I'm sorry, those bastards, those motherfucking bastards, why didn't they do a biopsy *then?*"

Katie and Alta stood in the middle of the kitchen floor holding onto one another as though the world had disappeared and all its familiar landmarks. The only landmark now was a stunning, piercing grief; so powerful they could hardly breathe. As they stood together, holding on, the first wave of grief slowly subsided.

They separated. Katie sat down on a chair as Alta found her balance against the sink.

"Do you want some wine? I made some tacos. Are you hungry?"

"I'll take the wine."

April and Ian were home and Doug's voice called out. "I saw these two walkin' home and decided to give 'em a ride. Is

Katie . . . " Doug stopped short as he saw her. "What did they say, Katie? What's wrong?"

Katie looked at Doug, but she couldn't bring herself to answer him.

"What the hell's wrong, Katie?" Doug raised his voice angrily.

"April, Ian, please go to your room," Alta said, taking them away.

Katie took a deep breath and held it. "I've got cancer, Doug, and it's spread all over my body. There's nothing they can do. I have maybe six months. That's what they just told me." Tears continued to fall down Katie's face, but the sobs, the great grief had been gotten through for the moment.

Doug's face became enraged as he looked at her, as though she could only be lying. "I don't believe it! Goddammit, I don't believe any of this! What about the kids?"

"They can go with my parents, Doug. I don't expect you to stay with me." Katie's voice was harsh with sorrow, and her eyes never left Doug's face. "But I've got cancer and I'm going to die."

Doug picked up a kitchen chair, holding it up high over his head. "I don't believe it! I don't believe it!" He began to cry, his face contorting into a terrible red mask of pain and rage. He brought the chair down to the floor, and it exploded, splintering all over the room. He shoved the kitchen table to one side, spilling sugar all over the floor, as he reached for another chair.

"Stop it, Doug, stop it! Stop it right now!" Katie was on her feet screaming at him, but she was utterly afraid to touch him.

"Stay here and don't come out," Alta told April and Ian. They were speechless as she slammed the door.

"What in hell's going on here?" Alta yelled, seeing the broken wood everywhere. It was total chaos. Doug had another chair in his hands, and Katie was pleading with him to stop. It was as though Doug's eyes had ceased to see. "That's my goddamned chair, Doug, put it down or you're paying for it!" Alta shrieked. "Can't Katie be sick for Christ's sake, you god-damned coward!" Her voice lost all control.

Doug put the chair down, slowly. His eyes began to focus, not on Alta or Katie, but on the room itself. "I'm sorry. I'm sorry 'bout all this." His voice was strangely calm. "I'll pay for the chair." Doug turned and stumbled, as though drunk, toward the front door.

"Doug!" Katie called after him.

"Leave me alone, just leave me alone. I can't deal with it right now."

Katie banged the table with her fist and yelled, "I'm the one who's dying, you bastard! I'm the one that's got cancer! Get your shit together and get out!"

Ethan stood at the kitchen door, staring at his mother with terrified eyes. "Are you sick, Katie?" he asked in a clear, brave little voice.

Doug drove straight to a waterfront bar and, without ac-knowledging anyone, began to drink. He remembered:

"I'm not a woman anymore, damn it! And the damned thing hurts so bad," his mother said hopelessly.

"You've got to start exercising, Mom—that's what the doc-tors said—so the muscles under your arm get strong." Doug's voice was firm, the way she'd been with him. He towered over her, six feet at fourteen.

"They took more than my damned breast, Doug, damn it! They took who I am." She turned her face from him and let the hot, held tears fall.

He'd heard his father last night when he came home drunk. "I just can't stand to look at it, that's all. I just can't help it, Mary. Just don't badger me. Just don't badger me, goddammit anyway."

He heard his mother crying, muffling her voice into a pil-low. He hated his father for saying it, and he hated his mother, just as much, for crying.

"Mom, you've got to pull on these weights. You've got to start doing these exercises, do you hear me, Mom?" Doug began to raise his voice as he'd never dared to do.

"I can't. It hurts too much. You don't know what it's like. I'm going to go rest. I'm so damned tired." She turned, without any trace of spirit, to walk away. Her hair needed washing, her usual hair style, and she hadn't even applied lipstick for over a month. A little makeup had always been important to her.

"So you lost your breast, what's the big deal? Do you want to be a goddamned cripple?" He was yelling now and his mother began to cry. Now he knew what he had to do.

"I just don't care, Doug. Don't you understand?" She looked at her son. "No, you don't understand. How could you, anyway?" Her voice was flat and indifferent.

"Okay, then, show it to me. Show me this thing you're making such a big deal about." Doug's voice was insistent with a distinct edge of cruelty, and his eyes were unyielding as he stared at his mother.

Her face registered shock. "Doug, I can't show you this, for God's sake. Don't you understand, my breast is gone! It's been cut off! There's nothing there but an ugly scar, damn you!" Now her voice began to rise with anger.

"So you lost your tit, big deal. That is, if you did, because I'm starting to think you made the whole damned thing up, that's what!" He stared at his mother.

Hot fury filled her. It felt like she was on fire, head to foot. She could kill him. Then she remembered: "I fed you from that breast, Doug. I fed you from both of my breasts." Her voice was choked, but she met his gaze. "Do you still want to see it?" She reached for the top button.

Doug ran from the room and, taking his bike, headed straight for the desert. When he got to his secret spot he sprawled in the absolute silence and wept as he hadn't since he was six. That time his father had taken a belt to him.

"Don't you think you had enough there, Doug? You gotta get home, right?" The bartender didn't want to serve him anymore.

He could see it was a feat for Doug to stay seated, much less walk.

"Come on, Larry, what's it t'ya? Gimme another or ah'll kick yer ass. Shit, ahm payin', ain't I? Filler 'er up agin. Ain't my motherfuckin' money good here or what?" Doug could barely keep his eyes open. Even thinking cost him his balance.

"Right, you're gonna kick my ass—wouldn't want that ta happen, man." The bartender poured him another. "Don't say I didn't try ta warn ya, Doug."

"Does yer wife ever threaten ya with bein' sick an dying an all that shit? Ya know, gettin' one up on ya. Bitches, man, a bunch a natural born bunch a bitches." Doug tried to stand. All he could remember was trying to grab onto the bar and falling quickly toward the floor, as though the floor had come halfway up to meet him. Then the pain.

Alta had picked up the check the last few weeks; Hugh was cold and distant, but the matter of the money seemed settled. He'd left for the weekend once. Alta was tempted to challenge him, to find out where he went, but now she felt that since she had the money she should leave him alone. His thin male pride was stretched taut.

The job is okay, Alta thought, but it's not what I really want to do. Well, what do you want to do? The familiar question brought its usual terror. Leaving Hugh, the second fantasy on her list; and the children? How would I even pay the rent? Now her possibilities narrowed down to a long, dark tunnel, giving her barely enough room to breathe or light to see by.

The phone rang: "Mom, I'm at Katie's. Guess what, Mom? Guess what happened?" April's voice was high and excited.

A wave of anxiety slapped her full to the present. "What happened, April? Why aren't you home? Ian's been home for half an hour. I was just about to go look for you."

"I'm at Katie's, Mom. I got it. You know, I got it." Now April's voice was low and shy.

Alta suddenly understood. "You got your menstrual? Why didn't you come straight home, April? Did it actually start?"

"Just some spots, but I thought I'd stop at Katie's and get a Kotex, but she doesn't have any. Can you come and get me?"

"Sure, honey, I'll be there in about ten minutes. Do you feel okay and everything?"

"Yeah, I'm okay. Just kind of funny in my tummy area, but it's neat. Does this make me like a woman and everything?"

Alta could hear Katie laughing in the background. "Damned right. And everything. I'll stop at the store and pick up some Kotex. Ask Katie if she needs anything." Alta's spirits sunk as the question left her lips. Katie needed a new body. One that wouldn't kill her within six months' time. The radiation therapy was hard on her, wearing her down slowly but surely. She'd cut her hair to make the process easier, knowing she could very well go bald under the treatment. Paradoxically, her short, fire-red hair made her look younger. Alta had cried seeing her hair short for the first time. "You look like a little girl, Katie," was all she could say.

Alta stopped at the store and bought some milk and coffee for Katie and the Kotex for April. April opened the door with Ethan right behind her.

"Well, I believe this box of Kotex has your name on it," Alta said, taking it out and handing it to her daughter.

April snatched it from her mother's hands and ran for the bathroom. "These glue onto your underwear, right?" she asked, slamming the door behind her.

"Do you want some coffee or some wine, your choice," Katie called from the kitchen.

Alta walked back to the kitchen and, sitting down, met her friend's eyes. There were dark circles of fear under her eyes, but the clear light of her courage shone from their centers.

"I'll take some wine. How're you doing?" Alta paused. "I mean, how're you really doing? That therapy's a bummer, isn't it?"

Katie poured the wine. "Yeah, it is, but what else can I do? Maybe it'll give me a couple of extra months; now we're talking about extra months." Her heart began to pound. "I guess I still can't really believe it yet."

Katie ran her fingers through her short, stylish hair. Little fringes framed her face, making her look especially young and vulnerable. "Well, April made my day by stopping here first. She was so cute. For a minute there I thought she was trying to tell me she's pregnant." Katie laughed and the darkness fled. "Well, I must say, I feel honored somehow. It seems like there should be a ritual we should do for her. The older women, you know?"

"That's what I was thinking. We don't have any rituals, do we?" Alta said quietly.

Katie's breath caught in her throat, and she looked out at the soft summer air. The end of summer. Her children had played all day in the backyard with their toys after she'd come home from the hospital. Juanita, a neighbor, watched the kids for her whenever she needed her, even at a moment's notice. Katie's parents would be coming at the end of the month from the Orient. They were cutting their trip short to be with her. Though Katie missed her mother, she dreaded seeing her. The reproach in her mother's eyes. She was supposed to be nearly perfect—healthy, intelligent, resourceful, brilliant—but certainly, most certainly, not dying.

"Not for the living or the dying," Katie murmured. "Well, here she is, the grown woman. Would you like some coffee and a donut with us old ladies?"

"Do you have any tea?" Pleasure washed over April's face.

"Three kinds. Come here and choose." Katie looked at Alta. "You know, if this keeps up you could be a grandmother in no time."

"I don't even like boys yet," April said with embarrassment. At the same time she was pleased. "I don't even know if I want kids. I mean, ever."

Suddenly, Katie was stunned as she realized, looking at April's new womanhood, that she, herself, Katie, would never know. And her babies, her boys, would be men without her.

The dress began to take shape. It was made of fine muslin and it was long. The special lace went on the sleeves, the neckline, and at the hem. Alta was almost finished with the rainbow solar plexus sun she was embroidering on the midriff section. She hadn't sewn for April in years, and this would be the last dress she'd make her: her coming of age dress, she called it.

Jackie knocked twice and then let herself in. "Alta, it's me!"

"Who else would barge in but you?"

Jackie laughed. "What a beautiful dress. It's for April?"

"It's her coming of age dress, for her first menstrual. I'm sure she'll tell you all about it." Alta smiled.

"So she finally got the curse. Maybe she was better off without it," Jackie muttered. "Anyway, do you think she'll actually wear it? It's not exactly the style."

"Probably not for school, but for something special. Hugh's going to take her out to dinner by herself and all."

Jackie's face softened. "I like that. I wish my father'd taken me out to dinner for my first one."

"Me too. I guess that's why I suggested it. Hugh's getting into it, actually. You know, taking out his *grown* daughter. Where's José?"

"I'm off early today, so I pick him up in an hour. I had a hell of a weekend. Saw three guys in a row. One for Friday, Saturday, and Sunday." Jackie giggled, hugging herself with self-satisfaction.

"Do you worry about herpes?" Alta paused, then went on. "Or even AIDS. I mean, that shit's out there."

"Hell, Alta, what about Katie? There she is being good and all that shit, and she's dying anyway. Do you know what I mean? I mean, why are so many people *getting* cancer? What the hell are we eating and breathing every day like a bunch of dorks? What about the fucking nuclear arsenal? What about Chernobyl spraying that poison in the air and all the other nuclear reactors that're bound to go sooner or later? When those hotshot bastards split the atom, they split our cells while they were at it. Jesus, don't get me started." Jackie tried to smile. "Sometimes I think I'm pissed off at the top boy scout, God."

Alta put April's dress down.

"I want to go out smiling, stoned, and sexually satisfied. Yeah!" Jackie burst out laughing, seeing the worried look on Alta's face. "Do you have any chilled wine? Anything will do."

"Well, I just hope you don't get a case of herpes. There's some wine in the fridge. Pour me a glass while you're at it. Why don't you get José and stay for dinner?"

"That sounds good to me." Jackie hummed as she poured the wine. "You know, you can get all that shit secondhand from someone else. Do you think Hugh's seeing someone else?"

"Sometimes I do and sometimes I don't. He's been home the last couple of weekends, so I guess I'm in the I-don't-cycle." Alta picked up April's dress, fingering the bursting rainbow rays of the bright yellow-gold sun. "Probably some easy pickup, something like that. Like Carl has affairs—long, drawn-out affairs—but I think Hugh keeps whatever it is superficial and impersonal. Anyway, that's what I think."

Alta picked up the red strands of thread, laying it against the fabric. Yes, red is perfect, she thought, and then it's done.

"Well, how is it for you? Sexually and all." Jackie watched Alta's face carefully as she waited for an answer.

"It's the pits. Do you want to know what it feels like sometimes?" The words rushed to Alta's lips as she clutched the red thread of her daughter's bright, feminine sun.

Jackie met her gaze and waited.

"Sometimes it feels like rape, that's how it is. Like if I'm not completely submissive he can't get off. I don't know anymore. It feels like I'm sleepwalking, and things seem a little unreal. Then I look at Katie and I realize I don't have any real problems, you know? Just this lousy marriage of mine."

"Joe pulled that shit too. That's how they break your spirit. Makes you feel like a week-old hamburger, doesn't it? The old total control bit," Jackie said angrily. "Does he hit you?"

Alta sighed, folding April's dress. Hugh would be taking her out to dinner Friday night. "No."

"Do you want to leave him?"

"More than anything sometimes."

"Then why don't you?"

"I guess I'm afraid. Maybe after I get my degree next year. Maybe then." Alta looked at Jackie, clutching April's dress tightly, as though once April wore it she'd never be able to leave her, ever.

"Katie'll be dead by then," Alta added in a murmur.

"What's the best days to visit her? Do you think she'd mind if I came by?" Dwelling on sorrow just wasn't Jackie's style, her own or anyone else's. She got up to pour another glass of wine.

"Just give her a call. I know she'd love to see you. She looks a little bit different though, so don't be too surprised. She's cut her hair and she's starting to lose weight."

"Is it depressing?" Caution crept into her voice.

"Of course, it's depressing," Alta said irritably. "But she's coping with everything. Suing the hospital for Doug and the kids, dealing with Doug, going to radiation therapy . . . " Alta's voice trailed off. "She's even writing a little journal so her kids can read it when they're older."

"God-fucking-damn, that lady has some guts." Jackie quickly emptied her glass. "I'll go get José and be right back. Anything I can get?"

"Dessert, if you want. You know, Jackie, I think most of the women I know have that kind of guts only we don't know it." Alta felt like flinging herself on the floor and weeping, but instead she smiled. "Yet."

The red tights peeked from beneath April's dress and the white lace at the hem rested against them, adding an almost fairy-tale charm and contrast. Her shoes were small red heels, "Like Dorothy," April laughed with excitement.

Carefully, Alta put a subtle smear of lilac eye shadow on April's eyes and a light coral on her lips. The color and contrast against April's dark skin was stunning. April's hair hung loose past her shoulders. Alta could see her daughter was beautiful and, for an instant, she was jealous. Just for an instant.

"Do you want to wear my long cape with the hood? It'll look beautiful with the dress."

"The reservations are for seven!" Hugh yelled from the front room. "If we don't get there we'll probably have a wait!"

April walked ahead of her mother with the cape around her shoulders. Her face shone with absolute happiness as she walked toward her father.

"Everyone's going to think I'm a dirty old man taking such a beautiful young woman to dinner." Hugh smiled with pleasure.

"I have eye shadow on, Dad." April was unable to hide her delight.

Ian sat on the couch watching television and for once he stopped himself from saying, "Bet your bra's stuffed."

"I need the money, Alta," Hugh reminded her angrily. "Give me at least a fifty."

Alta rushed to the bedroom, choosing three twenties. Hugh snatched it from her hand. He turned toward April, placing his hand on her shoulder and guided her toward the door.

April turned. "Bye, Mom." Her eyes were twin pools of liquid excitement.

Alta waved and walked to the window. She watched them walk to the car and drive away. She couldn't deny it; Hugh hated her. The thought made her sick to her stomach as though she'd swallowed the vilest poison.

As Alta finished her homework the phone rang. It was Steve wanting to make sure they got one class together next semester. They ended up talking.

"Did you ever feel like someone truly—I mean, truly—hates your guts? It's a kind of stunning, sickening realization. I mean, I think Hugh really hates my guts, you know?"

"He's a white man, Alta. The man hates his *own* guts, man. When're you ever goin' to *understand that?* I guess I found that out 'bout age four, though my mama tried to smooth it away. Truth is, you can't."

"They're back, gotta go. How about lunch tomorrow off campus?"

"Good enough. Take care a yourself."

"April rushed to her room. Hugh threw off his coat and then flung himself beside it on the couch.

Alta's stomach clenched. "What's wrong with April? Is something wrong, Hugh?"

Hugh looked bored, angry, indifferent. He got up to turn the TV on, ignoring her.

"Hugh, what's going on?" Alta raised her voice over the television.

Hugh leapt to his feet and stalked to the refrigerator, pouring a full glass of wine. "The little bitch ordered something she couldn't eat, that's what, and I had to fucking pay for it. I told her she was acting like a spoiled little bitch, so she ran to the bathroom and didn't come out for about a half an hour. Then she wouldn't talk to me to top it off." Hugh's eyes held a deadly expression. A ripe violence.

"Do you mean you yelled at her there in the restaurant?" Alta could only think of the dress and what it meant to April and herself.

"Damned right I did! Shoulda slammed her too! *She* wouldn't talk to *me.* That's rich!" Hugh said with disdain and, ultimately, a superior satisfaction.

"Don't you understand that this was her coming-of-age ritual, her dinner with you, you stupid asshole!"

Hugh stepped forward quickly as though to hit her and then walked into the front room. He'd gotten the desired effect; Alta had cringed.

April was already undressed and in bed as Alta opened the bedroom door. The lights were out, and a nearly full moon made her daughter's face clearly visible. She was trying not to cry.

"April, I'm sorry it turned out like this." Alta sat on the edge of the bed. "Do you want to tell me what happened, honey?" Alta's voice was gentle, but there was a gathering rage at the bottom of her throat. It tasted like the bitterest bile. Without knowing it, her daughter and her mother became fused in her mind: women betrayed. Why am I shaking? she asked herself. Why am I so damned helpless?

"Oh, Mom," April turned her face toward her mother as her tears began to fall, "all the way over in the car Dad kept telling me I looked so pretty and everything; I felt so big, you know?" April's eyes implored her mother for understanding.

"I know." Tears started down Alta's face.

"I ate most of the beef stroganoff, but it tasted kind of funny—not like yours, Mom. But I ate most of it, I really did." April's face contorted with the effort to say it. "He called me a spoiled little bitch in front of everyone, and he told me to go to the bathroom and wipe my makeup off 'cause I was just a baby anyway." Now April sobbed.

Alta stroked April's hair while her mind screamed. She forced her voice to be soft. "April, this isn't your fault. Your father should apologize but he won't. You didn't do anything wrong, do you understand? You look beautiful in that dress, you really do. Do you know that I love you?"

April's voice was muffled but audible. "Why does Dad hate me?"

Steve's words came back to Alta. She answered in a choked voice, "I think he only hates himself." Alta stayed with April until she began to sleep fitfully on her side. The moon continued to spray her daughter's face with light as she closed the door behind her.

Hugh was in bed and the house was silent. Alta opened the back door and stepped out into the darkness. The stars were bright over the crisscrossing of clotheslines. The buildings across the way were as tall as the redwoods, she realized, looking up at them. The puppy scratched on the back door trying to get out. She hated Hugh intensely at that moment.

The buildings across the way were no comfort to her the way the redwoods might be. As she looked at the lit and the darkened windows she could only imagine the women behind them struggling with some jerk of a man: husband, father, lover. Son, she almost added, then Ian came to mind, innocent Ian. What happened to men? she wondered.

She thought of Katie dying, courageously, three blocks away. Do I have that kind of courage? she asked herself. Tears of utter frustration, anger, self-loathing, streaked down her face. I don't even have the courage to leave Hugh, much less die.

Something rustled in the yard, jarring Alta to attention. She thought of her grandmother, an old, brown Indian woman with piercing white darts of light in her black eyes, fading somewhat with each new humiliation in the county home. The cracks in the window behind her bed, the pneumonia she caught, and, finally, her decision to die as she coiled downward into herself, until no voice could have—even if it had wanted to—called her back. She had died into the windy morning sun with Alta at the foot of her bed open-mouthed, wide-eyed, calling her back at the top of her lungs. But something *had* come back, not right away, but later ringed with light. A gentle presence in the dark night, like a rustle in the bushes.

Only two lights remained lit in the building opposite her, and her own eyes wanted to shut with sleep. As Alta stood up to go, a shiver of fear ran up the length of her spine.

Hugh. She dreaded him.

Alta sensed he was awake before she eased into bed. He reached for her, seizing her breast too tightly. His breath was sour in her face. "I want you to suck me off, okay, Alta?"

She lay still facing away from him. "You don't care how April feels, do you?"

"Come on, put it to rest. Come on, Alta." Hugh's grip tightened as he tried to turn her toward him.

"You know, Hugh, if you just want someone to suck you off, why don't you pay someone to do it." A cold revulsion swept through her; his hands held no warmth.

Hugh felt her body withdraw into itself, shutting him out. Anger pulsed him erect and hard. "I pay you every Friday, remember?" He forced her onto her back, spreading her legs with his knees pinching the soft flesh of her inner thighs.

"You're hurting me! Do you hear me? You're hurting me, Hugh!" He was nearly inside of her, but she was dry and his erection was painful to her as he tried to penetrate her, ignoring her completely as though he were deaf, dumb, and dead. Truly dead. Dead in spirit. He just wanted to be inside of something, someone alive.

Alta brought her arm up, elbowing him in the side of the face.

"What the hell're you doing? That damn well hurt, you bitch!" Hugh got to a kneeling position, holding his face with one hand.

"Get off me, now! Right now! Get off!" Alta wanted to cry with fear and frustration, but her rage superseded everything.

"What do you mean, get off, you fucking bitch!"

Then it rose, deep from her childhood; the little girl in the park rose into Alta's eyes. Everything was clear. "You're trying to rape me! Goddamn you! You're trying to fucking rape me! Get off of me, Hugh! I'm warning you!"

Hugh loomed over her. "So what're you gonna do, kick my ass? Stop being so damned hysterical."

Alta tried to sit up and Hugh pushed her back down, trying to pin her arms behind her.

"How the hell can I rape you after two kids? Give it up, Alta." He started to laugh, losing the grip on her arms.

Quickly, Alta brought her knee up into his testicles. She said nothing, leaping up as he doubled over. She watched him catch his breath. She wanted to run but she didn't know where to run to.

Suddenly, Hugh jumped to his feet and grabbed her, pinning her up to the bedroom wall. Alta screamed as he punched her in the face. The tissues around her eye exploded into pain as though cement were being driven into bone and soft flesh.

"Let go of my mother!" April screamed. "Let go of my mother, you bastard!" She began to cry with terror and anger.

"Go back to your room, April! This is none of your business! This is between your mother and me!" Hugh dragged April back to her room as Alta put her hands to her swelling face.

"Don't touch me! Don't touch me, you bastard! DON'T TOUCH ME!" April screamed. Ian began to cry from his bed.

"Don't you call me a bastard, young lady! Don't you dare call me a bastard! I'm your father!" Hugh yelled, forcing April down to her bed.

Alta rushed to April's room and the sight of his large body overpowering hers—April's cries were becoming sobs of helplessness, whimpers—drove her wild. "Goddamn you, let go of my daughter! Now! Right now, you son-of-a-bitch!" She had no weapon but her fury, but she grabbed April from his grip. Alta faced Hugh, holding her swelling eye up to him, and placing herself in front of April she said, "Well, go on and hit me again! Go on! But I'll tell you this—you'll have to sleep, and if you stay here I'll stab you, I swear it, I'll kill you while you sleep, you motherfucking bastard!"

Then an unexpected thing happened; shame crossed his face and stayed there. And he believed her. He stared at her face, her eyes, and he believed her. Hugh turned and lurched from the room. He put some clothes into a pillowcase and slammed the door behind him.

Alta began to tremble and shiver at her own daring—what she'd just dared to do. She thought of the knife going into his sleeping back—the pain in her eye and the side of her face pulsed—and only that comforted her.

"I'm going to double lock the door, April, so he can't get back in, so don't worry. Try to go back to sleep."

"Are you okay, Mom?" Ian's terrified voice was small in the darkness.

"I'm okay, Ian. Stay in bed. I'll be right there, okay?" Her voice sounded unusually loud and full to her, as though it weren't her own. At the same time she recognized it as her own. Her own real voice.

April looked at her mother and winced. "Mom, your eye's swelling up. Do you think you should go to the hospital or something?"

"Maybe I will tomorrow, but right now I'm going to put some ice on it. April, thank you for doing that. You were very brave, kiddo." Tears sprang to Alta's eyes, burning the nearly shut one.

"Would you really kill Dad?" April asked in a thin, frightened voice.

Ian watched his mother through the darkness, waiting for her reply.

"If he ever touched me like this again, yes. I think I have to leave your father, April. Do you understand?"

"Yes," April murmured with a strange sigh of relief. The moment was vivid as though she'd learned something of great importance. The paradox of such illuminations is that they're often, instantly, forgotten. As though such gold must be dug with one's own stubborn hands.

"Yes," Ian whispered as he fell back to sleep, escaping the nightmare that had interrupted his dreams.

By the third day her eye began to open. Everyone had come by: Steve, Jackie, Rita, Katie, Doug, and a friend of Hugh's she had never met or heard of: Bill. The doctor had reassured her nothing was broken, though the bridge of her nose was still twice its size. Alta had, as the saying goes, a shiner, but it wasn't funny; it was horrifying. It was absolutely humiliating. She felt ugly, exposed.

From time to time, she'd catch herself beginning to blame herself—hadn't she kicked him in the balls? Wouldn't any other man do the same? Then what Hugh had done to April came back to her freshly, and the little girl would rise to her eyes again clearly, and she was surprised the world had changed so much since she was seven. First the little girl stayed for a minute, then three minutes, pretty soon ten minutes. The trouble was she was frightened much too easily.

Well, Alta thought dismally, as she looked into the bathroom mirror: My black eye could be eye shadow, but it sure isn't close up—and what about the nose . . . "Shit," she muttered angrily. And I made an appointment to see a therapist. A woman. Next week. Now Alta began to wonder if she really were crazy. But, then, she knew she was, only no one else knew it. Yet.

Tomorrow she'd take Katie to the hospital while she got a radiation treatment and wait for her because Doug had exams. Hugh hadn't even called, and she had no idea where he was, though she knew he was working. The secretary had told her when she picked up his check.

Suddenly, Alta felt like calling the therapist and cancelling the appointment. The idea terrified her. Hadn't she worked things out so far? No one in her family had ever gone to therapy: a shrink. Sure there were some crazy people in my family, Alta told herself. But isn't going to a shrink *admitting* you are? Alta sighed. Maybe I am crazy after all this shit. Self-pity alternated with anger and anger alternated with fear.

Tomorrow morning she'd take Katie to the hospital to see if her therapy might give her two more months of life. Alta began to cry. She didn't really know if it was for herself or Katie. Maybe it doesn't matter, Alta thought. "Fuck it!" she said out loud to no one.

Katie moved over to let Alta drive. "Your eye sure is down. You can hardly see it. Is the asshole back yet?"

"I guess I wish he wouldn't come back, you know, just make that decision for me. I think between my part-time job, and if I get welfare and some scholarships, I might make it." Alta's voice lacked conviction, but it felt good to say it out loud to someone.

"Hugh'd have to give you money too, you know."

Alta glanced at Katie's face and her heart sank at its unnatural paleness. "I sure can't count on it. I mean, he's so bitter now, and it only seems to be getting worse or something; it wouldn't really surprise me if he just disappeared. You know, paycheck and all. Katie, have you been getting in the sun at all? After this, why don't we stop at Golden Gate Park for a while?"

Katie smiled. "Good idea, but I might have to sit a little in the shade. The sun really bothers me. Was Hugh always like this?"

"No. I used to really love him. He was my first love and all that. He was playful, funny. Gentle." With the word *gentle* a deep pain engulfed her eye as though to remind her.

As Katie went in, escorted by a nurse, she turned once and met Alta's eyes. She looked like a woman at the moment of childbirth, but this child's name was Death.

Alta sat down, grabbing a magazine. An unbelievable anger filled her. It was an aimless, yet consuming, anger that had nowhere else to go but to the tips of her hair, making it crackle; at least she could hear it, its angry energy. Like snakes. Like Medusa. Like an angry Goddess that turned the living not only to stone, but the impassive stone to life. Alta had no image for this anger, Medusa or otherwise, and so her anger turned back against her, filling her with an unutterable despair.

She had no name for her anger; she had no Goddess to turn to, no mother. She had no image of strength; no feminine image of strength, no wholeness, no knowledge of such perfection. No real power filled her in the wake of such anger. She and every other woman, Alta thought, feeling the despair now tangibly— in her wounded face, in her breasts, in her womb, in her vagina—was alone, motherless, on the face of the Earth.

The sound of the machine filled Katie, not with hope, but with dread. She was losing her hair; she was losing her color; she was losing her life. "My babies," she murmured. "My little boys." Tears slid from the edges of her eyes, soaking into her scalp.

"You aren't picturing that meadow, are you?" the technician called out over the speaker.

They were in the semi-shade, in the middle of falling golden leaves under an immense oak. Katie lay on her stomach, rubbing her face on the thick green grass. "This grass smells so good I almost hate it," Katie said softly.

Alta was staring up at the tree, watching the large, golden leaves filter the light like thin, spun honey. It was a balm to her and just what she needed, so Katie's words jarred her. "What do you mean?"

Katie turned over on her back. "I guess I mean that anything that's too vivid—you know, too beautiful—reminds me that I am, in fact, fading." Katie touched her short, thinning hair that still held a memory of the old fire as the sun shifted through it. "It'll never grow back again—not in this life, anyway."

Alta felt the profound anger beneath Katie's words. "Do you think we come back again?"

"Yeah, I do. I mean, I know I've known you before. We're important to each other, don't you think?"

"It feels like that to me too. We certainly met under strange circumstances." Alta smiled at Katie.

"I owe you the next time around, okay?" Katie smiled back and the first hint of color came to her face, but it vanished just as suddenly.

"It's a deal."

The wind blew in swirling gusts, bringing a fresh golden harvest down all around them. The sounds of their dry stems cracking filled the air.

Alta stared haphazardly at the trunk of the tree, and then she saw it. "There's a woman in the tree!" she said excitedly. "Do you see it?"

Katie sat up, staring at the trunk fixedly. "Yeah, I see it. Or, rather, her. It's like she's dancing with her arms in the air. Do you see the arms?"

"I kind of saw that as fire. Like she's standing in fire. How about dancing in fire? How's that?" A strange, dark joy coursed through Alta.

"Perfect. You know, oak is a symbol of strength." Katie paused and looked over at Alta. "Next week is my last therapy, then we see what happens."

"Well, not that it's even on the same level, but next week's my first therapy session—and not that I have a bitch or anything, but I hate to do it."

"Think of the lady in the oak tree." Katie drew in a deep breath tasting the inevitable merging of leaf and earth. "Doug's really trying hard now, no bullshit. Isn't it too bad I have to fucking die to finally get it?" She allowed one tear to escape, but she commanded the rest to remain in the shelter of her body. Who would stop me once I started? she asked herself. Not mother. Not father. A well-brought-up girl like me. A well-brought-up girl wears underwear, bras, panty hose, remains calm, keeps all feeling under control.

A well-brought-up girl doesn't die, Katie almost said out loud. Not without permission anyway. Like getting a bathroom pass. Permission to pee. "We should probably get going," Katie said faintly, not really meaning it. Though it disturbed her, the fresh, moving air brought the complexity of her sorrow to life. And, so, life stirred within her, vividly.

Alta had been silent, trying to make sense of it, but no matter where she ended up, there were no tidy conclusions, no answers. She stood up, looking at the image of the woman in the tree. She looked at Katie. "Do you think the fire's necessary? And, if so, why the hell do we have to dance?"

"It must be a test." Katie began to laugh softly as they slowly crossed the meadow.

"Mom, what's therapy?" April studied her mother's face. Things were back to normal, but April could see something in her mother's face she hadn't seen before, and she couldn't begin to describe it. She could only ask, "Mom, what's therapy?"

"Don't forget, Jackie's picking you guys up after school today, and I'll come and get you after my appointment. Jackie's going to make you dinner." Alta hesitated, then went on. "Therapy's somewhere you go to talk to someone, like a doctor, about what's bothering you, and then maybe you can finally change things around."

"Is Dad still alive?" Ian finally asked his burning question.

Alta laughed. "He must be since I picked up his check and he left me a note saying to leave him a hundred."

"Did he say to say hi to me or anything?" Ian persisted.

"Dad creamed Mom in the face. I don't want him to say hi to me," April said defiantly.

"I just wondered, that's all." Ian's hazel eyes held his father's expression.

Alta wanted to lie and say, yes, that Hugh had mentioned Ian and April in the note, but he hadn't. "He didn't mention anything in the note but the money he needed, Ian. He didn't even say hi to me. I don't think I can live with your father anymore, but that doesn't mean he isn't still your father." Alta sighed at the truth and the lie inherent in her words.

"Okay, come on, we'll all be late. Grab your lunches and I'll see you both later at Jackie's."

Mom's different, April thought as she opened the front door, and she really wasn't sure if she liked it. Or trusted it. This change.

It'd been a long day—first her morning classes, then the preschool in the afternoon. She loved the little kids, but she had to admit it: she was tired, deep down, of the tediousness of caring for small children. Caring for their needs, their endless needs, since she herself had been fifteen, while a great, sucking need of her own ached through the center of her being. It threatened to devour her, especially in the predawn hours when the silence of the world spoke to the void, the need, of the clamoring hunger that terrified her beyond belief. It left her sweating and trembling alone in the huge bed.

Is this all I have to look forward to? she asked herself, this disgusting, never-ending fear?

The therapist sat in a chair facing an empty chair where Alta was supposed to sit. She was blond, her hair pulled into a full bun straight off her face, making her pale blue eyes focal points of her expression. Her lips were thin, almost angry. She was somewhere in her forties.

"Have a seat. I'm Cheryl Gann." Her voice was low pitched and direct, almost disinterested. She didn't smile. "What brings you here, Alta?"

Alta surveyed the woman with guarded, unwavering eyes, and she realized she didn't like her. "My whole damned life."

"Would you care to fill me in? Like what brought you here now?" She could've been asking a butcher to weigh a chicken.

Alta steeled herself; she wouldn't cry in front of this woman, no matter what. "Well, my husband punched me in the face the other night. We've been married ten years, and I have two kids."

"Why did he punch you? Has he hit you before? Is this a pattern?" Still the same tone of voice.

Alta suddenly hated this woman intensely. Why should I pay twenty dollars an hour—sliding scale maybe, but sliding scale treatment?—Alta thought, adding, fucking white bitch, internally.

"Look, I kicked him in the balls because he was trying to rape me, believe it or not, and no, he never hit me before though he always made it clear he could if he wanted to." Alta paused to gather herself and then she saw a flicker of amusement, for a moment, in the therapist's pale blue eyes.

I should know better than to just walk in and talk to someone with blue eyes, Alta groaned inwardly. The old bitterness welled up in her. My grandmother wouldn't have trusted her for a second. I may be a liberal, but they're sure not.

"Look, Cheryl, or whatever your name is, I've read a little bit about this method in my psych classes." Alta gauged the impact of her words against the pale blue eyes. This'll get her, Alta realized. "Isn't this the Fritz Perls method where the patient actually enjoys being mentally abused?"

The therapist's face was beginning to turn red from anger, and her thin lips bit down on themselves.

Alta stood up. "Well, I, for one, don't have to pay to be abused. I can get beat up for free, thank you."

"I don't even know who this Fritz Perls character is, to begin with. Now, if you'll sit down, Alta, we can get on with our therapy session." The indifferent tone in her voice was gone as it shook with an unmistakable anger.

"If this is therapy, you can have it!" Alta turned the door knob. "You're just a rude, snobby, overeducated, white bitch!" She slammed the door behind her.

As Alta pulled onto the freeway she saw the truck in the lane she was trying to enter. It was an immense truck going at least seventy. It looked like a dark, grey beast with its mouth wide open. It would eat this little car that Hugh and she fought over. It would eat her. She would cease to exist if she didn't pull out of the way—now.

It was that simple. It was very private. She would be in an accident.

The truck roared by as Alta broke into a sweat. She picked up speed again and carefully entered the lane while an angry voice in her head repeated, *coward*. April and Ian came to her clearly, and their eyes questioned her, Why? They would grow up and question her. Why? Alta asked herself. "Why am I so alone?" Alta asked the leaden sky.

There were some old tranquilizers that Hugh kept on the top shelf. She wondered if they were too old to work. She'd soon find out. There were ten. Alta got the chilled Chablis from the refrigerator, as well as a small square of hash Hugh was saving. She'd never smoked hash, not even grass, so she had no idea how to start a pipe.

"While other kids were smoking dope and drinking I was being a responsible mother," Alta muttered. "I don't even have a mother. Or a therapist," she added. Alta swallowed the chunk of hash and half expected to die right there. Then she took a sip of wine. She got up to four tranquilizers and finished the glass of Chablis. She poured more Chablis. She was beginning to feel a kind of darkness around her eyes.

Alta fingered the fifth tranquilizer and walked over to the phone and called Rita. The phone rang twice. "Rita? It's me, Alta. Look, I think I'm trying to kill myself."

Rita and Carl were there in three minutes, banging on the door.

"Show me the tranquilizers!" Carl demanded. "What else did you take?"

"I just swallowed a chunk of hash." Alta's speech was slurred. Her tongue felt thick and funny. She imagined her face must look out of proportion. Ugly. Terrible. The real me, she thought.

"Should we take her to the hospital?" Rita asked. She looked desperately from Alta to Carl.

"How many tranquilizers did you take? Do you know?" Carl was speaking in a very loud, commanding voice.

"These were pretty old." Alta held up a tiny pill. "This was number five, I think, but I called you guys instead." Alta's stomach fluttered and she began to sob.

Rita held her. "Go ahead and cry."

"They'll just pump her stomach. I don't think four's going to do anything."

Alta stumbled to the kitchen sink, got a paper towel and blew her nose. She wet another, putting it on her eyes—her poor, old eyes that were so tired, so very tired of looking out at the world. The little girl was gone, entirely.

"Let's take her out to the beach and walk her around. That'll probably do it. The hash and the tranquilizers will wear off." Carl gave the impression of being totally in control.

He was the doctor here. He even looked like he'd chosen what to wear for this event, whereas Rita obviously had come the way she'd answered the phone: in jeans and a sweatshirt. Carl had on a striking sweater with socks that matched. Beautiful leather sandals set them off, and his jeans fit him perfectly.

"Here, just lay your head on my shoulder." Rita gently placed Alta's head down.

"Don't let her fall asleep, for Christ's sake! Put her window down! Stay awake, Alta!" Carl shouted.

"Maybe it'd do her good to sleep a little, Carl," Rita said softly.

"Keep her awake!"

The wind whipped Alta's hair in every direction, but she slept anyway. They had to drag Alta out of the car, and at one point Carl's hand was poised to slap her to consciousness. Alta's eyes flew open. "You can just forget that movie stuff, I'm not dead yet."

"I'm just trying to help you, Alta. Then, come on and walk." Carl was angry now. The tips of his ears were red, which made him look silly to her.

"Take it easy, Carl," Rita said with an unexpected anger of her own. "Don't you think she's been clobbered enough lately? Here, let me help her out. Get out of the damned way!"

Carl composed himself, moving out of Rita's way. Now he'd sulk and remove himself from this little theatrical mess. I hate it when people pretend they're going to kill themselves, all the time just wanting some cheap attention, Carl thought with disgust. His mother had done it all through his childhood.

"Carl, you can give me a hand now!" Rita was yelling at him.

"I thought you had it under control." He made no effort to hide his contempt.

Alta stood up on her own, facing the sea. "It's just like being a little drunk, that's all." She began to walk toward the beach.

"Hold it, Alta! Let me hold your arm! Carl, get the other side! Come on!"

Carl sulkily complied and the three of them walked back and forth on the beach as though under orders. The ocean was steel grey, choppy with wind and unfriendly.

"Where's the oak trees?" Alta asked.

"We're at the beach, Alta," Rita answered her.

"She knows that, for Christ's sake. I'm hungry. Let's get a hamburger or something," Carl complained.

"Where's the woman in the tree? I'm just kidding, Rita. Katie and I saw a woman in an oak tree the other day. She might help now is what I mean." The ocean at that moment looked deadly with its immense waves, but the thought of the thick oak tree with the woman standing—or was she dancing in the fire, Alta tried to remember—comforted her.

"Oh, great, now the crazy act," Carl muttered, letting go of Alta's arm.

"Are you hungry, Alta?" Rita asked, ignoring Carl.

"Sure, let's go eat. I'm freezing my ass off out here." Things were still moving kind of slowly, but the terror of the darkness was subsiding; the darkness she'd felt behind her eyes.

"I'll take a strawberry milkshake," Alta ordered.

Carl frowned. "You ought to have coffee."

"And I'll take a chocolate milkshake and fries." Rita glared at Carl.

"Suit yourself." His ear lobes were red again. Carl ordered a full course hamburger dinner as though he were in a gourmet restaurant. Then, with exaggerated seriousness, he got up to go to the bathroom. A few feminine eyes followed him as he crossed the room, restoring his easily bruised ego.

The room was warm and sunny, but the harsh glare of late afternoon, the sound of the wind howling outside, and the thought of the steel-grey sea beating everything to death depressed Alta. The tranquilizers were wearing off, but the hash gave objects a secret glow.

"Why do you stay with that stupid little white boy? Since I just attempted suicide, I may as well go all the way." Alta

109

stared at Rita trying to gather her thoughts. "What I mean is, there're guys who're blond and fairly normal, but Carl's a White Boy. How do you stand him?"

"Not now, Alta, he's coming back." Rita didn't know who to be angry at, Alta or Carl.

Their food arrived and they ate in an awkward silence. Alta was glad she just had to maneuver a straw, because everything, including herself, felt wooden and unreal. Suddenly, an intense shaft of sunlight blazed down the center of the room.

Alta began to laugh, spitting her strawberry milkshake all over the table. She laughed uncontrollably, putting her face in her hands.

Rita handed her some napkins. "What's so funny, Alta? What's so funny?"

Alta paused long enough to choke out, "Look, look at that bald guy's head in the sunlight. Isn't that great?"

Rita burst into laughter almost as loud as Alta. They howled with laughter, doubled over, holding their stomachs. The man's head was a spotlight of joy, a joke on death. It mocked Alta's sadness, her anger, her emptiness: perfectly.

Carl wiped the milkshake spots off his sweater. His entire face was red. "I'll see you both in the car." He stood up and stalked away angrily.

They laughed even louder.

Now Alta sat in the therapist's waiting room with its four chairs and one Chagall print of a bride and groom flying through the air; it hung on the wall opposite her. The bride held a spread, black fan close to her womb, and the groom held the other side of her womb. The air was thick with color, and Alta liked it though the obvious joy of the painting made her rather sad sitting there in the bare room. Not even a magazine.

Hugh had come home, late, the night of her suicide attempt. Alta had forgotten to double lock the door, but she knew it was him as she heard him collapse on the couch. Yes, Hugh was home and she was alive, but they were not the magical bride and groom flying through the colorful air, and Hugh had no desire to touch the dark mystery of her womb.

The therapist had called early that morning. Her voice had sounded loud and determined as though she were forcing herself to speak. "It's me, Cheryl Gann, the therapist you saw yesterday. I don't usually do this, but I think I owe you an apology." She cleared her throat and continued. "I'd like us to work together, that is if you still would like to. Anyway, maybe I come on a little too strong sometimes."

Alta was speechless as she stared at the fine drizzle outside the front room window. The room smelled of Hugh's alcohol and sweat as he slept undisturbed.

"Well, how about it? Do you accept my apology?"

"I suppose so," Alta answered in a cautious voice. Yesterday seemed far away and she felt almost peaceful. However, Hugh's presence bit that peace in half. He slept with his work boots still on, face down on the couch. Alta looked out at the rain, trying to ignore him.

"Would you like to come in this afternoon? I have a space at two o'clock if you can make it."

Ian had stopped to look at his father as he passed the front room on the way out to school. His expression was that of children at the lion's cage—that unmistakable mixture of fascination and terror. The desire to know and the dread of knowing. Ian slammed the front door and ran to meet his friends.

April only said, "Are you going to let him stay with us, Mom?" She refused to look at him as she walked past. He smells like a bum, April thought to herself. She walked slowly to school, staying behind by herself. The leaves were beginning to fall and the rain was cold. A little brown sparrow washed itself, shuddering awkwardly as though it were all alone in the world, standing on a branch as April looked up at it, feeling the rain on her face.

Something happened to Mom yesterday, April thought. That's why she was so late. Everyone's pretending everything's okay and being so phony. I'm not a little kid anymore, she thought angrily. The other kids had reached the top of the hill and were probably approaching the gate, so April looked at her shoes, dark and wet from the rain, and walked a little faster up the hill.

As Alta sat down across from Cheryl she noticed Cheryl looked a little different from the day before. She wore a light lipstick, gold hoop earrings, and an attractive knit dress that hugged her slightly plump figure. It suited her, as well as its turquoise color that complimented her eyes, and her hair lightly framed her face. Now her eyes, though still clear and direct, were softer, more human. Concerned.

"How are things with you today?" Cheryl smiled slightly but with a genuine warmth.

"Well, I made a pathetic attempt at suicide yesterday, believe it or not." Alta returned her smile.

"Tell me about it," Cheryl said, leaning forward.

Four

"She wants you to come in too, Hugh."

"To see a shrink? Give me a break, will ya? You're picking up the check and I'm not bothering you, am I? I said I was sorry about hitting you, didn't I?"

Almost two months had passed and each one of Alta's sessions brought more tears as she talked about her childhood, her mother, her children, Hugh, and the unutterable loss of her grandmother, the one magical being in Alta's life who had connected her to her dreams; sunlight through leaves; rain puddled on the thick, green, growing grass; the wonder of picking cilantro, squash, and beans grown by her grandmother's own hands; the rainbows in the sky that were always "buena suerte." The one person in her childhood that knew how to love and then abruptly died with her secret.

Finally the words had stopped, but the tears wouldn't. Cheryl had said in a voice Alta would always remember—a mother's voice, a midwife's voice: "Go ahead and cry. You don't have to have a reason. I'll just sit here with you."

"Hugh, I don't want to live with you anymore if this is how it's going to be. You're not happy either, are you?"

Hugh's head jerked up angrily. "How're you going to pay the rent and the rest of it? Have you thought about that?"

Alta met his eyes and asked, "Are you going to come with me? I want you to come tomorrow. We have a special appointment for six o'clock. I mean, we don't make love anymore, and I don't know where you go when you're gone for days at a time." She wished intensely that she could read Hugh's mind. "Are you seeing anyone? Is that it? Just tell me."

"Look, I'll go with you tomorrow, but I'm not promising anything. I guess everything is pretty well shot to shit. Maybe the best thing would be to split and give you some money." Then trying even harder to shift the topic—Alta had never asked that question before—he added, "Are you still thinking of that master's thing? Takes money, you know." He knew money matters and her uncertain future always made her brain lock into neutral, her fear giving him the upper hand.

"Are you seeing someone? Just tell me. I don't even know if I care anymore. I just want to know." Her brain hummed along as Hugh's eyes darted toward the door.

The phone rang. It was Katie, in tears. "Doug just spanked Erin for not going on the toilet. I can't stand it, Alta. He's too little. He's just too little to be spanked for that. Will you come up and talk to Doug? Please? I just can't tell him the right way or something, and I just can't stand it." Helplessness and rage mingled in her anxious voice as motherhood slipped away from her.

"I'll be there in ten minutes. Take it easy." That's easy for me to say, Alta thought and banished it, trying to be practical. "Have you told Doug yourself, Katie?"

"He doesn't listen. He just doesn't listen and I'm too tired to keep saying it. I'm so fucking tired, Alta." Fresh tears choked her voice.

The radiation therapy, if anything, worsened her condition. Now Katie looked like she was dying. It was as though her stored vitality had been unleashed only to feed the emerging monster that had been concealed. She had increasing pain now and so a hospital bed had been placed in the front room to give her comfort and relief night and day. She used morphine now at the worst times, which was a lot.

The first time Doug helped her to the bathroom Katie cried with shame and anger after he left the room. Hadn't she always said she'd rather die quickly in old age than go through such humiliations? And liar that she was, she was struggling for a few more months at twenty-seven. She'd flushed the toilet, waiting for a few minutes to call him to help her back to bed, and then she wondered if there'd come a time when he'd have to stand there and prop her up so she wouldn't fall. The pain shot through her body in terrible ripples—almost like an orgasm, she thought bitterly—but they subsided once she lay down.

Doug answered the door, smiling sheepishly when he saw Alta. "Don't tell me, you're here to give me the word, right? I'm such a macho bastard asshole, I think I should have a brain transplant or a dick transplant. Or something, Christ. What's your advice? Do you have any? Sure could use some, like now." Doug's voice was low pitched and trembling.

Alta waved at Katie as they passed the front room. Katie smiled, saying thank you silently with her eyes.

"I just put the kids to bed. I put a double diaper on Erin, by the way." Doug's eyes were weary, not with booze as they often were, but with sorrow. A sorrow he himself hadn't expected.

"How 'bout some vino, there, Alta? I hear you been seein' a shrink." Doug's relaxed drawl returned somewhat.

Alta nodded yes.

"So speak! Are you goin' ta bawl me out or what, woman?" Doug sat down opposite her, handing her the glass of wine.

Alta smiled, gathering herself, and, as gently as she could, said, "Doug, Erin is her baby"—she kept her voice low; she didn't want Katie to hear her—" and she isn't going to live more than a few weeks, right?"

Doug clenched his fists and looked away out toward the night where the moon shone in the weed-choked garden. Some late rose blossoms were in full bloom, ripe and red, but no one had seen them; only the butterflies, hummingbirds, and sparrows enjoyed the roses. Ethan and Erin no longer played in the backyard because Juanita, the older Mexican woman who watched them during the day, found it too exhausting to walk up and down the stairs. Juanita's ample breasts and loud laughter were familiar to Alta like a long-lost aunt, her laugh growing even fiercer with her years. She reminded her of her mother, but only the laugh, the best of her mother's spirit. But Juanita had the magic ingredient: the ability to love.

Erin's wooden pull-toy train, the one he'd looked for crying, "Erin's trainey!" was under the blossoming rose bush. Ripe and red, the roses would unpetal onto it soon. And Ethan's small metal cars glinted under a trailing blackberry vine holding the remains of the unpicked, rotting harvest.

"Let him be her baby these last few weeks." Tears slid down Alta's cheeks. She reached over and touched Doug's tense arm. "Anyway, it's hard to toilet train anytime. Give yourself a break."

Doug looked at Alta. Seeing her tears made him tremble. He hadn't expected her to cry. "I hear you. Don't worry, it won't happen again." Then Doug fastened his eyes on her, daring her to glimpse his depths. He kept his voice low but it sounded like a shout. "I haven't told the boys she's dyin'. I just can't seem to bring myself to. I guess I'm a fuckin' coward. Well, it's obvious now; she ain't gettin' better. It's obvious to everyone, even the kids. She's fallin' fuckin' apart." Doug's eyes filled with tears, but instead of allowing them to fall he wrenched his eyes away from Alta's.

Doug stood up and walked to the window, and then he heard the owl he'd been hearing the last couple of weeks singing to its prey, singing to the waning moon, singing to his shrinking courage. Singing to Katie's fragile soul, he thought darkly. He longed to walk in the high desert with only food and water in his pack, with only silence, sun, and wind surrounding him. Then he'd be able to tell Ethan and Erin their mother was dying. But hasn't the owl been trying to remind me of my old courage? he asked himself finally.

"I guess we're all goin' ta die sometime. Some sooner, some later." Doug's voice was hoarse with tears. "I'll talk ta the boys this week. Katie's parents'll be showin' up this weekend." He paused, making a distasteful face. "Prepare yourself. I'm sure you'll meet 'em. They're the gen-u-ine Palm Springs type, if you get my drift."

"Do you want me to be with you when you tell the boys? I'll come up if you want. I mean it, Doug." Alta searched his face for an honest response. She sensed he was trying to change the subject with Katie's parents.

"Since you usually say what you mean, I believe you." Doug walked over to Alta and touched her shoulder, but he was immediately embarrassed and pulled away. "You will be with me, you know, thanks," he blurted out.

"Call me if you change your mind, okay?" Alta stood up to go.

"Will do. Are you gonna talk to Katie?" Doug met Alta's eyes. "I love her, Alta."

"I know you do." She wanted to ask him, for purely selfish reasons, she realized, why he hadn't known before, as though it might explain the flying bride and groom in Cheryl's office. Their joy, and why did it go away? That was the mystery. That was the secret of their flight. Their joy. Her hand holding the dark fan, shielding her womb; his hand covering her womb protectively. Their joy. How has death brought you joy? Alta wanted to ask him.

Hugh hates my womb, Alta thought suddenly, as she walked down the dark hall toward the living room and Katie. And it isn't because I'm Mexican; it isn't even because I'm me. It's because I'm a *woman*. The very idea made her dizzy, and, for an instant, it felt like her mind teetered on the edge of knowing something she desperately needed to know, but her mind collapsed and shut its doors as though that knowing would destroy her.

Alta stood silently, watching Katie sleep on her side in a fetal position, and the terror of *not knowing* made her forget the flying bride and groom in Cheryl's office. She felt dazed, and the only reality she could grasp was Katie lying in her sleep like a newborn when, in fact, she was dying.

"She wanted you to take her to the hospital Friday, if you can make it," Doug whispered. "It's at two and I can't make it."

"Tell her it's okay. Friday's okay. Good night, Doug." Alta welcomed the cold north wind, though it made her cringe. A large, dark bird swooped noiselessly, with its wings outstretched, directly in front of her. She held her breath, wondering what it was.

She started the motor, letting the heater warm the car, but her trembling was no longer from the cold. She doubted that

117

Hugh meant what he said about going to Cheryl's tomorrow, and if he did show up, what would they talk about?

"The size of that bird," Alta murmured, staring out at the night as the car heated up. "What in the hell could be that big and graceful?"

After class Steve insisted on taking Alta to a Japanese restaurant. She followed him in her car. The car was mainly hers now since Hugh had bought Tony's old pickup. As they walked into the restaurant she was aware of scrutiny. She could always tell when Steve was tensing up; he laughed loudly as if to say, "Kiss my ass, white folks!"

The lunch and the sake arrived. The waitress already loved Steve. His expansiveness and laughter were hard to resist.

"So what's this shrink shrinking? Don't get too damned mellow now, Alta. Can't stand those vibratin' white folks," he said, laughing and pouring more sake.

"First of all, she isn't your standard shrink. Like some of her wisest comments are, to quote, 'What a bunch of bullshit!' " Alta laughed. "But I've also sat there and cried my heart out as well, and she's hung in there with me. You know, you can tell if it's for real. Well, this lady's for real. I like her."

"You're for real too, Alta. When you goin' ta come ta your senses and be my main squeeze?" Steve's eyes were intense, but laughter still played in them. He was beautiful in his darkness, and the center of his eyes seemed to gather light as he spoke and laughed. He was a large man with a large man's confidence. And here was a man, Alta realized, who likes women. The way he talked about his mother and his sisters always touched her; the obvious affection and warmth that came to his face and voice.

Alta's womb stirred, bringing with it a peculiar loneliness, a sense of absence. Hugh didn't love her womb.

"You know, someday I might take you up on these casual offers of yours." Alta smiled at Steve.

"This is not a casual offer, Alta. I like your hair in braids."
Steve reached over, touching her left braid. "Makes you look
like a real Indian, girl." He brushed her cheek with the tips of
his fingers, and she shuddered with pleasure.

"Why're you wastin' it all on this fool, anyway?" Steve
stared at her hard.

Alta sighed, looking away out the window to see if the fog
was lifting, but it was still thick and blowing hard. "This fool
and I are supposed to meet in a few hours at Cheryl's office. You
know, the shrink. If he doesn't show up, Steve, I'm going to ask
him to get out, this week."

"You mean it?"

"Yes, I mean it."

They were silent for a while and then Steve said without
threat or brag in a calm, clear voice, "If that fuckin' fool
touches you again, I'm goin' to give him some instant therapy. I
don't care what you say next time."

Alta smiled and took one of Steve's large, broad hands in
hers. "I don't know why, but that makes me feel wonderful.
Thank you, Steve."

Hugh walked in, still in his work clothes, but he'd washed
up. He almost smiled at Alta; instead, he looked away, glancing at the bare room. "Bare necessities, huh?"

Instantly, her brief relief and pleasure in seeing him disappeared. "We're the main attraction here, I'm afraid."

"Why did you want me to come?" Hugh sat down like a kid
in the principal's office. Then he slouched and spread his legs
defiantly.

"I don't know. Maybe I want things to get better if they
can," Alta answered in an exasperated voice. She clutched herself nervously, hugging her midsection. She hung onto herself.
That's all she had.

"Maybe I want you to tell me the truth or something." Alta
looked at Hugh, but he wouldn't look back at her. "Why does it
always feel like you're lying to me?"

"Come on, Alta. I don't want to talk about this shit here. Anyway, there's nothing to talk about." Hugh felt trapped, as though Alta had purposely brought him here to confess. What I do is my business, he told himself angrily. Doesn't she get all the damned money I bust my ass to make?

"Then why did you come at all, Hugh?" Alta's voice trembled from anger. She looked away, glancing at the only object worth looking at in the room: Chagall's bride and groom flying through their swirling air. She placed her own hand protectively over her own womb and looked back at Hugh.

"I was just asking myself that very same question." Hugh stood up to leave as Cheryl opened her door.

"Glad to meet you, Hugh," she said, walking over to shake his hand. "I'm Cheryl." There was something steely in her voice. She knew he wanted to leave and she wasn't going to let him. "Come on in, both of you." Cheryl met Alta's eyes, acknowledging her briefly.

They all sat down. Hugh and Alta sat side by side with Cheryl facing them. Hugh moved his chair a little closer to the window and farther away from Alta by dragging the chair with his elbows and kicking it with the back of his calves in an angry, violent gesture.

"Obviously, Alta's told me about you, but in my experience there's always two sides, and I'd like you to feel free to say whatever you want here. I'm not going to censor you, and Alta won't censor you. Not here. Do you understand what I'm saying, Hugh?"

Hugh's body was pitched forward as though it were taking all his control not to lunge at her. "I don't really have anything to say. I suppose Alta's filled you in, and I guess whatever she's said's the truth. I'm here because she told me to come, that's all."

"Oh, I see, you're here because mommy told you to come. Is that it? I'd say you outweigh Alta by about eighty pounds."

Hugh clenched the arms of the chair, and, for a moment, he imagined he felt a rope cutting into his wrists. Sitting at the edge of his seat, he rubbed his wrists and looked up at Cheryl.

"Look, I don't have anything to say. Think of me as a witness or whatever."

"How in the hell can you be a witness when you've been a part of my life for so fucking long?" Alta said, almost yelling. "When're you going to tell me what's going on with you?" Now she began to cry. "Look, you can leave. You don't have to be with me anymore. I can make it without you." Her tears stopped abruptly and she glared at Hugh, wiping her tears away in impatience.

"Tough chick, aren't you?" Hugh raised his voice. "You're just one tough cunt!" He darted his eyes to Cheryl. "Very disgusting, aren't I?"

"You are really pissed off, aren't you?" Cheryl said in a soft voice. "I mean, you are so pissed off you could just about kill someone, right?"

Hugh began to tremble with rage. "Yes!" he yelled. "I am goddamned pissed off!" He pounded the chair with his fist.

Cheryl stood up. "Come on, Hugh. Follow me into this room." She looked back at him. "Come on, it's okay. It's an art therapy room and no one's there right now." She looked at Alta and said, "Come along with us."

Cheryl walked up to a small clump of clay on a large clay-covered table with the dry dust of old clay splattered in every direction, and ugly, awkward, childish pieces filled half the table. "Here, Hugh, pound away," she said quietly, pointing at it.

It looks like a scene from a nuthouse, Hugh thought. Not like Bill's studio where every shelf and fixture has some meaning and order, and beauty. Hugh looked at the small lump of clay, walking toward it. He brought his fist down once and it was flat. "Bill," he muttered, letting the name escape him.

"Okay, look, wait a minute," Cheryl said, running toward a closet.

Alta stood in a corner of the room watching Hugh's rigid body. For some reason she felt incredibly embarrassed for him, for herself, as though some terrible vulnerability were being exposed against his will. He continued to stand there with his entire weight on the flattened clay, staring at the raised veins on his hands.

Cheryl struggled with an immense piece of clay still wrapped in plastic. "Here, take the whole damn thing. Tear it up. Go for it," she said, dumping it on the table.

There was a moment of absolute silence and stillness as though the world were going to be ripped apart, and then Hugh cried out, unintelligibly, ripping the plastic off in quick, jerky movements. He pounded the clay with his fists in a pistonlike motion. The clay was thick and sturdy and didn't give easily. He took off his shirt and continued to pound and then he began to cry soundlessly, as sweat dripped from his body. His world was destroyed and he knew it.

"Bill," Hugh gasped softly. "Goddamn it, Bill." He sank to his knees and continued to cry.

"Is Bill your father?" Cheryl asked gently from a distance. She was afraid his anger might explode again. At the same time she wanted to touch him, but she was afraid. She asked him again, "Is Bill your father?"

"Yes," Hugh sobbed, standing up. He gathered the clay together, picked it up, holding it over his head, and threw it across the room, hitting the far wall.

Alta's entire body jerked to attention. She knew Bill wasn't his father's name. *Then who is Bill?* she wondered, but she didn't dare ask. She'd forgotten the older man who rang the front doorbell and courteously asked for Hugh.

"Mom, is Katie going to die soon?" April asked in a quiet voice, studying her mother's face. Everything felt wrong, like something terrible was about to happen now that her father was back. He'd tried to talk to her a couple of times, but the truth was she didn't trust him anymore. And now Katie was dying and she looked like an old lady with her short hair and dry lips. Plus she kept losing weight.

But Katie's eyes were always happy to see April, like they both knew a great joke or a really great secret, and then Katie would ask her endless questions about her friends, school, books, even boys. So, they never talked about cancer or dying. But Katie had given April a book about a girl named Anne Frank. Her diary. A young girl who'd been killed by the Nazis in the Second World War for being Jewish. Katie had told April, "I read it at about your age. See what you think." April was coming to the end of the book, and it was the saddest book she'd ever read. She decided to take the book to Katie's next time and maybe talk about it. That is, if Katie wanted to.

Ian put his bowl in the sink and, grabbing his lunch, ran out the door. He didn't want to hear the answer. The bright morning sun was warm on his face as he ran up the hill, and he wished he didn't have to go to school. He thought of the creek with the rope hanging close to the water, and in his mind it was still and inviting, dangling over the cool, flowing creek.

"Katie has maybe two more weeks or so, they think, honey. When you're young like Katie the cancer cells multiply faster."

"Who's going to take care of Ethan and Erin and everything?" April's eyes filled with instant tears.

Alta walked over, taking April in her arms. "I guess Doug will take care of everything. Maybe we can help him out too. Right?"

"I guess I like Doug better now, but wasn't he kind of a creep before and all?"

"Yeah, I guess Doug's changed since Katie's gotten sick. You better get going, kiddo, or you're going to be late." Alta watched her daughter open the door and then shut it—the bright spray of sun on the hall floor and then darkness. She heard April leap the four steps to the cement, and the thought of the little girl attempting to manage the emerging woman made her throat swell with a peculiar anguish, bringing brief, stinging tears to her eyes.

The cab driver honked twice, impatiently, as Alta slammed the door behind her. Katie looked almost propped in the back seat, but she smiled as Alta opened the door.

"Limousine service for the sick and dying," Katie joked. "Not bad, huh? And for free, yet." Katie's lips were dry with a white spittle caked at the corners of her mouth. The effort it took to leave her house was becoming more difficult each time. Her eyes were especially large now that her face was becoming thinner, and an intense luminosity shone from them, as well as an intense weariness and sense of unrelenting pain. But still the humor would not leave them, not entirely.

Alta laughed, kissing Katie's cheek. "Does James know where to go and all?"

"James sure does," the cab driver answered irritably.

"I was just kidding." Alta rolled her eyes and Katie giggled for a moment like a little girl behind Daddy's back. "Spare me," Alta said in a low voice. "How're you feeling? Are you feeling okay?"

"I feel better already seeing you, my friend. I took a little something to help me along, so that helps. I have to remember to bring water next time. I get so thirsty," Katie said, licking her parched lips.

"You ought to wear chapstick too. Do you have any? Can you wait to get a drink at the hospital?"

"I gave up on chapstick." Katie smiled. "Yeah, I think I can make it. How's Rita doing?" Katie leaned her head back against the seat, letting it roll as the cab turned and stopped.

"I still can't believe Rita has cancer too. But, of course, you can," Alta said softly. "She's scheduled to have her breast removed, but she'll live. That's something."

"That's everything, I'd say." Katie stared in to Alta's eyes with a terrible longing. Gently, she turned her head to look out the window at the crowds of people that seemed so alien to her now; all their noise, their hurried movements, meant nothing to her anymore.

"Tell Rita I always knew she was an amazon." Katie laughed softly.

The cab driver lurched to an abrupt, sudden stop, nearly throwing Katie from her seat and banging the length of her forearms as she tried to protect her fall forward.

"Damn it! Can't you slow down? The woman back here is very sick, and you're going too damned fast!" Alta yelled angrily, as she helped Katie up.

"They're all sick, lady," he mumbled in a surly voice.

"If you don't slow down, I'm going to take your name and report you. Do you understand?" Alta was livid with sudden rage and her voice trembled slightly. She locked her eyes on the right side of the driver's face.

He didn't answer, but he slowed down, hunching and sulking in his seat. He looked into his rearview mirror once, glaring at Alta.

"I don't have to go back anymore for those fucking visits," Katie sighed as she got into the hospital bed. It felt so good to have her street clothes off again and slide between the comfort of clean sheets.

"Do you want another pillow?" Alta asked.

"I'll just prop the back up here a little. Would you bring some fresh water from the fridge? I'm going to take another pain killer." It was a terrible relief to not hear the children playing in the house, reminding her each time they went to Juanita with their needs that she was unable to fill them. At times it made her feel dead already, and a terrible hatred would fill her because they were young and a lost or broken toy took all their attention. And then a terrible love would come in its wake, neither giving her any comfort.

"When are the kids coming back?" Alta poured a fresh glass of water, handing it to Katie.

"Juanita's bringing them back around four. Will you stay with me for a while?"

"Of course. We haven't had a good visit in a week at least, right?" Alta smiled reassuringly, sensing an edge of loneliness and desperation in her voice. And who wouldn't be? Alta thought. "Would you like some tea with me? And how about some sandwiches?"

Tears filled Katie's eyes. "I called some old—good friends, I thought—anyway, friends, to come over. Juanita made some snacks. I love that woman. And do you know only one woman showed up, and she was so nervous and embarrassed she couldn't look me in the eye. I mean, it's not my goddamn fault I'm dying. I'm just dying."

Alta stood in the doorway. "It could be me, Katie. Look at Rita—now she's dealing with it. I mean, I could die crossing the street going to my car, right? There's no guarantees. Anyway, I don't understand why they couldn't at least be honest with you—but then that's why they didn't show up." Facing death means facing your truth, Alta realized. "Did they actually say they'd be here?" Katie's pain filled her heart, and then her own fierce anger took its place.

"Every one of them. Alta, come here," Katie said, motioning her closer.

Alta walked over, standing next to the hospital bed.

"You know, I notice even Doug doesn't like to touch me anymore, like death's contagious. Like he might die if he touched me." Katie smiled, looking up into Alta's eyes. "Like right now though you're standing close to me, you still aren't touching me."

Alta met Katie's gaze and, reaching over, she touched her shoulder. "Maybe you're right. Maybe it's the unconscious fear of the healthy. If you felt me doing it, I'm sorry because it's really nothing but bullshit." Alta stroked Katie's forehead.

"Alta, would you lie next to me, just for a while? I know it sounds a little weird, but I'd really like you to. Do you mind?" Katie's eyes pleaded.

"Do you have enough room there, girl?" Alta laughed. "I guess you are getting a little skinny there, so I guess there is," she said, settling herself comfortably on her right side. Alta looked into Katie's face and she remembered, with sudden clarity, the times she and her mother had lain in bed talking when she was little, in the mornings.

"Is it terrible? I mean, is it terrible being this close?" Tears fell automatically from Katie's eyes as she continued to face Alta.

"No, it's not terrible. It's not terrible." Alta began to cry, holding Katie to her, cradling her head on her shoulder. "What would be terrible would be if you didn't ask, or if I were afraid to lie here with you."

Alta stroked Katie's face, forehead to chin, her fingertips becoming wet with Katie's tears. Alta sighed deeply, as her breath caught itself like a in mid-sob. "I love you, Katie. If I become an old lady—if I live that long—I'll always remember you. Do you understand?"

Katie clung to Alta. "Yes," she murmured.

They were quiet for a while, watching the afternoon shadows shift on the white living room walls. A mockingbird sang from the sapling tree in front: a tree Doug had planted last spring. A small, white butterfly gingerly touched the window; then, surrendering to a gust of warm wind, it was gone.

"You know, my first lover was a woman, or really, we were girls. We were sixteen and she was my best friend. I had my first real orgasm with her. It was wonderful. Does that shock you?" Katie studied Alta closely. The morphine gave her time now to remember.

"Maybe just a little. I guess I just have to catch up here just a little." Alta's heart was beating fast and her ears felt plugged up. Take it easy, she told herself. Just take it easy. What am I, a baby? Alta slowed the racing of her heart, and Katie's face came back into focus.

"Does it make you uncomfortable? I'm sorry, maybe I shouldn't have told you. I've never told anyone else. I mean, no one. Not even Doug." Katie met Alta's eyes knowingly.

"Well, then, I'm glad and honored that you told me." Alta smiled shyly. "Your secret's safe with me, okay?"

"Have you ever made love to a woman? I guess you haven't." Katie returned Alta's smile.

"No, you're right, I haven't."

"In a way, you are now. I mean, just in a way. Does the idea repulse you?"

Alta thought about it, remembering Katie's lovely, red hair that had stopped just above her full, womanly breasts. "Not really. I've always found, you know, beautiful women attractive. What's it like?"

Katie lay her head back on the pillow and gazed up at the ceiling. "It's like making love to your mother, finally." She paused. "Am I shocking you again?"

"No," Alta answered, staring at Katie's lips the way she had when her mother had told her stories.

"And it's like making love to yourself, in a way, discovering the taste and feel of yourself in another woman. The taboo breasts, Mom's nipples." Katie giggled softly. She was floating from the morphine, but she was conscious. Almost acutely conscious with Alta lying next to her, stroking her face now and then.

"The inner labia. You know, the cunt. Its juices, or rather our juices. And the feel of a woman's orgasm on my tongue was like a miracle, but, then, so was mine. It was like fusing bodies. Souls. It kind of helped me become a woman. In my soul." Katie looked at Alta with unusual tenderness. "It did," she added softly as she remembered her lover, vividly.

"Why did you get together with Doug, and where's your friend now? Two loaded questions, right? Sorry." Alta returned Katie's tenderness with her eyes, but at the same time she wondered what Doug would think if he walked in right now.

"I promptly fell in love with men's bodies, their differences." Katie licked her lips as the white dryness at the corners of her mouth began to irritate her. She reached for the water.

"Here, let me clean the sides of your mouth," Alta said, dipping the edge of a paper towel into the water.

"Gracias. I'd do the same for you, you know." Katie's voice was suddenly fierce, but her eyes remained gentle, tender.

"I know you would," Alta murmured.

"Where was I?" Katie smiled.

"Men's bodies, but not chocolate dipped, right?" Alta laughed gently.

"Right. I still want to do that. I wonder if I have time?" The humor in Katie's eyes blazed. "Anyway, I fell in love with Doug, and, to his credit, he wasn't afraid or disgusted by the 9taste of my pussy." Katie laughed. "In fact, he professed to love it. How could I refuse?"

"Did I tell you that when I kicked Hugh in the balls he was trying to rape me? He eats pussy, now, anyway, only when I'm in bondage." Alta expelled her breath in a rush as though she were ridding herself of something. "It wasn't always that way. He was gentle once. I mean, I think he loved me."

"I'm sorry, Alta." Katie stroked Alta's hair. "Motherfucker. When're you leaving him? You've got to. Is that what your suicide attempt was about?" Katie locked eyes with Alta and they burned with fierceness. "No one's worth dying for. Do you hear me? No one. Fuck that Christ complex. You know, Isis . . ."

"Who's Isis?"

"An Egyptian Goddess. Anyway, yes, a real Goddess who puts her dead lover back together, since he was cut into pieces by finding his dick. The point is, he doesn't stay dead forever on the fucking cross." Katie's voice was soft but fierce.

"I'm getting ready to do it. Don't worry. You have enough to worry about. I'm not the martyr type, really. And this Isis, I have to remember that and maybe find out more. And this dick stuff. It sounds intriguing like chocolate-covered men." Alta felt light, like laughing, like all the darkness in the world had fled before this strange name. Isis. It stirred her as it had seeing the woman in the oak tree, but now she had a name, and she was a Goddess. And Katie'd made love to a woman: amazing.

"You can have Doug. He's improved, you know. A new and improved model," Katie said, smiling. Her eyes burned clear.

Alta laughed. "Thanks for the offer. You say he likes pussy and all?"

"Definitely." Katie lay back again. She was becoming tired though she desired, more than anything, to stay awake and talk to Alta.

"And what happened to your friend, your first lover?" Alta asked, gently. She could see Katie was tiring quickly.

"She died in some foreign country by herself, a suicide." Tears sprang to Katie's eyes, and her skin, dry as any desert, soaked them up. "She thought she'd failed everyone. That she wasn't normal; a normal woman, that is. And she was brilliant. Brilliant."

Katie looked at the shades, pulled down to keep out the harsh warmth, and it occurred to her that it felt like there was a sun inside of her trying to escape and expose itself, as though her body had always been the healthy shades of her inner sun, and now it was breaking through as she disappeared. She began to sweat, and she knew the ice water wouldn't quench her thirst, but she reached for it anyway.

"How do we stand it? That's what I wonder sometimes. Like sometimes I actually forget Hugh was trying to rape me. I start to think maybe I made it up, you know?" Alta held Katie in her arms, unaware she was rocking her. "Why don't you take a nap and then we'll have that snack? Just close your eyes for a while, okay?"

"Only if you promise to wake me up in thirty minutes. Do you promise?" She hated to close her eyes, but the sun inside was growing brighter. Katie closed her eyes for a moment. Then why is it so dark? she thought, wishing she could ask someone who might know the answer. Quickly, she opened her eyes. Alta was still there.

"Yes, I promise." Alta started to get up.

"Do you want to hear something funny? I've got to tell you." Katie put her hand over her own breast. She felt her heart beating steadily and it comforted her. Almost as much as having Alta next to her.

"Paula—that was her name—sent me her clipped pubic hair wrapped in red tissue, tucked into a beautiful, hand blown goblet, for my wedding present." Katie laughed softly. "Don't you love it?"

Alta laughed. "I love it."

"I've never let anyone else drink out of it, you know?"

"I wouldn't either." Alta wet another paper towel and wiped Katie's lips, then her face. "Thanks for telling me all this. Don't you ever feel sorry you did, okay?"

"Okay." Katie's eyes were closed. She fell asleep almost instantly.

Alta took her tea into the backyard. The wind had picked up, and it matched her inner turmoil almost perfectly. At the same time she felt an inexplicable excitement. A cluster of butterflies exploded from a purple thistle flower. Butterflies, she thought. Yes, that's what it is. Butterflies.

Katie's revelation about her woman lover had taken her by surprise. But hadn't Katie been one of those beautiful women she'd always been drawn to? Alta thought. Katie's long, thick, red hair grazing her full, soft-looking breasts, her once limber walk, the sway of her hips. "Bird of paradise," Alta murmured, "you were so beautiful. So goddamned beautiful."

Alta went in to make the cheese sandwiches. She thought of tomorrow night. She and Hugh were going out to dinner; something they hadn't done in almost a year. He'd asked her out in a strangely formal way, saying he had to talk to her about some important things. Who's Bill? she'd wanted to say, but she couldn't bring herself to do it and she didn't know why.

Bill's not your father! she'd wanted to scream. You fucking liar! But she hadn't, and she didn't know why. Now, she supposed, they'd go out to dinner tomorrow night and talk about splitting up and how they'd do it.

Cheryl wanted Hugh to come back, if not with Alta then by himself. Hugh had just nodded his head mutely and walked out the door, his violence almost spent. Almost.

Alta was still stunned, in awe of it. It was as though he'd wanted to kill the entire cosmos as he flung the raw wedge of clay against the wall. It was strangely beautiful and it stirred her. At the same time it frightened her. Who does he hate that much? she asked herself. Who does he love? Not me. Certainly not me. What will we talk about tomorrow night? she wondered. How will we say everything we have to say? How will I let my first lover go? Not a woman—a man, my husband, father of my children. A man who's tried to rape me, who's split my face open. My first gentle love.

Alta cut the sandwiches in half, the neat, green lettuce showing on the edges. Mayonnaise, smooth and tasty, squirted out from their centers. Her stomach began to growl. It was almost forty-five minutes, so she walked into the front room to wake Katie up.

Katie only nibbled hers, and she sipped the spicy cinnamon tea slowly. Alta sat next to her on the bed. Only the sound of an occasional car broke the silence. The neighbors upstairs were still at work, so not even a footstep could be heard.

"You know, I'm a junkie now. Remember that guy you ran over? I bet he was a junkie. Full circle, no? I mean, I don't think it's his fault or anything me ending up a junkie. I just think it's apt. And, anyway, that's how I met you. Do you want my half? Go ahead, take it." The nap had revived her somewhat, and she decided to wait until she couldn't bear the pain to take the next pill. It gave her relief, but it made the inner sun burn brighter, making the darkness in its wake even more terrifying.

"I could wrap it up for later. I don't see you as a junkie. I see you as having cancer, but I guess I understand what you mean."

"No, go ahead, eat it. I'll have some soup later."

Alta reached over and took the half sandwich. "Thanks. I have to go pretty soon. It's almost four-thirty. I told the kids I'd be there by five. Juanita's probably on her way."

"Just help me to the bathroom before you go. At least junkies can make it to the can, right? Jesus." Katie turned to her left side facing the windows. The sun was beginning to set, leaving trails of gold on the far wall. Alta had raised the shades midway.

"It's perfect, isn't it?" Katie stared at a beautiful scroll painting her parents had sent her from Japan. There was a range of mountains tipped with gold at their heights and small pine trees in clusters, some by themselves threading their way to the top. A waterfall ran down the center of the scroll, and a small human figure, dwarfed by such beauty, made his way by the waterfall toward the mountains. Or, rather, he paused in the silence gathering that wonderful sight. The choice was up to the viewer at any given moment, and *the moment was now.* The moment when stillness and movement, death and life, hatred and love, reconciled themselves in a strangely perfect equilibrium through the witness: the human soul. The result was always beauty.

Katie sat up a little bit straighter in her mound of pillows. "Isn't it perfect right now, Alta? Look at the gold on the tips of the mountains—they're shining with the gold from the sun. That's me walking there. That's me with the short hair," Katie said, smiling, and her skull-like face shone like the sun.

"It is perfect, absolutely perfect," Alta whispered, not wanting to disturb what she saw on Katie's face. What she heard in Katie's voice—a kind of transcendence. A fearlessness. Peace. "I knew that was you. You didn't have to tell me."

Doug opened the front door, jarring them in that still moment. He strode into the front room. "Well, what's this, a pajama party? What're you two concocting up there in that bed together?" He laughed loudly, bringing everything to the present in a rush.

"You'd be surprised," Katie said, glancing at Alta and smiling. The intense light was gone from her face, but her eyes still held their unspeakable peace.

"Yes, indeed, you would," Alta laughed softly. "I suppose I'd better get going, so you're right on time."

"I gave you to Alta after I'm gone. I thought you'd like to know. It's a good idea, isn't it?" Katie smiled as she gazed at Doug.

Doug blushed deep red. "Katie, don't say things like that. Come on, have some sense, will you?"

Alta started laughing, though Katie's frankness startled her as well. She was joking, after all. "You asked what we were concocting, so that's your mistake," she said, winking at him.

He caught the wink and relaxed a little. "Okay, ladies, very funny. Are you coming for dinner Sunday to meet Katie's parents? They're flying in from the Orient tomorrow."

"I guess so. What're you making?"

"Stew. What else?" Doug laughed, mainly at himself, but there was a hollow echo to it, and when he looked at Katie he tried to look only at her eyes. She was so thin . . . "I can make a mean pot of chili beans too. What do you think?" He looked at Alta, noticing the swell of her hips, her small breasts, and Katie's words were no joke. He felt instantly ashamed as though the women could read his mind.

"Do you want me to bring a salad?" Alta asked, sensing his discomfort. "If you do the beans I'll bring fresh tortillas and some guacamole," she added in a supportive gesture.

"It's a deal. Gracias." Doug smiled as he sat down on the couch opposite Katie. "Bring a lot of patience too. Her folks can be a pain in the ass. You don't mind me saying that, do ya, Katie?" He looked at Katie, at her eyes. They were peaceful. Unusually peaceful, and they seemed to be able to see the contents of his soul. He looked away, out the window.

"It's the truth," Katie said. She looked at herself in the scroll and smiled.

Alta leaned over and kissed Katie on the forehead and rubbed her neck briefly. "I love you, Katie."

"I love you, too," Katie whispered.

"Doug, this woman could use a massage, in case you didn't know. You know, tender loving care and all that good stuff. Bye, Doug." Alta kissed him on the cheek and left.

The sun had set and a thick, massive fog bank was rolling in over Twin Peaks, bringing a chill winter wind with it. As Alta stood on the landing she remembered a teacher, when she was in the fourth grade, telling the class that the Indians of the area believed Twin Peaks to be a woman lying down on her back. Of course, Alta thought, seeing her breasts clearly. I wonder what they called her?

Suddenly, she felt exhausted and cold, and she knew the kids were waiting. And Hugh. "Isis," Alta murmured, thinking of Katie and her woman lover. Then she ran for the car.

They dropped the kids at Jackie's. Hugh tried to kiss April goodbye, but April pulled away quickly, following Jackie into the kitchen. Ian hung back, waiting by the door, waiting for something he couldn't even articulate, but he waited, gazing shyly at his father. Hugh rubbed his head roughly, saying, "See ya later, guy. Don't drink too much beer, makes ya piss."

"Yeah, right," Ian answered sulkily. He waved goodbye once to Alta and slammed the door behind him.

The transition had been so subtle that neither Hugh nor Alta noticed it: Alta was driving the car. Hugh was almost courteous, but distant, and though they still slept in the same bed, they touched only by accident—a foot, a hip, a shoulder. Then one or the other would quickly pull away as though they'd broken some rule. But it was more than that; the space between them was poisoned, polluted. Taboo. There was no love, not even physical desire. It was like the islands the major powers bombed, testing their weapons; no life could live between them anymore, and the radiation was unbearable.

The immense fountain was still in the middle of the restaurant, splashing continuously onto the floor and the closest diners. Fresh flowers were in small vases and candles burned on each table. The murals on the walls looked as faded and old as the first time they'd come four years ago. Alta felt suddenly happy sitting down at their table closest to the fountain. They'd always sat as close as they could get. Tonight the fountain was right next to them.

"Maybe we'd better move the table over a little, Alta, unless you're into soup." Hugh laughed nervously.

"Okay, just a little. We've never sat this close." Alta blushed awkwardly. "I mean, someone's always sitting here. Well, it's been a long time since we've come here, hasn't it?" Alta said, picking up her end of the table as they moved it

135

slightly out the way of the water's spray. She refused to meet Hugh's eyes.

"Do you want to order?" A waiter asked, wiping the table dry, but it wouldn't last. "Comes with the territory, I'm afraid," he added in a sullen voice.

Whenever they came here they ordered crab cioppino, which always arrived in a huge earthenware bowl, steaming in the most delicious sauce and spices. So they automatically ordered it again.

Hugh looked at Alta. "You don't mind eating out of the same bowl with a bastard like me?"

Alta glanced at him, then shifted her gaze to the flowing water. The sound of it captured all of her attention for a moment. "No problem, I'm hungry," Alta said dryly.

Hugh laughed, throwing his head back. Alta looked up in surprise. She hadn't seen him do that in years. At least a couple of years, she realized, but she still refused to meet his eyes.

"In a matter of survival anything goes, right?" Hugh broke off a piece of the warm French bread and, buttering it, stuffed it into his mouth. It was fragrant and delicious.

"They always have such fresh bread here, they must get it straight from the local bakery. Do you remember I used to shop for our coffee, pasta, and bread in North Beach?" Other memories flooded her, and she wished she hadn't said anything.

"I used to come sometimes, remember?" Hugh played with the drops of water forming on the table, connecting them and watching the candle's reflections spread over their scattered mirrored surfaces. "Yeah, I like this neighborhood. Anything goes." He looked at Alta and then at the flickering chaos he'd haphazardly created, and in one movement wiped it dry with his napkin.

Two men chose the table next to them. Both of them had a very feminine quality, and they both wore diamond studs in their ears. The taller, dark-haired man had a diamond stud in his right ear with a gold star above it, while his blond friend wore diamond studs in both ears. Both men were extraordinarily handsome, almost beautiful.

136

Hugh glared at them. "Just what I need, a couple of fags." Then he looked away, fidgeting with his damp napkin. Again, he wiped the table dry. "You wouldn't catch me dead in earrings," Hugh said loudly. Bill doesn't *look* like a fag, he thought with unexpected anger.

"They aren't trying to pick you up, so why don't you cool it?" Alta retorted irritably, with embarrassment. She thought of her talk with Katie, imagining how shocked Hugh would be to know about her lover. She glanced over at the men and the dark-haired one smiled at her. His smile was sensual and feminine, yet masculine. She smiled back shyly.

"You know, I like men with earrings," she said, looking at Hugh for the first time in the face.

"Since when?" He met her gaze with a certain hostility.

"I don't know. I guess I've never really thought about it, but I do. I think men look attractive in earrings."

Hugh felt unnerved by her admission and it bothered him that Alta was watching the men with interest. What if she knew I'm a fag? he thought sullenly. She'd hate my guts, that's what. I wouldn't last two minutes on the steel with an *earring*. And Bill, what about Bill? His stomach clenched with sorrow.

Their dinner arrived. The crab floated in a rich, red sauce and it smelled delicious. Maybe they're not even gay, Alta couldn't help thinking—or they're bi. Anyway, they're gorgeous, she decided. The blond, smaller man was almost as striking as the dark-haired man. And if they are gay they must be worried about AIDS all the time. The dark-haired man turned and, catching Alta's gaze, smiled at her again. Alta's stomach fluttered and her vagina clenched with longing—it'd been a long time since she'd made love.

"You know me, if you don't eat your half, I'm going to eat it for you," Hugh said playfully, but there was an edge to his voice.

Alta looked at him, trying to imagine him with an earring. "Yeah, I know you," she lied and eagerly began to eat the spicy, succulent crab with her fingers.

The salad was gone, the crab was gone, all the bread was gone, and the wine was nearly gone. The two men next to Hugh and Alta talked and ate with an orchestrated ease, breaking out into hilarious, spontaneous laughter now and then. While Hugh and Alta had eaten with an appetite, they were still hungry for something unsaid. They'd eaten the delicious food in silence.

"Why did you ask me out to dinner?" Alta's voice sounded thin and brittle from disuse, and she wished, immediately, that she hadn't spoken.

Hugh lunged at her words with relief. "What do you want to do now? I guess that's what I want to know."

"I guess it's time to call it quits, isn't it?" The words spilled out of their own volition.

"I guess it is," Hugh echoed.

The two men got up to leave and the lovely, dark-haired man leaned over, nearly touching Alta's shoulder: "Cheer up, nothing's that bad, is it?" He smiled full in her face. The small, gold star looked huge from that distance, and it seemed to twinkle in the candlelight for her benefit.

Alta laughed. "Okay, I'm cheered up." His unexpected gesture caught her by surprise, and she was at once startled and delighted.

Hugh started to stand, but the men turned and walked out the door. He looked at Alta with an expression of utter frustration, but at the same time he was relieved they were gone. An intense energy overtook him as he thought of the two men going home to make love. And then he thought of Bill and terror filled him. He heard himself saying, "Do you want to go dancing?"

"What do I have to lose but the blues? Sure, why not?"

"Cheerful, aren't you?" Hugh couldn't help smiling.

"The only thing we have to do is die, right?"

Hugh winced. "That's the truth."

"Then let's go dancing." Alta finished her wine. "Fuck it, I'm ready."

The floor was crowded as they stood up to dance. They didn't touch or look at one another, but the music was good. They ignored each other, listening only to the beat of the music. Soul music. For a while Alta forgot about Katie, and Hugh forgot about Bill, but mainly they forgot about each other as they climbed each note, its beat, leaving the other further behind.

They drank quickly as though their lives depended on it, waiting for the music to begin again. The band jumped right in to "Soul Man." Hugh motioned the cocktail waitress for more of the same.

As they danced Hugh's movements became more and more sweeping, taking up a large portion of the floor because of his size. It seemed the band began to play to him. His sudden joy was contagious, and the other dancers stopped to watch.

Alta danced with him, but at a distance. She felt awkward next to his size and grace and also because everyone had stopped to watch him dance. Hugh's movements were becoming wild as he waved his hands over his head, sweat dripping down his face. The other dancers clapped for him and then began to dance again. It was as though a storm had broken, and now it was clear and fresh. It was a moment of change.

"What was that all about? Jesus! I've never seen you dance like that before." Alta laughed as she mixed her black Russian with her finger. Hugh looked boyish with pleasure. Almost feminine, like a beautiful woman, she couldn't help thinking.

A slow dance started. Hugh put out his hand to her saying, "Do you want to? May as well, our last dance and all." He smiled provocatively.

The three black Russians made her slightly dizzy, fusing the dancers and the music together in some strange way. And somehow Hugh's dance seemed to make everything possible, for the moment.

Alta stood up and, still holding his hand, followed him out to the floor. As Hugh put his hand to her waist, holding her to him, and Alta put her hand to the back of his neck, they fused. It stunned them both with its unexpected intensity. It was almost like making love and any small, subtle movement was an ecstasy in itself. They moved against each other slowly, as though trying to prolong their mutual orgasms. They were completely unaware of anything but the music which ran through their bodies in ripples.

They made love slowly, as though morning would never come. As though their past no longer existed, as though language itself didn't exist. Only this terrible longing existed, this terrible desire. Only this kind of passion, when everything real was renounced, was born from great mutual pain. And it, the pain, and its twin sister ecstasy, were almost unbearable. Almost.

Alta lay curled on Hugh's chest, stroking his neck and watching deep colors gather under her eyelids. She could find no words for her orgasm. No words.

Dawn prepared itself in the lingering darkness.

"Alta," Hugh said softly. "Are you asleep?"

"No," she managed to say.

"I have to talk to you. Are you listening?" There was a strange desperation in his voice. Hugh gathered himself and opened his mouth.

"I've been seeing someone since I was seventeen. I'm a homosexual. That's what I am, a homosexual. And the man I've been seeing has AIDS. He's going to die. I went to get the test and I'm negative, so you're negative too. Do you hear me?"

Alta's breath left her body, and an eerie silence made Hugh's words echo with precision. His voice was like a recorded message, and she wished she could hang up and not hear anymore. But now the intense pleasure she'd been filled with a moment ago turned neatly into its opposite. This pain was unbearable.

She opened her mouth to speak, but only inarticulate sobs escaped. She was drowning in this pain. She sat up and stared at him. She couldn't recognize him. She tried, but nothing about him was familiar. She willed herself to name him, even silently: Hugh. But she couldn't.

He was dead, but he spoke anyway. "I'm sorry. If it means anything, I'm sorry that I've hurt you." He waited for her to speak but she was silent. "Do you hear me, Alta?"

His body was unusually pale in the darkness, and it occurred to Alta that Hugh didn't have any blood. How could a vampire have blood? How could a vampire get AIDS? She started to laugh until she couldn't breathe anymore—and then the long, hoarse cries of betrayal began to issue from her crooked mouth like an angry volcano. Her lava flowed and flowed, red and hot, into the foggy sunrise.

Five

"Hugh, you can't stay here. There's nothing you can do." Bill's face was tired and drawn, but implacable. His eyes glittered like steel shards as he met Hugh's downcast eyes. He forced Hugh to look up.

"We've got a nurse to take care of us," Bill said, indicating the next room where his lover was, "whether it's six weeks or six months. You're young, you're negative. Go out and live your own life. You were going to leave Alta, weren't you?"

Hugh couldn't talk. His anger was overwhelming.

"Maybe it's time to be honest with yourself." Bill's eyes softened. "Maybe it's time to live with a man."

Hugh jumped to his feet, knocking the chair over, scratching the wooden floor harshly. "That's easy for you to say. How am I supposed to be a fag and an ironworker? Besides, I have kids."

Bill's eyes glittered hard again. "How long are you going to run from yourself toward a father that doesn't exist?" He held Hugh's eyes. "I'm dying, that's all there is to it," he said in a low, clear voice. "Find someone to love. Shit, love yourself."

The tears started at the bottom of Hugh's gut, rose past his heart into his aching throat, filled his eyes and fell, salty and fresh as the sea, and they stung him. They stung him with their truth.

"How in the fuck am I supposed to do that?" He looked at Bill as though he were far away and blurry, and though he wiped his eyes quickly with his hands, the impression wouldn't leave him.

"I guess you know that using those rubbers saved my life," Hugh said, trying to reach Bill with his voice.

Bill smiled and said, "I was afraid to catch something from you."

A sense of shock, like being engulfed unexpectedly by an immense, powerful wave, hit Hugh, and Bill seemed even further away and indistinct as though the room itself had lengthened, expanded, and the sound of the sea was deafening. "I thought you loved me," Hugh managed to say.

"I did."

Bill's voice was underwater now, and Hugh turned and ran from the house, leaving the front door open. Maybe it would float away, maybe it would flood, maybe death would just walk in. He didn't care anymore. He had to save himself.

Hugh started the truck up and pointed it north.

"He'd signed up for the Marines. Did I ever tell you that?" Alta asked, looking up at Cheryl's listening face. Alta's eyes looked old and listless as though all the joy had been sucked out of them.

"Well, it didn't last very long. He went AWOL and they put him in Leavenworth for a year." Alta looked down at her hands, and for some reason they looked especially small and helpless today; the way the right hand covered the left hand, almost protectively. She squeezed her hands into fists. They still looked small.

"Anyway, I lived in some projects—an almost all-black project—out by the Cow Palace. The walls were about an inch thick so you could hear your neighbors cough, or fart for that matter. Anyway, I lived there for a little over two years by myself. I was pregnant with Ian there, all of seventeen, and April was almost two. "Alta's expression was grim, and the tone of her voice was flat as though she didn't really care about what she was talking about, but she had to say it anyway.

"So, when my labor started I had to take a cab to the hospital, and the nurses took care of April until a friend of mine named Jackie came to get her. I mean, Jackie was just graduating from high school, so I was kind of her living nightmare, so I didn't have too many visitors in those days. And, then, it was one of those military hospitals, and this fucking doctor's in a hurry because he says he's late for an appointment."

"He actually said this?" Cheryl interjected.

"That's what he said."

"Fucker," Cheryl muttered. "Weren't there any nurses in the delivery room . . . "

"Believe it or not, no. Just me and him, so he gives me a saddle block and pulls Ian out and his head's all long and bruised. Then, they wouldn't bring babies to privates' wives. One black woman was too weak to get up, and the assholes wouldn't bring her baby. So, I found out her last name and went to the nursery and asked for the baby. 'You aren't the mother,' this robot nurse tells me. And instead of saying 'No shit,' I tell her in a calm voice that the woman's too weak to get up, and all she wants is to see her baby. She's very angry and all, but she lets me take the baby. 'You have to bring him back, you know!' she yells in a nasty, loud voice, and instead of answering, 'I didn't think he could walk back,' I answer, 'I know.' "

"You know, Alta, you've been through a lot of shit, but you've handled it. I mean, you've prevailed. Do you know that?" Cheryl met Alta's eyes and smiled.

"I suppose so. But why don't I feel like I've prevailed? I feel like I've had my ass kicked, and I'm laying on the street and fucking bleeding to death." Alta looked down at her hands, and they'd gone back to their protective gesture all on their own.

Cheryl felt Alta's despair, acutely, and so she asked, "How did you survive the projects by yourself?"

"I met my neighbors and they kind of looked out for me. One neighbor, about three doors down, was from Jamaica. She had a beautiful accent. Anyway, she had four kids and two of them were blind twins. Imagine being black, on welfare, with four kids of which two are blind. But she bitched and moaned and got her blind kids in special schools, and she had a boyfriend who gave her money on the side—an old, white guy. It was all part of the job, survival. She was an amazing woman. Donna was her name. She saw me bringing in diapers one time after dark, and she came over and told me that if I kept that up I'd be raped. 'Do it in the daytime, girl. Diapers aren't that important.' " Alta tried to mimic the accent but she failed.

"Anyway, she was right. The next week as I'm having dinner with April in the kitchen there's this terrible scream. A girl was raped right in back going home. Donna used to tell me, 'There's a rape in this place every night. Lock your windows, girl, and don't put your head out the door.' My neighbors next door to me, they were a young, black family, about my age, seventeen or eighteen. They'd just had a baby. One night they started really fighting, I mean violently, and she runs out of the house. Sonny, the guy, who's about six foot six, stands at the door yelling, 'Bitch, you better come back! I can't feed this kid!' Then silence. In about an hour his friends are over, and the stereo's blasting away downstairs. I feel like banging on the wall and shouting to turn that noise down, but there's a bunch of heavy looking black guys in there, including Sonny." Alta paused, looking into Cheryl's face. "I haven't thought of all this in a long, I mean a long, time. I mean, I'm sitting here wringing my hands." She tried to laugh, but it caught in her throat and died there like a dry, useless thing.

"I can tell. Keep on going," Cheryl encouraged her.

"Then I heard the baby start to cry. You know, that squeaky newborn cry. The baby was upstairs. These were downstairs and upstairs things, but very primitive with cement floors. Anyway, the baby continued to cry for about an hour off and on, and as its cry became a scream the stereo went up. I couldn't stand it. Something clicked in my head. Ian was about three months old, so he was asleep and I told April to stay on the couch. I went to their door, and, without even bothering to knock, I walked in and there was this roomful of black guys smoking dope, drinking, and whatever. All conversation ceased. I mean, they were silent, and there I was in my flannel nightgown. They all looked stunned as I said, marching up the stairs, 'Your baby's been crying for over an hour. I'm taking him to my place.' I picked the baby up and he's soaked and I can't find any diapers, so I grab what I can. The baby's body is rigid from crying, but he stops as I pick him up and whimpers with the effort to catch his breath. Then I'm walking down the steps, heading for the door. Still, no one's moved or spoken. I say in the silence, 'And keep that music down! It's too damned loud! You should be ashamed!' I yell and leave. I changed his diapers, put him in some of Ian's old clothes, fed him some formula, and lined a drawer with some blankets like I'd seen in the movies. It worked. He fell asleep on his stomach. The next day Sonny's wife came back, and he came over for the baby. He was so tall he had to duck to get in the door. He asked me if the music bothered me anymore and I said no. He thanked me for taking the baby and then he told me if I ever needed anything at all, anything, he said, 'You jes bang on this wall an ah'll be right over. You know, anyone messin' wich ya or if the music's too loud. Ya hear?' I thanked him. I knew he meant it. I found out later he was the biggest drug dealer in the area."

"That's an amazing story. So you survived again by the strength of your courage. Your caring, really. Do you notice how in both of the incidents there was a baby?"

Alta thought about it. "I guess you're right."

"Why do you suppose? Any ideas?"

"I guess I can't stand to see something or someone helpless, something small, suffer." Alta looked at her hands, small and helpless, and she hated them. She hated herself for being helpless.

Cheryl got up and placed an empty chair opposite Alta. "Alta, I want you to try something. I'd like you to picture yourself as a little girl and then I'd like you to talk to her. I'd like you to tell her how you feel about her."

"I can't do that," Alta said with sudden embarrassment. "I mean, the chair is empty."

Cheryl let the silence settle between them and then she repeated her request, adding, "Just try it, please."

"Okay, but I feel pretty stupid." Alta shifted in her seat, trying to avoid the empty chair.

"Try describing her."

"Who?"

"Yourself as a little girl," Cheryl urged.

"How old?"

"You decide."

Alta looked at her feet. She couldn't bear to look at the chair; it made her feel ridiculous. Then she saw the scuffy tennis shoes, the dirty, limp socks that hung around the ankles and refused to stay up, pretty and fluffed out, the way the well-cared-for girls' did.

Then, without realizing it, Alta placed the girl in the chair.

"What does she look like?" Cheryl asked softly.

"She has these raggedly tennis shoes on with falling down socks that expose her skinny, brown ankles," Alta answered in a stunned voice. "She has dirty jeans on that should be washed and a T-shirt and a flannel jacket over that. She has short, boyish hair, and a boyish face, but her mouth is—well, it's soft, though it's angry." Alta bit her lip. "And her eyes—she's scared. She's eleven."

"Why is she scared?"

The question hung in the air. Alta's heart was racing with it, and then she knew. "Because no one loves her. No one loves this little girl who's trying to look like a boy, who's trying to be brave and fake everyone out. She's scared shitless, that's what." Tears were streaming down Alta's face as the child sat, vividly, opposite her. "Her grandmother's dead and no one loves her anymore. She's all alone now."

"Do you love her?" Cheryl's voice was tender.

An intense sorrow and longing filled Alta; so intense she almost lost consciousness for a moment. It was the child's pain. "Yes." She saw her hunger, the shame of her poverty, the color of her skin, the sound of her Spanish being ridiculed publicly in a five-year-old's memory, and an Indian language her grandmother spoke sometimes flickered like a vague, comforting dream that left her desolate because she could never remember, never remember, never remember.

Then Alta remembered the cries of her mother, the defense of her mother, the betrayal of her mother, the longing for her mother. Her mother. Her longing for a father had stopped at eight, and now she craved only a mother.

"Tell her you love her and that you're old enough now to take care of her and that she doesn't have to be alone anymore. Tell her, Alta."

The defensive girl/boy continued to avert her eyes from Alta; her posture was of flight. Fear. As Alta began to speak, she turned and looked at her with large, very large, dark, frightened eyes in her thin face. She was utterly vulnerable, stripped of her anger, as she paused in a rare split second of trust.

"I love you. You're hard to love, but I love you, I do. I'm a grown woman now, and I'm going to take care of you from now on like April." Alta's voice broke as deep sobs convulsed her body, but she held the child's eyes, afraid to lose her. "You're my little girl and you'll never be alone again because we're together, now, forever and ever. I promise."

The child's eyes became soft, almost gentle, but something was held in reserve. A certain fierceness that shone like a light from the center of her dark, now fearless eyes. Alta saw that the child's hands were opening, and that they were small like her own, but strong from use.

"You are my child." The words started from the soles of Alta's feet, coursing through her body with a power of their own. They issued from her mouth like a command.

Then the child disappeared.

"Did you see her?" Alta asked.

"Yes, I did." Cheryl was weeping. They sat in the silence a little longer as the scent of birth lingered in the air between them.

It was a hot day in early spring.
Alta, pregnant, carried April with a
map in her hands. A dark circle
surrounded her grandmother's
grave. April was nearly two
and beginning to walk. Finally,

Alta found it; it was so
quiet. Sweat and tears mixed
as they ran down her face.
She'd brought roses, but they
were wilted. She placed April

down on the green grass
and she gave out a cry of delight.
The grass was cool, thick, and
alive.

* * *

It was a little after eleven o'clock when Jackie got José to sleep. April hadn't heard Ian cry like that since he was little. She stuffed her pillow over her head and fell asleep with a groan. Ian slept through José's protests peacefully.

"There's a program called 'State of Emergency' on in an hour. It's supposed to be about nuclear issues, global destruction, normal stuff like that. Do you want to watch it?" Alta asked as Jackie climbed into bed next to her.

"It sounds depressing. I mean, here we are, two freaked out women in the middle of the night. Do we need to be depressed too?" Jackie laughed a little sadly.

Alta sat up and looked at her friend. "I'm not freaked out. Shit, I'm relieved. My test was negative."

"I can't believe that motherfucker was cruising back and forth between you and that fag. Maybe even *fags*. Jesus." Jackie shook her head in disbelief. "Look, I brought some vodka and some joints. Do you want some? I mean, *I* need a drink."

"Yeah, why not? There's orange juice in the fridge. Would you make me a screwdriver? With ice?"

"What do ya think I am, a beginner?" Jackie laughed and left the room.

Alta heard the refrigerator door open and shut and the sound of glass gently bumping against the sink. She heard Jackie struggle with the ice, muttering, "Fuck, what is this, super glue?" She was glad Jackie was here with her, making the silence of the night warm and human.

Jackie held a large glass in each hand and a joint in her mouth, wiggling it with her lips until Alta took it from her. "Shall we light up right away or let these triple shot babies take effect?" She handed Alta her drink.

Alta laughed and took a sip. "Holy shit! You must be kidding! One of these is enough to knock my goddamn socks off. Forget the joint."

"Take your socks off, mujer, who cares. Go barefoot for a while," Jackie said, stretching out on the bed, curling her toes. "Tomorrow morning's cartoons, and, besides, April can get breakfast for once, right? Come on, relax." She could see some anxiety on Alta's face.

"Look, you go ahead and smoke. I think I'll pass." She took another sip, a long one. "I love screwdrivers," Alta sighed. "Anyway, my socks are off, aren't they?"

"You know, I've never seen you smoke a joint."

"I tried it once and I nearly choked to death. Also, I remember my grandmother talking about some uncle being caught smoking Mary Juana, and everyone going crazy because there was a drug addict in the family." Alta laughed at the overblown memory and took another sip of her drink, watching the ice cubes float toward her.

"Yeah, my mom was the same. I guess first and second generation are like that. Fresh off the boat." Jackie lit the joint and it smelled rather sweet and delicious. She held the smoke in her lungs which made her face become extremely serious.

"You look like you're trying to fart." Alta burst into laughter.

Jackie exploded with choked laughter, swallowing some smoke. Her chest burned for an instant as she pounded herself for air. "Don't say things like that when I'm smoking. You trying to kill me or what?" She handed it to Alta. "Just take a little, just a little, and hold it down for ten seconds."

Alta looked at it.

"And don't talk," Jackie added, smiling.

Alta liked the sensation of smoke in her mouth and the taste was rather nice. "Listen, if I go crazy tie me to the bed, okay?"

"You know, you worry too much about being in control all the time. That's your problem. I seem to have the opposite problem." Jackie offered Alta another hit but she refused with a nod. "This is strong stuff. I'll put it out for later, okay?" She looked at Alta, taking one last drag.

"Okay, maybe later when I see if I'm still coherent after this drink."

Jackie saw Alta eye her drink, which was almost gone. "Yeah, I drink too much. But I *am* going to school and working part-time. I'm going to be a goddamned nursie." She laughed loudly at the idea of herself in a pure, white uniform.

"What's so funny about that? I think it's a great idea. It sure beats typing for the rest of your life for chicken feed."

"Oh, I don't know. I just saw myself with this prissy look in a starched little nursie's uniform." Jackie closed her eyes. "Maybe with a screwdriver in my hand." She smiled widely. "There, that's better. So, what about you, my dear slut?" she laughed loudly as Alta wacked her with a pillow. "What is your plan, *professionally*, that is?" she managed to say between fits of laughter.

"Hey, bitch, where does 'my dear slut' come from?" Alta demanded a little angrily.

"Just kidding. Lighten up. So, what're your plans, mujer?" Jackie forced herself to rearrange her face into a somewhat serious expression, but a gale of laughter was trying hard to escape.

"Next semester I'm taking a couple of advanced psych courses, and I thought I'd take a pottery class. Some self-therapy, I guess." Alta answered cautiously, seeing Jackie's hilarity in her large, dark eyes. The grass, no doubt, Alta thought, knowing Jackie's sense of humor was naturally outrageous and always waiting in the wings of her sorrow. In fact, she thought further, most of my friends are pretty funny women. Maybe it's better than crying all the time.

"How can you take pottery after you know that joto was a potter? Or is it potter-er-er? You should go over there and break his pots." A smile began at the sides of her mouth. "And his pee-pee too," she added, sending herself over the edge into an uncontrollable fit of laughter.

"Jesus, you think you're hysterical, don't you?" Alta couldn't help laughing with her. The image of breaking his pots was not only funny but appealing. Since she hadn't heard anything from Hugh, she guessed he was with him and there was nothing she could do about it. Not really. Because he was already dead. A vampire . . . Without realizing it Alta mentally changed the subject and thought of Katie.

Jackie sense a change of mood and turned on her side, facing Alta. "What's up?"

"Katie's in the hospital. She's fucking dying in the hospital where she didn't want to die. Her mother called an ambulance and carted her off, even though Katie kept asking her not to. Doug was too freaked to do anything. Apparently, the pain wouldn't subside and rather than call the doctor her mother decided to ship her there." Alta glared at the blank TV screen.

"I can't stand that woman. Upper middle-class white bitch! You know, everything in its place. One doesn't die in one's front room, you know?"

Jackie sighed and finished her drink.

"When I met her that night for dinner she actually told me, when we were alone, that she and her husband had done the grave error—right?—of making friends who weren't their *equal*—can you imagine? And she said it with nasty emphasis while looking me right in the eye."

"Gross."

"You said it. And her old man's not a hell of a lot better. I am so sick of racist snobs! They sure ain't pretty close up, that's for sure."

"Makes you wonder how Katie came out so good with a couple of slimeballs like that for parents." Jackie sat up. "Want another?" She indicated Alta's glass.

"Sure, why not? Do you want to go with me Saturday to see Katie?"

"Is she really bad?"

"Yeah."

"I don't think I can. I guess I'm a coward that way. Me and my nursie plans," Jackie said with disgust, but she knew it was true. She couldn't bear to actually see someone deteriorating. Dying. I'll work in maternity, she thought sullenly. "How're the kids?"

"They don't know what hit them." Tears came to Alta's eyes as she thought of the lovely bird of paradise turning dry and brown, her purple and orange glory gone and only the dry rattle of seeds in a secret pod hinted of life. Were the seeds her children or Katie herself?

Jackie touched Alta's shoulder. "I wish I could go with you, but I really can't." She paused, picking Alta's glass up. "You were always stronger than me, Alta."

Alta's head jerked up in surprise. "That's not true. You've always helped me too. Like tonight. Aren't you here?"

"If I weren't here, I'd be drunk, probably with some jerk. You *handle* things better. You're a fucking rock and you don't know it."

"Well, I'm glad you know it," Alta laughed.

"Yeah, yeah, yeah." Jackie walked toward the kitchen. "So, are you going to be a shrink?"

"Cheryl thinks I should be. I certainly have enough psych units." Alta turned on the TV. "Maybe that's it," she added in a whisper. Then fear clutched at her; she might not be good enough. She might fail.

"Do you have these things in super glue or what?" Jackie pounded the ice tray on the sink and they all fell out. "All or nothing, that's my fucking life," she muttered in a strange, sad voice as she looked out at the fog, hating it.

They lay dazed with the information the program had just given them, and the hopeful ending showing a dark circle becoming a circle of light only added to their mutual sense of doom.

"I think I'll start smoking a pack of cigarettes tomorrow and drink only straight vodka from now on."

Alta looked at Jackie's tired face. "Good idea." She smiled weakly. "I wonder if children in the next century will have a chance. Leukemia by four and AIDS by eight. That is, if the nuclear arsenal doesn't wipe us all out."

"Fuck, I told you we shouldn't've watched, didn't I?" Jackie saw Alta's face register a tremor of hurt. "Anyway, I'm so stoned I'll forget all this tomorrow."

"I took notes. I'll remind you."

Jackie groaned loudly.

"It's worse than I thought. Have you heard of the hole in the ozone layer over Antarctica? Right over Antarctica, miles wide like a tear and possibly growing. There're scientists down there checking it."

"Aren't you even a little drunk yet?"

"Well, have you heard of the ozone layer?"

"You answer my question first."

"Slightly."

"Time for more dope." Jackie lit the half-smoked joint. "Anyway, yes I have. More work for nursies when people start being unable to tolerate good old natural sunlight. Like cancer'll by synonymous with tans. Maybe then being our color'll be fashionable, by default, of course."

Alta laughed and took a hit of the grass, letting the smoke out slowly. "Do you suppose that because the earth's shield, the ozone layer, that is, is falling apart—you know, what keeps us healthy—it's hard to explain. It's just an idea. You know, a feeling. I mean, why so much cancer, leukemia, and now, AIDS? I mean, maybe the hole in the ozone layer is symptomatic of the holes in our immune systems, like our shields. Do you know what I mean?"

"Yeah. Maybe it's the grass, but I do," Jackie said, handing the joint back to Alta. "Did you ever make love stoned?"

Alta shook her head.

"It's really nice. Intense."

"Those screwdrivers were strong, but they didn't really affect me." Alta began to cry. She turned over on her stomach, laying her head on her arms.

"What's wrong, Alta?"

"Hugh, AIDS, the ozone layer. My kids and Katie's dying. How in the hell am I supposed to do it all, Jackie?" Sobs rippled through Alta's body.

"You will, girl. You will." Jackie reached over and touched her long, shiny, dark hair. "Do you want a back rub? Remember, we used to give each other back rubs? A hundred rubs each?"

"I remember," Alta murmured. She felt Jackie's hand on her shoulders. It felt like a child's hand: soft and tentative and utterly gentle. Then Jackie's hand began trickling up and down her spine in a waterfall motion and her sorrow waned with her child's tender touch. Alta surrendered to an old trust. Mother, child: daughter, mother.

Jackie pulled up Alta's top and her long, brown back was beautiful in the dim lamp. The slight curve of the small breast excited her. She'd never really been excited by a woman's breast. Or have I? the thought occurred to her. The thought disappeared and Jackie lightly traced it. She felt Alta quiver, and she shuddered at Alta's response. Response, Jackie thought lazily through the lovely grass high. A woman's response. But then she thinks it was just an accident probably.

This time Jackie traced the soft bulge of her breast with two fingers and Alta turned her face toward Jackie and just looked at her. Alta felt like the middle, the very middle, of a dark, dark circle where the fire was kept. The secret fire. The healing fire that smoldered even in the presence of death. In that dark circle.

She turned on her side facing Jackie, and, reaching up quickly, she turned off the lamp. She could still see Jackie's face, and it was sad and tender like she wanted to apologize or cry.

Jackie cupped Alta's breast in her hand and it fit, perfectly. She heard Alta suck in her breath sharply and hold it.

Then she lowered her head to the erect, pointy nipple and sucked it so gently she thought she would come as ripples of pleasure spread simultaneously from her clitoris and cunt, radiating out to every part of her body—toes to fingertips. And a part of her mind felt on fire where only ice had been before: a loneliness. A daughter's loneliness for her mother. For the mother who could not love herself, much less such a strange and needy child: daughter. That terrible reminder of the self.

Alta held Jackie's head cautiously as Jackie clasped her other nipple with her soft mouth, feeling the tongue caress and circle it.

"Oh, my God!" Alta whimpered.

Jackie lifted her head and stared into Alta's eyes. Her eyes were strangely fierce. "Oh, my *Goddess!*" she hissed, with a trace of a smile.

Their mouths met, and then their tongues.

"Goddess." "Goddess." "Goddess," each one gasped and moaned like a long forgotten prayer. And they remembered. Everything.

Their hands swept over each other's bodies, their faces, again and again, as each woman shuddered with an excruciating, sharp, unimagined pleasure.

Then Jackie placed her hand over Alta's warm, flowing cunt, and a hoarse cry of shock and pleasure flew out of Alta's soft, open mouth. Her mouth was completely open as though she were dying of ecstasy.

Alta placed her hand over Jackie's soft, secret cunt, and Jackie cried, "Yes, yes, please, please do it. Oh, mama, don't stop! Oh, mama!"

Jackie plunged her entire tongue into Alta's mouth, and her fingers eased, gently, into Alta's warm, tender, cave flesh.

Alta slid her fingers into Jackie's hotness and moaned at the discovery of such secret warmth. Such nourishment. *Such secret softness.*

Jackie got to her knees, moving her fingers slowly, feeling the soft cave flesh clasp her fingers as she watched her friend writhe underneath her, and she began the journey, the endless journey, of her tongue down the center of Alta's body. This body that had received Hugh, given birth to a daughter and a son. This woman's body, like her own. A mother's body, like her own.

Alta reached for her, bringing Jackie's feminine, sea-stinging warmth to her mouth. And they remembered. *Everything.*

They came in circles of sorrow, in circles of joy—crying, then laughing together. Circles of ecstasy electrified their bodies from head to foot, and they came again: mouth to cunt, tongue to clitoris, soul to soul, woman to woman. Without man. They died, slowly, into swirling pools of utter pleasure. They remembered a woman's selfish, hungry, howling, singing pleasure to be food, to be fed. Without man. They searched for the hot, life-giving, creative, and golden sun. Without man.

The golden rings between their legs spread themselves, rippling and rippling, extending ever outward to the void—and in the utter void, the utter darkness, their sun was born: pale gold with the promise of the matrix.

Jackie woke up first in the morning. She nearly leapt to her feet though it was only six-thirty. Alta's pubis was hard against her hip. It was soft and moist and furry, but this morning it didn't excite her; it frightened her. The afterglow of the screwdrivers, the grass, their intense lovemaking, lifted, leaving her confused and alone. She forgot she felt like this with men as well and blamed Alta, in that moment, for being a woman.

She should've known better, Jackie thought angrily, as she slid out of bed. "I ain't no fucking lezzie," she muttered as she showered in the hottest water she could stand.

Alta heard the shower running. She looked out at the small patch of grey at the end of the lightwell and thought of Jackie's soft, round breasts—much larger than hers—and their taste. And the taste of her feminine juices, and the small, fleshy thing on her tongue that had given electric jolts to her own clitoris, again and again. Their wild, yet gentle, orgasms had been almost simultaneous. Alta wondered if they'd make love again, and she felt strangely shy in the morning light, like a little girl who wanted her mother's approval.

By the time Jackie was dressed Alta had made the morning coffee and bacon was cooking slowly in the skillet. Jackie heard Alta in the kitchen, and her strongest impulse was to avoid her, but she knew she couldn't. She walked into the kitchen. A low pitched classical piece played on the radio perched on top of the refrigerator.

"Want a cup?" Alta turned from the stove, ready to smile. Jackie's face stopped her. It was cold, distant. Angry and embarrassed.

"I should be going. I've got a million things to do today, and José has to be at his *father's* at ten." Jackie placed an unusual emphasis on the masculine as though to set things straight. She was a normal woman, after all, her tone conveyed.

It felt like a direct blow to Alta's abdomen. She fastened her gaze on Jackie's eyes. "Are you sorry about last night?"

"Well, aren't you?" Jackie looked away toward the front door longingly.

"No. I don't think so." Alta paused, turning the shrinking bacon. Her hunger disappeared. "Look, Jackie, no one has to know as far as I'm concerned, but I don't think we did anything wrong. Do you?"

Jackie heard the wound in Alta's voice and she almost relented. But could she really fly into another woman's arms? Could another woman really protect her? No, a familiar voice, full of authority, answered her, and she recognized it as her own voice. Her own *no*.

"Look, I don't know. I think I'd better go." Jackie walked away. As she carried José, half-asleep, to the car she started to weep. "I told you you were a rock, Alta. I told you, girl, didn't I?" Then she remembered Alta's musky, sweet taste, her secret skin, their spiralling moans that had reached the stars and moon, and she cringed inwardly with shame, and disgust took the place of sweetness.

158

Though she turned the windshield wipers on high, the fog kept gathering, obscuring her vision, making everything distorted. She could hear the sharp blows on her mother's softness.

Alta sat down with her second cup of coffee. It burned her mouth and throat as she drank it without caution, making her angry with herself. She got up to pour some more cream in it and the phone rang.

"Alta, it's Doug." His voice was tired and sounded like a man who'd finally let go of a rope that he'd thought would save his life. "She died last night around three in the morning." His voice broke. "I wasn't even with her. She was alone, Alta. God, she was alone."

"Doug, where are you?" Alta asked softly.

"I'm here with the boys. The most beautiful woman in the world has died, and I don't think I can stand it." He began to sob in a dry, hoarse manner. Alta said nothing until he was done.

"Do you want me to come up?"

"Yes, I'd like that." Doug's voice was choked with tears, but he'd gained back his composure. "I'm sorry. I thought I could call you and not do this."

"Don't be sorry. I loved her too." Alta strained not to cry. "Look, I'll see you around noon. Is that okay?"

"Sounds good."

"What's wrong, Mom?" April asked as she walked past her mother on the way to the bathroom.

"Katie died last night." April ran to Alta's arms, and Alta held her as they wept together without restraint.

The kids played quietly on the front room floor. Katie's hospital bed was gone. In its place was a maroon armchair with Katie's mother sitting in it. She met Alta's eyes with cold indifference when Alta entered the room. Juanita had answered the door, briefly hissing to Alta, her eyes angrily indicating the front room, "The old bitch's in there, Dios mío!"

Alta almost laughed, but laughter, at that moment, seemed alien. Impossible. She walked over to Doug and stood next to him, touching his shoulder once.

"Will you be able to watch the kids as usual during the week?" Doug asked Juanita. He acknowledged Alta with his eyes, feeling the warmth of her hand through his T-shirt.

"I'll be here Monday morning. Tomorrow I'll bring you enchiladas, so don't cook. You hear me?" Juanita's eyes were dark and tired, but a young woman's passion gave them an unmistakable life. She'd always known who she loved and who she hated. She apologized for neither.

Doug's face softened. "Gracias, Juanita, por todo."

"De nada, hijo, de nada." Juanita dismissed his gratitude while she quickly hugged Erin and Ethan. "Hasta luego, Alta." She glanced over at Alta and headed for the door without speaking to Katie's mother, Barbara.

"Doug, I think it'd be best if they came with me for a while. Stu will be up tonight and we can all fly back. It'll give you some time by yourself." Barbara's voice was coaxing and soothing with an underlying tone of command.

"I don't think I want to be alone, Barbara. I think I just need to be alone with my kids. Shit, I should take next week off and stay home with them."

"That's a good idea. I think you should take at least a week off." Alta lowered her voice and asked, "Are you going to have a service of any kind? You know, so we can all say goodbye."

Doug looked at her with hollow eyes and started to speak. "We've been thinking about it . . . "

"We decided it wouldn't be good for the———" Barbara mouthed the word "children"—"and she'll be c-r-e-m-a-t-e-d. Her father and I will take the ashes home." Her voice and tone were businesslike. Detached.

Alta searched Katie's mother's face for the sorrow she knew she must be feeling, but she could see no trace of it. She didn't like this woman at all, and apparently, Barbara didn't care for Alta either. "Maybe that's exactly what they need," Alta answered her.

"I have some things for you," Doug interjected, indicating the next room. The queen-size bed took up most of the space and a table lamp was on as if someone was about to read. Doug followed Alta's glance. "I didn't sleep last night."

"Doug, don't you think it might be good to have a little something for Katie, even if it's going to the beach and making a fire or something? Maybe you could sprinkle her ashes on the tide. The kids know she's dead, don't they?" Alta instantly wished she hadn't said it. Doug's eyes filled with tears as they began to fall rapidly.

"You know, it's so hard, goddammit! I guess I was relieved she was out of that pain and now I'm sorry I was relieved. Now I hurt so bad, Alta." His last words ended on a choke of sheer anguish. Doug looked large and helpless with his open hands fallen to his sides.

Alta drew Doug into her arms, letting him cry against her. His large body felt strangely light against hers, and for the first time she caught his scent and it was strong but pleasant. Familiar. Like Katie. But of course, Katie's scent was still in the room.

As her arms encircled his back she became aware of his muscles and how they led to his slim hips, and, without any conscious choice on her part, she realized how she might comfort him best. Last night's orgasms with Jackie, Katie's death, and the sudden desire to comfort Doug—to feel his body completely naked next to hers—merged in an overwhelming moment, making her moan softly. It was inexplicable. It was sex, love, and death coming to meet in the ripeness of her body. Alta imagined his erect penis, ready to enter her, and, though she grieved for Katie, she trembled with the thought of being filled with his life. To feel him hard against her, *inside* of her, with his hard, stirring life. The penis, like the womb, like the cunt, is life, Alta thought with a shock as though she'd never known it before.

Alta sighed, pulling away from Doug, but not too quickly. He towered over her, and as he looked down into her eyes she saw his longing. It was naked on his face. He looked away awkwardly and reached for a small bundle.

"She wanted you to have these."

The goblet was on top, wrapped in tissue. Clippings of Katie's hair were stuffed inside. The thick, shiny, deep red hair was so full of health and vitality, it made no sense that Katie was dead. Alta forced herself to remember what Katie looked like the last time she'd seen her, but then the red-haired Katie, the healthy Katie, superimposed herself on Alta's memory. In her mind, as sharp as a portrait, she saw Katie's sea-green eyes laughing and looking at her.

"Goddess," the word slipped out unselfconsciously, "she was beautiful. The bird of paradise left me her beautiful, red feathers," Alta murmured so softly it sounded like a long, sustained sigh—like the wind at sunset, like a leaf being rustled by that wind.

"Will you help me clean out her closet, later maybe? I mean, later." Doug longed to be held again, but he was ashamed to have imagined Alta's response.

Barbara appeared in the doorway. "The kids are hungry, Doug. Do you want something too? Would you like some coffee, Dougie?" Her voice was sharp and almost angry, except for the "Dougie," which seemed inappropriate as though Doug too were now one of her children. She eyed Alta and Doug, and being a clever, manipulative woman, she grasped the recent intimacy between them.

Doug looked at Alta and then at Barbara and said, "What I need's a shot of whiskey with a beer chaser."

Six

These guys up here would kill me if they knew I was a fuckin' fag, Hugh thought, as he watched the men he worked with joke around. It's all over for me, that's all, and Alta can bring the kids up here. Oregon's nice and healthy, what the hell. They probably don't have much AIDS up here—shit, maybe it was the city making me crazy as hell. He walked to his car and headed home.

The one-room cabin was in back of the main house, but so far back they couldn't see each other. It came with a wood stove, refrigerator, basic furniture, and a phone.

Hugh placed a collect call. Alta answered. "Do you accept the charges?" Hugh heard the operator ask. Alta paused and finally said, "Yes, I will."

"Alta, I'm up in Oregon."

"It's been over two months, and I haven't had a penny from you or heard from you. Nothing." Alta felt strangely calm and stunned at once.

"Well, look, I'm calling to ask you and the kids to come up here with me." Hugh's voice was flat but confident.

"You must be kidding."

"I could look for a place and then come down and get you."

"Why haven't you even written?" She felt like a ghost talking to another ghost, but she had to ask.

"I haven't had the time."

It was so predictable.

"But you do have time to call me collect, don't you, Hugh?" She said his name, but the name was vague, causing her no great sorrow. All of that was abstract, hearing his voice over the phone, without a moment's pause, because of a technology she'd never understand: abstract, like love, death, sex. At that moment.

She had no desire to imagine him.

Hugh was silent as he breathed out heavily.

"No." Alta placed the phone down gently on its hook.

Hugh ripped the telephone out of the wall, throwing it and shattering it against the far pine-panelled wall. Little brown plastic pieces flew in every direction. Then there was silence, a resounding silence.

He saw the axe by the wood stove, propped by the stacked wood.

"Goddamned bitch cunt! I could fucking kill you! You goddamned diseased cunt!" Hugh screamed hysterically. Grabbing the axe, he stalked out to a stand of pine and, choosing the largest among them, began to chop in an absolute frenzy as he cried and sobbed inarticulately, "Bitch, bitch, bitch, bitch . . . " with each wild stroke.

"I mean, Cheryl, not only did he almost give me AIDS, then he wants me to have a case of amnesia and just follow him up to Oregon or whatever. It felt like the twilight zone, you know?" Alta and Cheryl had become friends as well as therapist and client, and so Cheryl often talked about her own life as well.

"Have I told you how I met my old man?"

Alta shook her head no.

"After the good doctor molested my, or rather our, daughter, I drove over to Sausalito to see about hiring a hit man to kill that motherfucker. Anyway, I ended up in this bar talking to one of the musicians on his break, and he talked me out of it. 'Why you wanta fuck up your own soul?' he asked me with those intense eyes of his. So, in short, we got together, and my mother and my family won't have any niggers in their house, so fuck them." Cheryl laughed. "Yeah, life is definitely like that. The old twilight zone. Anyway, I took my first husband to court and he can visit her only in my presence, which he's done only twice since he can't stand my killing vibes."

"You were actually going to kill him? Though I'd want to do it myself if anyone ever messed with April, so I certainly understand." Alta's blood boiled at the thought.

"Yeah, and, you know, that's the one thing women are never forgiven for: their anger. It's *not nice* and all that load of bull. Don't let anyone ever talk you out of it. You've got a beautiful anger, Alta, just like me." Cheryl's eyes glittered with a playful malice. And then in an even, almost soft, voice she added, "It's your power, and don't you ever forget it."

"It's funny, the other night when I hung up on Hugh I felt so strangely peaceful and remote."

"That's because you lived through your anger, fully. That kick in the balls did you wonders. No, there's always someone, usually some man, giving us this forgive and forget bullshit. There are some things we shouldn't forgive in this life. Understand maybe, but forgive, no. Absolutely not. It only drains our power. Leaves you talking to the kitchen sink." Cheryl sat back and lit a cigarette. "Forget it."

"The other day in pottery I cut two broad strips of clay of equal length and placed them on a coil pot, like a cross. I don't know why, but as I did it, it felt almost taboo. Like I shouldn't be doing it or something. It was so strange. And then I looked at it, completed, and I felt wonderful. Like I'd done something wonderful. You know, I've dreamt making a cross before in clay or something soft. I can't explain it, Cheryl, but it still makes me feel wonderful."

"You know, before the Christians messed it up, it was an ancient symbol of healing. And, of course, you are healing, you really are."

"I made love to my best friend." Alta blushed with embarrassment and at the same time with secret pleasure.

"Well, well." Cheryl smiled. "How was it?"

"I've never had an orgasm like that before. I mean, never. It was as though my whole body caught fire, over and over. It was so," Alta paused, "so tender." Tears came to Alta's eyes. "Do you know what I mean?" She wondered if she'd ever stop this crying, a little angry with herself. But relief always followed, so she let them fall without ceremony.

"Yes, I know what you mean," Cheryl answered, remembering the woman she'd loved. "How are things with your friend?"

"She's avoiding me like we committed the original sin or something. I guess she just couldn't handle it."

"That's bullshit, you know, about committing any kind of sin."

"I know," Alta echoed.

Cheryl leaned forward, touching Alta's knee. "Remember that orgasm, Alta. That's what your body wants. Don't forget."

Alta smiled as she wept, nodding yes wordlessly.

"My grandfather raped me beginning when I was ten until he died," Cheryl added softly. "If it hadn't been for another woman, I don't think I could've made it. This is our secret, Alta." Softness and strength merged in her voice. "Love her. The one inside." Cheryl's eyes burned in the dim office light. "To quote a black woman poet: 'I found god in myself and I loved her, I loved her fiercely.' "

There was a loud banging at the door. It stopped and started again even louder. The clock said three in the morning. Alta sat up in bed. It's Hugh, she thought, and her mouth went dry with anxiety. She ran to the door; she didn't want the kids to wake up. "Who is it?" she asked in a threatening tone.

"Alta, it's me." His speech was slow, but precise. He was drunk. "Doug. Let me in, will you?"

She didn't really want to. It was late and he was drunk, but she opened the door anyway. He stumbled past her and landed on the couch. Doug's long hair hung over his face as he bent over, his face in his hands. Alta stood waiting in her flannel nightgown in the chill air outside her bed. His size, at three in the morning, drunk, without Katie, frightened her, but she waited for him to speak. He remained silent as though he'd forgotten she was there.

"Doug, do you want some coffee?" She couldn't keep her voice from trembling; she was cold and unsure. "Doug, do you hear me? Do you want some coffee? Doug?"

"Kids're gone. Said they could take better care of them." He choked on his words and rubbed at his eyes slowly, as though he were asleep. "I can't stand it. I just can't stand it anymore, Alta."

Alta walked over to Doug, feeling like a little girl in her bare feet and sat next to him, placing her hand on his shoulder. He began to sob at the touch of her hand. He was utterly helpless. He was the child. He smelled thickly of alcohol and his hair was tangled.

Alta went to the kitchen and wet some paper towels, bringing some dry ones as well and handed one to him. "Doug, here, blow your nose. Come on, blow your nose. Now lie down. Yes, just lie down."

"I can't stay here," Doug mumbled.

"Yes, you can. I want you to. Okay? Just lie down. There, that's it." She brought a blanket and covered him, and she wiped his face with the wet paper towels.

"You don't have to do that. You don't have to . . . "

"I want to. Now be quiet and go to sleep. In the morning you can take a shower. Go to sleep, Doug." Alta slipped off his tennis shoes and looked at him. He was out.

"Is that Doug in there?" April asked.

"Yeah, he came by at three in the morning a little drunk. Just be quiet so he can sleep."

"Do you think he's going to kill himself, Mom?" Ian asked somberly.

A chill went through Alta's body. How astute children are, Alta thought, looking at Ian. "We won't let him, that's all."

When Doug woke up Alta was in the kitchen studying. He went directly into the bathroom without speaking to her. He looked into the mirror. You look like a goddamned wino, he thought with disgust. Then the pain overwhelmed him again, and his life, as he stared into his blank, red eyes, trailed ahead of him—bleak and frightening and utterly without hope. Katie was dead. Period.

It took all of his control to not smash the mirror with his clenched fist as he looked away and turned the shower on. Hot. He wanted to become the steam if that were possible and disappear without any conscious effort.

When he came out Alta was preparing to leave. She had a class in twenty minutes, then work, and she still had to cash in her food stamp voucher for the little books of phony money that bought their real food. She was just making it. The idea of forcing Hugh to give her money repulsed her and, beyond any rationality, it injured her spirit to even think of it. She wanted to divorce him—that much was clear.

"Sorry 'bout last night. I didn't even know where I was this morning. Musta gotten here on automatic pilot or somethin'." Doug looked young and vulnerable as he stumbled over his words in his embarrassment, and his wet hair, nearly to his shoulders, made him look almost feminine. It'd begun to curl as it dried into large, silky sandy-gold curls. He pushed his hair back with his hands, revealing his small turquoise earring.

I always leave the hair down when it dries." He looked at Alta and smiled apologetically.

"You have beautiful hair." Now Alta blushed and added, "I like your earring too. What is it?" she blurted out. She handed him some coffee.

"It's a bird. A little carved bird an Indian friend made for me. We used to live on the wrong side of the tracks in Palm Springs, close to the reservation, so I was always in and outa there. I always wondered how I even met Katie, her bein' high class 'n all. Guess I had promise, as they say." Derision and sorrow played in his voice and across his face, and at the mention of Katie's name they became silent.

Finally, Alta spoke. "Doug, you've got to get your kids back, you know." Her voice was gentle, but firm. "You love them, don't you?"

"What do you think?" he said angrily, looking into her eyes. The blue of his eyes leapt out at her like cold fire. She returned his gaze.

"Then do it."

Doug sighed. "Barbara's not going to like it," he said in a crisp, clipped tone.

"Tough shit for her. They're your kids, aren't they?"

Doug started to laugh, but it sounded so awkward he stopped, embarrassed. "Pathetic, ain't I?"

"No, not really, just going through some heavy shit. You shouldn't drink so much though."

"Yeah, you're right. I'll call Barbara tonight." He paused. "I want my boys."

"Do you want to come for dinner tonight, around six?"

"Whatcha havin'?" Color came to his face.

"Tostadas."

"Wild horses couldn't keep me away." He couldn't help smiling.

"Alright, see you then. Gotta go, I'm late for class." Alta kissed him, briefly, on the cheek, and the bristles of his beard surprised her.

Alta's kiss caught Doug off guard—it felt personal, meant for him somehow. He thought of that day Katie had jokingly given him to Alta, and he dismissed it immediately as Alta closed the front door behind her. She wouldn't want to take up with anyone so soon. Besides, she ain't interested in me, she just feels sorry for me. Sorry for me: the words echoed in his mind, and his self-disgust returned.

"You know, I haven't eaten since the boys left, or if I did I can't remember what the hell it was. I haven't had tostadas like that since I don't know when." Doug felt painfully shy with Alta suddenly, now that they were alone in the front room. A guitar piece played softly, but it didn't soothe him. The silence just made him realize how awkward he was.

Alta sat on a chair across from him. She was tired but alert, watching his turquoise bird earring in the lamplight as it flew in the sky attached to his ear. It's crazy, but his earring makes me want to trust him, Alta mused. Doug's hair was pulled back into a ponytail. He looked away trying to avoid her gaze.

"Did you call Barbara?"

"Yeah, well, she was mad, I could tell, but she said to come on down and get them if I want. I'm goin' down day after tomorrow. Tomorrow I'm goin' ta clean everything up and go out an' buy some food. Stuff like that." Doug's voice was tense. It trembled as he spoke, though he was trying desperately to create the illusion of ease.

Alta smiled at Doug, gently. "Great. That's great. We'll have to have a welcome home party, okay?"

Doug took courage from her warmth and asked, "Will you come shopping with me and give me a hand buyin'? I'm kind of a klutz with the shoppin'. I'm prone to buyin' three kinds of chips rather than the edibles." His hands were trembling in his lap.

Alta got up and sat down next to him, putting her hand over his. "Sure, I'll come with you. Are you okay? What's wrong?"

Doug sat stiffly, tears starting to gather and fall, and his hands trembled violently under Alta's. He couldn't speak. He just couldn't speak.

Alta turned, facing him, took his face in her hands, and slowly kissed his eyelids, both his cheeks, and then, seeing the startled look in Doug's eyes, she kissed him softly on his silent lips.

Doug groaned loudly and reached his arms around Alta, feeling her strong, slender back with his hands, clutching her to him, feeling her living woman's warmth. He felt like crying for joy: her touch, her touch. He felt like worshipping her. He felt she might disappear. No, no, not that, he pleaded silently. He buried his face in her neck. And then he smelled her woman's smell, her juices gathering, hidden, but he could smell it.

He was afraid, but he had to do it; he would die if she wouldn't let him enter her body. If she wouldn't shelter him, he would die. He put a hand over her breast, caressing her softly, and she quivered, throwing her head back with a cry of pleasure. He began to kiss her neck gently, then with wide open sucking motions, tasting her. He licked her neck, lifted her sweater, and he saw she wore no bra and her breasts were brown and beautiful, almost girlish. He sucked them, being careful not to lose control because he felt he would devour her if he did.

Alta shut the front room door with her free hand and then, extending herself fully, lay back on the couch inviting him. They kissed again and again. Neither spoke. This was the Braille of compassion and sympathy. Human comfort.

Doug tugged at her jeans, unbuttoning the top and lowering the zipper. He exposed her belly and plunged his tongue into her belly button, and she began to move under him. Her smell was stronger now. He was closer. He slipped the jeans down past her hips and carefully lowered the silky, red panties. Seeing her woman's hair, he moaned, spreading her thighs with his large hands. Then he opened the plum colored labia and saw the fleshy queen waiting to be kissed, to be stroked, to be sucked and licked. To be worshipped.

And he was more than willing. His excitement mounted as hers mounted, and the more he ate her, the more he wanted her, so when she came, shuddering violently and crying out, his penis, his prick, was in pain.

He lifted himself to enter her blindly, but Alta stopped him. "Wait, take your clothes off and lie on the rug. Please," she asked, looking into his eyes.

Alta stripped everything off and when she turned to face Doug, he was lying on the rug with one leg up trying to shield his erect penis as though he were suddenly embarrassed by its swollen presence. She knelt down, taking it into both her hands, feeling its heat, shaft to tip. A small bit of sperm was gathered at its tip and she licked it, trailing her tongue down the rough underside. She marvelled at its stiffness, putting it between her soft breasts, and then she sucked it gently.

"Let me come inside you, Alta. I can't stand it," Doug pleaded, sitting up, braced by his elbows. His face was diffuse and lovely. His penis was long and lovely. Lovely. Full of sperm. Full of life. His life.

"Take the rubber band out of your hair." Doug's thick, golden hair spread luxuriously over his neck. It was exactly as Alta had thought; he was beautiful.

Quickly, she mounted him, putting his penis at the opening of her cunt and teasing him by holding it there. Her opening was hot and inviting; she wanted him. She smiled at him. "Do you want to come in?"

Doug's head was thrown back, his thick hair spread on the rug. He gripped her ass, and his arms and chest revealed their strength. He locked eyes with her, almost angrily. "What do you think?" he answered huskily.

Alta lowered herself, as Doug moaned and cried out, sobbing wildly, until he filled her completely with his life. And then they fucked. Ripples and ripples of unending pleasure flowed between them as she raised and lowered herself, watching his cock disappear; and he, for a moment, becoming a woman like herself; and she, with his hardness, for a moment, becoming a man; and then she utterly feminine, being penetrated; and then he utterly masculine, penetrating; and then peace. And then they fucked again. This was the comfort of the living. Woman to man. Cock to cunt.

How could this end in death?

"I'm just going out for a little while, Rita. Maybe play a little pool or something. Anyway, I told you yesterday I was going out tonight." He thought of Dora waiting with chilled wine, probably wearing a silk nightie. And though he actually felt slightly ashamed for thinking it, he couldn't help it; she had both breasts.

"Besides, the kids go to bed right after this program. Can I get you anything? I told them to put themselves to bed, okay?" Carl's patience was wearing tissue-thin after months of slavery, as he considered it.

The flesh itself was healing, but the muscles across her chest and right arm were extremely tender as though the absence itself were a wound. Rita stared into Carl's implacable eyes; this was usually when she relented. His need over hers. Of course, she knew where he was going. There'd been an escalation of phone calls that hung up at the sound of her voice.

Bitch! Rita cursed silently, but then what was Carl? A mother-fucker, as Jackie would say. A motherfucker afraid to fuck a mother. She has no kids, Rita guessed.

Carl turned away impatiently. "Okay, I'll be back around eleven or so. I'll tell the kids one more time to get into bed. Goodnight."

"You mean one or so, don't you, Carl? Is she waiting for you right now? Scared she's going to call?"

Carl whirled around. "What're you, crazy? I'm just going to get some air. You've been watching too many soaps."

"I don't watch soaps, Carl. You're my soaps. Why don't you stop lying for a change?" Rita's anger surfaced so quickly it nearly suffocated her. How many times she had imagined do-ing this. Just saying it.

"You've been fucking other women since I was pregnant with Blanca. I may be crazy, but stupid I'm not. If you go out tonight, don't come back. Do you understand me?" Tears streamed down her drawn face, fast and warm.

"Who in the hell told you this load of shit? Just where do you get your information, Rita?" Carl yelled. His face was beet red, making his eyes a neon blue. He couldn't believe she'd challenge this; this was his *freedom*. The unspoken contract be-tween them. She was his accomplice. She'd *allowed* him to do as he pleased, hadn't she? It was her fault too; he'd always felt like a spoiled child, and now *he* felt betrayed.

Rita struggled to control her tears in order to speak. "You never were careful, Carl. It was as though you left notes and things in your pockets on purpose. Like the time you used a let-ter for a bookmarker and left it there." A cry escaped her throat and she couldn't go on.

Carl was silent and his color was returning to normal. He felt absolutely no pity for her. Absolutely none. They're all ballbusters, he thought with his usual sense of cool eventual-ity. It always came down to this. And now she was mutilated as well, and the idea of making love to her made him physically sick. Haven't I been a good husband *and* father? He looked at her lying there, feeling sorry for herself, not thinking of him at

all. Haven't I given everything up? Everything worth anything: myself.

"You're just like my father," Rita said in a low voice. "You
don't care about anyone else. Just your own good looks and the
head of your dick." She paused, gathering herself. She saw the
sheer hatred in Carl's eyes. It was naked and exposed for once.
"He made me feel like it was my fault too all those years. Why
do you think he doesn't come around? Why do you suppose?"
Rita's voice was filed to a murderous edge.

Carl watched Rita as though fascinated by how far she
would go. His eyes glittered in a hard way, and he wanted to
smile.

"He molested me for years, since I was five. It was our secret. I thought he couldn't help it because I was a bad girl, and
then I thought I was a good girl because I let him. And then
when I was ten he began to rape me, and then I began to dread
it."

"Rita, do you know what? You've flipped out. This opera-
tion's made you lose it. I don't believe any of this!" Carl was
shocked and excited at the same time: her father.

"I tell you he raped me! Just like you're raping me!" Rita
screamed.

"Quiet down! You'll scare the kids, Rita! Come on!" He'd
never seen her this way and it frightened him.

"I am not crazy, you bastard!"

"I'm calling the doctor. Now shut up and I'll put the kids to
bed. Damn it all, anyway!" Could it be true? he asked himself
as he walked to the phone. Her father? Carl thought of Blanca
at five, her large, brown eyes—trusting—and he turned his
mind away immediately. Could it be true?

Carl called the doctor and he prescribed a low dosage tranquilizer. "Yes," the doctor told him in a confidential tone,
"women sometimes imagine a tragedy to equal the loss of the
breast. You understand . . . Most women are weak, impression-
able and, ultimately, hysterical: poor things. We men have to
help . . . give her the tranquilizer."

Then Carl called Dora. Now Dora was angry. She didn't believe him. He was trying to avoid her. She knew it. I'm surrounded by crazy women, Carl thought with exasperation as he hung up the phone.

Rita stared at the ceiling. She was stunned by Carl's hatred and disbelief. Somehow, she'd always thought if she just said the truth everyone would simply believe her. Not only does Carl not believe me, she thought, feeling the smooth sheets underneath her, he thinks I'm crazy. And he's actually denying everything. Rita sat up with sudden renewed rage, breathing in shallow, quick breaths. She could hear the children being put to bed; the door shut.

"How dare he say that I'm crazy!" Rita whispered, spitting the words into the air. "How dare he! Maybe I've lost my breast, but I haven't lost my goddamned mind! Damn him! Damn him! DAMN HIM!" And then she knew Carl would have to change or else leave, and that she had to confront her rapist, her father. And that she wouldn't rest until he apologized. And then she wondered, as this new rage filled her and the long suppressed urge to kill him rose to her shoulders, down to her arms and hands, what possible apology could ever be enough? What can he say that would ever be enough? Her left nipple shrivelled from the slightly chilled bedroom air, and it felt soft and vulnerable to her. Rita started to weep, but the image of the scarred, vacant side where she was flat and hard as bone made her stop. It filled her with a strange and unexpected strength. She thought of Alta and Jackie jokingly slicing off their breasts, heating the knife over the camp fire, to become amazons.

For an instant Rita saw herself in leather and steel, with a breastplate, her breast exposed; her right side slashed and scarred.

Carl opened the bedroom door. He was surprised to see Rita sitting up, and she looked almost calm. "Look, I'm going for some tranquilizers. I'll be right back."

"I'm not taking tranquilizers." Rita's voice was even, calm.

"Look, the doctor wants you to, Rita." Her composure unnerved him.

Rita turned and looked directly into his face, fixing her eyes on his. "You take them, Carl. You're the one who needs them."

Doug was in Palm Springs getting Erin and Ethan. He'd come by briefly before he left to give Alta Katie's journal. "Hang onto this for me, will ya, Alta? I don't know why, but I just want to leave it with you, okay?" Doug's eyes had searched her for reassurance.

"Sure, no problem," she'd said, taking it, feeling strangely shy. Their lovemaking had been so intense and immediate, as it had been with Jackie. A deep, hungry part of herself was filling up, and she didn't know whether to call it love. Hadn't she always called it *love?* Alta looked at Doug. His eyes probed hers, and she smiled in a careful way, afraid to give more than she intended.

"You can look through the journal. I know Katie wouldn't mind. I'll call you when I get back. Wish me luck." He'd pulled her to him, kissing her, moving his lips suggestively, promising her more.

The kids were asleep, but she couldn't sleep. She waited for no one. She tried to remember Hugh's face clearly, but she couldn't. All the years erased; no, not really, Alta thought. Just Hugh's face. She opened Katie's journal and read:

Naked Ladies

> I won't live to see the naked ladies,
> summer is too far away—
> I do not grieve, not really,
> not anymore, except that
> I've never picked naked ladies
> with my children—how will
> they remember me when I am no more?
> When my flesh is gone, and my bones.

Will I sprout, at last, in their fertile
imaginations? Dressed in pink,
a tender stalk.
My naked, living love.

For Ethan and Erin

April (such a beautiful young woman now) brought me
naked ladies today, fully blossomed. They won't last very long
(like me). I wish I had the time (the talent, the courage) to
write something that would last like *The Diary of Anne
Frank*—what a brave little girl. Yes, she was right for all of us
(and so damned wise)—I believe people are good at heart, she
said just before the Nazis killed her. My boys, my little boys,
when you read this and your voices are low and there are
beards on your faces and girls that you love, know that I leave
you both with that same basic trust in life. Know how much I
wanted to know you both, Ethan and Erin. Remember all death
is followed by spring and summer—a birth, a bright, glowing
sun I'm beginning to see day and night, so I'm not afraid. I think
I'm dying into that sun—dying has stripped me bare, has
taught me such love. So stark it is, so utterly beautiful, and terrible too. And so perfect, like my love for you—though I'm not
perfect, no, no. Only love is perfect . . .

Alta could tell Katie was censoring herself for the future,
for the boys, because she never spoke about her constant pain.
She'd also left them little morning notes, little humorous greet-
ings to be read to them, but, apparently, Doug hadn't opened
them. They were neatly folded in fourths.

Finally, Alta fell asleep after coming to the conclusion that
Doug was still Katie's. Of course, he still loves Katie, Alta
thought. I still love Katie. "Katie," she softly whispered.

*A woman is burning in an intense fire. It starts at her feet, grow-
ing to her hair, which leaps with pure, blue flame. Everything
crackles, including her bones. Everything is swept away. Clean.*

Alta woke in a terrified sweat, forcing herself to focus on her surroundings: her bedroom, almost dawn. She went back to sleep almost angrily.

"Thanks for coming with me. I wouldn't blame you if you didn't want to," Jackie said as she walked into Alta's kitchen. The abortion was scheduled in a couple of hours. She was terrified and tears filled her eyes. She hated the idea of killing a child; she hated the pain she'd have to feel. Worse yet, she hated the reality of another child. How can I have another and get on with my life? she told herself sternly. All those right-to-lifers fighting food stamps and welfare to the same unborn. Spend that money on something sensible like Star Wars . . . "Fuck," Jackie sighed.

"You knew I'd come with you." Alta sat across from Jackie. "Do you know how you got pregnant? I guess it really doesn't matter, but I can imagine how hard this is for you. Double up on your contraceptives, girl." Alta smiled.

"I'll tell you what I'm going to do. I'm going to stop drinking, be semicelibate, and kick ass on my life." Jackie looked up at Alta's warm eyes. "I'm sorry about my bullshit."

"It's me, too, it's okay. For the record, I'm glad we made love that night. I wouldn't have had the courage if you hadn't. We're still friends, right?"

"Yeah, we sure are."

As Jackie got up at the sound of her name being called, she paused, bent over Alta, and kissed her softly on the lips.

"My house burned down. I mean, the goddamned bottom flat went, and then mine went. You know, all that food we bought?"

Alta nodded her head.

"All of it—gone. Jesus-fucking-A-Christ. I wonder if I'll be crippled next." Doug was standing in the doorway. The kids were in the car, looking up with lost, frightened faces.

"I can't believe this, Doug. Well, get the kids and come in. Is everything gone?"

"Just about everything, including their toys." Doug struggled to retain his reserve. His dignity. He went and got the boys.

"Why don't they play in the front room with the blocks and stuff? How would you guys like some hot chocolate?"

Ethan and Erin nodded their heads gravely, yes. They looked like they'd forgotten how to smile.

Doug followed Alta to the kitchen. "How 'bout if I go get a pizza?"

"Sounds good. April and Ian will be home in a couple of minutes. I'll chip in for an extra large."

"I'll buy it." Doug sat with his knees spread apart and his body pitched forward.

She just said it. "You can move in here, Doug."

Doug looked up at her as though he'd been struck across the face, but he almost smiled.

"Doug, I don't love you like I did Hugh. Maybe I'll never love anyone like I did Hugh. I just don't know. I just want to be honest with you."

Doug got to his feet and walked the few steps between them, taking her into his arms. "Shit, I don't care."

Part Two

Seven

It was March 1999, nine more months to the new century.
Alta sat bleeding her warm womb's blood into the soft, fertile
Earth, in the warm, spring rain, in the blossoming apple orchard, naked. The hospital had just called to tell her Hugh
was dead. He'd called her four months ago to say goodbye.
"Have you forgiven me?" he'd asked. Now he was dead. Now
she was alive and bleeding in the warm, spring rain. Naked.

When she and Doug moved here that first spring, they'd
slept outside and in the morning were covered by the white and
pink, thick and sensually fragrant, apple blossoms. It'd lasted
five years, three of them very good. They'd fixed up the old
house, raised chickens and steers, and learned to prune and pick
the apples at the right time. Then Doug began to drink heavily, dropping out of law school. Alta kept going and got her
counseling degree. She'd gotten a second mortgage and given
Doug the money, and he had left. She kept the house and the
eight acres of land. She'd kept Ethan and Erin for two more
years and then they'd gone to live with Katie's parents. She'd
gotten them over their mother's death, and life had made
them smile again, but, ultimately, they weren't hers. Katie's
lawsuit money would be released to Ethan in a couple of years
when he turned eighteen, and then to Erin. They wrote and
called from time to time, but she hadn't seen or heard from
Doug in years.

Now Hugh was dead: AIDS. Rita was dead: cancer. Her
mother was dead. Alta had been with her mother a week before her death, sitting with her without the pretense of the
mother-daughter bond. Their bond had been a pain borne by two
women, two strangers. Her mother had allowed no intimacy to
the end, but once, unguarded, Alta had seen a kind of wonder in
her mother's eyes and she'd wanted to ask, "What are you

thinking?" But she hadn't, and now she was alive and bleeding in the warm, spring rain, naked.

Ian was in college full-time, clear across the country. April was married to a man who reminded Alta of Carl, and her first child was due in four months, coinciding with her BFA in photography. April had her own darkroom in spite of her husband's objections and obvious disapproval. He considered April's photography an expensive, useless hobby, although she was unmistakably talented, and he resented Alta's encouragement. Alta was proud of April; she knew her daughter would survive intact. She knew her children had to live their own lives now, as she did.

Alta was thirty-eight and alone. She had friends, a few good ones, and her work, her troubled people as she privately called them, and she cared about them. There were the couples playing tug-of-war with their love, the single people looking for someone to play tug-of-war with, the three young children sexually abused by their own fathers, an older woman who'd been raped by her grandfather until he died, and the two people dying with AIDS. These were her troubled people. She wept with them and she laughed with them, but she continued to doubt her capacity to love, and to be loved, and it continued to wound her in innumerable small, and large, ways. Each wound bled, and where her blood fell life quickened, but her love still lacked the full joy of consciousness. Choice. That strange paradox of strength and surrender that was at the heart of conscious choice.

Now Chagall's bride and groom, his hand still over her womb, hung in Alta's office, as well as some prints of Frida Kahlo's work—her favorite, of the artist lying full length on a barren Mexican landscape, with thin bloodlines flowing from her body as though to feed the soil, the soil of Alta's grandmother. There was a giant aloe vera like the one her grandmother had moved from place to place, cutting it carefully to heal burns or cuts. Now she had a giant aloe vera; now she would be a grandmother.

The rain had stopped and streams of thick, gold morning sun poured through the old, fertile apple trees, warming the ground. Alta's body filled up with a familiar longing, the longing to fill up with life: a child. She laughed out loud. There was a man, a lover, in her life. He was younger than her by ten years, and he reminded her of her old friend Steve. Alta was training him, in the final stages, for his counseling degree, to work directly with clients. He was solid and sensitive, and she respected that. And he was dark and lovely. Alta shivered with a jolt of desire, which started in her womb, as she thought of him, his gaze that met her own. "Let's have a kid sometime," Michael had said, laughing. Only Alta couldn't imagine living with him. In the morning she could, but not at night and every day.

And Jackie. Jackie was bringing her first book of poems up next weekend. She was married to a nurse she'd met working with AIDS patients. AIDS could be curbed, but not cured, so the dying continued. The shields of the Earth were weakening.

She limited her time in the sun. She didn't trust the wounded ozone layer to protect her entirely. She didn't trust love to protect her entirely. "We're all troubled people. Me, a grandmother, an orphan." She liked talking to herself.

Alta put her face up fully to the sun, feeling its warmth flood her. She spread her legs to it, throwing her head back as chaos invaded her, the chaos of spring. It was always the chaos of spring. Who could explain it? It just was.

Is.

"Isis," Alta said, getting to her knees, "I want to love." She smoothed the earth with her hands and, taking a thin twig, drew a circle. It looked empty. She drew a line down the center, then one across. It looked familiar, strangely personal, but she didn't know why. Last night, she made herself remember, she dreamt the birth of her grandchild, a girl, and then in a flash, a large, dark, terrible bird soaring toward a bright light, and, as it disappeared, the child began to cry with hunger.

Alta broke off a twig covered with wet apple blossoms and, smearing the blossoms with her womb blood, placed it upright in the circle's center. Bright lights played on the fragile rain-drops, and she knew the beauty of these blossoms wouldn't last forever. "Katie," she whispered, remembering her long dead friend as her own life force surged through her like a music only she could hear, loud in her ears. And the blossoms, wet and fragile, smeared with her womb blood, were utterly beautiful, though in that moment they'd ceased to bloom.

The goblet, full of Katie's deep red feathers and perched on a shelf in Alta's bedroom, caught the sunlight, and they flared with their old fire.

Alta looked up at the ripe explosions of apple blossoms shivering and swaying in the warming gusts of wind. Some of them began to flutter down silently, like an exquisite, fragrant snowfall onto the damp, rich earth. A few of them clung to Alta's hair like a blessing, and the wind caressed her as she surrendered to a molten softness, a fierce fertility in her womb.

Alta placed her hands protectively over her sore and tender womb. She was the bride and the groom. "Hugh," she whispered to the wind, remembering her wound, and his. "Goodbye, Hugh. Forever." And the wind carried her words to the waning crescent moon. It hung delicately as it prepared to set at the edge of the world, where she had arrived, and she wasn't lonely.

She was the child of her own endless longing. The time is now, the scattered blossoms seemed to say to the wonder in Alta's eyes. "The time is now," she whispered, alive and bleeding her womb's fierce blood in the warm chaos of spring, in the warm womb of spring. Naked.

*   *   *

Jade turned the lights on at the end of the studio as she entered the classroom. She glanced at the looms in their various stages of completion. It was hard to believe that so much had happened since she last saw her students. And they'll be here soon, Jade reminded herself, walking back to the sink to put on the water for coffee and tea for the three-hour class.

It helped to make everyone comfortable, and a certain intimacy had developed between the five women and the one man. At first Jade worried he wouldn't fit in, or even keep coming to the class, which was what usually happened with her few men students, but he was younger than the women, and boyish and likeable. Men, she thought. Men. She hoped no one would ask if she'd had the flu; even trying to attempt small talk about why she'd been absent last week might start her crying again.

Enough is enough, she told herself, toughening her mind. She hadn't even called her mother after the rape. Rapes, she reminded herself. Rapes. And her lover, her ex-lover, was in Bali, exactly as she'd promised herself. Yes, Grace is gone, and there's no one to really talk to. How can I tell my mother about this, or anyone? Anyone at all? I can't even describe it to myself, though I keep seeing it over and over . . .

"Hey, Jade! Missed you last week! Were you sick or taking a vacation from us?" Gary laughed and threw down his pack next to his loom.

The mug Jade was holding dropped to the floor, shattering into sharp-edged pieces at her feet. His voice had cut through her false sense of safety and solitude. The picture in her mind of the two men raping her became real at the sound of Gary's male voice, and her body felt the horror again so vividly that her mind threatened blackness.

It's only Gary, she told herself; it's only Gary, catching her breath and hanging onto the edge of the chill white sink. She willed herself to stop trembling.

Gary reached for Jade, holding onto her arm. "Are you okay? Hey, what's the matter?"

Jade tossed her head back as though her long, black hair were down, reaching to her waist. She had it pulled back into a single, thick braid. Her dark, Asian eyes, almost black, met his as she pulled herself away from his touch. "You just startled me, that's all. I wasn't expecting anyone for at least ten minutes." She forced herself to smile. "Water's almost ready, help yourself."

"Are you sure you're okay, Jade?" She'd looked so terrified, but her voice was calm now.

"Yes, really, I'm fine. Thanks, Gary." Only her hands trembled ever so slightly. She could hear the women talking as they walked down the hall toward the class. Jade spooned a large dose of coffee into another mug with a teaspoon of sugar. No tea and honey for me tonight, she thought—coffee, and more coffee. Or a bottle of brandy. No, enough booze—drunk three nights in a row. Jade poured the boiling water into her cup, letting the steam reach her face.

"There you are!" one of the women called. "Got some fresh-baked brownies tonight, ladies!" She glanced at Gary and laughed. "And gentlemen. Do you bake, Gary?"

"Hey, next time I'll bring a pie. I promise." He laughed with the women and went over to fix his coffee and get a brownie. He looked at Jade and handed her one.

"Thanks," she said, taking a bite. "These are great, Ruth. What a treat."

"Had the flu, I bet. My kids all have it. Bet I'm next. Oh well, what can you do, walk around in a bubble?"

Jade jumped at her words, but she smiled and said, "I just hope that's it for this spring," silently wishing there were such a bubble to protect her. She'd gladly stay in it, never feeling another human touch, as long as *that* never happened to her again. Ever, ever again.

Alta watched Jade move from loom to loom, pausing to comment and assist if needed. Her face was masklike and her usual graceful movements were slightly wooden, forced. Alta always had a kind of afterimage of a black orchid whenever she looked at Jade. There was such a composure about her, and a fragility, a kind of rarity. They'd had a glass of wine a couple of times after class and talked, but when Alta had mentioned she was a therapist she felt Jade recede, just a little.

"I like the colors you've chosen, Alta. I think the pattern's going to be really interesting, from what you've shown me. But look," Jade said, taking the shuttle, "try it this way."

Alta smiled. "That looks a little easier, thanks." As she took back the shuttle she touched Jade's hand, and she saw it was trembling. Instinctively, Alta reached for her hand and held it. Jade's eyes filled with tears, but she quickly forced them down.

Not here, Jade told herself sternly, and turned to leave.

"Jade, can I talk to you after class?" Alta held Jade's eyes. "Please."

Jade nodded and left.

"I'm glad you're finally here," Alta smiled. "You know, I've asked you over twice now." For the first time she noticed Jade's hair was in a braid. She'd always worn it loose almost to her waist. Her carved jade earrings—delicate, stylized horses rearing up—were clearly visible.

"Oh, I guess I've got this teacher hang-up. When I started teaching I was so young I felt I had to keep it together to keep my sense of authority and all." Suddenly, in spite of herself, Jade felt relaxed in Alta's front room filled with pillows, plants, pottery, some paintings, and a most curious, almost ugly, she thought, print over the fireplace. She got up to look at it, sipping some chilled colombard. But watch your step, she told herself, she's a therapist, trained to get it out of you. Jade sucked in her breath sharply.

"You teach twelfth grade, right?"

"Yes, and it's challenging, as you can imagine. Sometimes I think I should switch over to college level full-time, if it becomes possible. But, then, I also really love some of those crazy teenagers." Jade found herself blushing. I really shouldn't talk so much, she caught herself. It's been so long since Grace and I talked. Grace. Even her name means so much to me: beauty, gentleness, and, yes, strength. So much roared through her as she stood staring at the bizarre print on Alta's wall. She hated Bali because Grace preferred Bali to her; she hated the world, a world that produced men that rape and hurt, rape and hurt and kill. They even kill each other without a qualm. Bitterly, the word *men* took the place of *Grace*, but at least she could go on now, standing there like a rational human being. Anger took the place of sorrow, grief. Fear.

"Do you like Frida Kahlo?" Alta asked, standing next to her.

"Frida Kahlo. I've never heard of her. Well, actually, I have, I think, but I've never seen this. It's almost ugly, isn't it? I mean, it's really almost ugly." Jade stared, fascinated by the picture in front of her: a dark Indian woman with a blackened mask-face—no eyes, no visible soul stared out of her face—with blunt, straight black hair, cradled a girl-child's body with an adult head in her strong, brown arms as she suckled her, barely, letting the white milk drip from a large brown breast with a lacy x-ray of the white milk covering it in arteries, tentacles, of delicate, white flowers, while all around, all around, a milk-rain, droplets of milk-rain surrounded the Indian woman and the child as they sat in the middle of giant, green leaves, a jungle. Underneath it said, "My Nurse and I."

"I guess it takes getting used to. I love it. It makes me feel strangely safe to look at it, you know?" Alta glanced at Jade's profile just in time to see tears rolling down her cheeks.

"But why is her face so ugly? Why is her face so terrible?" Jade whispered, almost to herself.

Alta put her arm around Jade's shoulder. Her shoulders are so small, she thought, and vulnerable like a child's. Like my own, she realized. "Maybe because love has a terrible face."

Jade began to cry softly, with her hands to her sides like the child in the painting, and then Alta took her into her arms, holding her, telling her, "It's okay, Jade, it's okay, go ahead and cry, I'm right here," as she stroked her hair and back, again and again. Then her cries became sobs, then inarticulate moans and screams. Jade began to shake violently as though gripped by a seizure.

Alta led Jade to the couch and made her lie down on her stomach. She began to massage her body as best she could with her clothes in the way, starting with her back, waist, legs, up again to the neck and face, until the trembling subsided.

"If you take your things off I'll give you an oil massage. I'm a trained masseuse, you know." Alta's voice was low and gentle, feeling Jade's delicate balance. "Here, let me help you, okay?" She took off Jade's skirt and blouse, leaving her panties on. She wore no bra and her breasts were small and firm like Alta's, and her body was slender and very white as though the sun never touched her.

Jade lifted herself up, stretching her arms over her head, letting Alta undress her, but she couldn't speak or it'd start again, the seizure.

"Are you warm enough?"

Jade nodded, closing her eyes.

When Jade woke up Alta was lying in a sleeping bag by the fireplace. Supported by her left arm, she stared at the fire. Her face was exposed, almost childlike. Tender.

Jade's body, the whole of it, felt rested, at peace, for the first time since *that afternoon*. She touched her breasts and her belly, and they felt like her own. She put her hand over her pubis, feeling her short, scratchy hair. Almost, she thought, almost. The violence still lingered there and in her mouth. She touched her mouth with both hands as though she were blind and trying to figure herself out. She touched her eyes, her cheeks, her nose. She rested her hands on her face for a moment. "Maybe love has a terrible face," Jade whispered. "My own face."

"Are you awake?" Alta asked, turning to face her.

"Yes. What time is it? I didn't mean to fall asleep, I'm sorry."

"It's two o'clock and there's nothing to be sorry about. Why don't you stay the night? I'll get you a nightgown." Alta held Jade's eyes and waited.

"Sure, why not? Tomorrow's a holiday anyway." Jade's voice was sleepy but her mind was becoming alert.

Alta got up to get the nightgown. "Do you want some more wine or some tea?"

"I'll take a half-glass of wine. Thanks, Alta. Where's your bathroom?"

"Right down the hall," Alta answered, pointing to it. She glimpsed Jade's nakedness as she stood up, pulling on her blouse. What happened to her, she thought again. What happened? Rape, I bet, she answered herself with a shiver. I bet it's rape.

After Jade was settled again on the couch with her wine, Alta built the fire up to a blaze. "Apple wood smells so good, doesn't it? I almost hate to throw on the oak."

Jade nodded silently.

Alta sipped her wine. "Are you Japanese and something else? I've always wanted to ask you. Hope you don't mind."

"No, I don't mind. My father was Japanese—he's dead now—and my mother's Navajo and Spanish. Quite a mixture. What're you?"

"Mexican, with lots of Indian, as you can see," Alta smiled. "My mother died last year, and my father died in the Vietnam war when I was three. My grandmother raised me. Did your mother raise you?"

"Yes. She taught me to weave. She's a master weaver, and she taught grammar school for twenty-some-odd years in a little place in New Mexico. That's where I grew up. Only a slight oddity there, really, being part Japanese and all, and I think I look more Asian than anything else. You know, the land bridge theory." Jade smiled to herself, and Alta saw the strange and beautiful black orchid where Jade should be.

"Where does your name come from?" Alta murmured. The fire on her face soothed her, and it was a pleasure to look at Jade, like it was a pleasure to look at Michael. He too was beautiful. Black, sleek, male, and a jaguar like herself: fierce and catlike, yet wonderfully tender. Playful. He'd been her only lover for over two years. They quarrelled occasionally, but nothing life-or-death. They moved apart and moved together in a well-orchestrated dance. She the teacher, he the student, but that too had given way to equality.

"My father named me. I was as precious as jade, he said. An *ornament*," her voice took on an edge of bitterness, "to his manhood or whatever."

"I've always loved your jade earrings. Do you always wear jade?" Alta couldn't help asking and then she felt immediately silly. Well, why should I censor myself, she thought. I'm not with a client.

Jade didn't answer, sipping her wine. "He killed himself when I was fourteen, samurai style with a sword." She looked directly at Alta and in a falsely pleasant tone, she said, "Dramatic, isn't it?"

"Why did he do it? Do you know?" Alta's voice was low.

Jade held Alta's eyes with a terrible expression—a mixture of anger and defeat—that made Alta want to look away, but she didn't.

"He used to beat me as a kid. I was headstrong, that's for sure. You know, independent, and it was hard on him, I guess. When I started to develop he began to rip my clothes off as a kind of humiliation, and only when my mother wasn't home. Then, when I was fourteen, he not only ripped my clothes off, he raped me. He killed himself the next day."

Alta sat silently, feeling Jade's anguish, her pain.

"After he raped me he cried; he apologized; he said he loved me, that it would never happen again. I told him he was ugly, that he couldn't be my father, that I hated him." Jade's voice was calm, but tears ran down her face. "He begged me not to tell my mother. He begged me, but I told him I was going to tell everyone, everyone I could. This time I was going to tell. After the other times he would dote on me, buy me anything, call me his precious Jade, and I'd forget about it. But this time I knew I couldn't forget. He killed himself the next day."

"You know, Jade, it's not your fault, your father's death. He raped you and you had to tell what happened to you." Alta's voice was gentle.

"I never did. I never did tell anyone, except Grace, that is."

"Who's Grace?"

"She was my lover." Jade watched Alta's face for shock, but there was none, and she sighed with relief.

"Is that what you're still so upset about, your father? You were just a frightened little girl, Jade." Alta leaned forward. "I mean, earlier I was really worried about you, you know."

"I know." Jade's voice was soft. "I keep telling myself that. No, I was crying earlier about something else."

Alta waited.

Jade finished her wine and began: "I was raped last week by two men. I was bike riding, around sunset, when these two guys pulled over and dragged me out to a field. I tried to fight, but each one held me while the other one raped me. They laughed at me when I cried and pinched my breasts to shut me up. They kept me for hours and forced me to swallow their sperm till I gagged. They fucked me in the ass. 'Chinks like it like this,' that's what they said." Jade's voice failed her.

Alta took Jade into her arms and held her as she began to cry again, but this time her sorrow was less violent.

Then Jade continued, her words pouring out: "They talked about killing me for a while and how they'd do it. I was ready to die at that point. They said they had a shovel in the car, and they'd bury me right there. And then they threatened to start their party, as they called it, again, but I was really ready to die so I didn't respond. Then the younger one, the blond one, said, grabbing me by my hair and pulling my head back— they'd held me by the hair through the whole ordeal, like guiding a horse or dog—" Jade's voice shrunk to a whisper, but she continued. "He said, 'If you want to live, you bitch-chink, you better keep this to yourself!' Then they left me there. I got dressed, got on my bike, and drove home in incredible pain."

Alta wept with her, tears streaking her face and hair. "Did you get treatment? Did you go to a hospital? Did you report this to the cops?" Alta could hardly believe that two men would willingly brutalize this fragile woman that rested against her. But, then, she knew better. She was working, even now, with two little girls, two fragile little girls, and an equally fragile little boy, all with sexually abusive fathers.

Alta expelled her breath, feeling secretly helpless before such senseless cruelty. Where does it end? she asked herself. Her usual question.

"No. I just went home and took care of myself, and I don't want to deal with police reports and all that. And what about those two men? I know they'd kill me. They'll find me and kill me." Jade's voice was exhausted. Alta's warmth was all she needed right now. Just her warmth.

The sound of the small, flowing creek was vivid in the silence. It was almost noon and the wind came in strong, springtime gusts, whipping Alta's hair in every direction and making the small orange butterflies take refuge in the tall ground cover. Birds pecked at the last of the apple blossoms, and the trees were fully leafed. Jade gazed out over the valley. From this vantage point there were only apple orchards and the wide, endlessly green valley.

"I sleep here sometimes in the summer. Nothing but stars and crickets all night," Alta said, languidly.

"Are you safe here?" The beauty all around them ebbed for a moment for Jade. Her mouth felt dry with anxiety.

"This is about as safe as you can get. Private property seems to keep the creeps at bay around here. I gave up bike riding a couple of years ago when some guys tried to run me off the road. Actually, they did. I had to dive off the side of the road into some damned bushes. I guess I'm lucky they didn't do anything else." Alta reached over and touched Jade's hand.

"Look, whenever you want to walk or get out in the open, come over here. You don't have to call, just come over. I really mean it, okay?"

"Thanks, Alta. Thanks for saying it. And I will, thank you." Alta had given her another oil body rub in the morning after breakfast. Once, when she pressed down on her belly area, grazing her pubis, her clitoris stirred with desire. But Alta's not gay, she reminded herself. Jade gazed at Alta's tongue as she spoke, imagining its gentle, insistent pressures on her body, but she made herself stop.

"Why don't you come to the beach tomorrow with Michael and me?" Alta felt herself blush and it made her laugh. "He's been my lover for a while. He's a really sweet guy, a really good man. Also, we do some team therapy, kind of his last leg toward his counseling degree. He's an excellent counselor, very tuned and sensitive. Anyway, I like working with him too." Alta laughed with pleasure.

Now Jade was curious. "Maybe I will. But, look, no team therapy for me, okay? And please don't tell Michael about all this. I just wouldn't be comfortable."

"Okay, fair enough, if that's what you want. But I wish you'd consider reporting what happened to you. I mean, you know this, but these men are dangerous, and it'll probably happen to other women. Do you remember what they look like?"

Jade turned away and looked out over the wide valley. Just remembering their faces made her nauseous with fear.

"I'm sorry, but I really think you should. I'd help you in any way I can," Alta said, running her hand along Jade's long, black braid.

"I remember their license plate, a custom one: COCKEY. Of course. Bastards. It was a red pickup truck. And I remember exactly what they look like. Exactly." Now Jade's breath came short and shallow, and her heart felt small and exposed to every danger, trapped inside her chest behind the softness of her left breast.

"I just can't do it, Alta. The truth is, I'm scared shitless. Those men will kill me, I know it. You should've heard them talking about it—rip me open, cunt to mouth, things like that. One wanted to cut off my tits, as he called them, for a souvenir." Jade began to tremble, though she willed herself not to. "I just can't do it. I just want them to leave me alone, that's all."

"Look, just think about it, and, if you can, imagine them doing that to other women. You've been through a hell of a lot, but you're strong, I can see that. How old are you?"

"Twenty-nine. And you?"

"Thirty-eight." Alta smiled, soothing a stray piece of hair from Jade's face. "I really like your hair down, you know."

Jade looked at Alta closely. They were nearly touching shoulders. "Do you?"

"Yes, I do. In fact, you have some of the most beautiful hair I've ever seen. It's so long and thick. Do you plan to let it loose again? I hope so." Alta's voice was soft as though someone were sleeping nearby, as though she were telling Jade a secret.

The sun was directly over their heads, and the wind only seemed to be gaining in strength. Jade leaned over silently and lightly kissed Alta's half-open mouth. She tasted like the wind. Jade waited for Alta to get up and leave, to be angry, but she did neither.

"Do you plan to wear it down again?" Alta smiled with pleasure.

"I'll think about everything you've suggested. I promise. Do you mind that I kissed you, Alta?" Jade held her breath.

Alta leaned over and kissed Jade, feeling her soft lips with her tongue in a tentative fashion, and Jade's tongue shyly touched hers in silent greeting. Alta felt incredibly tender toward this woman, and she didn't know why. Then Alta kissed Jade's cheeks and eyes, and pulled away.

Michael slid out of bed, trying not to wake Alta, but she stirred, opening her eyes briefly. "Where're you going?" she asked, pulling the covers higher around her neck.

"Going to start some coffee," he whispered. "You know me, can't lie in bed after sunrise. Go on back to sleep, Alta." Then Michael added, deep in his throat, with a soft laugh, remembering her warm flesh next to his, "Lazy woman."

"What time is it?"

"Seven, that's all."

The day was warm and cloudless, and the early morning chill would soon be gone. A pair of red-tailed hawks spiraled together in the innocent morning sun. Then they shot down, first the large female, as large as the male, and plunged toward the green, waking valley, hungry for prey. Their eyes worked effortlessly, scanning the Earth for movement, their wings cutting in, resisting, submitting, to the west wind that carried the ocean inland to the wide, fertile, achingly green, fields. The male hawk followed the female, still playing more than hunting, but to a hawk hunger is a mixture, a paradox, of necessity and play. Their hunger called them out to play, and with senses sharp and acute, they searched now for their kill. The west wind, gentle this morning, made little puffs of dirt, circles of wind, in the freshly turned soil of the apple orchard, row upon row. The rotted apples and green manure smelled so clean, so rich, all rotted and rotting now under the dark soil.

Now the hawks were far away, miles away, as movement caught the female's eye. She turned sharply, and swooped, missed, and rose again. The male went on in an easterly direction toward some hills which the sun had cleared an hour ago. The male screamed once, high and shrill, just for pleasure in the high, blinding air.

Carrying his fresh, hot coffee, Michael stopped to watch Alta's steers graze in the fenced-in field. She ate some and sold the others. The last one still filled the freezer halfway. He heard her horse snort and shuffle with excitement at the sound of human feet and the scent of his presence, so he walked toward her field. She slept outside now that the frost was gone. He stopped to fill her bucket with grain. He sipped his coffee; it was strong and good. Perfection, he thought.

"Yeah!" Michael said out loud, placing the bucket next to the horse through the fence. He ran his fingers through her mane carefully, trying to avoid the knots, and then he scratched her beautiful, black ears. Her body shivered with delight and she raised her head to look at him, and then bent again to the sweet grain.

"Hey, Night Mare, how'd you sleep? Sleep okay out here by yourself? You've got it made, yeah." Michael stroked the sides of her cheeks, watching the sun glint off her black body. The shine on her smooth blackness created a spectrum of deep colors. Wide bands of rainbows rippled as she moved and tossed her head.

"Why don't you ride her?" Alta approached, carrying her coffee, dressed in old jeans with a warm flannel shirt hanging out. Her hair was in braids, and silver, crescent moon earrings swung as she walked. "Go ahead, just ride her bareback. She likes it better that way, anyway." Alta smiled.

"I always feel sorry for her when I have to saddle her for a long one. The bit and reins and all that shit."

"Don't have my jock strap on, remember?" Michael laughed. "I've got one of those dangling things. What're you doing up?"

"I smelled the coffee and I missed you." Alta smiled into Michael's eyes. His hair was cropped short all around his head, revealing a strong, beautiful bone structure, a wide jaw and expanse of face. His large deep green eyes—sensual, fully lidded eyes—were startling against his dark, chocolate-brown skin. Eyes that could turn absolutely cold like hard, green stone when he was angry, and a slightly flaring nose. Whenever he spoke his nostrils flared and shut, with one passion or another, and his mouth, his lips, were dark and full. His body was lean and graceful and muscular. Like a jaguar, Alta thought, like a beautiful, dangerous, black jaguar. She loved the blend of femininity and masculinity, the integration, in his body, and her eyes swept over him with fresh, intense pleasure. A small, star-shaped diamond earring in his left ear absorbed the sun's new light. It glittered against his darkness, sending silent messages to Alta of the night's physical pleasures, their shared sleep.

"You can ride her if you're careful, O studly one," Alta teased, laughing with a kind of sheer delight his presence gave her. She felt there was nothing she couldn't tell him. He would understand. The boundaries of friend and lover blurred and a nagging voice asked, But do you *love* him?

"Nah, I just feel like being still, I guess. I fed her some grain." Alta leaned against Michael, and he cupped her breasts gently, sniffing her behind the ears. "Why do you smell so good, huh?"

"You didn't like my farts last night." Alta laughed softly.

"I would say that's different, wouldn't you? Go on, you ride her so I can watch. That's what I feel like doing, watching you ride your Night Mare."

"Maybe I will," Alta murmured, placing her hands over Michael's hands that cupped her breasts.

"I dreamt my brother last night." A sadness crept into his voice, but just slightly. He was too happy now to be entirely sad about anything.

"Which one?"

"My older brother. I dreamt him dying again. You know, being beaten to death, but this time he changed into me. It was my face." Michael shuddered inwardly, pulling Alta even closer to him, wrapping his arms around her. "I guess that's your run-of-the-mill nightmare, right?"

Alta turned to face him, looking into his now fierce, green eyes—fierce with anger and sorrow, and he looked back at her without fear or the defensiveness most men couldn't help feeling when faced equally with a woman. He had long, thick black eyelashes and beautiful, thick eyebrows. Michael's natural beauty and gentleness made its first impression in the realm of the feminine, yet his masculinity was whole and healthy, assured.

"You were kind of talking and whimpering in your sleep last night. I held you for a while and then you stopped. You haven't had one of those in a while, have you?"

"A couple of years, I guess. I have long periods where I actually forget, but last night was so vivid." Michael's eyes hardened. "That's a terrible way to die, to be beaten to death. Here in the United States of America, not South Africa. Right here. And it wasn't even *personal*, Alta. He just happened to be black and they just happened to be white."

Alta thought of Jade and how that too wasn't personal. Violence, random violence, was escalating, coming to some kind of terrible peak as they approached the new century. She often couldn't help thinking of it as a sort of collective cleansing, a meaning in the madness. A cleansing for the next, for the new phase of human consciousness. But at what price? she wondered.

"All or nothing," Alta murmured.

"What did you say?"

"I said all or nothing. You know, the nasty question of human survival. The violence to your brother and the violence to women and the violence around the Earth and to the Earth. We either don't know any better, or we're sure trying to learn. I just hope the learning process speeds up, you know, for April's baby's sake. The ones to come. I guess I feel a certain irrational relief that my children are grown at least."

"Look, I'm sorry to bum you out on such a really beautiful morning. Go on and ride Night Mare instead of talking about them." Michael's eyes softened as he smiled. "And, besides, I still think we should have a kid sometime."

"You know, the woman we're going to the beach with today? Jade?" Alta breathed deeply, changing the subject.

Michael nodded, shifting his weight, trying to rid himself of ghosts.

"I'm not supposed to tell you this, so don't say a thing, but maybe you can help, Michael. She was raped by two men recently, pretty brutally. They threatened to kill her, and she's scared shitless, and not that I blame her. Anyway, she hasn't reported it, and, frankly, I'm worried those creeps will do it again and again. Plus, I think she needs to do something about it, damn it. They shouldn't get away with what they did to her. It was pretty bad."

"Motherfuckers," Michael muttered, clenching his teeth.

Then Alta added softly, "Jade was raped by her father when she was fourteen and then he killed himself the next day. How's that?"

"Well, I guess we've almost heard it all, right? But it sure doesn't make it any easier. It just makes me wonder where these guys keep springing up from. But, of course, you know I have my theories." Michael smiled sadly, expelling his held breath sharply. He looked toward the horizon for a glimpse of the hawks, but there was nothing moving in the sky.

"I just want you to know, but don't say *anything* unless it comes up somehow, unless she should bring it up, okay?"

"I hear you. They threatened to kill her?"

"Yeah."

"Is she okay, more or less?"

"I think so, she's pretty strong. Special somehow." Alta walked over to Night Mare and began stroking her face. "Look, I think I will take a short ride over the first hill. Do you mind starting breakfast?" Alta kissed Michael lightly, taking in his morning scent. She unfastened the gate and slipped the halter over Night Mare's head.

"No problem." Michael watched her ride away, over the knoll, until she disappeared. At the sound of the high, shrill cry he turned his head up just in time to see the fan of a red tail filtering the sun's rising light. Alta had taught him to sight-name birds, like this hawk, and she'd given him a bird guide-book the first year they'd met. She's taught me a lot, Michael thought as he stood in the deep, humming silence.

An easterly wind blew now, a tugging, fitful wind. But we each have to ride our own nightmare, right, Alta? Right, he answered himself, walking slowly toward the house.

Jade was already sorry she'd come; Alta and Michael's intimacy was obvious, and now she felt excluded even though they both meant to make her welcome. What would Michael think, Jade mused, watching him open a bottle of wine, if he knew I'd kissed her. Twice, during the night, she'd sat bolt upright at a harmless sound, but nothing was harmless anymore. Nothing had ever been harmless, she realized. Being a woman is being raped as a child and being raped as a woman, and then killed if it suited them. "We'll cut you cunt to mouth, chink bitch, cunt to mouth," the words echoed in Jade's tired mind. She made herself look out at the blue, moving ocean and the incredibly blue stretch of sky, but the day refused to lighten for her.

"I'm so glad we got this spot," Alta said, handing Jade a glass of spumante. "Once in a while someone gets here before me. It's a great spot, shielded from the wind. I even brought some wood for later if we want to have a small fire."

"I've never been here before. I usually go to the more crowded beaches myself." Immediately Jade was sorry she'd said it and hurriedly added, "I guess you have to really know where it's at, being such a small beach and all. I like it." The tide was out, and the exposed tidal pools lay helplessly in the warm, noon sun. Jade looked out at the wide expanse of low tide, and, though it was beautiful, without knowing why, it made her anxious. It made her long for the tide to come back and cover the fragile, naked life.

"Yeah, Alta and I have talked about how hard it is for women to just *be* where they want without carrying a machine gun or hiring body guards." Michael smiled at her. "Being one of the dangerous gender in question, I apologize, collectively, you know?"

Jade took two fast sips of the spumante and the bubbles stung her nose. Now she felt ludicrous and exposed. She wondered if Alta had told him. I asked her not to, damn it, she thought, betrayal settling in her stomach. Well, I hardly know her. What should I expect?

"You don't have to apologize for all men, Michael. Don't you think that's kind of silly? I mean, it's not your fault I can't go to unpopulated places." Anger crept into her voice and she was sorry again. But, strangely, his naive apology touched her, disarming her slightly.

"Well, maybe. Being a black man I've got an idea of what you're talking about. The dangerous gender, when it's white, tends to be a little more dangerous. Then we have a very dangerous inflation of the creature in question." Michael laughed.

He paused, seeing Jade's pain pulse under her thin anger. "But it seems most men, when it comes to dealing with women—

white, black, brown, or zebra—treat them like the perpetual nigger. Personally, I think it's envy and fear, in that order."

Alta was on her stomach staring out at the ocean, but obviously listening. The sun felt good on her legs and she enjoyed hearing Michael speak. She only hoped he wouldn't be too obvious or push it too far. She could feel Jade balancing on the edge of trust and distrust, and, for Jade, it was agony.

"Envy and fear?' Jade shot back with more skepticism than she'd intended. "What makes you say that?"

"What I believe probably stems from my father and mother. Of course, I could tell you theories I agree with and all that. About the unbonded male, unbonded even from the Earth he springs from, and how female children have more of a chance for that bonding. It's built in more to feminine nature, and men see it and want it any way they can get it. Like rape." Michael paused, seeing Jade recoil at his words. "Anyway, even in the very beginning, when the chromosomes are being arranged in the fertilized ovum, all life is female, and, then, by a quirk, one chromosome tilts the balance for the fragile offshoot male. Anyway, my father told me that—he's a doctor. My father has a natural reverence for women. Like he says, 'It's not Adam that made Eve—it's the other way 'round. All life springs from the feminine, boy,' he'd say. And it wasn't a phony reverence either. He treated my mother, always, like the equal she is. She still works with him as a nurse. It's really hard to tell who's the doctor and who's the nurse. She's a nurse practitioner and takes over the office, quite competently, as my father would say. She takes no shit, my mom."

Michael laughed and poured the rest of the wine out among the three of them. "Besides, those two love each other, and both of them with tempers too." He laughed again.

"I met them once, so I can vouch for that," Alta said laughing and sipping the lovely, slightly sweet spumante. She considered sitting up, but she didn't want to alter the dynamics, maybe making Jade feel self-conscious with both of them focusing on her. Michael, you are beautiful. Alta closed her eyes and hoped her thought would reach him.

Jade looked directly at Michael, searching his eyes carefully. "Well, then, you were lucky, weren't you? Being how things are, it rather makes you a rarity, I'd say. Maybe even a freak, wouldn't you say?"

Alta glanced up at Jade's face. It was reddening with intensity. Michael registered hurt, only for a moment, then understanding.

Michael laughed softly and said, "Well, if I'm a freak, that's good. The so-called normal ain't normal no more, and what's needed is more of us *freaky* men. Like in my family, all my brothers love and *like* women. I mean, how could we not with our mother being who she *is*?" Michael's dream about his brother, his older brother, came to him now, vividly: his bloody body, his brother's face becoming his own.

"There were three brothers and one sister. My older brother's dead, beaten to death by some white men," Michael spoke softly. "And my sister was raped by a group of them going back to her dorm from a lecture."

"Oh, Michael, I'm so sorry," Jade whispered, tears rising to her eyes, but she stopped them. "I'm so sorry."

"Now, see, you're apologizing for all humanity." Michael smiled. His eyes were gentle. "I guess that's it when you get down to it—we're all human and trying to apologize for and understand each other's cruelty and stupidity. Like my brother— only one of the men is still in jail because he finished him off with a gun, and maybe that was an act of kindness." Here he paused to gather his thoughts; he'd never said this out loud. "And my sister's rapists are out now, but I think she taught them a lesson. They served four years, not much, but for privileged white boys, that's a long time. She's a practicing lawyer now, and she's married to a good man. She's healing. But, I suppose, my brother, he's the one I'm still trying to understand." Sorrow made Michael's voice thick as he remembered his brother's unpredictable sense of humor, his loud belly laugh that could fill a room. He remembered his brother teasing him and, just as suddenly, comforting him with the words, "Cat got your tongue?" His brother had read him most of his childhood stories, being eight years older than him. *Horus,* Michael moaned his name internally.

"Why don't we walk out to the tidal pools and check out the sea anemones?" Alta stood up and stretched. "Come on, you guys. Up." She offered one hand to Michael and one hand to Jade. Then Michael took Jade's other hand, helping her to her feet.

"Well, we have a little circle," Alta said with a laugh. Then they separated and walked, still in a group, to the tidal pools. The ocean was beginning to return, but the fragile life clung to the dark, slippery stones beneath their curious eyes.

"Look at this starfish! It's a purple one. The only thing is if you take them home, they die, so I don't do it anymore," Alta said, admiring its beauty. "Do you know that starfish can grow their organs back? They can actually regenerate."

"Yeah, that's a beauty." Michael bent down to touch it. The starfish was so delicate underneath as its pink tentacles tasted the air. "Horus," he murmured, thinking of his brother's mutilation. Tears rose to his eyes, but he forced them down quickly.

Jade froze where she was. She could hear the sea life screaming for the sea, for the sea's protection. Strong and sudden, wavelike ripples went through her body, and she began to sob in spite of her desire not to. Michael rushed up and held her, and Alta joined them, stroking Jade's long, black braid, her neck, her exposed cheek wet with fast, salty tears.

The first cluster of stars imposed themselves on the hazy purple twilight. They shone with a gentle preparation for the fierce, dark night ahead, when they would glitter without mercy for the dreamers and the ones who dreamt no more. The sea swept the sand possessively; the tidal life was safe again, and the three humans sat close to the fire watching the flames, speaking softly and occasionally, as the warmth of the small fire convinced them of everything sane and good, at bottom, of their own kind. The human race.

"We'll come with you, if you want. I know what a hassle cops can be," Michael said, sipping the dark, rich cabernet, the last of it.

"Are you going in Monday?" Alta asked.

"I guess I will," Jade whispered.

"Let us come with you, okay?" Alta placed a seasoned apple branch in the fire's center and, keeping her silence, watched it catch and blaze.

The men's license plate flashed on and off in Jade's head: COCKEY, COCKEY, COCKEY. "Okay, I'll take you both up on it." Jade closed her eyes and listened to the waves arriving and receding and to the sound of the fire and the presence of her friends, but she was still terrified. The tidal life no longer screamed. Now the scream was in her.

"They aren't going to get away with it, Jade. They may be out on bail, but there's still the whole trial process ahead, and if you hang in there like my sister did, it'll happen. You're a teacher and you have so-called credibility. They picked them up, didn't they?" Michael paused.

"But they're *family men* and they have to go to work tomorrow. Plus, they have clean records, or just kid stuff, as the sheriff said. I bet it's rape," Alta said darkly. "Your lawyer can look all that stuff up, you know."

They sat around the table eating the chicken crêpes Alta had prepared. They sat outside on the patio, facing a gentle, green slope that opened out to the apple orchard. Four white, lotus-shaped candle holders held a small, contained flame, and one brown moth danced between them, unable to make up its mind, unable to choose its particular death. It flew and flirted and danced, sizzling once into the center candle's flame. Each diner had a candle and the extra flame was in the center of the table. A sudden wind threatened to extinguish the candles, and their faces—Michael, Jade, Alta—blended for a moment with the night. Crickets could be heard everywhere at once, and the frogs in the small, flowing creek had begun their nightly chorus to the deep, dark night that sheltered them.

"They're going to get me," Jade almost whispered. "Did you see their faces? They took me apart right there. And they probably have friends, good old boys, just like themselves."

"They don't dare touch you, Jade. They're in big trouble, like right now, man!" Michael said angrily. "We're your friends. You know, the good old people," he added, trying to laugh and change the tone.

"Look, I'm not trying to change the subject, not entirely, anyway." Alta reached over and touched Jade's arm. "But Michael and I made a little fire and slept outside on the summer solstice last year. We prayed to Isis."

"And Osiris, her brother," Michael interjected.

Alta smiled at him. "Nothing elaborate, just a small, personal tribute to the Earth/Sun rotation and the Goddess. We light candles, drink some wine, and count shooting stars." Alta didn't mention their lovemaking when she imagined herself Isis and Michael Osiris, her brother. When she imagined her womb swelling with his child, her belly full of pleasures, the pleasures of the full moon and the Earth tilted toward the sun.

"That's next month, isn't it? The end of June. My mother called her Corn Mother and Changing Woman. It's the same, isn't it?" Jade's face softened in the candlelight remembering her mother talking about such things. She remembered her mother's weaving of Changing Woman; only one, and she kept it in her bedroom. She tried to capture the wonder she'd always felt at the sight of Changing Woman standing in the night with stars dangling down her long, black hair and a golden crescent moon, pointing upward like horns, on the top of her head. In her hands, close to her womb, she held a yellow sun. But it was hard to recapture the wonder because the taste of terror lingered in her mouth.

"Here, have some more wine. This is some good zinfandel, isn't it? Got a case of it from Bruce. You know, the guy who works at the vineyard." Michael poured Jade a glass.

"A Goddess is a Goddess is a Goddess. Gertrude Stein." Alta laughed. "The story goes that Osiris is killed and cut into pieces by his brother, Set, the negative masculine, right? And Isis wanders on the water, the river—the embryonic waters of life, shall we say. I love that image. Well, anyway, she wanders looking for the pieces of him to bring him back to life, to put him back together."

"Here's the best part," Michael said, laughing shortly. "A God is a God is a God."

"You should tell it." Alta smiled at him.

"No, go ahead, I'm listening."

Alta continued. "The only part of him she can't find is his penis."

"Maybe his brother ate it. You know, penis envy." Jade gave a little laugh.

"Probably exactly what happened," Michael said in all seriousness. "That negative masculine has a hard time tolerating the positive masculine, especially nowadays." He mumbled the last words, more to himself, and now his face grew solemn as he waited in the darkness for Alta to finish her story. He'd never told Alta. Only his family knew. His brother had been castrated that night, and the thought that always tormented him was—was he alive when they did it? The thought made a part of his mind blank out. He could go no further. Michael waved the brown moth away angrily.

"Isis makes a penis from the river mud and brings him back to life. That's quite a concept, wouldn't you say?" Alta looked at Jade, then at Michael, with a shy, triumphant smile. "Only the divine feminine, the Goddess, Isis—" Alta looked into Jade's dark, almond eyes and held them for a moment— "Changing Woman, can bring the positive masculine back to life. She *makes* him a penis. I'd say it was men who had penis envy, not women." Alta laughed softly and shook her head the way she'd seen her grandmother do when she'd stated the obvious, but the obvious had to be said for its own sake.

"That's the truth," Michael murmured to himself.

"What'd you say?" Jade asked.

"Why don't you spend summer solstice with us crazy pagans?" Michael's voice was a little too loud, so he quickly lowered it. "Tell us stories about Changing Woman and drink wine."

"You'll be safe out here. I sleep out by myself almost all summer. Besides, Osiris will be with us." Alta giggled wickedly.

Again Jade sensed their sensual intimacy, and, again, she felt like an intruder. The Changing Woman stories she'd heard from her mother had only women in them, and, come to think of it, Jade thought, she wove Changing Woman after *he* killed himself. Jade gave a deep sigh. "Look, two's company, three's a crowd, and besides, I'll probably just end up ruining it for you both. I'm not ready to do something like this right now, that's all."

"I have a high-powered pellet gun I keep for roving dogs. I'll take it with us. Jade, we both want you to come. I mean, there's no wrong way or right way to our little ritual. It's just a small gesture to those immense forces out there. Join us, okay? Isis will be pleased." Alta laughed, looking out at the moonwashed orchard.

"Osiris would be pleased," Michael echoed in a joking tone as he looked up to the bright, hot stars. He didn't see the moth extinguish itself in his candle.

"Are you sure it's no hassle having me stay like this? I guess I feel like a baby not going home, but you can bet those bastards have figured out where I live by now." Jade began to cry. "Maybe I should've left it alone, you know, Alta?"

"I don't know, only you could make that decision, but I'm glad you did it and like I said, or rather like I'm trying to say, I *want* you to stay here till you feel okay about it. Anyway, I'm really used to living with people. I've always had kids, since I was fifteen. I had April at fifteen," Alta said with a slight smile. "I mean, I like, even love, being alone, but I'm not a fanatic about it."

They sat on the couch, facing each other. The small lamp in the corner was on, otherwise they were surrounded by darkness.

"It gets pretty dark here at night, doesn't it?" Jade began to dread going to bed by herself in all that darkness, and at the same she reprimanded herself harshly. Grow up, Jade, little baby, come on and grow up, damn it. "Do you have any outside lights?"

"There's a couple, but I keep them off at night. It's better camouflage actually and, besides, the stars come closer. I only use the outside lights for guests once in a while."

"Do you plan to sleep outside tonight?" Jade asked nervously.

"No, but I can see a sky full of stars from my bedroom windows. Come on, I'll show you."

Jade followed Alta into the bedroom and faced the sliding glass doors; Alta had placed her bed right next to it. "Do you close your curtains at night?"

"Haven't you noticed? I don't have any curtains. When I lived in the city, San Francisco, I dreamed of a place like this—a place where I wouldn't have to have curtains, so I don't."

"No one's ever bothered you?"

"No. I'm almost a mile off the road, if you can call that one-lane thing a road. It's funny, that's why the place was so cheap, you know, the bad roads. But that's exactly why these places are so safe, their relative inaccessibility."

"I suppose it's true. Being that my place is in town I've got to have curtains. I even have a couple of street lights, how's that? But I think I'd still have curtains here." Jade shivered, looking out at the silent hills. A half-golden moon was about to set.

"Why would you want curtains here?" Alta asked, glancing at her. "Look, you'd close all that out. I mean, just look at those stars, the moon."

"Stars make me lonely. In the desert you could swear they hiss at you." Jade made a gesture of shielding her eyes with her hand and continued to speak in a low voice. "My father hated the stars. He used to call them 'The Immortals.' I guess they just reminded him how mortal he was. My mom would soothe me with the wind, with songs about the wind, so that, even now, the wind makes me feel safe like a blanket. 'The wind is an Earth blanket,' she'd tell me. Blankets, curtains. I guess I need them."

"That's beautiful," Alta murmured.

"My mother wove a rug with Changing Woman on it, with stars all down her long, black hair. I guess my mother loved the stars, Alta. She told me, when I was little, that our souls go back home to the stars after we die and that little children *come* from the stars." Jade looked up toward their faraway light. "I wonder why I remember my father's hatred more than my mother's love?"

"The point is, you're remembering her love right now." Alta touched Jade's long, thick braid. "May I take your braid out? I'd love to brush your hair. May I?" Alta's eyes were soft in the darkness, and her own dark hair was long and full around her face.

"Okay," Jade whispered, shivering at her touch. She looked out at the stars, staring at the darkness between clusters and then at the brightest ones. She wished she were a newly arrived, innocent child, instead of somewhere in the middle, lost and stranded.

"I've always thought of you as a black orchid," Alta laughed softly, undoing Jade's braid and running her fingers through its length that ended bluntly at her small, subtly curved hips.

Jade couldn't speak. Alta's words and hands were overwhelming to her. No one had touched her hair this way since Grace. No, she reminded herself. No, those men touched my hair. They held me by the hair. Jade's hands flew out, and she caught herself on the wide windows.

"Are you okay?"

"I just remembered those guys holding my hair," Jade gasped.

"Forget them, Jade. Forget them for right now, okay? It's just me going to brush your beautiful hair. May I?"

Jade nodded yes.

"Why don't we sit?" Alta suggested. The deep-toned wind chimes moved in the wind as Alta began to brush Jade's hair, crown to hip, crown to hip, over and over. "How long did you live with your lover?"

"Three years," Jade murmured. "Two years in New Mexico and one here. I don't think Grace liked it here, not really. She's in Bali now."

"Why didn't you go with her? Do you still love her?"

"Yes, I still love her, but I couldn't go with her." Jade surrendered to Alta's hands, to their gentleness. In that moment she decided to trust her. "I think she wanted to be with men again. I mean, I think she still loved me, but I just wasn't enough anymore, that's all."

"Have you ever made love with a man?" Alta asked gently.

"When I was very young, but it never really pleased me. It was too brutal—always that physical fear of being penetrated too deeply and being hurt, and I guess they were gentle, but it was always like they wanted you to say ouch, it hurts, so that they'd know they were so big. I just couldn't stand it anymore and then I met Grace, and everything was different. But my mother couldn't accept it, so I left."

"I know what you mean about the penetration bit. You know, I think you have the most beautiful hair I've ever seen or touched."

"Thank you," Jade said, arching her neck forward under Alta's soft touch.

"Michael and another lover are the only ones, thus far, to not ever hurt me. It's like they don't need to hurt a woman to *be* a man. I must tell you, Michael's one of the most gentle, and the best, lovers I've ever had, truly."

"Do you love him?" Jade's voice was high and thin like a child's.

"I don't think I could help but love him, he's such a fine, fine man. I've lived with two men. My first husband, the father of my kids, was a complex but decidedly cruel man. I'll tell you about all that sometime, but not now. I don't want to ruin our time. Anyway, the second man I lived with was rather simple, and not as cruel, but cruel nonetheless, and what it was, really, was that neither of them loved women, or liked them for that matter. As for Michael, all I can say is that he's not cruel, though he's both complex and simple." Alta gathered Jade's curtain of silky, black hair in both hands, holding it up for a moment, feeling its weight. Then she let it drop, spreading it back around her shoulders.

"Well, the moon's gone for the night." Alta sighed suddenly.

"Have you ever made love to a woman?" Jade asked, closing her eyes. She made herself breathe in and out as evenly as possible.

"Yes, a long time ago with my best friend. Unfortunately, it freaked her out so we never did it again." Alta's breath was coming fast now, and her nipples hardened against her cotton dress so pleasantly.

"Did you like it?" Jade's mouth was dry with excitement. "Yes, I did very much, in fact." Alta's hands followed Jade's hair down to her breasts, her small, soft breasts, and rested them there. Then, slowly, Alta began to trace Jade's nipples through her silk top, feeling them harden like her own.

Jade moaned, throwing her head back. Then she remembered Michael and said, "But what about Michael? Won't he mind, Alta?"

"I don't think so," Alta said, moving around to face Jade. She looked into her open gaze. "I really don't think so, and, besides, at this moment, I don't care."

Jade moved forward, meeting Alta's moist, open mouth. Quickly, she found her tongue and, like friendly snakes, their tongues played with each other. They discovered each other's mouths, the electric messages of their dark, moist hunger. Now they were both on their knees, facing each other, coming together, and undulating against each other like the ecstatic snakes in their hungry mouths.

The phone was ringing. Alta reached for it and missed, but got it the second time on the fifth ring. Jade had gone to work, and her first client was due in two hours. Michael, she thought. He was taking part in the sessions today.

"Mom, it's April. Were you awake?" April's voice was loud as though she were speaking over a bullhorn.

"Almost," Alta answered thickly. "Could you lower your voice two notches?" Alta laughed. "You sound like you're down the street. How're you doing?"

"I'm thinking of coming up to see you tomorrow. Would that be okay? I feel so fat and restless, so I thought I'd come up before the steering wheel gets in the way. I stopped throwing up, but now every time I move the way he or she doesn't want me to I get kicked in the ribs. Jesus, does it get worse? Like I have two more months to go, and I'm starting to wonder if I can stand it, and then it's got to come out, as *you* know, and I have a hard time imagining that part. But then if I just calm down and have a little talk with him, or her, I feel like such a monster, first, and then I feel like such *a good mother*. Mom, I think I'm going totally nuts. And sometimes I just *hate* Steve," April's voice caught for a moment, "like just the way he even smells or eats his food, and when he makes some stupid comment, like last night, about how some women never lose the weight they gain being pregnant, and I can tell he's enjoying it, like really enjoying it, Mom, I could just *kill* him. I mean, here I am trying to be a good mother, right now, though I'm not entirely sure I want something like this to happen to me, and this *asshole* starts telling me really shitty things about my goddamned weight, and now that I'm seven months pregnant I'd say it's too late for shit like this . . . "

"April," Alta interrupted. "April, I've always thought Steve was an asshole, remember? But you loved him and he loved you, and so you got married. I hope I'm not saying I-told-you-so, but I guess I'm trying to say, *remember?* Anyway, yes, you, or I sure did, feel bad enough in the last months." Alta paused to give her words emphasis. "Pregnancy is hard work. You feel bad enough being pregnant sometimes without the man you love, or in other words, the man who made you pregnant—" Alta laughed gently, trying to soften the situation; she knew it wouldn't help April now to inflame her frustration— "making crappy comments. Look, come on up and bring your camera."

April began to cry. She was angry at herself, and then she was angry at her mother, as though her mother had failed to save her from herself. And a part of her was already sorry she'd confided so much. Now she knows everything, April groaned inwardly. Well, almost. She blew her nose and shifted her position on the kitchen chair.

The child rolled in her womb like a captured seal, and then she rolled again, readjusting her frail, but strengthening limbs in the wonderful, close darkness that had no name, no fear, no desire, in the wonderful liquid that merged exquisitely with the absolute darkness. And the constant sound of the universe, her mother's heart—that was not separated from the darkness, liquid, warmth, the fleshy boundaries—permeated the child's body in a terrible bliss.

"Look, we'll talk about the baby coming out. Every woman feels that way. It's our moment of truth, like the matadors, only instead of killing something, you're giving birth. Anyway, there's a lot I'd like to tell you, but, frankly, April, you haven't asked, and I guess I've been afraid to intrude on you. You know, your own life and all. So I'm glad you called and we've talked, okay?" Alta imagined her daughter's face. It blended, so easily, into the twelve-year-old's, the daughter of April's childhood, not the grown-up daughter that defined herself in sharp opposition to what her mother was, and wasn't.

April gained control of herself and said, "I'll be there at one probably, and I'll spend the night if that's okay. Should I bring anything?" April saw her mother's eyes staring at her, sizing her up, over the telephone.

"Bring what you like, April, but just bring yourself. A friend of mine's staying here for a while, but, as you know, there's plenty of room. Her name's Jade. I think you'll like her. Anyway, in case I'm with a client, just let yourself in. You know where everything is."

Jade, April thought to herself, another exotic person, like Michael and his earring. Her old anger crept up on her—Why can't she be normal, why can't things ever be normal? "Why did you name your horse Night Mare, anyway?" April instantly regretted her question.

Alta laughed loudly. "I'll tell you about that too, if you want." She paused. She never knew anymore whether to talk to her daughter like she used to. "Better to ride your nightmares than be ridden by them. Better to let your nightmare be your guide, April."

"Oh, Mom, I never know what you're talking about," April said with exasperation.

"Oh, yes you do. Don't forget your camera."

As Alta made the bed an envelope fell to the rug. It had her name on it. From Jade, of course, she thought, opening it. "Please wear them, Jade," the note said. Alta opened the paper towel tucked into the envelope and found the twin jade horses, rearing up in their perfection of stone. She walked over to the sliding glass doors, opening them wide to the risen sun and cool morning air. A fine fog lay in the valley, but it would soon burn clear and the day would be warm. Though the day would be beautiful, she longed for more rain. "More rain for the summer ahead," she sighed, thinking of the old women, her apple trees. The first time she saw the apple orchard, on a rainy fall morning before the trees had been pruned to bear fruit, they'd been covered with Spanish moss—bright, deep greens, lacy like shawls—that had hung gracefully over their ancient limbs. That's how Alta always thought of her trees, though now they were pruned to bear profusely, like young women.

Alta walked out to the small deck to watch the emerging pale gold sun—the young, feminine sun—spread its light from the clearing matrix of the sky to the Earth matrix—fertile, yielding, unyielding, wild—below. Alta put the jade horses up to the sun's clear light to let them dance with translucence, the true color of their souls; their tiny hooves pawed the pale gold light with wild joy. Alta laughed out loud with sheer delight and placed them, one by one, into her ears.

Michael was engrossed in the couple's problems, their inability to communicate even the simplest things to each other, and he felt their pain. It was real pain. But he was tempted, very tempted, to tell them, "Look, you just don't love each other anymore. These things happen. It's no one's fault, really, and only evolution matters, so why don't you try evolving here a little bit and at least be *kind* to one another and keep loving your children, or, rather, *learn* to love your children, at the very least, and you might just learn to love each other, yourselves. Damn, shut up and stop that mindless bickering, the endless bickering about who's right and who's wrong and who's goddamned *fault it is*." Instead, he watched Alta respond to the woman's usual flood of tears, and he noticed the jade earrings swaying back and forth as she spoke.

"Chris, Laura's trying to tell you something here. *I* can see you tuning her out. Okay, what's going on with you?"

Michael leaned forward. "I think most men shut off when tears start. We're afraid of all that emotion. We're afraid *we'll* cry. What do you think, Chris?"

Chris looked up at Michael, startled at being revealed to the quick, and curiously angry at this man's betrayal. A black man with a goddamned earring, he noted in defense. What does *he* know about being a *man*, Chris asked himself, linking hands with his race, the race of White Men. He looked down at his shoes, examining the leather's grain.

"I suppose," Chris paused, insinuating his disbelief and emphasizing his generous patience overall, "that's probably true on some level, but, to be honest, Laura's tears bore me. I'm sorry, but it's true."

"I see. Why do you think she's crying?" Michael asked. Command crept into his tone.

"She's got it too damned easy, that's what I think."

"Would you understand if she had had an affair?" Alta asked in a quiet voice.

"I don't think that's relevant here," Chris shot back angrily.

"Oh, yes it is relevant! It sure as hell is relevant! You get to fuck up and I get to clean up!" Laura yelled, crying louder.

"Oh, for Christ's sake, we have every goddamn cleaning appliance known or invented by man, Laura! Grow up!" Chris felt his rage overtake him in front of these strangers and he hated Laura, intensely, for dragging him here. Stupid cunt, he thought, blowing her stupid nose, forever crying about some fucking thing.

"I think what Laura's telling you is that she feels things aren't equal between you." Alta kept her voice low. She glanced at Michael and continued. "I'd say you have most of the power in this relationship. What do you think, Chris?"

"I think that's the stupidest thing I've ever heard. What power? I don't have any power! Just because I'm a man doesn't mean I have power, come on!" Chris clenched his fists with the effort not to punch something.

Everyone sat in silence. Alta signalled Michael with her eyes to be quiet. He signalled back with his, okay. They waited. They all waited.

Finally, Laura spoke. Her eyes focused on the window and the blur of the blue sky beyond. "You've got power *over me* and you don't even love me. You've got power over the children and you don't love them either, not really." Laura's voice was strained with the effort not to cry again. She was a large woman, tall and pretty and blond like her husband. She buried her strong, graceful hands in her lap, and, turning in her seat, she faced her husband. She tried to force him to meet her gaze, but he refused.

"Chris, do you love me?"

"I come home every night, don't I?"

"That's not an answer." Laura's tears fell again of their own accord as her strong, graceful hands fluttered to her face.

The silence resumed.

"How would you like some pork spareribs tonight, my treat?" Michael asked, bringing Alta a glass of chilled Chablis. "I'll barbecue out here."

"Sounds good to me. I'll clean up." Alta grazed Michael's cheek with her hands and touched his star earring as he bent forward. She wondered if she should tell Michael about Jade. "My daughter's coming tomorrow. You know, Miss Prim and Proper," Alta laughed.

Michael tapped one of the jade horses, lightly, with his finger. "Well, are you and Jade lovers now?" His eyes stared into hers without blinking, but Alta saw his hurt. He reached into her where she had allowed him entrance, and he wanted the truth.

"Yes," the words came, "but I love you too, Michael. In fact, if anything, I love you more. Do you understand?" Alta got up and walked the few steps between them, taking him into her arms.

Michael stood up to meet her, tears on his cheeks. "Then why, Alta? Why?"

"I seem to care about her, and I guess I needed to, but I do love you, Michael, I do. Do you understand, at all?" Alta began to cry.

He didn't answer. He couldn't answer.

"Look, I'm sorry if I've hurt you. I'm really sorry. But we've never talked about not being with others, have we?"

Michael just looked at her, holding her by the elbows, and, without speaking, he picked Alta up and carried her into the bedroom, slamming the door behind him with his foot.

"What do you want? What do you want, Alta?" Michael had made her ask for his penis after his tongue had made her explode with ripples of orgasms. Ripples and ripples of orgasms, from the first eruption, so intense it made her see white light, bathing them in a shimmering, white light. But first she'd tried to make him come in her suddenly hungry mouth; her mouth so hungry for his hard gift. She'd wanted to taste him, but he'd refused. Instead, he'd withdrawn himself, facing her, making her face him, asking her, "What do you want? What do you want, Alta?"

"I want you to fuck me. I want you to fuck me, fuck me, fuck me . . . " And he had fucked the white light back into her. Back into her body with his lovely, alive penis, never hurting her; not ever hurting her. And fucking the white, shimmering, white light into her, Michael fucked his own soul, and so he couldn't hurt her, not willingly, because in that moment she became his soul. And that was what so many men really hated, resented, killed for, raped for—their own feminine soul.

Alta guided Night Mare toward her favorite field, the one with the wild iris, Indian paintbrush, and the small year-round spring. The late afternoon sun was warm, and the horse's mane reflected its heat onto her as she lay flat against it. The animal's rich, musky smell comforted her, and some of the black mane filtered across Alta's eyes. She clung to her horse like a child, feeling her gait and the uneven earth beneath them. Alta loved the rhythm of her horse; it was better than her own.

Later as she'd lain in his arms, Michael had asked her if she was going to make love to Jade again. "Do you think it's wrong for a woman to make love to another woman?" she'd asked. "No, certainly not. Like any real connection, it's perfectly fine. But I've been your lover and *we've* shared a lot, haven't we? That's what I'm talking about, not if it's right or wrong." "Of course, you're right. You have every right to ask me, of course."

She'd traced his profile with her fingers, feeling him with a sense of great luxury as though she were blind, and he'd turned his head toward her and looked at her, knowing what her answer would be. She'd have to think about it, and she would, and then she'd be as honest as possible. Then he realized how much he loved her.

"Do you love me?" Michael had asked.

"Yes and yes again, I love you, Michael."

"Then why do you need Jade?"

"Do you really want to know?" Her tone had grown serious, cautionary.

"Yes," he'd insisted, but gently.

"I think she's exquisite. There's something terribly exquisite about Jade, like a part of myself I can't see, but I can see in Jade. It's like I know she's feeling what I feel, sometimes, so strongly, and I know she feels me feeling her. I think with a mother and a daughter that's often terribly threatening until they're able to meet on a par. And in our culture, patriarchal culture, as you know, that meeting's discouraged, mainly because the feminine tends to be crippled. They cripple her and women, many women, continue to go along with the crippling. Well, we've talked about all this, but women help cripple other women, their own daughters, so that if they have to be threatened, it's only the men threatening them. A woman getting her own power breaks that agreement between women."

Alta stopped to look at Michael, to see if he was following her. He was, she could see. "You asked, Michael." She could also see his pain.

"Please, go on, I'm listening." He watched her mouth move and her face relax and grow concentrated as she continued.

"Okay, well, beyond the gut level fact that I find Jade very attractive, beautiful even—do you think she's beautiful?"

Michael smiled, slightly. "Yes, I do."

"Well, beyond that basic fact, truth, admission, this is what I'm feeling. In other words, not only is Jade exquisite, she is strong. She's *present*. Like in class, I kind of loved watching her just move around and talk to everyone. I think I had a crush and didn't know it." Alta looked at Michael's face, but he just looked back at her.

"I guess I've never gone all the way with that one, in the sense of sustaining it, that deep intimacy with a woman, or really, daring it and having it, that intimacy returned. It's like I've known it in my head, from observation, but not from my own experience. Oh, I don't know—a little, or a lot, with Jackie, some other women friends, and my daughter, and I continue to dance around it, but April and I aren't quite on a par, not yet. And then again, intimacy with sexuality really is another dimension, and I've never fully experienced it with a woman. I guess I sense this possibility with Jade the way I sensed it with you, Michael. The way we empower each other, do you see?"

"You want it all, is that it?" Michael laughed deep in his throat, with admiration, and envy.

"Have you ever made love to a man?"

"I told you before, no."

"Do you ever think about it?"

"Occasional fantasy, but the truth is, I'm not into it, that's all. Maybe it's because my dad sat me on his lap till I was twelve and hugged me, and hugs me to this day, and he read me stories, lying next to me without any self-consciousness whatsoever. I don't know, maybe that's resolved for me. Or maybe I just plain have different needs. Maybe it's as simple as that." Michael laughed, pulling Alta to him. "I like women. I like what makes you different than me. I love your pussy, your smell, your womb all secret up inside you. Yeah, I love it all, woman." Then his face and voice grew solemn. "I can understand how you feel about Jade, but I don't know if I can handle it, your making love with each other. I just don't know, Alta. I mean, it's got to affect us eventually, don't you think?"

Alta slid down from Night Mare, running her hands down the length of her smooth, dark body as she began to nibble the fresh, sweet grass. It was greenest and thickest around the spring. Alta cupped her hands and drank, splashing the icy water on her face and neck. She imagined Michael preparing the meal, cleaning vegetables for the salad. She imagined Jade bringing wine for the meal, coming into the kitchen. But she couldn't imagine them speaking to each other. "What will they say?" Alta asked out loud.

She took the water bag from her shoulder and filled it, listening to the water flow from deep beneath the ground. Clusters of open, purple iris smiled at her. In the distance someone started a chainsaw, but it was faint.

The icy, flowing water, deep from within the Earth, was wise. It only said, "Drink, my child, drink."

"I brought a couple of bottles of red and white wine," Jade said, putting the bottles on the kitchen counter. Jade felt shy alone with Michael.

He stopped cutting the onions and looked at her. "How're you doing with everything? Have you talked to your lawyer?"

Jade began to open a cabernet. "It's coming along, I guess, but she said it'll probably be pretty sticky because I waited the two weeks to report it. Do you want some of this wine, Michael?" Jade watched him move to the refrigerator with his usual slow grace, and she saw how his hands were gentle with everything he touched, yet firm. She relaxed as he turned and smiled at her.

"Sure, sounds good. How're you doing? I know it took a while for my sister to feel like herself again." Michael saw the smooth line of her cheek tremble, and for some reason he thought of Alta's cheek, not as smooth as Jade's, but still beautiful.

"Did your sister get pregnant?" Jade whispered.

"I'm sorry, I didn't hear you."

Jade met Michael's even gaze and, raising her voice slightly, asked again, "Did your sister get pregnant, Michael?"

"She was on the pill, no. Are you pregnant? Is that it?" Every defense he thought he'd keep in reserve to keep himself from getting too involved evaporated as he watched Jade's body slump forward, nearly dropping her wine.

"Here, let me take that. Goddamn it, Jade, are you pregnant?" Michael took her in his arms, feeling her smallness, her exquisiteness as Alta said, he thought, against him. Jade began to cry. Her arms were limp around his waist, but she let him hold her.

"I found out for sure this afternoon. I'm scheduled to have an abortion next week. When does it stop, Michael, you know?"

"I know, I know," Michael murmured, stroking her long, black braid over and over.

The sun was beginning to set as Alta started home with the filled water bag slung around her back. Night Mare was just as comfortable in the dark as the day, and Alta often rode at night with her over the hills and out to some neighbor's hills that overlooked the Pacific, about twenty miles away. Or, rather, the Pacific could be seen as a smooth shimmer in the distance on full moon nights. Alta had always wanted to ride Night Mare to the ocean and take some camping gear and spend the night hidden in the dunes.

The smell of the sea drifted in on a westerly wind, teasing her nostrils. "Do you smell that, girl? That's the ocean, remember? We'll go this summer, just you and I, Night Mare." As Alta crested the hill the lights of her house came into view. She could smell Michael's barbecue and she smiled to herself.

Jade had tied her backstrap loom to a hook set into the giant oak that dominated the main patio. The hook was meant for a hammock that hadn't been set out yet. Jade rolled the finished cloth toward herself and continued her pattern with the promise of calm it always gave her. Weaving, to her, was always peace. Her face reflected the deepening sunset colors, and the tiny jade and turquoise birds that dangled from her ears held still with her concentration. Michael's words lingered in her gathering calm: "I've got these green eyes because some white guy over a hundred years ago raped some scared shitless, young black girl. So, here I am, right?" "Are you saying I should have this baby?" Jade's body had stiffened and pulled away. Michael had gazed at her with his deep green eyes, an infinite tenderness. "No, I'm not saying that. I'm just saying what's true.

I think women should be in charge of human evolution from here on out as much as possible. Definitely have your abortion."

Jade glanced up at the streaks of magentas and reds and saw Night Mare and Alta, a merged black mass, coming slowly toward the house. She untied the rope from behind her back and rolled it carefully into a bundle.

"She's coming, Michael. Let me help, okay? I even feel hungry smelling that stuff."

"I felt her coming."

"Did you?"

"I almost always do."

"I see," Jade sighed.

Eight

Jade spread her legs. Her slender, milky-thighed, soft-thighed, leading-to-her-womb-thighed, legs. She spread them voluntarily. In fact, she was paying for it. She was paying to be delivered from life. From the life that had wedged itself in her womb. The small, innocent life that had uncoiled itself from the unspeakable violence of rape. Jade spread her legs, wide, very wide, and wept, welcoming death.

The sound of the machine was terrible. Never, ever, will I allow machine or man to enter me again, her mind shrieked. "Never, ever, never, ever," she murmured very, very softly.

The last client of the day was gone, and Jade slept in April's old room. Nothing of April's remained in it, but Alta still thought of it as April's old room. When it had been April's, the ceiling had been a bright sun-yellow with white walls; now the ceiling was a pale moon-lilac with soft cream walls. A black flower-patterned futon took the place of her white lace-quilted brass bed. Kerosene lamps and two strong spotlights overhead took the place of her assorted table lamps covered with white, lace hankies she'd found at secondhand stores. Where April had hung white lace table cloths for curtains, Alta hung a plain muslin Japanese draw-shade. In the far corner of the room, by the window, was a large black vase with tall, purple Japanese irises from the front of the house. There was a large Navajo rug with bold, black patterns against a deep purple-red background on the smooth wooden floor.

Jade's Japanese and Navajo, Alta thought, looking in on her, surveying the room, its blend of Japanese and Navajo. Perhaps the room was meant for her. Perhaps the room was always meant for her. Alta breathed deeply and expelled her breath in a long sigh, because she couldn't imagine not making love to Michael—his lovely, erect penis—his compelling, green eyes—his mouth, his soul.

April had spent the night in her old room. Jade switched to the guest room, gladly relinquishing April's old room to her for the night. "These masks are pretty spooky, Mom. Do you expect me *sleep* with them in here?" Her laugh had been almost angry, as though her mother's insistence on nonconformity was a betrayal, a personal betrayal to her. Her daughter.

"I'll take them down if you want, April. I guess you have to get used to them, but they are beautiful."

"Where'd you get them?" April asked in an accusatory tone.

"Michael gave me this one," Alta pointed to the monkey mask. "And we bought the jaguar mask on our trip to the Yucatan." Alta saw the resentment in her daughter's eyes.

"Do you and he ever plan to get married or anything like that? Like live together? It must get lonely here." April sounded like the older one, like the mother.

"I'm not lonely, and I don't think I'll ever marry anyone again, though I do care for Michael a lot. So, how's this child coming along?" Alta asked, changing the subject, feeling the beginnings of anger in the center of her chest.

"Here, feel," April said, taking her mother's hand and placing it on her great belly. "Do you feel him rolling around?" April laughed. "I sure don't want to do this again. One kid's enough for me."

"She's a good swimmer. I bet she looks like me." Alta smiled with sudden pleasure, feeling the child's movement like a jolt of electricity, almost sexual, from the new life that hid in her daughter's dark, warm womb.

"Why do you say *she*, Mom?" Exasperation edged her words.

"I dreamt you had a daughter. Remember dreaming, April? Have you dreamt your child yet?" Alta's eyes indicated her rippling belly. The baby stretched against the limits of her mother's flesh, listening not only to her mother's heart, but to the voices too. The voices that rose and fell. Certain tones made her cringe and certain tones made her expand. Now she was becoming restless in the shrinking space, the god space, the dark, beautiful space that once cradled her with its dark welcome: creation. Now she was readying for expulsion into the world of light, breath. Life.

April's eyes filled with tears. They rolled, wet and hot, down her splotchy-red cheeks. Her thick, black, shiny hair was cut short to her chin line, and a hair clip held one side away from her face, revealing a gold hoop earring. It looked heavy on her ear lobe as it pulled downward, stretching the lobe slightly.

Alta put her arms around April and held her. "What's wrong? Oh, what's wrong, April?" Tears stung Alta's eyes.

"Everything, Mom, just everything."

"What do you mean, everything?"

"I don't know, everything." April knew Steve was fucking someone on the side, and he was endlessly critical of her now, but she just couldn't tell her mother. No, it's bad enough, April decided.

Alta felt the baby kick in rapid, furious movements against her own belly, as she held her daughter, and she remembered her own pregnancy with April, unmarried and alone at fourteen. Barely tolerated by her mother, on welfare, Hugh avoiding her. Alta knew about *everything*.

Isn't this a great place to have breakfast?" Alta indicated the large greyish-blue, ghostly bird, so thin that when it turned to face the onlooker it disappeared. Beyond it was the tide. And beyond that the thin line of the horizon. And beyond that Hawaii, Japan. Japan—where Jade's father had come from when he was twenty-four to get his doctorate in biology research from Stanford. Alta remembered Jade's words: "His father, my grandfather, was killed in Hiroshima. My father should've been with him, but he was being punished for something he did at school. So, because of his punishment he lived. He could never get over that, I think. That because he'd been punished, he'd lived. They lost a lot of family in Hiroshima. A surviving aunt, his sister, later gave birth to a monster that died shortly after birth. So, he became a research scientist and came to the enemy's schools to learn their secrets. That's what he said once. And marry a true American, right? My mother, Changing Woman . . . " Alta remembered Jade's sad, gentle laughter.

"Great blue herons. I love to watch them fly. They're so silent." April gazed out at the bird, peacefully.

"Remember the time when we first moved up here? You and I came to the beach one morning when you played hooky with my permission—" Alta smiled. "—and we saw our first great blue heron together. Remember you tried to get a photograph of it, but it didn't turn out too good. Remember as it flew away, it was so huge and silent?"

April nodded. "Yes, I do. It was kind of foggy, wasn't it? Too bad I left the camera at the house, shit. I wish something would scare it up so it'll fly." Maybe remembering is almost as good as a photograph, she thought. Liar, you just flaked out, but I do wish it would fly. I *will* photograph my birth for my photo thesis, and because I *want* to. Steve can just shove it with his reasons why I shouldn't, stupid bastard. I wish it would fly, right now. Come on, April urged the awkward, graceful, silly, lovely bird. Come on, she urged it in her mind—fly.

"Do you like living in the city?" Alta asked, breaking the silence.

"Not really. It feels more dangerous. But, then, look what happened to Jade right here. Of course, if there's a nuclear holocaust, I'll go first, but from what I've heard about survival, I think I'd prefer it that way." The child inside of her readjusted herself, forcing April to sit up straighter. She sighed with discomfort. Then she remembered she was no longer singular, but two: a child and herself. She closed her eyes. She could imagine her own death, but not the child's. April opened her eyes, forcing the thought away from her. Not the child, she told the great blue heron silently, willing it to fly, but it ignored her.

"How long's Jade going to be staying with you?" April asked, trying to neutralize a gathering sense of sorrow.

"I guess till she feels safe again. Besides, I have plenty of room. Probably a few more weeks." Alta paused, trying to read her daughter's eyes, but they were guarded as April stared at the unwavering bird perched on its slender legs in the powerful, invisible wind.

Alta continued. "It's a crime we have to think in those terms, about how it'd be better to die immediately in a nuclear exchange, war, or whatever they call it. I used to worry about you and Ian having a chance to grow up. Now, I suppose, you'll have to worry about your own child. Some legacy."

The wind outside was strong, smoothing the sand dunes of all human footprints. Alta could see the calm they surveyed was possible because of the window that shielded them from the wind. Only the bird was unshakable, because it gave no resistance to the wind.

Alta leaned forward as though to tell April a secret. "Don't laugh, I just want to say this—if it ever happens, you know, the holocaust, think of the great blue heron and so will I." Her eyes were intense as she took her daughter in, pregnant, as though for the last time. She tasted that sorrow and then switched it firmly back to the present.

"Why don't you stay another night? I'd like that. We'll cheer up, no more sad stuff." Alta smiled at April.

"It's a deal, about the great blue heron. I'm glad you said it—I was thinking it, really," April said in a toneless voice. Now the secret to her sorrow refused to be silent. Love was like that; it had to know everything.

"Steve would love me to stay another night," April blurted out. "Another night with his honey, and here I am in the final stages of pregnancy." She began to cry.

"Do you want a Bloody Mary? I'd like one." Alta placed her hand over her daughter's. "You know, April, I've always had a secret name for Steve. You know, my own secret name for him?"

April looked up at her mother. "What?"

"Steve the Slime, or Slimeball for short."

April looked at her mother's serious face, and as the first contortions of laughter shook her body, she repeated the word *slimeball* until it became a gasp between breath and tears.

"Jesus, take it easy. You haven't even heard the worst of it," Alta said, laughing with her.

"You mean there's more?" April managed to ask.

"Honey, that's just the tip of the iceberg. But first I'm getting some Bloody Marys. You want one, don't you? Then we'll tear that sucker apart." Alta stood up and noticed the couple, a man and a woman, next to them, horrified by their exchange. In public.

"Shit! Just make it strong!" April continued to laugh by herself. Then she noticed the baby was still and quiet. She placed her hands on her enormous belly. "Your daddy's a slimeball, honey, I'm sorry to tell you."

"A real class show," the man said loudly.

"Is there a problem?" Alta asked with a false calm.

"We came here for a peaceful breakfast, if you know what I mean." The man strove for authority. The woman sat like a statue, without any expression.

April suddenly looked embarrassed and blew her nose. She looked at her mother and held her breath. Here it comes, she thought, and almost began giggling again.

Alta felt like picking her water glass up and dumping it on his well-to-do head. Instead, she said, "Hey, man, that's life. You know, like tough shit. Or as they say in Russia, tough shitsky."

"Or as they say in southern Russia, tough shitsky, you all!" April added. Their gales of laughter returned, and all April saw was the couple leaping to their feet and rushing away. "I forgot about that one, Mom. God . . . "

"Goddess."

"Oh, Jesus, okay, Goddess, I love those old stupid jokes. Remember Ian used to drive me up the wall with them?"

Their drinks arrived. Two tall, chilly Bloody Marys.

"I ordered double shots. Are you ready?" Alta laughed. "Go ahead, you toast. You know, you're going to have to do something eventually about Slimeball. In the meantime, I want you to take care of yourself. Right?

April nodded her head. Then she lifted her glass and said, "Here's to all the old stupid jokes. May they save my life. And fuck 'em," her eyes indicated the empty table next to them, "if they can't dance!"

The great blue heron rose awkwardly, but once in the air it became the color of the air as it skimmed the dunes and disappeared. Neither April or Alta noticed the bird fly away.

Michael fingered Jade's backstrap loom and asked, "Is she almost done? It looks like it." He indicated the multicolored, thickly fringed panels lying across the back of a kitchen chair.

"One more panel and I have a poncho with a hood. Isn't it amazing, these patterns? She can do so much with a little backstrap loom, and I'm still struggling to get the big one to work my way. Last week was our last class, but I'm planning to take summer session." Alta knew Michael had something to say. She could feel him gathering himself.

"Wasn't that curry delicious?" Alta finished her glass of wine. "You want some more?" she asked, indicating the half-empty bottle of wine.

"Sure. How's Jade doing being back at her place?" Michael watched Alta's hands. He reached into his pocket and brought out a joint, lighting it. It was mild and sweet, his own harvest.

"She's okay, I guess, but she's still in a lot of pain and worried about those guys. They're just out there roaming around at large, right?" Alta took a small drag, held her breath and exhaled the gentle smoke. "I like homegrown. It doesn't make you cough to death, and the strong stuff clouds my brain for a couple of days. Besides, I don't like helping big business," she laughed. "This is nice. Anyway, I asked her to stay longer, but she said she was beginning to feel like a baby. Plus, as she said, she's paying rent and all."

"Are you sorry she's gone?" Michael took another drag and waited.

"Well, she's not exactly gone, like forever. She'll be here for the barbecue Saturday. It'll be low key and she can meet everyone." Alta knew what Michael wanted to ask, and she already resented him for it.

"Did you make love to her while she was here?" His voice was calm, but charged with the tension to make it so. Alta took another drag and let the silence settle between them.

"To tell you the truth, *she* avoided *me*. She did say something about you, though. She said, 'Michael really loves you, you know.' "

"Well, it's true." Michael smiled with secret pleasure.

"What if I had?" Anger crept into Alta's voice. "We don't even live together, and I don't demand absolute fidelity from you."

"We've never talked about it—I just assumed . . . Look, I'm jealous, I guess. It's been just us, Alta."

"Come on, let's go for a walk. I'm too stoned to argue with you. In two weeks it's the solstice. Maybe the solstice will tell us what's up, our yearly human confirmation. The flesh. Flesh and blood." Alta laughed softly, musing, slightly stoned. "The winter solstice is more of the spirit, don't you think?"

"The spirit seeking flesh," Michael murmured.

Alta nodded and then she stood up and waited for Michael to join her.

"Is Jade still coming?" he asked.

"I think so."

"It won't be the same—for us, I mean." Michael stood up, facing her.

"Michael, we asked her, remember? And I'd like her to come."

"Why?"

"Well, because I care about her, and she could use the experience of sleeping outside in a safe place, and it seems the solstice is the one reason she might do it. She needs that healing, Michael."

"Do you love her?" Michael felt rigid and forced, but he couldn't help himself.

Alta knew she didn't have to answer him, but she did anyway. She knew she could've said, I don't really feel I can talk about this now, or I don't think this is a fair question at this time. Instead, Alta said, "I guess I do, the very beginnings, but it doesn't seem to be going anywhere. Don't you think the real question is, do I love you? And I do. Come on, let's go for a walk."

As Alta shut the back door behind her she thought of Jade. She felt like calling her to see how she was. Then she decided to call her early in the morning. She remembered Jade in the morning, coming out for tea, her long, dark hair spread around her shoulders, down her back like a thick, black shawl, and her face, fresh from dreams, like a child's.

I do love Jade, and I do love Michael, Alta thought with clarity. There was a sensation of a tearing in her abdomen as Alta acknowledged what was in her heart. But it was a gentle tearing, an exquisite sort of pain/pleasure.

The night was dark, and the first hint of a summer warmth was in the air. The slender crescent moon was a pure, pale white. Soon it would set, leaving the stars alone with the night. Soon it would set, leaving Michael and Alta, exhausted, in each other's arms till morning. But first Michael would insist on entering her, almost violently, possessively, pressing Alta against the smooth, mossy bark of the old oak, standing up, moving against her, and she against him, completely abandoned to the cover of night—the wind moving against them, gently—the silence surrounding them, gently. They moaned, they screamed, they cried. They surrendered to the other's desire, completely.

Anyone witnessing their lovemaking would've been struck by the protective gesture of the tree, immense and spiralling upwards toward the sky over their heads, yet joining them in their fleshy human pleasure, giving them shelter and adding its awareness to their own, gentling Michael as the crescent set into the far hills.

Trembling, Alta received his quick, hot sperm.

As April drove home her mother's face began to recede from her mind's eye until she became a safe, dark dot in the distance like her conscience, as a child, when she needed to do something she knew her mother would never allow. April looked in the rearview mirror, and the silver crescent earrings her mother had given her startled her with their newness. They were light and dangled freely without stretching her lobes or reddening the wounds, the open wounds, that held the silver crescents. But these are hers, not mine, April reminded herself, and Steve may be a slimeball, but at least he's not a queerball. At least we have money, and I have my own car. At least he won't die of AIDS.

April pulled over on the freeway and, leaving the motor running, pulled off the silver crescent earrings. She put on the heavy gold hoops, locking them into place. For an instant, she was tempted to throw her mother's earrings out the window, but, no, she couldn't do that. She placed them in the zippered compartment of her purse where she put everything she just might need in the future. The compartment that never fails to surprise when it's emptied just before the purse is finally thrown away.

April's daughter kicked and thrashed at her mother's hunched position. "Sorry, kiddo," April muttered, as she pulled back into the speeding traffic with her usual fear of dying, of being hit, of being in the wrong place at the wrong time, of not going fast enough, of going too fast. Soon she'd be home.

During lunch Jade sat by herself in the teacher's lounge safely away from students, and now she hoped no one would try to speak to her. Please, she almost said out loud, pouring hot tea from her thermos. Alta's call that morning had touched her. But it's better to do it this way, Jade thought numbly, than have Alta change her mind later on after she really means a lot to me. Like Grace. No, I really can't stand that again. Two more hours then home. I probably shouldn't have accepted dinner tonight. Big baby, she punished herself for her lack of discipline, the one thing her father had always prized in her. She'd always had extraordinary discipline, her father had said, even as a young child. "Without discipline, nothing can be realized," Jade remembered her father's words. She'd always wondered what her father had done at school that day he hadn't gone with his father to Hiroshima, but she'd been unable to ask. Maybe he forgot to do his homework or put it off too long so he could play. The thought of her father as a child wanting to play was painful to her. She'd known him as a somber, serious man, driven, with rare moments of joy. Then the rape and his suicide. He only wanted a good excuse to die, Jade thought. And then the words came to her, *the undisciplined bastard*. Rape and death, rape and death. I want an end to it. Anger and sorrow filled her simultaneously and, so suddenly, she forgot to breathe.

A brief, sharp image of her father as a child came to her. He was flying a kite in the wind, looking up at it with excitement and joy. At the same instant, to the right of the image, the bomb was being dropped on Hiroshima, and that part of the sky was red. Jade had forgotten her father's love of kites until that moment. In fact, it had been then when she'd glimpsed his brief flashes of joy, as his face looked up at the soaring kite, far from Earth for a while. And those times he knew he'd taught her something, joy would flicker and then swallow itself with shame.

Then she remembered the time he'd put the kite out as far as the string allowed. He'd handed it to her—she'd never been allowed to handle a kite. "Do you feel the wind?" he'd asked her. He hadn't looked at her, but stared, face up, at the kite. She'd answered, "Yes, Daddy, it's strong." She remembered vividly, as though she were still there with her father holding the living kite, the unexpected happiness she'd felt like an eruption inside her body, but at the same time the connection to the kite, the wind, the clouds.

Then, it was gone, flying away from her, and the wonderful, pulling tug of the wind, the living kite, was gone, and her body felt horribly vacant. Empty. Raped. But she hadn't even known the word *rape*, and so she'd looked at her father for an explanation, and she saw the pocket knife in his hand. She'd been too startled to cry. Later, he asked her if she wanted to learn to fly a kite. She could see he was sorry. "No," she'd said. "I never want to fly a kite," and he never took her again to his kite flying place.

Jade put her lunch away. She decided to walk out to the athletic field and get some air. It was windy but warm. She walked quickly, and as she looked up at the sky she whispered, "Father," to the enormous, retreating clouds.

The first thing Jade saw were the words CHINK CUNT sprayed in a garish red on her living room wall. They'd taken a chicken out of her refrigerator and sprayed it with the blood-red paint, putting it inside of her panties, and they'd sprayed them as well. A trail of red led room to room, clothes strewn in the bedroom; her woven wall hangings and a favorite watercolor of the mesas, its delicate sunset colors ruined with the horrible red. The old Navajo rug that had been woven by her grandmother lay underneath the words DIE BITCH. To the bathroom, more obscenity, to the hallway, the same and the same.

Her heart was in her throat, in her ears, in her eyes, but she had to look, to see what they'd done. She was trembling as she walked toward the second bedroom, her studio, following the trail of red. What if they're in there, waiting for me?—a part of her mind shrieked at her, but the part that made her walk and see was strangely beyond fear as though she were already dead, as though the words DIE BITCH, sprayed on her walls, had already killed her.

Jade opened the studio door, and then she screamed a long, high, shrill scream for the massacred, as though a roomful of young, beautiful children, bloody throats slashed, had been slaughtered and piled together like garbage. They'd torn apart her mother's loom, piece by piece, ripped the weaving she'd been working on into shreds, and every weaving that had hung on the walls lay on the floor in shreds. Then she saw it, and it was worse, much worse than the death of all the children. It was the death of the Grandmother. The Grandmother's vision. Her grandmother's vision. Timelessness. Eternity. What she always had imagined was the true source of her own power. Her grandmother's puberty weaving, the weaving of her first moon, her first blood, lay in shreds, and every part of it was sprayed in the garish blood-red. Around the walls were the words DIE CUNT DIE CUNT, over and over and over.

Jade screamed again, but this time a pure kind of sorrow flowed from her still raw, healing womb; the child, *their* child, wept with her, and through her, until the violence of her sorrow ebbed.

"Michael's going over there to meet the police, and they're sending someone over here to talk to you, okay?" Alta sat next to Jade, stroking her hair as Jade lay under the thick quilt trying to regulate her body temperature that kept going from hot to cold.

"Do you have some ginger tea? I'll be alright in a minute," Jade said, beginning to sob again.

"Don't talk. I'll get the tea. Look, if you're not well enough to talk to the police now, you can talk to them tomorrow."

"No, I'll talk to them now. The tea will help, thanks." Everything seemed distant, unreal, especially herself. She felt invisible, disembodied. Empty. Only Alta's face, when she got close to her, seemed substantial, maybe real. But now Alta was by the door talking about tomorrow, and she was saying the words *tea* and *thanks*. And soon disembodied people would come to ask her questions, and she would answer them, pretending she was real, and she would pretend they were real, though now she knew that the insane men had succeeded in killing all the children in the world—the Indian children, the Japanese children, the Jewish children, the African children, all the brown children, even all the white children were dead. Therefore, there was no more hope. But she'd pretend there was out of sheer, stubborn habit. Because human speech required human echoes, and that's what she'd do, she'd echo coherently for *their sakes*. But first the tea, Jade thought. Then the immense sorrow for all the dead children, the dead hope, settled itself on her, and she lost consciousness.

"Hey, Mom?" Ian's voice was full of his usual exuberance. "I thought I was going to get your answering machine again, so I was getting ready to hang up. What'd ya know, a human voice!"

Alta couldn't help laughing at the sound of her son's voice. He was the one who'd always known how to make her laugh in spite of everything. In fact, he secretly prided himself on it.

"Oh, my gawd, it's the college man! When're you planning to visit your old mother?"

"This summer, after summer session, that is. I decided to rack up some extra units, though I think I'm really out of my goddamned mind. I almost joined the Peace Corps last week, no kidding. I was thinking, if I'm going to be a doctor, I should see what it's like *out there* instead of being holed up in some crowded lecture hall, watching some dot talk to me. You know, I can't see their facial expressions. So, I thought, why not go to some desperate Third World country where I can at least give shots and health information . . . "

"Are you going to do it, join the Peace Corps?" Alta asked, interrupting him.

"Would you mind?"

"First of all, you're old enough to make that decision, but since you're asking me, no, not if you really want to. I mean, maybe you could use the experience. If the mechanics are leaving you dry, I suppose the travel and reality might really be an education. On the other hand, I hear you saying you want to help people, the ones that're having a hard time helping themselves, and you might be able to do that best as a full-fledged doctor. It just takes so damned long. Anyway, I can imagine how you must feel." Alta paused, seeing Ian's face, watching him internalize her words.

"Well, that's what I kind of came to, but I did go to talk to some Peace Corps people, just in case, so now it feels kind of like my ace in the hole. Sometimes I don't know if I have the mind for physics, but I seem to do okay once I get started, and I do like some of the theories they throw around. Sometimes I feel pretty stupid—was I stupid as a kid or what?" The words poured out to Ian's embarrassment and, ultimately, relief. If anyone knows if I'm stupid, it's Mom, he thought. Maybe it's a goddamn family secret.

Alta started to laugh. "Ian, you may have been a pain in the ass, but you were never, I mean, ever, stupid. You're just over your head in work, and this is when a lot of people just say 'Screw it' and become a mortician or something. No, you are *not* stupid."

Ian laughed softly, breathing out his frustration sharply. Last night he'd dreamt of being at bat and hitting the ball so far it seemed to take on a life of its own, sailing over trees, houses, freeways, and he'd watched himself run the bases, around and around, counting home runs, with no one to stop him. And, then, this morning before the chemistry test the dream faded, but now it returned unexpectedly. Vividly.

"So, you're saying that, as my mother, you can certify that I was not born stupid or anything."

"Absolutely, I checked you out very carefully. Ian," Alta said gently, "everyone feels ignorant while they're learning. That's why it takes so much courage. I remember when I was in my early twenties, before I went back to school, I picked up a magazine article and actually was unable to understand it, any of it. In fact, the words were swimming together. It was as though I'd forgotten how to think. How's that for stupid, huh?"

"Did that really happen?"

"I wouldn't lie to you, yes." Tears came to Alta's eyes as her old sadness surfaced unexpectedly, wounding her again as though she were still twenty-four, with her fear swallowing her whole. Alta thought of Jade in the next room, and her heart slowed down. Jade. Now fear was stalking Jade, she reminded herself. Jade. Poor Jade, those bastards destroyed her loom . . .

"Thanks for the courage part. I guess it's true. I'm writing it down," Ian laughed, "so I can remember that. I guess that's why you're a shrink, right, Mom? I guess I feel I can call you, and you're not going to bullshit me or anything. And plus, I can trust you, you know? There's not a lot of people you can really trust or really talk to. There's Mike and Rob, but they can get pretty flaky on me. Who knows, maybe I'm flaky. Maybe it's being in my twenties, and Marcia's even younger than me. The blind leading the blind. Okay, enough about me. Have you heard from April? When's she having that kid, and when's she getting that degree? . . . "

Once Ian got on a roll he could talk for hours, and now that he had his mother's ear again the questions and comments poured out. Besides, she usually hits the nail on the head, Ian thought. He was about to add, "What's she planning to do with a photo degree, anyway?" And, "Does she have her darkroom finished?" when Alta cut in.

"Do you want an answer, Ian? Earth to Ian," she joked. "Earth to Ian."

"Yeah, lay it on me. I'll shut up." Ian's voice was happy, unrestrained. "Moon to Mom, moon to Mom!"

"Excuse me, is it my turn?" Alta laughed and continued. "Okay, April's child and degree are both due next month. Supposedly, the child is due after the degree, but who knows that kind of thing, really, so the race is on. However, she's made a deal with the photo department to complete her photo thesis by taking pictures of her birth. She plans to have a tripod ready to go and a hand-held one as well. She's been taking pictures of her pregnancy from the beginning, some in the mirror, some from eye vantage point. I think she's onto something."

"Is the hospital going to let her set up a tripod in delivery?" Ian couldn't help smiling. Whether April knows it or not, she's as quirky as Mom, he thought. Their last conversation, a few months ago, had been sprinkled with complaints about Alta: "Like when's Mom going to grow up?" April had said. "Don't you think she ought to get married or something?" And, "Can you imagine Mom as a grandmother?" They'd both laughed like little kids.

"She said it's all set to go. Her doctor set it up for her. She loved the idea, April said. In fact, they're going to work together as much as possible . . . "

"Wonders never cease," Ian quipped. "Old sis, the prude. Maybe there's hope for Marcia even." Marcia was Ian's girlfriend.

"The darkroom's pretty much done, and she's developing all her own black and white. Right now it's kind of crummy with her and Steve, or in my own private code, Slimeball."

"Did you tell April that? I wouldn't if I were you." April had mentioned that she didn't think Alta liked Steve because he was so status quo oriented and made a lot of money as a rising young executive. And all that crap, Ian added to himself.

"Well, we talked about some hassles she's having, but I think she ought to tell you."

"What's he having affairs or something?"

"Something like that, yes, but anyway, *she* should tell you if she wants. Do you understand, Ian?"

"Well, yeah, that's great. Here she is, knocked up and all. I'm not having a kid until I get all that shit settled. Like sometimes when I think of Dad, it's still hard to believe." Ian lowered his voice. "What a way to go, with AIDS. Do you think of him much?"

"Not as much, but sometimes I do. I guess I always will from time to time. Do you think of him?"

"Once in a while, but three visits in all that time sure doesn't make for fond memories. I think, in a strange way, he wanted to die from AIDS or he'd of been more careful. You know, condoms? I guess I just wish he'd had more sense or something." Ian paused. Thinking of his father, with any seriousness, always meant an attack of temporary depression. So instead he made the presence he'd come to feel as his father go away, and gathering a burst of energy, he said, "Hey, why don't we do some backpacking again this summer, up to the mountains? I'll talk your ear off. We can even fight."

"You're on. When?"

"Early August. Is that guy Michael still around and all?"

"Yes, I'm still seeing Michael. He's my colleague, remember?"

"Get off it, Mom. No, really, I think he's alright. You ever going to tie the knot again?"

"Probably not, Ian." Alta felt herself getting tired. Aren't the parents supposed to want to run their kids' lives? she thought a little angrily.

"You know, the other day," Ian said, changing the subject, sensing Alta's annoyance, "I was looking up different names just for the hell of it and Michael's name in Hebrew—I remember it 'cause it was so weird, right?—means, Who is like God?, with the question mark and all. Did you ever hear of that?"

"Who is like God?" Alta echoed. "Sounds like Michael, question mark and all. I especially like the question mark, I think. I like that, yes."

"You know, Mom, I'm really beginning to worry about the next century, like next year, and there's so many damned *little wars*, as they say, and all these little countries building their nuclear arsenals, and then I ask myself, what difference is one puny doctor going to make, anyway? The whole world'll be a Third World country, probably worse—a No World, period. And just when's the ozone layer going to return to normal, if it ever will . . . "

"I know, Ian, I know." Alta's head began to ache, a small, warning throb over her right temple. "These are the questions I batter myself with. But if we don't keep trying, no evolution . . . "

244

"It depends on what you consider evolution to be, like whose point of view. Like maybe the universe would be better off without us noisy, stupid, warlike humans. Like maybe everything could relax for a while without human words—spoken, printed, or thought even, you know?" Ian felt himself strangling, for a moment, with an intense anxiety, but he continued in a smooth rush of words.

"Like maybe evolution's really better off without us, like who am I kidding? I'm not even as smart as a single cell, which *knows* exactly what to do . . . "

"Hey, Ian, Earth to Ian!"

"Yeah?"

"I love you."

"Yeah."

Michael decided to go home before going over to Alta's. He was still trembling with rage and fear. The words CHINK CUNT DIE CUNT DIE CHINK DIE DIE, repeated themselves, over and over, flashing hideously in the bright, unnatural red on the walls, in his mind. Blood is red on contact with oxygen, he thought—red blood no matter what color you are. Horus, did they make you watch your blood leave your body? Horus, how long were you kept alive? Horus, oh, Horus, your beautiful blood gone forever, just gone.

He felt like ripping down his walls with his bare hands so that no one would ever write on them or desecrate them with their obscene red paint. He felt like throwing open his front door and screaming an invitation to any violent, diseased, insane white men who wanted to see a black man bleed to death to come in now and just try it while he was ready for them, really ready for them. He felt like being in a world of only colored people, people with color on their bodies; natural color, not the fashionably tanned versions trying to be brown while despising *color* itself. Then he thought of the little white boy, only eight years old, he and Alta were counseling. Michael saw his large blue eyes, trusting, finally, after months of work. His foster mother said he was sleeping through the night without the nightmares, the terrible screams, the bed-wetting. Michael remembered the day he'd told the boy, "Your father did bad things to you, but it will never, ever happen again, Tommy. Ever. Those bad things won't ever happen to you again." The boy had flung himself into Michael's arms, and Michael had cradled the small blond boy in his arms, rocking him like his own child for a long, long while.

Instead, Michael went to his bedroom, picked up his bamboo flute and thought of Tommy's blue eyes, his thin, white arms encircling his neck, asking to be picked up and carried like a baby, which he did with a real joy. No, Michael reminded himself, they don't *start out* that way—they end up that way, some of them. They *learn* how to be full-fledged monsters.

Michael thought of red apples, the apples on Alta's trees. He thought of her favorite rose bush—the queen roses, she called them, because they were almost purple they were so red. Purple tinted their edges, but their centers were pools of deep, rich red. Michael put his hand to his heart and felt it thumping steadily, pumping his blood to every organ, to every tissue and cell of his body.

Long ago Michael's father had made him fall in love with his heart, the way he'd explained it to him. His father had given him a plastic human model of all the body organs and he'd taken them apart and put them back together by himself by the time he was eight. "The heart will keep you alive even when the brain's gone. The old heart really loves to live, so it pumps that blood from the time you're in your Mama's womb, listening to her heart. It's the original symphony, the heart," his father told him. Michael remembered the time his father took a blood sample from his finger and put it under his powerful microscope; that was the time he'd fallen in love with his blood, but first it had been his heart, what he couldn't see, what he'd never see. And his penis, that he could see, that he could hold, that filled with blood, rich with the blood pumped from the tireless heart. He'd learned to love it too, even earlier than his heart. But Michael couldn't think of that now because

246

he would think of Horus, mutilated, and so he thought of his heart, the original symphony, the small, plastic organ that fit in the plastic body so perfectly each time, and he began to play his flute. He called for Comfort; he questioned the silence of the afternoon; he blocked out words and then Comfort came crawling on its belly and laid its head at Michael's feet, and Michael played, extending his notes in sorrow, unexpected joy, bursts of anger, stretches of pure peace. Michael played and Comfort rested for a while in the growing darkness. Michael played and Horus was alive and whole in the tangible warmth of Comfort's presence. It raised its sensitive, wet nose to the first, pale star as Michael played, and it placed its massive head between its paws, ever so gently.

Then Michael remembered his mother's voice: "Your father and I would like you to be a doctor. We always hoped you'd want to be one, of course. But it certainly doesn't mean you have to be one. No, Michael, you've got to live your own life. You've got to decide what's important to *you*. That's what life is all about. I guess you've got to break our hearts and we've got to keep on loving you, because you *must* live your *own life*, just as we have." He remembered his mother's expressive, brown eyes, holding his with their impact of an almost inhuman strength. It was this strength he'd searched for and found in himself. Her words: "You've got to find your own way."

It was she who sat with him patiently, showing him where the plastic organs belonged, helping him sound out their names and placing them on the appropriate parts of her body and his, asking, "What belongs here?" "Do I have a womb too?" he'd asked his mother as she placed the small plastic womb against her body. "No," she'd answered him, laughing gently. "Jana and I have wombs because we're women. Women make babies in their wombs." Michael remembered Jana's little girl's face proud with pleasure. Now Jana was a lawyer in Los Angeles, and though she was married, nearly six years after the gang rape, she still had no children.

"But you have testicles, see? That's where the semen is made. They're like fast-swimming little fishes, and that's what fertilizes the woman's egg that will grow in her womb." How simple, how logical it had all seemed listening to this mother's calm, reasonable voice. It was she who had revealed the secret of the large plastic heart that came apart, naming the chambers and explaining them. It was she who believed in the impossible, who taught him not only to call Comfort, but how it stayed of its own will. She'd set him free, even after what happened to Horus.

"If you surrender to fear, you're as good as dead. We black people are on intimate terms with our fear. It makes us cry, but it makes us laugh too. After we finish crying for Horus, we'll start laughing remembering his silly ways." Her face was calm and her voice was firm. "Horus's body is dead, Michael, but not his soul."

Michael still hadn't laughed with remembering, but once in a while he smiled thinking of this and that. "Cat got your tongue?" Horus's words echoed playfully; the words he'd used when Michael would become sullen and distant. Then Horus would usually wrestle him to the ground, making Michael fight back, making him laugh. But the dream of Horus being beaten, and, now, the face becoming his intruded on the possibility of laughter. Fear clutched at his stomach and chest, and Michael felt Comfort rouse itself to leave.

Now Jade's in danger, he thought. But at least she's been warned. Michael took the flute from his mouth and, without turning on any lights, walked out to the garden. Comfort followed him and stood at his side panting, as he silently wept. "Horus," Michael whispered his brother's name out loud. "You were supposed to be the doctor."

Now his flesh and blood heart broke again, but, miraculously, it kept on, and on.

"I was beginning to wonder if you were coming. I called you a couple of times but your machine was on," Alta said, pouring Michael some wine. They sat in front of a small fire and talked, touching each other from time to time.

"After I saw Jade's place I had to be alone for a while. It was pretty ugly stuff, believe me. Did the cops come here?"

"Yeah, but she was asleep, so I asked them to come back tomorrow. She got up once to go to the bathroom and went right back to sleep. She's really exhausted, if not traumatized." Alta sipped her wine and stared into the fire. "I'm going to suggest she move here until this whole thing with these assholes clears up. I don't think she's safe by herself. What do you think?"

"Well, you know how I feel about you and her, and I assume we'll be honest about all that, but I think it's the best thing to do, other than going back to New Mexico and just coming back for the trial. Or, really, just going somewhere else, period. But then she'd have to get a new job and everything else. She'd be running from them." Michael threw in a small apple log and continued in a low, tired voice. "She shouldn't even try to go back to her place. This is probably the best place for her till some real action's taken with those motherfuckers."

"I'll bring it up tomorrow. You know, this die cunt stuff and breaking her mother's loom, Michael—well, you saw it, didn't you? It just makes me want to get a rifle and nail it over my door. Not a hand gun. You don't have to think about those as much. But a large, bulky rifle that I'd load, very consciously, and use if I have to."

"Do you think you could really use it?" Michael saw her rage and he knew that she would if she had to, but he asked her anyway.

"If those guys came here looking for any helpless cunt, I sure would. There's a limit to everything, and I think they've hit my goddamned limit. I'm going to buy one tomorrow."

Michael laughed, holding her. "Just shoot straight and blow their asses off. Can you shoot, girl?"

"Doug taught me. I'm no hotshot, but I'm pretty steady."Alta finished her wine and poured another. "Do you want some more?"

Michael nodded yes and said, "I like your hair down like this." He kissed the inside of her neck, smelling her feminine essence. He loved the way she smelled. Whenever they made love he felt her scent, her essence, melt into him, and for days after she inhabited him.

"Can I stay tonight?" Michael asked softly.

"I was going to ask you to." Their mouths met, long and deep and soft. Relentlessly. They separated for a moment, catching their breath, meeting the stranger in each other's eyes. "Let's go to my bedroom," Alta indicated Jade's bedroom door.

"Do you love her?" Michael asked in a strange, distant voice.

"Yes, I think I do," Alta murmured.

"It must be quite a predicament for you, then."

"I suppose so. Sometimes. But not at this moment." Alta stood up and waited for him. "Come on, okay?"

"I called my parents tonight. I'm going to visit them for a week in July. Will you think about coming with me? I want them to get to know you, I guess." Michael looked up at her and waited.

"Yes, I'd like that. Maybe for a couple of days. I think they're wonderful people."

Michael smiled. "They are."

"Come on, Michael, I want to make love to you."

Before Alta went to her bedroom she opened Jade's door to see how she was. Sadness and rage clutched at her mind. Tomorrow I'll get the rifle, she decided.

Michael was standing by the wide expanse of window, staring out. He turned as Alta entered the room and held out his arms. His diamond star earring caught the available light and beckoned to her. She walked into his warmth and thanked him, silently, for being a gentle man, a good and strong and fine man. A real man. She wanted to please him tonight. She wanted to nibble him and suck him until he came, and then she wanted to feel him come again slowly, very slowly, in her body. He would draw her orgasm out long and slow tonight, but she wouldn't scream with abandon because Jade was asleep in April's old room.

Michael and Alta floated in the ecstatic, amniotic fluid, in the warm womb of their lovemaking. Michael's right arm was under her head; she knew if he moved it she'd be lonely. Her left arm was flung across his chest; he knew it wouldn't last, but he wanted it to.

"When're you going to have my kid? A kid should be born from times like this," Michael murmured. A nightingale sang in the distance, forcing itself into his consciousness with its loud, persistent notes. It perched in an oak tree—the old one with its branches spiralling skyward, and it sang to the moonless sky without pause.

"I'm too old. Maybe I can't even do it anymore. You need a younger woman for this job, Michael," Alta teased him.

"I want *you*, girl." His voice was husky and low. His eyes were closed.

"Do you know you've never hurt me making love? Do you know what that means to me?"

Michael opened his eyes with effort and turned his head slightly to look at her.

"It means I can open my body to you, entirely, without waiting for that jabbing pain. I mean, I can open myself entirely to you, give myself up in trust, because you don't *want* to hurt me. And, you know, the soul follows where the body goes. I'm trying to tell you that I trust you." Alta buried her face in Michael's dark, sweet neck. She loved his scent, his male essence. She took it into herself, breath by breath.

"I just don't know if I could do it again. I just don't know."

"It's okay. It's just how I feel. It's just how I feel about you and me. I love you, girl."

"Ditto," Alta said, licking his neck and biting his earlobe.

"What do you mean 'Ditto'—say it, say, I love you! Come on—I love you, Michael!" Michael held Alta tightly with his legs and laughed softly.

"Ditto."

"Say it!" He turned Alta on her back, holding her shoulders down. He began to lick her face. "Say I LOVE YOU, MICHAEL!"

"You are crazy, but I love you, Michael!" Alta gasped, turning her head side to side, trying to avoid his wet tongue.

"You're crazier than me, riding a horse named Night Mare, but I still want you to have my kid. Any sex will do." He straddled her, licking her cheeks.

"Stop it! Do you want to eat me? Is that it? Cut it out!"

Michael let go of his hold that held her, kissing her mouth softly, softly, softly. "Yes, I want to eat you. I want to eat you all up, woman," Michael whispered. He kissed her again and his softness was infinite as he sucked her lips, her tongue.

"Eat me. Eat me all up," Alta begged.

The darkness surrounds them. Small, blazing fires begin to erupt in a circle, trapping them. Alta turns to Michael and he looks strangely unafraid. Then she turns to Jade. Jade wants to scream, but instead she smiles. Alta wants to run, but she finds herself paralyzed, utterly unable to move. "Get the rifle!" a voice shouts. Sweat erupts, everywhere, on Alta's body, and she runs toward the darkness, beyond the circle of fire.

Nine

"April has had false labor twice now. I hope I can make it down when it really starts," Alta sighed. She and Jade followed Michael, who was softly playing his bamboo flute. They were going to spend the night on the knoll overlooking the stretch of fertile valley. It was still a deep green as they approached the end of June. A precious, late rain had brought an abundance of wildflowers.

"That's another reason why I don't think we should sleep out tonight. What if tonight's the night? She can't reach you up here," Jade said, glancing at Alta with a desperation she struggled to disguise. She still felt terrified, even in the house with locked doors and windows. Now they were going to sleep outdoors, and though both Alta and Michael tried to reassure her about how safe it was, and how they'd slept out innumerable times in the summer, and that she couldn't let those men torment her the rest of her life—Jade was still terrified.

The police had brought the two men in for further questioning, but nothing could be proved; they'd manufactured their alibis, friends as witnesses as to where they'd been at that time on that day, and the court date was over a month away.

The day after the barbecue, Michael and Alta had gone with Jade to the apartment to pack what they hadn't destroyed and clean. The landlady had returned her full deposit. "It sure isn't your fault, honey, so don't you worry." The insurance company would reimburse Jade for the *damage*, as they called it, but how could they, or anyone on Earth, replace her mother's loom, the one she'd given her for her fifteenth birthday, the year after her father killed himself? How could anyone replace her grandmother's puberty weaving? The weaving her first menstruals brought. Her grandmother's vision.

Jade had called her mother, and her mother wanted her to come home. The words *come home* had almost made her lose her composure, had almost made her cry and tell her mother everything. She would see her mother for two weeks in July, just before the trial was scheduled to begin.

"I guess I can't wait by the phone until it happens, but I'd love to be with her. I'd love to see her, camera clicking, give birth." Alta laughed softly. She reached over, taking Jade's hand in hers, and they continued walking that way for a while.

Michael looked back once and censored himself for being jealous. She's her friend, he told himself. I'm her lover. Not quite, kid, he reminded himself. She's her lover too, or has been. His breath came short and the smooth, soft notes became staccato. Come on, man, lighten up. Besides, I like Jade, and besides that, no one can steal anyone away. Not really. His silent words seemed silly and hollow, but his breath returned to normal, and his chest began to expand, and the flute flowed smoothly again.

Jade's hair swung, brushing her hips as she walked. Alta had talked her into taking it down, out of her single, tight braid. "The rifle's up here, right?"

"I brought it up this afternoon. It's wrapped in plastic, under some wood. Look, we're almost there. I made a beautiful fire circle with some special fire stones, and there's plenty of wood."

"Is it loaded?" Jade's voice shook as she spoke.

"Michael has the cartridges in his pack. You know, I'm beginning to feel terrible bringing you here. Maybe it'd be better for you to stay at the house. Look, it's okay. We could walk back right now. It's only twenty minutes away." Alta put her hand on Jade's shoulder. "Really, it's okay. I could walk you back right now, if you want."

Jade's head jerked up in surprise. "You mean, you aren't afraid to walk back up here by yourself?"

"Don't forget, I've slept out here a bunch of times by myself, so that's why—and I know this land by heart." Alta stopped walking. "Look, just say so and we'll start back. Do you want to go back?"

Michael was at the ring of stones. He waved to them. He could see them clearly in the light of the rising full moon. It looked like something was wrong, but he decided to let them work it out.

"You really aren't afraid?" Jade asked, looking straight into Alta's eyes.

"Well, truthfully, I'm a little on edge, but that's why I brought the rifle, right?"

"Right," Jade echoed, as they began to walk toward Michael.

Michael placed the paper, kindling, and small pieces of wood into a carefully built pyramid. He worked intently and silently, pausing to look at the suspended fullness of the rising gold, a perfect, immense globe suspended in the darkness of the sky: the moon.

"The honor is yours, ladies," Michael said, handing a box of matches to Alta. He took out a small, clay flute from his jacket pocket and warmed it with his hands. He felt the snake and bird—Quetzalcoatl—that adorned the small, clay flute and remembered playing it for the first time in Teotihuacán at the very top of the Pyramid of the Moon. He remembered Alta's face, so peaceful, as the flute soared over the ancient city toward the Pyramid of the Sun. They were new lovers. "My ancestors are here," she'd said loudly as though to let the spirits know.

Jade looked anxiously at Alta, and then at Michael. "If anyone's going to spot us out here, it'll be with a fire, don't you think?"

"We're pretty far off the road," Michael answered her. "Someone would almost have to know we're out here to find us. I really think we're okay out here." He felt soothed and safe in this particular spot, and the tone of his voice conveyed that to Jade. "We sleep out here during the summer a lot. Just look at those stars, Jade." Michael put his head back and smiled up at them, then at her.

"But this summer you've got a couple of crazies out to get me. They are, I just know it." Jade's voice was low.

"I can't help but think they're trying their best to intimidate you, trying to get you to back down. Like your lawyer said, you can't prove anything and that's the bitch, those motherfuckers. Those cowards," Alta sighed with disgust.

"Look, we're okay out here, Jade. Really we are. Come on, let's light the fire." Alta put her arm around Jade's slender shoulders. She felt like kissing her and stroking her face, but she couldn't with Michael watching. She just couldn't.

"We brought some wine and cheese and some crackers, and some mushrooms. Some magic mushrooms, just a few pieces each. Have you ever had any?" Alta smiled at Jade in an attempt to convey all the warmth she wanted to give her.

"I've heard of them, but, no, I haven't. Maybe I'll pass, but you two go ahead." Jade sucked in her breath, drawing in her courage. "Okay, give me a match."

Alta kissed Jade on the cheek and hugged her. She glanced over at Michael, but she couldn't see his expression in the dark.

Michael began to blow on Quetzacoatl's flute, a long, sustained note. It was low and eerie, alone in the night. It was beautiful. He began to call the Man in the Moon. He began to call the Woman in the Moon. He began to call the Children of the Sun, softly at first, and then more loudly as the music took shape.

Alta and Jade struck their matches, kneeling on the ground, and lit the balled-up newspaper under the dry apple kindling. The small, quick fire blazed to the top of the carefully built pyramid. Alta placed two large pine pieces on top, and then she went and got the bag of food and a bottle of water, water from the spring.

They sat while Michael played for a while, listening to his tones break the silence, then become the silence, then sometimes, he'd let the silence win, making it even more beautiful. There were crickets everywhere, dancing in the long, silky grass, making the night thick with their music.

Alta poured some water and opened the napkin containing the mushrooms. They'd have wine and cheese later. "Well, this is why we asked you to fast today. We thought we'd surprise you, but you're thinking, enough surprises, aren't you?" Alta smiled, seeing traces of relaxation on Jade's usually tense face. Her thick, black hair was so long it almost looked like a dress covering the top portion of her body.

Michael stopped playing and joined them. "One mushroom each, cut into three pieces, is a light dose. It enhances understanding, but about four of these," he said, picking one of them up, "is the real journey. You know, the real journey to understanding. But these smell particularly fertile and powerful. Alive." Michael looked at Jade questioningly to see if she was following him.

Jade smiled at him. "I took acid a couple of times actually. Just twice, so I think I know what you mean. Yes."

"This is much, much gentler than acid, but it's really the same journey to truth." Michael laughed a little nervously. "I took acid more than a few times when I was younger, but I didn't really like how it affected me later. This just seems to decompose itself naturally in your system, leaving you with a much clearer vision." Michael shuddered thinking of the last time he'd taken a full dose of the mushrooms, a year after Horus was killed. When he'd gotten to Horus's death his mind had veered violently away and his journey had aborted. Since then he took only a minimal dose now and then. And that last vision of Horus, tied up and bleeding, was what he dreamt now.

"There used to be peyote rituals that lasted all night long, but they were very strict about who took part in them, so I never got to do it. How long do these last?" Jade asked, breaking Michael's horrible mental picture of Horus.

"One mushroom will be so gentle, it won't even matter," Alta answered Jade. "I took acid only once and I hated it— well, afterwards I hated it. The explosiveness of the chemicals. But these are gentle, even in a full dose like four." Alta lowered her voice and said, "They always bring me their gift of understanding. If I didn't think you were able to extract the same thing I wouldn't even suggest it."

Jade's eyes reflected the fire. She looked at Alta's eyes which reflected the fire between them, and then Michael's.

His, too, reflected the hot, living fire. I trust these two, she thought. And then she realized, I love them. "Okay," Jade smiled, "I'll give them a try."

Alta passed the water and the mushroom pieces to Jade and Michael. Michael began: "To the longest day of the year. To the Summer Solstice. To the Mother, Father." He picked up a mushroom and held it up to the rising moon, which was turning into a glowing, pale gold entity. Michael motioned to Jade, with his hand, to put the mushroom in her mouth as he was. They all ate their first piece slowly, sipping the fresh spring water.

Then Alta began to hum, deep in her throat, letting her voice vibrate at the very back of her throat for a while. Then she brought the hum up into her mouth and spoke: "To the oldest woman. To the Woman in the Moon. To the Mother of the Sun." She picked up her second piece of mushroom, holding it up to the Old Woman and then she laughed with a childish joy.

Jade stared down at her hands, and finally, she spoke in a clear, strangely detached voice: "To the Rainbow Woman born in the Solstice, from the moon and sun. To Changing Woman, the Grandmother, from where all life comes, and goes." Jade's voice faltered as tears ran down her face. "Change in me, Grandmother." She smeared her third piece into her salty tears and ate it.

They sat in silence for a long while. Michael added a thick piece of oak and the fire caught even hotter.

"I can feel it," Jade whispered. "I feel rooted to the ground, but it's wonderful. The fire is so perfect, isn't it?" As she looked into Alta's face, Alta's face became the moon, full of understanding. She knew Alta loved her.

The black orchid that sat next to Alta was pulsing with a soft, diffuse light. Alta leaned over, kissing Jade's lips lightly. Then she looked at Michael. Michael was watching them with open curiosity. "Isn't she beautiful?" Alta asked him.

"Yes," Michael answered, deep in his throat, "she is. And so are you."

"And so are you," Alta echoed Michael's words and a wave of tenderness engulfed her so completely she forgot to breathe. Michael's lips were on hers, pressing gently. Then Jade was stroking her breasts and moaning, and Michael's tongue was inside her mouth exploring her, and it all felt new, so new, as though she'd never made love before. A small fraction, a very small fraction, of herself began to censor this unbelievable, almost unbearable, pleasure these two people who she loved were giving her. No, it *was* unbearable, and she felt like thrashing and screaming and rolling into the hot, living fire, but she contained herself, and she simply stopped listening to that small fraction of herself that always said NO. That said, No one loves you and you love no one.

Then, as Michael kissed Alta's lips and sucked her breasts, taking turns on her breasts and her open, panting mouth with his tongue, his lips, his teeth, Jade lowered Alta's jeans and red silk panties and stayed there as Alta's body heaved and quivered. Until she reached the very edge of nothing, darkness, and flew higher, higher, higher into the pale gold light, screaming without restraint.

And then Jade watched Michael strip his clothes off and she thought he was beautiful. Even his penis is beautiful, she thought. Yes. It is beautiful. And then, as Michael entered Alta, Jade moaned with Alta, lying next to them, feeling their pleasure, watching his body rise and fall over hers, Alta's legs wrapped around him, their faces ecstatic with pleasure and joy—and then stillness as they wept. Jade stroked them with her hands very, very softly, weeping with them.

Michael turned and looked at Jade. He kissed her lightly on the mouth and asked, "May I make love to you?"

Alta's face was turned away and she was glad, because she was surprised at the unexpected shock of pain his words gave her. But immediately she understood and knew he was right, even as she felt his penis still throbbing rhythmically, magically within her. She turned her head to face Jade.

Jade's hair sheltered her face, so her expression was hidden. Finally, she spoke. "If it were going to be any man,

Michael, it would have to be you. But, no, I don't think so. I loved watching you make love to Alta, so I know how much pleasure you have to offer." Jade paused, brushing her hair from her face, exposing her eyes to him. "Your gentleness. But, no, no thank you."

Michael nodded his head silently and, then, turning to look at Alta, he kissed her. He felt expanded by a strange tenderness, as though he could make love to every woman on Earth: the old, the young, the beautiful, the plain. And, yet, as he looked into Alta's eyes he wished only to make love to her. She's every woman in the world, Michael thought, as he rolled off to one side of her, admiring her body, the tiny stretch marks on her hips from giving birth, the stretch marks on her small breasts from feeding her children. He looked at Jade and her body was beautiful and smooth and free of stretch marks, but he loved Alta's body more. He loved the whole of her: every wound, every scar, every healing that made her, her.

Alta reached over and began stroking Jade's belly and breasts, her soft, pointed nipples; nipples that no child would ever possess. Alta wanted to possess them. Jade moaned, her mouth falling open, her eyes closed. Jade's body sprouted tiny, little cell-fires, so intense and so sudden she imagined she was being consumed and would have extinguished them with all the ice in the world, with all the ice in her mind, if only she could.

Nipples sucked, licked, teased to sweet, tense points, and sucked again—Jade's moans and movements were beyond her control. Line of tongue, line of taste and spit, down the belly to the fur, to the creature in the fur that waited, so moist. Michael gently held Jade's shoulders. Jade looked up at him, wildly. He softly put his tongue in her mouth, tentatively. Jade growled, meeting his tongue with her own, fiercely, as Alta found the moist creature in the fur that waited, and Michael's tongue matched Alta's tongue until Jade was entirely, and utterly, inflamed by the one thousand billion cell-fires in her body.

In that moment Jade saw herself, clearly, shot out in a great circle—she entered the burning day-sun, and arching back, returning, ever circular, she flew through the coolness of the white night-moon, moaning, screaming, weeping, then laughing and, for the first time, during her orgasm, she didn't think of her father.

Jade, Alta, and Michael lay silently for a long, long while, staring up at the thick star clusters with Venus in the ascendant and the full, white, transparent moon. Full, and fully risen, the moon shone its truth for those with eyes to see. But there was no warmth to its light, just wisdom, and what wisdom brings: truth without clothes, truth without skin, truth without even a body. The most naked truth.

Michael got up once to place more wood on the ebbing fire.

They both wore ski masks, jean jackets, and gloves. Jim held the rifle as Ray tried the back door. It was open.

"That's real convenient," Ray whispered. He smiled under his ski mask and his eyes shone harshly.

"What if that other cunt's around?" Jim lowered the rifle and waited.

"One for yew, one for me, boy, what else?" Ray laughed and started for the bedrooms. He'd had more than enough to drink, so he was being unusually careless. He didn't see the piled cushions as he crashed to the floor.

Jim raised the rifle, listening for sound from the bedrooms. "Real smooth there, Ex-Lax," he muttered. He quickly entered Alta's bedroom and saw it was empty. "Look at this shit on the walls," Jim whispered, "must be devil worshippers. Shit."

"Wouldn't be surprised, Jim boy. Couldn't ya tell that chink cunt enjoyed ever' minute of it? All that fuckin' cryin's part a' the act." Then the other rooms: empty. Ray started to laugh. "They'd fuck the goddamn devil hisself if they could. Goddamn cunts." Phlegm caught in his throat. He gathered it up in his mouth and spit it on the mask in front of him—the Mexican skull mask. He laughed again.

"Where the hell can they be? Both cars in front. In fact, three," Jim said with irritation. "Maybe we got three crazy cunts up there somewhere. They got to be out there, stupid bitches, sleeping out in nature or whatever they fuckin' call it. Damn, these ugly faces make me nervous. Look, Ray, let's chuck it and go the fuck home."

"Sounds like an orgy for us, boy." Ray was fourteen years older than Jim, so he enjoyed calling him *boy*. He liked to think of Jim as an inferior: a son.

"If we do find 'em, what if we can't handle 'em or some-thin'?" Jim had gone along with trashing the house, and he'd enjoyed raping her until Ray started wanting to kill the bitch or whatever Ray'd kept saying about shooting her and cutting her up. He lowered the hunting rifle again and thought, Why the fuck am I carrying this mother, anyway? I ain't gonna hunt no fuckin' women! Wouldn't mind throwing a little scare into her, a little no-big-deal-rape, shit.

"Three cunts too much fer you, there, Jim, *boy?*" Ray's voice was harsh and slurred. "They're out there, somewhere. Ya gonna go cunt hunting, *boy*, or ya gonna crap out and go home ta yer mommy?"

"Fuck you, Ray! I kin fuck more cunt in an hour than you kin handle in a good week, man!" Jim decided, then and there, that when the whole mess with the bitch was over he'd have noth-ing more to do with Ray. Ignorant fool, just like my old man. I dare him to touch me now that I'm a grown-up man. We'll see who goes home cryin' to mommy. He beat her, he beat us. Kicked my ass daily, my old man, and laughed while he was doin' it. And that time he saw me pissin' into the creek, he laughed: "Call that a dick, boy? I'll show ya a dick!" It'd been huge and swollen to Jim's seven-year-old eyes, as he'd watched his father piss in a long, straight line into the creek. Into the creek he'd always imagined was his. That, somehow, when he'd pissed in it he'd made it bigger as he watched it flow away from him with boyish satisfaction.

Jim stalked out of the house and stood on the back porch. "Motherfucker," Jim muttered, gazing into the full moon darkness toward the hills in front of him. He felt like getting in the truck and leaving Ray stumbling around, drunk and lost. Tears rose to his eyes and he cursed them. Jim never pissed into the small creek again. Everything had belonged to his father. Even the creek had ceased to be his.

Ray lurched out and joined him. "D'ya want that fuckin' chink puttin' ya in jail? Gotta put the fear a God in 'er, boy, that's what. The fear a God!" He put his arm around Jim's shoulder. "After this we kin really tie one on, yeah, boy!"

Then Jim smelled it. Wood smoke. A fire, he thought. He stared toward the hills beyond the orchard, sensing the fire from that direction. His wife had threatened to leave him when the sheriff had come for him with a warrant of arrest. For rape. But now Connie believed him. He had a bad temper, and he'd hit her a couple of times. But why, he'd reasoned with her, would I rape pussy when I got free pussy right here at home?

"They're up there, asshole," Jim said, gesturing toward the hills with the rifle. "Can you walk that fuckin' far, old man?"

"C'mon, c'mon, don' take no offense! Ya take stuff too serious, Jim boy, ya know? Too goddamned serious!" Ray laughed loudly. "I kin walk and I kin fuck iny god-made day's what!"

Jim chuckled at the Sunday school brag. In fact, they both went to church nearly every Sunday, and if they didn't their wives and kids did. The people in the church blamed *those feminist bitches* for causing trouble. They said those words inwardly; outwardly they said, "Some folks just like to 'cause trouble, women like that . . . "

"Okay, fine, but walk *quietly*, got it, or ya ain't gonna get any pussy tonight. Not here, anyway, old man."

Ray grumbled and they began to walk toward the full moon hills. He remembered the first time he gang-banged a girl with a bunch of his friends out in the woods, her screaming and crying and pleading. We sure made that bitch bleed like a stuck pig. Just makes it all the better, he thought with the intense pleasure the memory always gave him. Yeah, that first time. Sloppy seconds, then sloppy eights. Makes a guy feel closer ta his buddies. Like me an' Jim's tight now. There was a full fuckin' moon the first time, he remembered. He smiled widely under the warm, scratchy ski mask, and he pulled it off.

"Hey, Ray, put that thing on when we find 'em, you understand?" Jim took his off as well.

Now the smell of smoke was getting stronger.

Alta poured them all wine as they sat facing the fire. "Are you two hungry?"

Jade was dressed, sitting up and staring at the fire. Michael lay back down on his stomach, enjoying the fire's warmth. He looked up at Alta and smiled. "Sure."

"Is the rifle loaded?" Jade asked. She continued to stare at the fire.

"Are you feeling nervous?" Alta asked.

"I don't know why, but I am. I guess I'd just feel better knowing it was loaded." Jade shivered, pulling her serape close around her, covering even her legs with it. She looked like a part of the ground, with her half-moon face floating over her body. The serape was a gradation of reds and the light of the fire gave it an unusual sense of life. Sitting there, she looked inseparable from the fire.

"Alta, I just remembered like a mental picture. I left the box of cartridges on the kitchen sink, on top of the flour canister, or at least I think I did. Do you mind checking my pack?"

Alta pulled everything out. "They must be on the sink. They're not here."

"Look, I'll go for them," Michael said, "but I think we're fine here. I'll go after we eat."

Alta could see Jade's face mounting with anxiety. "Why don't I go? I feel like walking anyway, and, besides, if I eat and drink wine I won't want to move."

The moon was so bright it could've almost been midday, except the moon's light, as it fell over earth, stones, trees and

Alta, was only concerned with clarity of light and absolute darkness. What it lacked in warmth, it compensated for with wisdom: the underlying, hidden truth. This was the feeling Alta always had as she walked at night, especially full moon nights like this. She knew this stretch of her land so well, and she loved it even more every time she walked on it. Suddenly, she was glad Michael had forgotten the cartridges.

Maybe I'll be able to sort out what just happened between Jade and Michael and myself. No, I'm not guilty, she told herself, and I don't think it's wrong and all that crap, but something monumental just happened and it's wonderful, and scary. What if Michael had made love to Jade? What if he's making love to her right now? Stabs of jealousy filled her so intensely that it surprised her. "Girl," Alta whispered to herself, "I think you love that man." And Jade? she asked herself. "Jade." You want them both for yourself, the words came to her. "But tonight something else had happened. She'd given up a part of herself to both of them, equally. Michael. Jade.

Alta stopped stock-still. She heard voices. Over the ridge, she thought, as a thick terror spread itself, all at once, throughout her body. Right over the ridge. She circled, widely, moving as quietly as possible toward a pile of large stones. During the day she'd often stopped here to lie on one stretched naked, fully to the sun. Now, her heart flew to her throat, and she hoped they would shelter her. She moved without a sound, stealthily, and, without realizing it, an old, unused instinct took possession of her. She followed it gratefully, smoothly as a panther.

"How old's yer daughter? Looks 'bout ten or so. She's a looker. Gettin' little tits." Ray laughed, seeing Jim's face darken.

Jim looked over at Ray, cradling the rifle in his lap. "You ain't messin' with your own kids, are you?"

Ray laughed loudly. "Ya takes stuff way too serious, Jim boy. Ya jus' be breakin' 'em in for mankind, the way I see it."

"Does your old lady know?"

"She knows an' she knows what's good fer 'er. Put the fear a God in 'er right away. Ahm the man, ain't I?"

Jim stood up, angrily. He felt like turning back, but his honor was at stake, or at least he thought so. His manhood. "Let's get this shit over with. All I know is I don't want to go to jail. Period." Jim began walking up the slope holding the rifle at a slant in his right hand. "Fuckin' A," he muttered. "Fuckin' pervert."

"Whadja say, Jim boy?"

"Not a fuckin' thing."

Alta waited for them to clear the top and then she ran at full speed toward the house. Tears of fear and rage kept wanting to rise and fall, but she pushed them down, hard. She needed to see clearly where she was going.

The cartridges were in her vest pocket. She'd called the sheriff. Now she mounted Night Mare bareback. Alta stroked her black mane and said, "We've got to do this quietly, Night Mare. Help me, Night Mare, please, please help me." Alta looked up at the bright moon. "Goddess. Goddess, help me." Tears rushed down Alta's face as she gave her horse the signal with her thighs to trot. She leaned forward into Night Mare's dark body, trying to blend entirely. Trying to become invisible.

"Quiet down! I can see their fire!" Jim hissed. "Come on! We'll circle 'round this way, behind 'em. Come on, old man, this way!"

"Yer just a little bastard, ain't ya?" Ray laughed softly.

Ray stumbled once and Jim hissed angrily, "Sound like an old woman! Keep it quiet!"

"Who's an old woman, punk?" Ray snarled. He didn't have to take any shit from some punk kid that treated his old lady like she was someone.

I feel kind of bad about Alta walking back by herself to get the bullets," Jade said. "I think I'll wait till she gets back to eat."

Michael swallowed some cheese and crackers and sipped the dry burgundy. "Have some wine at least. She wanted to walk. I could tell. She walks by herself at night all the time, Jade. She loves it. Actually, so do I. And so will you, believe me." He poured some wine in a tin camping cup. "You'll be camping out here by yourself by next summer, I bet."

"Okay, you two, stand up! Slow!" Jim yelled, jumping into the fire's light. He held the rifle straight in front of him, pointing it at Jade and Michael, but mainly at Michael.

Michael stood up. "Jade, do what he says. Stand up." His voice was low. The cup of wine had fallen from Jade's hands and she was trembling violently as she whispered, "No, no, no . . ."

"Listen, you cunt, I told you to stand the fuck up! Now, do it! Quick!" Jim's words were slightly muffled from the ski mask, drawn down over his face. He looked inhuman and terrible, and the fear on Jade's face confirmed it, making him feel strangely powerful like he owned them. Jim aimed the rifle at Jade.

Michael took hold of Jade's arm and helped her up.

"Did I tell you to help, boy?" Jim bellowed.

"Where'd the nigger come from, inyway?" Ray sneered. "Tie the fuckin' nigger up an' let's git on with it. C'mere, yew cunt! Bet yew think yew recognize us, but it ain't us, ain't that right, boy?" Ray laughed, directing his question to Jim.

"You got yourself a boy now, you old fool," Jim said, indicating Michael with his eyes. "So why don't you just shut the fuck up! Do what he says, cunt! Get your ass over here!"

Jade began to cry. Michael put his arms around her, holding her up. "What do you two want?" He kept his voice modulated and low, trying not to set the man with the rifle off. They're both crazy, he thought. Utterly crazy. Like those motherfuckers that killed Horus. But now Michael was more afraid for Jade. Alta, Michael pleaded inwardly, please don't walk into this trap, please.

"What's it yer business, boy!" Ray lurched forward, grabbing Jade by her long, loose hair.

Jade screamed, piercingly. Horribly. Michael grabbed Ray by the throat, pressing his fingers tightly around, throwing him to the ground. The rifle went off, scattering clumps of earth everywhere.

"On your knees, nigger! Now! On your fuckin' knees or I blow the bitch away!" Jim snarled, holding the rifle to Jade's head.

"Leave him alone! Just leave him alone! Leave him alone!" Jade was shrieking uncontrollably.

Michael got to his knees, as Ray kicked him once to the head.

Alta stood watching in frozen horror, but there was nothing she could do. I can't reach the rifle without them seeing me, she reasoned. In place of the first wave of overwhelming fear and desperation she'd felt, something like a calm, cold, calculating rage had taken its place, and her face was dry and tight. Set. The night wind had begun to blow steadily, and the fire was shifting and leaping in every direction.

I've got to wait, the calmness told her, and she obeyed.

"Hold onto her, I've got him. Take this nigger to that oak down there an' tie his black ass up. Got that rope, Ray?"

"Shor do. C'mon honey, jes wanna have a little more fun." Ray pulled Jade to her feet, grabbing her breasts. He held her by her hair with his left hand and ripped her jacket and shirt open with his right, exposing her breasts. "Now ahm gitting interested," Ray laughed. There was no inkling of mercy, no memory of mercy. Jade's cries, horrible to hear, were like his had been when he was two, three, four, five, but he had no memory, none at all, of his father beating him, raping him. It had stopped when he was five, when his father left.

"Come on, Ray, save it! Got to tie this boy up first, maybe rid him of his bothersome tallywhacker, huh?" Jim burst into harsh laughter and Ray joined him. Michael poised to run, and Jim shoved the rifle into Michael's back, hard, making him cry out. "Move it, nigger!"

Jade stopped crying and quietly pleaded, "Just let him go, I'll do anything you say, do you hear me, I promise, I'll do anything you say . . . "

"You'll do anything we say, anyway, bitch!" Jim answered, tying Michael's arms behind him and then he began roping him to the wide oak tree, around and around. He jerked Michael's jeans and shorts down, exposing his genitals.

"They ain't all that big," Jim said, handling them roughly. It gave him an intense pleasure, an unexpected one, to handle another man's penis and testicles in that way. To be handling them at all, without respect, without *fear*. Roughly. "They ain't all that big," Jim murmured.

"You plannin' on butt-fuckin' that nigger, boy, 'cause ahm gittin' hard's what!" Ray laughed, pulling Jade to him, handling her everywhere, but she remained passive, silent. She was terrified now for Michael.

"You hold on, old man! We're gettin' there!" Jim had no intention, consciously, of raping or castrating Michael. Not really. He was just enjoying himself, more than he knew. He got close to Michael's face and then he saw it. The diamond earring. "Got us a freakin' fag! Hoo-weeee! He don't need no balls!" Jim hooted.

Alta crawled on her stomach, without a sound, barely breathing, to the rifle as Ray held onto Jade and Jim tortured Michael. She slid the rifle out of the plastic bag and loaded it, putting extra cartridges in her jacket pocket. Her mouth was hollow and dry, but her hands were absolutely steady. She cocked the rifle, slowly, without a sound, and looked through the sights once. Then she got to her feet, concentrating, utterly concentrating, on not being heard or seen.

Michael stared past everything. He could see Horus now, like in his dream, with his own face becoming his. But this time the face remained Horus.

Jim jammed the rifle into Michael's groin and grabbed his testicles with his free hand, pulling hard. Jim's eyes were savage, and he nearly drooled as he spoke. "Want me ta get rid a' these things for you, nigger?"

Michael saw his brother clearly—his face unrecognizable with pain, his mouth wide open screaming, as they severed his testicles, his penis. Michael opened his mouth and screamed. And screamed. And screamed. Horus had been alive.

"Get over here, Ray! Gotta shut this nigger up! Here, hold this rope and tighten it, think he's gone crazy!" Jim began to laugh as he took off his jacket, and then his shirt, putting his rifle down. He kept on the ski mask.

Jade wanted to reach Michael, to comfort him. They would kill him, then her. She knew it, but she just couldn't move from where Ray had shoved her down, hitting her hard. Michael struggled against the rope as it burned into his skin. Welts of blood began to run down his body, but he was silent now in his struggle. Horus was alive, Horus was alive, his mind screamed for him.

Alta stood up fully, aiming the rifle, the tip of it. It was a long, silent second. "Who is like God?" she murmured, as she shot Jim once in the chest, exactly where she'd aimed. Then she shot him in the abdomen as he fell.

Ray started to run. She shot him too.

For a few, full seconds, Alta stood, looking up, at the spiralling branches of the ancient oak. It stretched itself upwards toward the sky, spiralling toward silence, spiralling toward time, toward the ancient stars and the void beyond. Then Alta made herself look down, down, down.

(In Alta's womb a tiny male child completed his brain. His future limbs, little buds sprouting like leaves on a plant, began to appear. His penis was barely distinguishable.)

Epilogue

Michael got up at Horus's first cries. He changed his diaper and brought him to Alta to feed. She smiled sleepily and placed the nipple of her warm, full, milky breast into Horus's small, eager mouth, and the crying stopped instantly as he began to suck. As Alta watched him suckle, forcefully now, she imagined she could feel her energy, like an electric current, like a thin, bright light, flow into him. She imagined energy flowing through her, from the sky, from the Earth, to him, in an inexhaustible circle.

"Little human being. Horus," Alta murmured.

"Do you want some coffee?" Michael asked, tracing the baby's soft brown cheek and then tracing Alta's breast, then the cheek again. They belong together, he thought, mouth and breast, and again, the fullness filled him so sharply tears streaked his face.

"In a minute. Sounds good. April should be here by ten or so with my granddaughter." Alta laughed softly. "Crying again?"

"Yeah. Just the usual. Because I love you two so damned much. You and Horus." Michael bent down, kissing her and the top of the baby's head on the pulsing, vulnerable soft spot. "The crown chakra," Michael said with a gentle laugh, "wide open."

There was a heavy frost on the ground and where his foot stepped ice creaked. The frost would keep his footprints until the midday sun made the ground muddy. He breathed the cold, sharp air carefully, as deep breaths hurt the sensitive, inner membranes of his nostrils. He thought of the fire in the wood stove he'd just built up to a blaze, and, for an instant, he almost turned back to have another cup of coffee. To touch Alta and the baby again.

Without thinking, he started for the ancient oak, following what was becoming a path. The land appeared dead and the grasses were brown and flat. The steers munched on the bales of hay, and little jets of steam blew rhythmically as they breathed in and out. They moaned in dutiful complaint as Michael passed by and then they immediately went back to the sweet, fragrant hay. The older two would be slaughtered this summer. They were just right, and they were healthy from the wild and planted hay, their unrestricted movement in the pasture.

He thought of the trial again. The terrible fear he'd had of losing Alta to prison for saving his life. He remembered clearly the suspended moment when the prosecuting attorney had asked Alta if she would shoot to kill again, given the same circumstances, yes or no. And Alta had answered, without tears or remorse in her voice, "Should I have allowed them to castrate Michael and rape Jade? Should I have allowed *them* to be killed?" "Yes or no," the attorney had insisted. Alta's face had hardened with anger. She knew what they wanted: a proper, false guilt. "Yes!" she'd nearly shouted. "Yes, I'd do it again!" There'd been gasps of outrage throughout the courtroom, but to Michael's amazement, applause and shouts of encouragement had drowned them out. But, still, he had been so afraid for her. "Alta, you've got to stop this. They're going to put you away," he'd pleaded. Their lawyer had advised, "Don't look so defiant, just look a little sorry. You know, repentant." But she'd refused to budge: "I will not pretend I'm sorry for what I did, Michael, because I'm not."

Then, miraculously, her complete acquittal, her pregnancy, everything, within a few short months. Jim had died and Ray survived. Now he was in prison. And, of course, Jim's wife and two children remained. "I understand, I suppose, what you had to do," Jim's wife had said to Alta after the acquittal. "He was almost always gentle with me, though. Almost always . . . " They'd decided to send four hundred a month for the children.

At first Alta had wanted to sell the place and leave, until one night at the winter solstice, carrying candles, Alta nearly full-term, they'd returned to the oak tree. "Do you feel it?" Michael had asked. They'd felt Jim's soul—what else could it have been—gentle and forgiving, and Alta had wept, "Forgive me, forgive me," to his soul.

As Michael came to the top of the knoll, the sun began to pulse on the eastern horizon. He sat on a rock to watch it rise. The new century had come and Horus had just been born two weeks ago, January eighth. He and Alta had spent New Year's Eve at a peace vigil in Santa Rosa in an auditorium filled with people. They'd brought a foam mattress and sleeping bags, and Alta had been fairly comfortable. There'd been poetry and music and singing all night long. And all night Michael had stroked Alta's immense stomach. Once she'd asked, "Do you love my womb, Michael?" Her voice had sounded so vulnerable, so naked, it surprised him. He'd looked at her in the dim light and seen tears in her eyes. Someone had been playing the guitar, and they'd been surrounded by people. "I not only love your womb, woman, I worship it."

Jackie had come up with her husband, Tony, for the peace vigil. Jade had gone to Bali with Grace. April had separated from Steve. Ian had gone snow camping with friends. Michael thought of his parents, and how they'd wept when he'd called to tell them the baby was born and that they'd named him Horus.

The sun was clearing the far hills and sending shafts of pale yellow light over the dormant valley. The apple trees were stark and bare, but they were beautiful in a sad, somber way as they stored their youth for spring.

Michael squinted his eyes at the exposed globe of the sun and let himself be blinded with its light. He imagined the orchard in bloom, and he could almost smell its suffocating, sweet fragrance and feel the soft, warm air of spring all around him. As he faced the rising sun he imagined its distant warmth filling his body with heat. Life. He began to sweat.

Piercingly, a hawk cried out with hunger and pleasure. The hawk screamed again as he circled in the sky in the innocent morning sun, over Michael's head. Then instinct moved the large, male red-tailed hawk toward the valley below, toward movement, toward life. Toward his kill.

"Death, you are graceful," Michael said to the vanishing hawk. The night before Horus was born he'd dreamt his brother like a picture. Horus had come to him like an immense vision of wholeness, and there'd been peace in his face. He hadn't spoken, but a wordless peace and wholeness had spoken from his clear, direct eyes.

Sweat poured down Michael's face and body.

Grey, quick movement below. Now it froze. Then it moved again. The hawk swooped, blinding itself with speed. His talons dug into the warm, nourishing flesh under the thick, grey fur of the stunned rabbit. The hawk ate.

As Alta watched Horus suckle, furtively at first, then more leisurely, his little face began to blur with light, and she was amazed again at being capable of such love. She was utterly grateful to be a woman at that moment. She'd become a grandmother and a new mother within the space of a year. And she'd killed. Alta uncovered Horus, entirely, to wonder at his wholeness. "How can you be so perfect?" Alta murmured, as his entire chocolate-brown body glowed with light. She could see it even if she blinked, but if she stared long enough the light would, momentarily, blind her. Then, carefully, she covered Horus up. He'd fallen asleep filled with the milk of his mother's body, and where there had been only darkness and the sound of the tide beating in his ears and through his entire organism, now there was such light and a strange silence. His small mouth moved in sucking motions, but the wonderful breast was gone.

Alta put Horus back in his crib and went to the kitchen to put water on for more coffee. The house was warm now, and the smell of burning wood in the wood stove permeated the house with its sweet, clean odor. She looked out at the thick, white frost and smiled at the harsh face of winter.

It'd been almost two months since she'd seen April and her granddaughter, Ramona Isidra—Isidra for her great, great grandmother. Alta had asked April if she'd name her granddaughter for her grandmother. "Isidra," Alta said out loud, "yo soy abuela, abuelita." She glanced up the hill for Michael, but she couldn't see him. Instead, she saw the frost on the ground begin to glitter like a harvest of spread jewels from the sun's long, pale fingers.

April would be staying for a week, a full week. She was freelancing and getting photography jobs, doing the bulk of her work in the darkroom at home. It was working out. Alta laughed out loud remembering April's call telling her that Steve had hit her. Her voice had been filled with rage and disbelief. "I kneed him in the balls and punched him out, Mom, after I put Ramona down. I mean, he actually hit me while I was holding Ramona!"

Jade's letter was open on the kitchen counter, and the picture of her and Grace together stared back at Alta. Grace was blond and taller than Jade, and they looked beautiful together, their arms around each other. Alta poured a cup of coffee and picked up Jade's letter, taking it back to the bedroom. Ian would be coming home for his spring break this year. He was applying to medical schools, and he was terrified and excited simultaneously. His new girlfriend was pre-med as well, and she'd be coming with him at spring break. Alta remembered his first words to her when he'd come home at Thanksgiving: "I always knew you were a killer, Mom!" Then Ian had picked Alta up in a hug, laughing, and she was surprised, as if for the first time, at his masculine strength.

"My girlfriend's a little straight, Mom, so you might have to be a little lenient. Anyway, I've tried to warn her about you and all," he'd teased.

"Do you mean Michael and me, like Michael being black?" Alta had asked with a hint of anger.

"Shit, no, Mom." Ian's eyes had become sober, gentle. "I just mean that she kind of comes from the old family TV sitcoms. She's a really good person, but she can be a pain in the ass with the straight stuff. Like her father's a nuclear engineer."

"I see," Alta had said.

"Life goes on," Alta muttered between sips of coffee. The house was utterly quiet except for the sound of the gathering birds waiting for their spray of morning seed. They perched in the treetops, on the ground, on the roof of the house, waiting for the generous, sudden explosion of flying seed.

Alta picked up Jade's letter and read:

Dear Alta and Michael,

I'll probably be in Bali for a few more months at least. It's so incredibly peaceful and beautiful here, it's hard to believe we've entered the new century sometimes when I wake up in our compound of grasslike houses. And the people go to the sea every morning to scatter flowers on the tide to honor the Goddess, imagine? You know, I'd like to live here, in fact, I'm trying to find a job teaching. So, I suppose, if I do I'll stay(!) Grace has her job nursing three days a week and that's all she wants. I don't know if it's permanent between her and me, but I do know I still love her. As I love both of you. I was a little disappointed Horus wasn't a girl, but indulge me (I've always, secretly, wanted a daughter). It's wonderful you've named him Horus after Michael's brother, of course. Life is really terrible, I know, but somehow it heals us, doesn't it? I don't think I'll ever forgive my father for raping me, but I do forgive the little boy who maimed himself for surviving his father's death. You know, I think he actually blamed himself for the atomic blast. Enough. If I do find a job (and it looks good) I'll come and visit in a month or so. I must see this baby (and I do miss both of you).

Alta, remember the first night I spent at your place and how I hated Frida Kahlo's painting of the dark-faced, masklike woman holding the child, feeding her from her enormous, brown breasts. I remember the drops of white, nourishing milk (and there was a rain of milk like a cosmic, impersonal sort of nourishment surrounding them)—coming from such a frightening, impersonal creature. I just thought I'd tell you that I love that painting now. Love is like that, isn't it? Terrible, impersonal, encompassing, *nourishing*. I think of that painting, now, and it strangely heals me a little more each day. All of us babies with our mouths wide open, trying to suckle that mysterious milk . . .

Okay, tomorrow I will pick a separate flower for each of you, including Horus, and cast them to the Goddess. I will say each of your names as I do it. I've never done it before, I've just watched, so I'm really excited. Maybe I'll add, "Forgive us, Mother. Forgive the child."

I know my letter is somber, but I also know you'll understand, both of you. I love you both as endlessly as Changing Woman is ever young, and at once older than death itself. Know that I feel fully ALIVE again, FULLY ALIVE. And grateful, no matter what will happen. I will never, ever forget the night you killed, Alta, so that Michael and I could live. I've learned courage, not bravery, but courage. Cour (more at heart) age. The age of heart. Here's to the new century, to the new Horus, to your new granddaughter, to all the new life that can't be stopped. To the flowers that float away on the tide, and to the Goddess who receives them.

All my love,
Jade

Alta stared at Jade's name for a long while. She thought of her mother and the conclusion she'd come to thinking of her mother's childhood stories: she'd been raped by her father on one of his salesman's journeys when he used to take her to cook for him. She'd said, "He used to just take me." Alta's mother had said this proudly, with the subtlest whisper of pain. But that subtle sound had echoed for years until, one day, pruning the apple trees, not even thinking of it, she saw her mother and her grandfather, vividly, in her mind's eye. She saw her mother, as a little girl, crying in pain as he raped her.

"Mother," Alta whispered. Then she picked up a pen from the night table and carefully drew a circle and a cross within. The room was mesmerizingly warm and cozy. Alta imagined hundreds of flowers, of every color and scent, floating on a peaceful sea. The pen dropped from her hand.

A beautiful woman, dressed in various shades of purple of a sheer material, is kneeling and working with her hands. She is holding a man's leg and attaching it to his torso. Then the other leg. Then the arms, the head. She takes mud into her hands and fashions it into a penis. She attaches it to the man, and the man begins to breathe. The beautiful woman turns. It's Katie, Rita, Jackie, Cheryl, Alta's mother, Isidra, Alta, Jade, April, April's daughter grown, and her daughter grown, and, then, in a flutter of millions of faces, every woman ever born and those to be born. She is Isis. She is. Then her face begins to burn, suddenly, into a terrible fire, and, at its peak, the face begins to pulse with a bright, white light. Into the inhuman, ecstatic quality behind her human woman's form. Into her divinity. Into absolute—encompassing destruction, creation—love.

* * *

"Hey, Mom, where are you?" April yelled coming in the front door. She held Ramona wrapped in a blanket. Ramona was naked underneath. She'd wet through all her clothing during her long sleep in the lulling car ride. She held an immense, wilted and battered, deep maroon Japanese iris and waved it in the air making noises of delight.

"I'm in here, April. In the bedroom feeding your brother." Alta laughed, seeing April holding her daughter, and she saw the light from her dream in her granddaughter's face. Alta laughed again, saying, "What the hell is that in her hand?"

"I grew some indoors. It *was* beautiful," April shrugged, looking at it. "I shouldn't have let Ramona play with it, but it is for you even if it's half dead. Holy shit, it's nice and warm in here." April removed Ramona's blanket and let the diaper bag fall to the floor. She loved feeling her daughter's sweet nakedness.

"Come on, Ramona, give the flower to your grandmother," April said, laughing. April bent toward her mother, encouraging her naked daughter. Ramona swung the dark iris in the air like a great rattle, and it fell into Alta's lap next to Horus.

"Thank you, Ramona Isidra," Alta laughed, picking the dying flower up. "Thanks for the beautiful flower."

Ramona began to cry. April sat next to Alta and began to nurse her. Horus had fallen asleep again, and Alta smiled, watching her daughter feed her granddaughter, unselfconsciously, from her full breast.

"I had an awful dream last week. I've never dreamt anything like it. In fact, I was wondering if I could dream anymore and then this one came in living color." April looked down at her daughter and then out the wide windows toward the harsh, January sun that made the stripped trees almost unbearable to her. But she wasn't really sad or unhappy, not really. Her life, now, felt filled with such hope, and she silently welcomed it to come.

"Why don't you tell me?" Alta's voice barely broke the silence. Ramona's sucking noises were punctuated with little gasps for air.

"I dreamt I was an old woman in a crowded city. It was after a nuclear exchange, what appeared to be what they call a limited one. But there was a feeling of devastation, a horrible chaos and turmoil. And I was saying to the people rushing past me, 'The radios no longer work, not even the clocks, the children are dying, the birds do not sing,' "—April's voice was low and measured. "But no one listened to me. I felt such despair, like I was a ghost."

Alta looked at April, and she realized there was so much ahead of her. That there would be a time when they would all be ghosts. Spirits. Spirits trying to warn the future, Alta told herself. *We are the ancestors,* she realized, and it took her breath away for a moment. She closed her eyes and saw vividly the view from the Pyramid of the Moon.

"You're trying to warn the future," Alta finally said. "That's an incredibly powerful dream, you know."

"So, you don't think it'll actually happen?" April looked at her mother with a little girl's trust. "It was so goddamned awful."

"Maybe you've already warned the future. No, I don't think it has to happen. No, I think as long as we dream dreams like that, the future's listening." Alta smiled, but apprehension clutched at her. A foreboding that she recognized as a foreboding for all life. For life itself. "Did you think of the great blue heron?"

"No, I didn't." April smiled, remembering.

Alta got up to put Horus in his crib. "If you dream a dream like that again, try to make yourself think of the great blue heron. It's hard to make yourself remember things, consciously, while you're dreaming, but it's very important. That's what I've been pushing myself to do. Anyway, I think with a dream like this, it's very important to balance it. Do you know what I mean?"

April nodded her head.

"Well, you're dreaming again."

"I sure am." April held Ramona loosely in her lap as she waved her hands in the air as though to an invisible playmate.

"I'll tell you about a dream I just had before you showed up, but first I'm going to put this in water." Alta paused. "This reminds me of a wildflower, you know, they come up toward summer . . . they're fleshy looking and pink like the new skin under the old skin. . . .

"You mean naked ladies, I think. It's almost dead, Mom."

"I guess I want it to live a little while longer," Alta murmured.